Joan Riley was born in St Mary, Jamaica, and now lives in Britain. Her other novels, *The Unbelonging* (1985), *Waiting in the Twilight* (1987) and *Romance* (1988), are all published by The Women's Press.

GW00642557

Also by Joan Riley from The Women's Press:

The Unbelonging (1985)
Waiting in the Twilight (1987)
Romance (1988)

JOAN RILEY

a KINDNESS to the CHILDREN

First Published by The Women's Press Ltd 1992
A member of the Namara Group
34 Great Sutton Street, London EC1V 0DX

British Library Cataloguing in Publication Data
A catalogue record for this book is available from the
British Library

ISBN 0 7043 4319 3 (paperback)
     0 7043 5062 9 (hardback)

Phototypeset by Intype, London
Printed and bound in Great Britain by
BPCC Hazells Ltd.
Member of BPCC Ltd.

Thanks to my children for three years of patience. To Bayo Riley for helping to print out the manuscript. Lethna Riley for reading, commenting and providing childhood insights. Beverley Huie for photocopying, collating and transporting. Kathy Gale for essential editing. And good friends for assistance and support.

Dedication

For Winston and my mother and for Aunt B, who cannot escape the prison of the past.

Chapter 1

The lush green slopes of the long-defunct plantation dominated the San Juanero skyline. Low-cost units from the first phase of the housing scheme – gaily painted for individuality – were sparkling gems in the cloak of uniformity. The land dropped with startling boldness, gentling out just enough to cradle the old plantation house, before sweeping regally down to the flatlands bordering coastal waters.

Sylvia stood in the shelter of her cousin George's verandah, gazing with tireless fascination at the view. Her eyes followed the sharp, extravagant line of far-off hills as she absorbed the impossible variety of green: from pale delicate limes and waxy ackee leaves to the deep, dense tangle of undergrowth. Across to the right, the town of Port Juanero nestled along the sweeping curve of the sea coast, while Sansee beach was a long ribbon of white sand. Brushed by the light blue waters of the Caribbean sea, it stretched out from the headland as far as the eye could see.

She took a long, deep breath, eyes closing as she savoured the combined scent of that rich nature.

So this is Jamaica! If she lived for ever she would never tire of this view, this landscape. She felt overwhelmed by emotion, an intense feeling that this was a place for her. It was hard to believe that she had never set foot in Jamaica before. It all seemed so familiar. New, and yet old and remembered. The town, the people, even the accents, well remembered from that tight-knit child-hood on Mostyn Road in the heart of Brixton, London.

Sylvia thought of the years her parents had spent trying to convince her she was British. If only they had realised what it would mean: to be here where no English voice intruded and most every skin was black. Where the heat and the sheer *big*ness of the empty land added haunting echoes to snatches of conversation, and gave extra meaning, even to the sound of cutlass cropping grass. No one could describe the sight, the sound, the taste of this country. This was something she had to *feel*, experience for herself.

A stray gust of wind nudged at the hot, scented air around her, enfolding her like a balm, a welcome and acknowledgement. Sadness was a brief dimming of the bright day coming on the tail of memory. Winston had always said he wanted to be buried in his own country. To lie side by side with his parents at the heel of the mountains that cast long shadows across the green cane and banana land. She thought of the sombre South London cemetery with its ornate carved stonework, its neat lines of graves broken by well-tended walks. She couldn't think of that place without seeing overcast skies and the bedraggled pink blossoms of ornamental cherries after hard, unseasonal rain. The memory brought an immediate pain, a sense of betrayal. He had wanted the heat and beauty of this land, and all she had been able to offer was a stark, grey headstone with a one-line message. *In memory of my husband.*

Sylvia blinked rapidly as tears filled her eyes. She squared her shoulders, straightening against the powder blue of the verandah wall. Hadn't she grieved enough? Winston was two years dead and she was here to try and understand something about the place that had made him the person he had been; and maybe come to terms with his loss.

Not that everything had gone to plan. Sylvia thought

with regret of the pretty white-walled villa she had hoped to rent in Boscobel. It certainly would have been more comfortable than the cramped, unfinished spare room in George's chaotic house. But Jimmy had asked her to look after his daughter when her mother had sent her to Jamaica alone. Sylvia felt the old stirrings of impatience as she thought of Jimmy's relationship with George's sister. Jean's behaviour was so increasingly bizarre that Jimmy didn't know whether he was coming or going.

Sylvia hadn't wanted to get involved, much as she sympathised with Jimmy's anxieties. Secretly she thought he should have left the woman to her own devices and brought the children to Jamaica by himself. As far as she was concerned, Jean's claims to hearing voices were just more ploys to get herself attention . . . like the drinking and the dramatic declarations of feeling suicidal. She saw too much of that in her working life to have any patience with it inside her own family.

But she had never been able to resist a request from Jimmy. Ever loyal to Winston's younger brother, she admired his quite calm and loving responsibility. He was so good to Aleesa and Davian. Right from the start he had been more mother to them than Jean had ever been capable of, despite her good intentions. Yet he had never once condemned his partner, still finding it in him to love her, despite her immaturity.

An off-key rendition of an old reggae song drifted up from the road and Sylvia was grateful for the distraction. She watched as the derelict who haunted the Port Juanero streets came shuffling into view. The ragged woman paused beside the road stairs, looked warily from left to right before bending painfully to poke through the debris clustered there. She snatched at something, cradled it with a crooning sound, then placed it with elaborate care into the fading, discoloured straw bag always in her possession. Finally, satisfied, she straightened, arranging the bagstrap on her shoulder, then setting off again on her slow, tuneless way.

A hail of stones and a string of curses from a nearby garden interrupted the rhyme of the song. The derelict froze, her fear radiating upwards to the woman gazing down from the high verandah. Then she scurried off at an impossible speed.

The crying of a baby claimed Sylvia's attention before she could register a reaction. Pearl appeared from the side of the house, hands dripping, a disconsolate look on her face. 'Sylvia, is the baby a hear crying?'

'Yes, do you want me to see to him?'

'No, don't worry, George still inside, he can tend to him.'

Pearl turned to leave, hesitated. 'Sylvia, a hope you don't feel a neglecting you today, through Mauvia not coming a having to wash Kaona things.'

The baby's crying increased in volume and just then George appeared. Pearl frowned. 'Dear, you can tend to the baby, through Mauvia don't come a having to rinse out the diapers.'

His bushy brows narrowed, a frown replacing the good humour on his face, as he hissed air through his teeth. 'Pearl, you don't see me this minute going through the door!'

Pearl looked embarrassed. 'George, if you could just give him the bottle, it ready cooling in the jug . . .'

He seemed about to refuse, his eyes seeking silent support from Sylvia.

She looked from one to the other, saddened. 'George, surely half an hour won't make a difference?'

He shrugged. 'Alright, but is only through you here and a don't want a next argument again.'

Sylvia felt irritation rising. Since she had come, not a day had gone by without a flare-up of disagreements between these two. At first she had sympathised with

4

George, taken in by his ready acceptance of her presence. His insistence she treat his home as her own had been generous and open, while Pearl was abrupt and awkward. But now, she was less certain.

'Dear . . .' Pearl's voice brought Sylvia back to the present.

George turned back resentfully. '*What you want now?*'

Pearl shook her head, the corners of her mouth pulling down, ageing her. 'Is nothing . . .'

The bitterness between them was almost palpable and Sylvia felt her own annoyance rising. All that recrimination and anger! Why couldn't they just be glad for what they had?

'Look, I'm going to pick up Aleesa . . .'

Pearl gave her an apologetic smile, as George went off to get the baby. 'You not to let we upset you . . .'

She didn't want to be dragged any deeper into their problems. It was bad enough having to put up with the way Jean and Jimmy were tearing *their* relationship apart. 'It's nothing to do with me.'

Pearl refused to let the subject drop. 'Sylvia, a just don't want you thinking is me one to blame for this thing with George.'

She swallowed back the words, strong in her determination not to get involved. 'Pearl, it's none of my business. Now I've got to get going . . . Aleesa will be expecting me.'

Pearl nodded automatically.

Sylvia picked her way gingerly down the steeply rutted road, absorbing the scents teasing up from the lowland. She slowed as she neared the old plantation-owner's burial plot. A stone mason, gleaming with sweat, sun-darkened to polished ebony, was perched on top of the highest memorial, relentlessly chiselling elaborate patterns into the blue-veined stone. Sylvia paused, watching for a moment, fascinated by the need that drove him to create such intricate beauty, and the pointlessness of his labour under the hot sun. George had told her about this man. An escapee from the mental hospital in Kingston, he had taken up residence among the ghosts. He spoke to no one, troubled no one, cut lawns and cleared bush for food; and each year carved a new tribute to a long-dead past.

The afternoon breeze did not reach the worn footpath at the back of Port Juanero school. The infants were swarming out when she reached the school boundary, though there was no sign of any primary children. Miss Berta, one of the stall-holders who survived on the school trade, hailed her as she reached the impromptu marketplace. Sylvia changed direction, going across to her shaky stall. 'Hello, Miss Berta, have they started coming out yet?'

Miss Berta shook her head, swinging her big straw hat lazily so it stirred up the warm air. 'Just the one, one that leaving early . . . So how you managing with the times so hot?'

Sylvia wiped at the rivulets of sweat trailing crisscross paths down her forehead and dripping into her eyes. 'Phew, I'm melting!'

'It hotter than normal, man,' Miss Berta nodded sympathetically, patting the space beside her on the rusty drum she was using as a makeshift seat. 'Here, rest yourself a minute. The way Aleesa slow she not coming out awhiles yet.'

Sylvia sat gratefully. This had become a ritual between them since the evening of the first day she had walked down with Aleesa. The little girl had taken her hand and pulled her over, introducing Miss Berta with an endearing eight-year-old dignity.

A fat woman sitting on the hard-packed ground with her wares around her interrupted her conversation with her neighbour to inspect the new arrival. 'Miss Berta, is the English lady this?'

Miss Berta nodded, sitting straighter in her import-ance. 'Miss Sylvia, this is Dorrie, she just come back down from town.' She turned back to the other woman. 'Is Aleesa auntie this.'

Dorrie's smile was friendly. 'A suppose things differ-ent from in England, with the drought we having in these times.'

Her neighbour kissed her teeth. 'Missa George get-ting water, man, me see water commission truck a full up him tank last evening.'

'So what!' Miss Berta came to the defence. 'If him buy water a fe him water, you can't grudge man for that: Missa Mackenzie have guest from foreign and young baby.'

The woman wasn't mollified. 'Plenty a we up a hous-ing scheme have young, young baby . . . should a get water first thing; but a so it stay inna this Jamaica, them only rate who can buy the something.'

'Me no think people should allow to buy water till any and everybody get . . .' Dorrie eyed Miss Berta warily as she added her support. 'You know is all eight month water don't come inna the pipe up Mountain district and is one day a week water truck come . . . then water done fore it reach top road, true man like Missa Mackenzie a get look after first.'

'You think that fair, Miss Sylvia?' Dorrie's neighbour demanded.

Sylvia was at a loss. Not so Miss Berta. She lapped her skirt between her legs and glared at the dissenting woman. 'Left Miss Sylvia out a this.'

'Well she a use water same way,' Dorrie's neighbour insisted.

'So what.' Miss Berta dismissed that with a kiss teeth. 'You a say if you did have water tank and the eight hundred dollars fe full it up you wouldn't pay fe do it?'

'But we no have water tank;' Dorrie persisted.

'Well what you a argue bout then?' A trader on Miss Berta's left joined in the fray.

Sylvia felt like the meat in the proverbial sandwich and she was relieved when the topic changed.

'You little niece have nice manners, man.' Dorrie's mood shifted with the flow, 'She buy one cheese trix from me recess time and you should hear the way she say thank you and please.'

Miss Berta nudged her and winked. 'Aleesa talk pretty, man, but she too trusting.'

'Is true she born and grow in foreign,' Dorrie volunteered, needing to have an opinion on everything, 'if you don't talk good and have manners you don't get through.'

Miss Berta gave her a sour look. 'When since you turn expert on foreign?'

'A have a auntie in England,' Dorrie threw out triumphantly, 'in Birmingham. She tell me all about the way how the white people hate black so bad, black haffe trust black or no trust at all.'

'Me know plenty people come back say the selfsame thing.' Miss Berta was not to be outdone. 'That is how come when them reach back and bad-minded smaddy in this Jamaica go tief them, it turn them mad.'

There was a murmur of agreement. A diversion, as the women swopped horror stories of people they had heard about who returned to Jamaica only to lose their sanity when they were cheated.

'You see, Miss Sylvia,' Miss Berta grinned her crooked, infectious grin, 'is not every and anybody you can just trust so.'

'Plenty mad people born and grow right here in Jamaica,' Dorrie challenged, 'look on Maddy and the way she just get a mind and set up down Trinity.'

'Them people should lock up, man.'

'Is true, you know,' Dorrie agreed, 'every day a seeing the counsellor for district and a telling him them

8

should send her go a Bellevue, but them man is just waste a time.'

Sylvia listened to the impassioned debate on the best way to rid Jamaica of the scourge of mad people. Listened to the prejudices and the fear behind the hate. She thought of the ragged woman who haunted the Port Juanero streets; remembered the stoning she had witnessed less than an hour ago and felt an abstract kind of pity.

Several primary school children and a few infants wandered over in a group. The women vied with each other for their custom, debate suspended for the moment. Miss Berta sold two bags of cheese trix, but the activity soon died down as the children wandered off again, and the traders went back to individual conversations.

Miss Berta rummaged in the coolbox at her side. A large brown fist emerged with a bag of multi-coloured kiscopop. 'Buy one a these noh,' she invited Sylvia, adding when she hesitated, 'go on, man, a know you don't business with sugar but the yellow one them not so sweet and the ice will help cool you down.'

Sylvia gave in, reaching gratefully for the frosted ice-pole. The heat down here was merciless without the hillside breeze and she could feel her scalp tightening, on the verge of a headache, under the protection of her straw hat.

Miss Berta selected another ice-pole, biting it open with strong certain teeth. 'Aleesa telling me Miss Jean and Missa Jimmy coming soon.'

Sylvia nodded. 'Saturday.'

'A bet she going glad to see her mada and faada again, is one month gone since she come noh.'

'Yes, Jimmy had some work to do.'

Miss Berta nodded. 'A meet him auntie down High-gate market, she was telling me say him write book

9

and everybody rate him from that . . . Pity him brother dead so young. Is you did married to Missa Winston?'

Sylvia blinked back a sudden rush of tears, as Miss Berta's words resurrected the old pain. It was much harder to ignore it here, where every street and turning seemed to house someone who had known her husband and his family. She forced herself to nod and smile, touched, despite herself, by the admiration in the woman's voice. It surprised her how much these people knew about Jimmy's life, her marriage, Winston's death, surprised her too how much they cared. Stories of childhood and schooldays hadn't given her that, and despite the pain, it made her feel warm and wanted.

'The baby coming down with them?' Miss Berta's attention shifted once again.

'Yes, they're bringing Davian . . . though he's not really a baby now, you know.'

'How old he is now . . . three?'

Sylvia grunted, scanning the crowd of children emerging from the school buildings. Thoughts of Jimmy and Jean brought back memories of how disagreeable and destructive her cousin could be. It made her uneasy, Jamaica seemed to have the effect of stripping things back to basics . . . and just suppose Jimmy was right – supposing Jean really did have a problem?

Miss Berta was chewing thoughtfully on her ice-pole in between serving the growing trickle of children streaming over to buy cheese trix and fruit buns. 'So what time in the day Missa Jimmy them coming?'

'Saturday night.'

The woman laughed. 'But him a Jinnal eeh! So that mean you going go church in the daytime?'

'No, I am not a Christian, Miss Berta.'

The woman nodded. 'Me neither, but Missa Mackenzie going get you to go a church fore you leave Jamaica.'

'No way, I haven't been since I came and I'm not going to start now.'

Miss Berta gave her a sly look. 'A betting say Missa Mackenzie no like that.'

Sylvia smiled, not bothering to answer. She wasn't falling for that one. It hadn't taken her long to find out that Miss Berta was an avid gossip, any little titbit she could glean, hoarded and treasured and traded for more. Sylvia knew the woman meant no harm, but she wasn't about to add to her store.

Miss Berta shrugged good-naturedly, turning to attend to the children who had started to mass around her stall. Sylvia watched for a few minutes, enjoying the by-play between Miss Berta, the children and the other stall-holders; but she was glad when Aleesa appeared and she could leave.

They walked back through the bare stony schoolyard to the road that led directly through the town, Aleesa chattering away about her day. Sylvia could only marvel at how easily the child had become acclimatised. In her blue school pinafore and short-sleeved white blouse, Aleesa looked for all the world like any of the thousand and one primary school children pouring off buses and being disgorged from local schools.

'Auntie, are we going to the beach today?'

Sylvia nodded. 'Let's just get something to drink and we can see if the ice-cream parlour have any ice-cream cake.'

Sansee was nearly deserted at this time of day and Sylvia was grateful for the stillness, after the fumes and bustle of Port Juanero's crowded main square and the volume of noise from the beachside shanty. Warm powdery sand stretched emptily to either side of them. Two runners paced themselves along the waterline; a rastaman sat smoking a ganja spliff under a coconut palm; and barefoot Headland farmers formed an antlike procession as they headed out to their provision grounds one last time before sunset. The fishing boats, green, gold, red and yellow, bobbed lazily at anchor offshore. Long rods, rising from their empty bellies, sent lines dipping into the still water and gave sharp-edged focus to the reds and oranges of the sun as it slipped away behind the rim of the island in the middle of the bay.

Most of the sea road was obscured by mounds of sand, leftovers of the hurricane two years before. They had to remove their shoes to scramble over them, their feet sinking ankle-deep in the hot gritty hillocks. Aleesa loved the freedom of the flat beachsands. She ran off down to the water's edge and did a little jig in the ebbing tide. Sylvia followed more slowly, juggling schoolbag and shoes. Down here, on the edge of that timeless landscape, it was easy to forget the passing of the days.

Sylvia had to remind herself how close Saturday was. She sighed; if only Jimmy and Jean weren't coming for another week. She had grown used to the pretence of having a daughter of her own. The thought made her feel sad and guilty at the same time. Of course it was good the child's parents were coming. Aleesa had never been away from them before, and Sylvia knew she fretted about the tension that had caused this separation.

As if on cue Aleesa suddenly turned. 'Auntie Sylvia, is it this Saturday Dad, Mum and Davian is coming?'

She swallowed hard. 'Yes, Aleesa.'

'Can I come and meet them with you and Uncle?'

'I can't see why not.'

Aleesa bubbled over, talking about all the things she wanted to tell her father, how she would look after Davian.

Sylvia gave her a puzzled look. 'What about your mum Aleesa, aren't you going to tell her too?'

The bright smile vanished, doubt replacing antici-pation. 'Mum wouldn't want to know.'

Sylvia was torn between preserving her cousin's privacy and her need to know. Curiosity won out. 'Why wouldn't your mum want to know?'

'Because she drinks too much.' Aleesa's response was matter of fact. 'That's why I had to come to Jamaica, because I was getting on her nerves.'

Sylvia was puzzled; whatever Jean's faults, she loved her children, even though she didn't always show it. 'I'm sure your mum didn't say that?'

'Yes she did . . . and she said Davian was stupid 'cos he don't talk and he's three.'

Her heart went out to the child, and she felt a sudden anger at her cousin. 'I'm sure your mother loves you really, Aleesa, maybe she and your dad is just having a bit of trouble right now.'

Aleesa looked uncertain. 'Is it because of me, Aunt Sylvia?'

'Of course not.' Sylvia was horrified at the thought of Aleesa shouldering that guilt. 'It's just that sometimes big people get a bit fed up with things and that makes them argue.'

'You mean like Uncle George and Auntie Pearl?'

'Yes, just like that.'

Lights were twinkling from the houses on Solon Heights when they finally got to the steep stairs from the road to George's house.

The angry tide of the argument crashed around them before they were halfway up, the barking of the dogs running down to greet them hardly dimming Pearl's pleading voice or George's impatient shouting.

'Dear, why you can't stay in tonight and be company for us?' Pearl sounded desperate, humbled.

'Pearl, you know I going up so to work.'

Aleesa's small hand crept into Sylvia's and she squeezed it reassuringly. But inside she wished she could turn and leave until the argument died down.

13

'How come you and Uncle Winston didn't used to argue?' the child asked sadly.

Didn't they? Sylvia was surprised to find that she couldn't remember. 'Everyone argues sometimes,' she answered automatically.

'But they argue *all* the time,' Aleesa contradicted.

Pearl's voice broke in, underlining the contention. 'Just one night, George, a sure it not going make such a difference.'

'Cho Pearl, man, you know is my best collecting day today and a can't afford to miss it.'

'But, dear, is the same thing you is always saying come Friday.'

'Pearl, man . . . *what* wrong with you, eh? Why you always have to causing trouble?' George's voice rose in bluster.

Sylvia felt a sizzling anger at him, as Aleesa's fingers tightened around hers. She stopped, stamping with her feet to shoo the dogs. Sitting on the rough concrete of the stairs she pulled the little girl down beside her. Why couldn't those two think of anybody but themselves? She could just imagine the other children, huddled to one side of the small verandah, forced to witness their parents tearing each other apart night after night.

'Dear,' Pearl was attempting to placate, 'I know you prefer to eat up at Lisa's and you going go down a Selsey to play domino, is not that a mind all the time but . . .'

Pearl, why you always do this, man? What wrong with you? You never give me no support . . . just unreasonable. Is no wonder I don't stay here. You think I can stand this pick-picking all the time?'

Sylvia couldn't just sit there and pretend it wasn't happening, however reluctant she was to get involved. She got to her feet, pulling Aleesa up with her.

'What are you going to do, Auntie Sylvia?' Aleesa

whispered so fearfully that Sylvia smiled and gave her a hug.

'Don't you worry about it, just stay on the verandah with your cousins until I call you.'

The three children, huddling on the worn wooden bench in the dark, clustered around Sylvia as soon as she appeared.

'Auntie,' Jalini, the youngest and boldest, clutched at her hand, 'you could walk out with we?'

Sylvia squeezed the small hot hand reassuringly, hiding her own nervousness, as one of the twins began to cry softly. 'Lutie, don't get upset, I'm sure your parents don't mean half the things they say . . .'

'They do, Auntie.' It was Dionne, the other twin who answered. 'Why they always fighting and shouting so?'

Sylvia wished she could gather them all and take them away; instead she turned on the verandah light. Fishing in her pockets for the icy mints she always kept in case Aleesa asked for a sweet, she distributed them liberally. 'Come on, you children stay here and . . .'

'Auntie, a don't like it.' Jalini grabbed her hand again. 'When Sister Rose try and talk to them, Daddy quarrel and make Moomie shame.'

'Don't worry, I don't think your daddy will quarrel with me,' Sylvia reassured the child, extricating her hand from the clinging fingers and wishing she really felt as confident as she sounded.

Bracing herself to enter the room, Sylvia felt the nerves knot inside her stomach and make her palms clammy.

Pearl and George were so engrossed in each other they didn't even notice her come in and that made Sylvia feel worse. Arguments always had this effect on her, and the thought of intervening scared her enough to make her want to run and hide. Instead she forced

15

herself to walk across the narrow room to the kitchen end.

'Look, you two, I'm not one to poke my nose in other people's business but don't you think this shouting is a bit hard on the children?'

George stopped in mid-sentence, both of them turning to stare as if she were some alien life form. Sylvia wished she was anywhere but there, and she had to steel herself not to back down.

'I don't know the rights or wrongs of this argument, I just know that shouting at each other and hurling accusations isn't going to solve anything.'

The silence stretched for a long minute, and Sylvia began to relax. At least they had not turned on her. Suddenly both erupted into speech, each clamouring to pour out their grievance into fresh ears, each demanding that she see their point of view. She stared from one to the other, at a loss. How on earth did she deal with this without appearing to take sides? The last thing she needed was for them to round on her.

The baby's crying was a welcome relief, slicing through the anger and the petulance. It stopped them for a moment.

Then George muttered something under his breath and moved to check his cosmetic stock laid out across the kitchen table. 'You better go tend to Kaona and stop bothering my soul,' he told Pearl provocatively.

Pearl tensed, making no attempt to answer, then turned aside, a determined set to her mouth.

'Go on no, Pearl, man! You can't hear the baby needing you?'

'Feed him, then. Is your son.'

George stiffened. 'Pearl, what wrong with you? Why you have to so unreasonable?' He looked so wounded, so unaware of his own insensitivity, Sylvia could have wept. She saw the explosion building up in Pearl, knew this time she could not avert it.

16

'*Unreasonable!*' Pearl practically spluttered. 'You think I enjoy getting tie to a next baby again! *Look at me!* Jali is eight, George! *Eight!* What use you think a having for a new baby? You think that is the limit to my ambition?'

'Nobody did force you to get pregnant, Pearl, or you forgetting when I find out?'

'George, a did it for you and you know it as well. You is the one was down on me, down on me to have boychile, and now he reach, is me you expect to sacrifice and do everything.'

'That not true, Pearl. Far as I understand it, we did agreed to set aside having a next child.' He stepped back from the table, spreading his arms helplessly. 'When you did have Jali you suppose was to get tie off. You even go a town saying is for that you was going so I never need to worry about contraceptive again . . . But it was lie, no true, Pearl?'

'You think you can throw blame on me?' she flung back, refusing to accept any criticism, too angry to see his reasoning. 'It take two, you know. You think I impregnate myself, ee, George? Is so? You think I one did it so you don't responsible?'

'Pearl, we decide after Jali not to have a next one till things ease a little. A never tell you was to get pregnant, you never even have little decency to discuss it with me . . . so don't cry bout Kaona now he reach.'

'You was glad enough to boast off bout your son . . . or you forgetting that? All that *thank you* and that fo-fool party, like that could make up for the pain and suffering I had was to go through.'

They were equally angry now, tearing at each other in the usual pattern.

'What pain?' George challenged. 'What suffering? Women have children all the time, what make you so special?'

'Nobody know what I go through, nobody but me

17

and my God, so don't come talk to me bout that. You have baby . . . you can get pregnant, ee, George? You can carry baby for nine months?'

'Man never design for that, so stop this foolishness and pick up the baby.'

She ignored that. 'So what they design for? You see you . . . You Jamaican man them, is one worthless set a people, all a you worthless. Well, this is one Jamaican woman you not going mash down in the ground.'

Sylvia could almost see his mouth setting into stubborn lines but she had heard enough. 'Just stop it, will you!' She had their attention now, forgetting to be nervous in a sudden rush of anger. 'I'm going to pick up the baby seeing that neither of you care enough about *his* suffering to do it, but just imagine how Jean and Jimmy is going to feel walking into this!' She didn't wait for them to respond, marching over to the stairs and going determinedly for the child.

The baby was wet, and she changed him before taking him down. He looked so mournful, she couldn't resist engaging him, and he was chuckling with glee by the time she returned to the main room. She was relieved to hear that silence had replaced the bitter, acrimonious words. George was nowhere in sight and Pearl looked subdued as she prepared dinner. Sylvia got the baby's bottle ready, taking him onto the verandah and asking Lutie to feed him.

'Can I come in now, Auntie Sylvia?' Aleesa gave her a hopeful look. 'I want to read my new book.'

'All right, but have a wash first.'

'Sylvia.' Pearl's voice halted her as she made to retreat up the stairs.

Sylvia sighed. 'Yes, Pearl?'

'A . . . sorry about earlier.'

'Pearl, as I said before, it's not really any of my business, but I have to say, it's not very pleasant for the rest of us who have to put up with it.'

18

Pearl sighed, 'A know you right, but things not really so simple as you thinking. A know it look like a picking at George all the time but is a bigger story than that.'

'I don't want to know it, Pearl, you and George must be able to work out your problems without dragging the rest of us into it as well.'

'You right,' Pearl's shoulders slumped, 'is not fair for Jean and Jimmy to come in this . . . a will talk with George when he come down from topside late evening.'

Sylvia didn't hold out much hope of an improvement but she nodded anyway. At least Pearl was showing willingness. The state Jean's relationship with Jimmy was in, this holiday could rapidly become unbearable.

Chapter 2

Jean sat on the plane with her small son, waiting. She was tight faced and closed in, red-rimmed eyes hidden behind dark lenses. The little boy, Davian, was tense with fright, fighting in jerky spasms to escape the restraining belt.

She soothed him at first muttering indulgent words, bending to drop a kiss on a stiff, averted cheek. But as the minutes ticked by she grew impatient. She shook him roughly. The child cried out, startled. Jean hugged him, feeling immediate remorse.

It happened more and more these days, the need to lash out, smash something. Someone close to Jimmy. And he had sent her off alone, with the children he loved as he should love her.

Jean dared not think of the pain that squeezed her skull recently, every time they disobeyed her or simply looked at her with their father's tilt to the head or frown on the face – shades of his disapproval, stirring an undisciplined rage.

As if that wasn't enough, the voice of her conscience had started plaguing her again. Driving her wild with reminders of how sinful she was, how unworthy of Jimmy. Sometimes the clamour inside her head was so bad, Jean wondered if she was going mad.

She swallowed hard, unable to face that thought. She had sent Aleesa away because of feeling so out of control. Jean had become increasingly on edge since

Jimmy's brother died, afraid his widow, *her own cousin*, would steal him from her. She saw Sylvia as everything she was not, confident, good with children. . . desirable. No wonder Jimmy was always asking her why she couldn't be more like her cousin.

The ready tears burned behind her lids and Jean gathered Davian close for her own comfort. He resisted briefly, then hugged her tight, confusion in the solemn eyes that reflected back her sadness.

'I love you!' she told him fiercely, desperately. 'Whatever Sylvia thinks, I love you children so much but I need your father too.'

Davian's lower lip trembled, and Jean forced a smile, trying to lighten her mood a little. Dyspraxic and without speech, the little boy was too quick to sense emotion, so vulnerable to her seesaw moods of the last six months; his ready smile had given way to silent watchfulness most of the time she was around.

She sighed. Jimmy kept saying that if she loved the children she would control herself. But what did *he* know? It was alright for him; he had been as natural to fatherhood as she had been scared by motherhood. He was the one who changed nappies and soothed the crying, while she looked on, miserable and ashamed, because although she loved her babies she was afraid of them.

Aleesa and Davian had grown up looking to Jimmy, while she, their mother, didn't understand them, couldn't work out what went on behind the solemn eyes. Although the children did not reject her outright, they would run to Jimmy whenever they were upset, burying their heads into him when she would have gathered them to her own breast.

Jean told herself it was a natural reaction, that Jimmy was the stay-at-home parent. But the rejection still hurt. That drove her further into the cold, forcing her to seek solace and affirmation of her worth by putting all her energy into building her career. She used to tell herself she made Jimmy's writing possible. That bringing in the income was as important as raising children. But now Jimmy's writing brought money in and she had been left with nothing. Maybe that was why she resented her children as much as she needed their love. Aleesa and Davian filled his time, took all his attention till there was nothing left to satisfy her need, and nothing for her to hold him with.

If it wasn't for the kids he'd still love me. The thought brought fresh remorse. A memory surfaced, slow frame replays behind closed eyelids. A child in the shadow of a blood-red cross, groaning in pain, the seep of blood and tears mingling with the grey concrete dust. Jean shuddered, shifting her mind away in near panic.

Ladies and Gentlemen, welcome to BA Flight 265.

At last! Thank God! The announcement eased some of the tension squeezing the back of her skull, banished the disturbing image and allowed her bitterness to coalesce.

All this . . . this out-of-controlness was Jimmy's fault! He was the one that took away the first good feelings she ever had about herself. She turned her head to look at the markings on the tarmac through the small sealed window, seeing little beyond her own misery.

Jimmy should be here with her now. He owed her! All those years! All that pain!

Nine years they had been together and she had dared to hope that one day they could be holy in the eyes of the Lord. Jimmy had always been there for her – once. He had held her hand and wiped her brow through the pain of labour, encouraged her to study and succeed in her career. Jean frowned. So how had she ended up like this, alone and abandoned, crawling back to family, because they were all she had left?

She felt a sudden tension at the thought of her brother and his church brethren with their village mentality and gossipy small-town ways. What would they think of her now she had been cast adrift to stumble along without the security of male support? They all liked Jimmy, looked up to him. He was a man who had mastered the Queen's English . . . crafted it into something fine, something black. They were proud of him, though they did not always understand why. Jean had basked in the reflection of Jimmy's glory for so many years, she had forgotten how to stand up on her own.

The plane was moving at speed now, lumbering along the runway, to the point of breathless pause where the wheels bumped up and the massive body left earth.

She needed a drink badly, something long, strong and extravagant: a triple gin and vodka. She could imagine the warm spread in her chest, the hazy well-being. Except she had promised Jimmy: not another drop. Four weeks she had been dry, four painful weeks so full of crowded images, sometimes her brain felt it would explode.

The No Smoking sign went out and she reached automatically for the call button. Just one small gin, surely it wouldn't hurt?

Jean gave herself a mental shake, determined to ignore that niggling voice inside her head. She remembered the last time she had yielded to temptation. Her own snoring had woken her, seeping into her dream and bringing her back to consciousness in a dizzying rush. She had lain sprawled on her back, afraid to move a muscle in case the queasiness in her stomach retched up into disgusting actuality. Her mind had staggered awake, groping sluggishly for time, place, day. All she remembered was that she had had something important to do. She had rummaged through her mind, coming up blank.

Then it had hit her: *Aleesa*! Her daughter was going to Jamaica, and she had promised to take her to the

23

airport. Jean had fought Jimmy for the privilege, wanting Aleesa to know she was not abandoning her, needing to communicate the love she had lost the ability to show. A squinting glance at the clock told its own story. She had let the child down again.

Jimmy had been furious when he had come back from the airport; and Sylvia had been quick to reproach her by talking about how brave Aleesa was to go off on her own. Jean had listened, hiding her anger behind a false penitence.

The rattle of the drinks trolley revived her nagging thirst. Jean breathed deeply, trying to ignore the lure of alcohol pouring, pretending she wasn't counting the rows till the flight attendant backed to hers. The tremors in her hands spread and she pushed them under her bottom on the narrow seat. Surely she was bigger than a glass of gin. She would have a Coca-Cola, nothing stronger.

The three men in front of her had rum, the woman in the aisle seat beside her, gin . . . *Temptation!* Jean's mouth watered for the taste and she bit on her bottom lip, glad the sounds in her head had quietened to a listening stillness.

'Something to drink, miss?'

'Orange juice for the child.' She listened to it pouring, watched Davian reach eagerly for the plastic glass, gulp greedily. It made her throat dry.

'And you?'

The drinks come free! Gin, vodka, you name it! Jean licked her lips and looked around. Had those words been in her head or did someone behind her speak?

'*Do* you want a drink, miss?' the attendant persisted.

Her palm was clammy with the effort, her mouth alive with need as it came out in a rush: 'A double gin and vodka, please.'

She drank it in three swallows, and signalled a refill

before the man could move on. What the heck, a couple of drinks wouldn't hurt her.

The woman in the aisle seat gave her a curious side-long glance, looking away quickly when their eyes collided.

Jean glanced furtively at Davian. She fancied that his big eyes watched her with reproach. Had he heard her whispering conscience too? Could he somehow see the things she imagined watching her from just outside her line of sight? She looked at the half-filled glass in her hand, restraining the impulse to justify herself to the silent child. Self-pitying tears filled her eyes and she chased them with another gulp of gin.

How had her happiness with Jimmy turned to this? She stared wistfully into her half-empty glass, thinking back to their first meeting. She had been two days out of college, visiting with cousin Sylvia while deciding between a new job or returning to Jamaica. And then he had walked into her life, irrevocably altering the course of what might have been. She could remember every detail of that meeting, the excitement of those getting-to-know-you weeks that had followed. Sylvia had introduced them, at one of the spontaneous parties that always seemed to be happening around her and Winston in the old days.

'Jean, this is my brother-in-law, Jimmy; Jimmy, my cousin Jean.'

He had smiled. The smooth dark skin crinkling around his eyes. 'How do you do, Jean?'

'Fine, and you?'

The smile widened into a grin. 'Likewise.'

She found the corners of her own mouth curving upwards, instant recognition.

Attraction was a sharp kick in the gut, warmth in some deep just-discovered place. Her body language said, *I like you . . . all of you.*

His responded in kind. 'What do you do, Jean?'

She wondered what it would be like to have a man like him. 'I'm starting work next week as a research officer in housing. What about you?'

'I write. One day I'm going to do a book everybody's going to want to read.'

No vanity, no boasting, just that bald statement; and she had believed him. She liked the open invitation in the slow, assessing grin, but hesitated to reciprocate. The miracle was that he had noticed her enough to show any interest at all.

They had talked on the phone every day for a week. Under his influence she was able to come out of her shell and explore her world a little. They discussed philosophy and world affairs. She with the fervour of the recent graduate, self-consciously important, with borrowed knowledge mistaken for her own. He, with the practice of four years' seniority and a mastery of language, wooed her with words, feeding her hidden snobbery. And underneath it all, her body itched with wonder.

By week two she was bold enough to seek him out deliberately. They walked, talked, saw plays to argue and disagree over. Laughed, touched, kissed. He brought her to a pitch of expectation. Her mind thirsted, opened to receive him . . . her first man.

Before the third week he made good on his silent promises. In the soft, warm intimacy of his pine-carved bed he initiated her into passion. There was a little pain but no blood, and he coaxed her past that nagging image of a small child, bleeding under the shadow of a crucifix. Jimmy said the tension was natural, fear of the unknown, a manifestation of her innocence. His patience and understanding reassured her and the image slipped away in the beauty of the moment.

His loving was slow, hot and sweet, lighting up the hunger she had once thought was a figment of weak women's inadequate imaginations. They explored each

26

other with soft sensual kisses and patient touches, whispered instructions for mutual pleasure, and daring experiments. Jean opened her thighs to receive him, as her mind had done before, discovering fulfilment, and more . . .

The mocking snigger of her conscience dislodged the memory, bringing the present back abruptly. Her fingers tightened, anger rising for a brief moment.

'It's that damn voice in my head . . . that's what it is!'

'What?' The woman in the aisle seat gave her a wary look and Jean shifted, embarrassed.

'Sorry . . . I . . . em . . . I was talking to my son.'

She wished she could shut off her conscience at will. God alone knew how it gained voice. Sometimes it was so persistent it seemed she had a whole army of people inside her head. No wonder she needed the odd drink with all that going on inside.

It seemed so long ago, that first stiff drink. The day she had come home to find Jimmy brimming with excitement because he had sold one of his short stories. Jean had seen the spectre of losing him come one step closer even as she had forced herself to hug him and try to mirror his excitement. If he earned money from writing where would that leave her? He didn't need her for anything else and despite all his protestations, without a ring on her finger she felt no security in their relationship.

Maybe that was why she had insisted on a small gin, an act of defiance in the face of Jimmy's surprise. Something to celebrate with, she had told him, as he insisted on inviting his brother and Sylvia over. The first glass had made her feel sick, but the second settled warmly in her stomach. By the time Winston and Sylvia arrived she felt detached enough to persuade herself she didn't mind the way they formed a circle with the children that left her out in the cold again. She supposed, in fairness to Aleesa and Davian, that they *had* run to her at the height of their excitement, but as soon as Jimmy called, they abandoned her as she fancied they always did.

Yes, that was the start of it, Jimmy pushing her out of the things that mattered. Then had come the next story, and finally the book. That was when her conscience had really begun to bother her. Friendly at first, it tried to comfort her and she had thought it was only her inner strength manifesting against the strain everyone was putting her under. That hadn't lasted though, not once Winston died. In her mind that was the beginning of the end. Jimmy just seemed to abandon her, taking the children over to Sylvia for weeks at a stretch. Jean hadn't even been invited, at least not what she would consider a real invitation. All right, so she was only Jimmy's live-in lover, but Sylvia was her cousin and Winston had been *her* children's uncle.

Davian was sleeping, his head lolling uncomfortably to one side, the earphones knocked even more crooked by the awkward angle at which he lay. Even with his bottom lip hanging loose he was beautiful, as only a child could be. Unbidden images of her own childhood came back to Jean as she gazed at him, bringing a brief and unexpected peace. Jean eased back into the narrow seat allowing remembrance to soothe her troubled mind.

Granny, Daddy's Great-aunt P, sitting on a fallen trunk under the shade of the old almond tree, fanning herself with the battered straw hat she wore over her tiehead to protect her from the midday sun.

Of all the people Jean had loved in the world, she loved Granny best. Better than Aunt Vi who could tell a wicked nancy story. Better than Tashi who would buy kiscopop and snow cone and take her to the market at Highgate during the school holidays. Most times she even felt she loved Granny better than Papa. Granny

28

was the only one who never told her she was too young for the things she wanted to do, or scolded her when she spilt a little water on Aunt Vi's clean floor.

If only Granny hadn't died. But then she had been so old – nearly a hundred, Papa had said. Jean sighed. Granny had believed in her. The old lady never dismissed her triumphs just because she was a girl. She used to encourage her to be as good as Noel and George. Not like Papa, who only looked to the boys, because they could carry on his name.

Jean could almost see her now, a dark-skinned woman with a well-worn face, full of humour, kindness and the sort of patience only decades of living could bring. Granny's thin body had been like a piece of history. The lines of age packed so closely on her face it was impossible to see where one ended and another one began. There had been something regal about her old great-aunt. An original Ife sculpture cast in living flesh and blood; as lost to faraway Africa as those long-dead sculptors of the bronzes Jimmy had taken her to see at the museum in London.

It was Granny who argued with Papa every time he brushed aside how well Jean did at school.

'Obadiah, this one is the brightest you have, why you can't give her some encouragement and rejoice with what she can do?'

Jean could remember standing to one side of the airless verandah, pretending the tears came from perspiration stinging her eyes. Her arm was outstretched, offering yet another of the flimsy school reports to her father's unresponsive presence.

Her father kissed his teeth, the frown gouging deep parallel lines across his sun-baked forehead. 'Miss P, don't do this, man . . . Jean know a will look at it later.'

'No Obadiah, you look on Noel and George report,

you even find time to give them quatty, so how come Jean must wait?'

Jean could still feel the pain of her father's reluctance. The way his work-roughened hands folded the big pages of the *Gleaner* newspaper so impatiently that they twisted out of shape.

The leathery palm opened, swallowing the small white paper, and she felt guilty for forcing it on him. But she wanted him to see she wasn't a waste of time; needed him to glow with pride, the same way he glowed when Noel came third in English and got seventy-five per cent in maths.

'A get ninety-seven per cent in English, Daddy.'

'Seventy-two per cent in maths, Jean, you telling me is all you could get?'

She flinched with the memory, concentrating on how tired he had looked. His eyes had been red-veined even then, his back bowed worse than Granny's. He had seemed old – not ageless like Granny, just old. Old enough for her to say a furtive prayer in the dark nights that he live until she grew up. She wanted him to be proud of her. Had vowed that one day he would boast of her achievements to everyone in Cromwell Land District.

'A come first in spoken English, Daddy.'

'How come is only thirty per cent you get in needle-work?'

'I can't pass without I sew a skirt.'

'Wha wrong with you mek you can't sew . . . How you so worthless?'

Words *can* hurt, words like 'worthless', 'disappointment', all the things she had known as her own special labels. It didn't matter how many times Granny had said 'never mind', or told her Papa didn't mean it. Those words remained sharp and hot like the sting of the pretty, scallop-tailed wasps which nested in the eaves of the concrete house.

Always Jean would rush into speech, needing to wipe the pain away, replace it with approval, liking, something with a value. 'Papa, a think a going to be a doctor when a get big?' She had waited, glowing in the stunned silence, expecting the first rays of his approval.

'What! *You?* Jean, chile, leave ambition like that to your brother. You going grow up to something fitting – teacher even, then you can married, and raise African children to the glory of the race – just like Missa Garvey did always say.'

All she wanted was for him to like her as much as Noel; to treat her like she counted for more than assistant cook, and trouble on his head.

'Daddy . . . a going to get a prize for English?'

Silence like the long heated hours of midyear days; 'You think you should get one?'

'Yes, Daddy.'

'Alright . . .'

'Dinah getting *What Katy Did* and Jeanette going get a Enid Blyton.'

She had said the wrong thing again.

The lines on the sun-baked face deepened. 'That is white people brainwash. A get a nice book when I was up in town.'

'What book, Daddy?' Her voice was small, swallowed by disappointment.

'Man name . . . eem . . . Cleaver, it call *Soul On Ice*. You have to start learn to support the race.'

It was raining hard against the small window, black clouds engulfing the plane as it descended for the short stop-over in the Bahamas. Jean watched the jagged lightning flash across the darkened sky and shivered.

Another memory. She with her greedy self saying the wrong thing again; goading her brother into another of his stupid, dangerous games. Noel the oldest, under the mango tree, stretching to the tip of his toes, reaching

31

for the last ripe fruits. She, angry because Granny had said they were for her.

'I going tell Granny you tiefing me mango.'

'A no Granny tree and Papa never say you can take them, anyway Granny gawn a town till day after tomorrow.'

'A going tell Papa, Granny say a fi me mango them.'

Noel hissed air through his teeth. 'You too fraidi, fraidi to come stop me.'

Jean balled her hands in frustration. 'Lightning going flash and thunder going kill you.'

'Stop talk foolishness. I not fraid of a little thunder.'

Rain dripping, dripping, pouring off the ridges in the new zinc roof, mini waterfalls, all over the hill country. 'You fava dying duck in a thunderstorm.'

Noel laughed. 'And your nose fava tunnel.'

'Me naw run joke with you . . . You no hear sey you no fe laugh after long man till you done grow?'

Lightning flashed right overhead, the thunder rumbling a warning. Fear now; Noel shouldn't joke her up by staying under a green leaf tree. Maybe she shouldn't have called God's attention by talking death. *God bless the mark and cross it off.*

'Daddy, thunder rolling and Noel under the Julie mango tree.'

'Jean, don't tell untruth on your brother.'

'Is not untruth, Daddy, he out there, and thunder shaking the ground.'

'Tell him to come in.'

'He say he not coming in.'

'Why you children can't live good? Is me one leave with the burden of your upbringing since your mother dead.' He sounded weary, sad, worse than the last time he had come back from farm work in the States.

Thunder rolled, a sudden clashing noise; rain driving hard against the small stone verandah. Lightning! One last jagged flash . . . the hand of God, not blessing the mark . . . refusing to cross it off.

The aircraft tilted to its final descent and Davian whimpered, grabbing Jean's attention. He clawed at her arm, raising welts and drawing blood with his sharp nails. She made a mental note to cut them, half irritated, half despairing at the spectacle he was making, as she prised the fingers away with an effort. Anger ballooned swiftly inside her head and she clenched her fingers into fists.

The little boy continued to look at her, tears dripping down the soft brown cheeks. Something in his mute despair reached through her anger; pulled past the endless months of gin-fuelled resentment to touch a chord deep inside and dissipate a portion of the swelling rage. Maternal feelings, long pickled in the bottle, stirred to life. She felt the pain of her own helplessness but for once resentment didn't follow. Jimmy would have known how to calm him, what to do.

'Don't worry, sweets, we'll soon be on the ground. Davian hush . . . it's alright.'

Meaningless words, dribbling across his fear, making little impression. She could feel her own frustration, her own despair. Then the last few screaming seconds, the impact of her own fear as they touched down, rolled, the roar of reverse thrust.

Davian was shaking and she wanted to gather him in her arms. Not allowed . . . She pulled his head against her chest, rocking him and crooning nonsense, as she had done when he was a baby.

Norman Manley Airport was its usual mixture of petty irritations and endless discourtesies. The potted plants in low, barrack-style corridors had seen better days, as though the drought Sylvia had warned her was gripping most of the rural areas had crept into water-glutted Kingston on some crazy equality mission. Soldiers in full battle dress stood on every corner, adding intimidation to the atmosphere. That was the main problem with Kingston airport. Everything was out of step enough to jar on travel-frazzled nerves. The air-conditioning was a little too cold, the corruption a little too obvious, the building a little too seedy for an international airport.

Jean felt the tension return, the ambivalence of this country, the only one habit and history allowed her to call home. She watched the Immigration officers on the visitors' desk with a sense of shame. Only black people were being stopped, questioned as if they had no right to foreign passports. The white tourists sauntered through, acting as if the days of Empire still existed and they were here to view the natives in the glass case of their own making. They only paused long enough to have their passports stamped, while the officials were at their most respectful. Jean felt lost and isolated without Jimmy. It was strange not having him to smooth the way for them.

She thought of Aleesa struggling along this same corridor, all alone. . . and felt her stomach clench as she coaxed Davian along. She had been too eager to send the child away, too off-balance and preoccupied with her own fears to consider the rejection the little girl might have felt.

Jimmy had been against Aleesa travelling on her own from the moment Jean had broached the subject, had been furious when he found out she had gone behind his back and booked the ticket anyway. Not even her assurance that Sylvia would be there within five days of their daughter could mollify him.

'You know what could happen in five days?'

'In Jamaica?'

'*Especially* in Jamaica.'

'Come off it, Jimmy, it's not like over here, you know.'

He had rounded on her. 'Jean, Jamaica is just another

34

country and if you'd just take your nose out of a glass of gin long enough to dry out, you'd realise that.'

His brutal observation had put her on the defensive, made her try and disguise the truth a little. 'I've only had a small gin.'

'Sure,' he was sceptical, 'and I suppose the two empty bottles at the bottom of the rubbish bag are spillage.'

She ignored that. 'Jimmy, Aleesa is going to be away from you for a month, surely you can live without her that long?'

He hadn't answered and with hindsight she realised that Jimmy had never intended to go to Jamaica. The little tell-tale signs had been there all along. His reluctance to turn down a conference invitation, his insistence that he booked the flight . . .

Immigration was only one hurdle, the first and the least. Customs and Excise had to be the worst. Jean thought of the Customs hall as a microcosm of the state of the nation, where colour gradation determined the degree of courtesy, or humiliation, allocated.

A multiplicity of sordid little dramas was playing out at the worn, old-fashioned Customs benches. It was hard not to flinch as the white tourists walked away with a cursory glance. Sensitive as she was, Jean fancied she could read derision, contempt, on their faces. She felt a renewed shame, as one after another the black people had their bags rooted through, their underwear strewn across the worn and peeling counter like some obscene insult.

Davian tugged at her t-shirt, resting his head wearily against her skirt. She smoothed her hand gently across his short-cropped hair and smiled reassuringly down at him. He responded with a tired half-smile of his own, before popping his thumb in his mouth, and she felt fresh resentment welling up against his father. Jimmy should be here to lift him up. Who the hell did that man think he was anyway, abandoning her and the children so he could spend the summer playing the big shot author?

The Customs officer rapped impatiently on the glass partition. Jean walked forward reluctantly, bracing herself for the violation, but the search never came. She could hardly believe it – a cursory glance, a sour smile and that was it. She gathered Davian close, angry with herself for feeling gratitude.

The baggage handlers rushed forward, vultures fighting over a fat carcass. *Held to ransom*, that was how she thought of it, a subtle form of extortion which officialdom either actively sponsored or, at the very least, permitted to go unchecked. You were not allowed to touch the luggage trolleys on this side of the customs barrier, and your relatives and friends were not allowed inside the airport building. So there was no choice; you had to use the official baggage handlers. Even when your luggage was within carrying capacity, it was removed from reach until you paid your dues. Today she felt too sick to make even a token stand, so she paid the appropriate levy without demur in the requisite foreign currency.

Sylvia could scarcely believe how packed the airport was. She looked at the teeming sweaty crowd, wondering how she was going to spot Jimmy and the others in this crush. It made her bright mood falter for the first time. Or maybe it was the thought that she would soon be losing Aleesa. She pulled herself up sharply. No, that was nonsense. Aleesa was never hers to lose. Something squeezed in her chest as she watched the way the child craned her neck from side to side trying to peer through the crowd, the small body in ceaseless motion as anticipation built up.

'Will they be here soon, Auntie Sylvia?'

Sylvia's fingers tightened round the small hand. 'The plane's landed, so I expect so.'

'Will they see us?' The child was suddenly anxious.

'I'm sure we'll see them, don't worry, you'll be with them soon.'

She looked around, wondering what had become of George. He had better come back soon, or she'd have to go looking for him. The mood he was in, he just wasn't fit to be let loose on his own. All day he had been like that, almost manic, full of his own fears and apprehensions about seeing Jimmy again.

It didn't take long to realise how much George looked up to the other man, the way he peppered his conversations with liberal references to the family connection. Sylvia supposed it wasn't so surprising. They had both come from the same beginning, yet now Jimmy had standing invitations from what George considered Jamaica's finest.

'Are they coming yet, Auntie?'

Sylvia reassured the child automatically, her mind still skipping restlessly from thought to thought; anything to stop her dwelling on the pain of passing Aleesa back to her parents' care.

She wondered how they were going to get back to Port Juanero. After the coughing, spluttering nightmare of the drive to Kingston, she doubted George's ancient Cortina could survive the return journey over the steep mountain roads. Not that the state of George's transport depressed her ordinarily. On the contrary, she found an enterprising spirit in Jamaica, an indomitable will that made her feel a warm glow of pride. No wonder Jamaicans were endlessly optimistic; inventive even when they were unable to acknowledge their own potential. Look at the way they moved around despite the ramshackle state of the transportation system.

It was like some giant board game. The ruling élite spent all their time devising ways to rip the heart out of the country; unable to accept the absence of a colonial motherland to which they could retreat after a tour of duty. And the ordinary people fought back, confounding them by surviving however reduced the circumstances, however high the cost. Jamaica was a revelation to Sylvia, far removed from the defeatism she was familiar with. The people impressed her, captivated her. It made her want to experience life through their eyes. She actually enjoyed squashing into ageing unofficial taxis; had become a seasoned traveller on the battered, rusting minibuses, elbowing her way on with Aleesa in tow, and learning to shout 'One stop, driver' with the best of them.

There was fresh activity at the airport doors and Sylvia pushed forward, sheltering Aleesa as she tried to get a better view. Baggage handlers emerged, unceremoniously dumping overburdened trollies before haring off for another lucrative load. The soft lilting sounds of conversation were punctuated here and there by cries of welcome as people recognised relatives and waded forward to greet them. Sylvia scanned the trailing passengers for Jimmy's short-cropped hair. She saw Jean just as George arrived. Her eyes moved past her cousin in either direction, looking for Davian and Jimmy.

'Is Dad there?' Aleesa had caught the excitement around her.

'I can see your mum but I can't see your dad yet,' Sylvia responded. 'Come on, let's go over to her.'

George was already barrelling his way towards his sister, and Sylvia followed in his wake, tightening her grip on Aleesa. Jean turned in their direction on George's second call, her eyes lighting with relief when they met her cousin's welcoming smile.

Sylvia breathed her own relief, remembering the bitter words that had marred their last conversation. Maybe Jean and Jimmy had worked something out after all. She looked around, wondering about Jimmy's non-appearance, but was swept into the exhuberance of the greetings. She gave Jean a brief hug before lifting Davian. The feel of his small arms around her neck was gratifying, though it resurrected the old pain. Why had she and Winston not had children? Of all her regrets that had to be the worse.

'Mum, where is Dad?'

Aleesa's disappointed voice sliced through the euphoria. Sylvia stiffened as she saw the way Jean closed in on herself, pretending she didn't hear the question. Something was really wrong.

'Jean, couldn't Jimmy get down with you?'

'He wanted to, but at the last minute something came up.' Jean gave a nervous laugh, avoiding her cousin's eyes. 'You know what it's like with those creative people.'

George looked disapproving. 'What kinda foolishness you telling me, Jean?'

Sylvia felt like swearing. 'I suppose it was a bit much expecting him to get away,' she offered diplomatically, 'especially with the book having so much impact.'

George's face had dropped. 'If you asking me, that is so much slackness.'

Jean gave him a sour look. 'Nobody was asking you anything.'

'You see you, that was always your trouble, if the man did married to you now.'

'For God's sake, George!'

'Move noh people, you can't see everybody waiting to come out.' A wiry taxi-driver swung a heavy case across his shoulder and pressed forward as Sylvia pulled Aleesa to one side.

'Sorry about that you hear,' Jean muttered, lifting a protesting Davian.

'No problem, lady, but if you not waiting a cab, you could just move aside mek the people come through.'

Sylvia waited until George started loading the car.

'Jean, why didn't Jimmy come with you?' she asked quietly.

'He thought we needed time apart.'

Her heart sank. 'Are you saying the two of you have split up?'

'Not yet, but it's on the cards.'

Sylvia wanted to say something reassuring but her mind came up blank. Jean was tense and brittle, with unmistakable signs that she had recently been drinking. Why on earth hadn't Jimmy given her some warning? What was he thinking of, anyway, sending Jean to be on her own with the children? Anyone with half an eye could see the woman was in no state to look after herself, let alone two kids.

Chapter 3

Pearl left the baby's bottle cooling in a jug, and went back to buttering water crackers for the children's lunch. The clock on the wall showed a quarter to eight and she felt rushed and harrassed. *Why I can't never get them ready on time?* she wondered in frustration. It didn't seem to matter what time she got them up for early morning devotion, by the time eight o'clock came, they were still only half dressed; and they had to be at school for twenty past.

The singing of the kettle brought her back to the stove. Pearl gave the bubbling pot of porridge a quick stir, before setting out plastic mugs and mixing Milo with powdered milk.

Mauvia, her helper, hadn't come again today and her mind was brimming with the hundred and one inconveniences the woman's absence was going to cause. The worst of it was the baby's dirty nappies. Pearl hated and resented having to wash Kaona's soiled linen as she never had with any of the other children.

If George never trap me a would never inna anything like this, she thought sourly, *four living children for Moomie, and I is the only one scraping dirt and making do.* She flicked a green lizard off the formica table-top and added Milo to another mug. *That man so stingy. If it wasn't for that we wouldn't in a this tribulation right now. We could pay a money and get things done proper stead a getting cut-price help like Mauvia who barely come from one day end to the next.*

Things had been different once; a long time ago, before Hurricane Gilbert knocked the prosperity from under them, when she had dared to dream of alternatives. They had a good helper, someone she could talk to. Janet had worked in town until she got pregnant, then came down to the country to have her baby. They could afford a town-trained woman then. In those days George's provision ground and his cosmetics sales kept them comfortable and able to pay for a better quality of life.

Other things were different too; the steep rising land at the back of the house had rough mud steps to access the lower reaches. When she felt sad, Pearl used to stand on that low slope – the boundary which marked the end of female access – and gaze at the steeply rising provision ground. She had dreamed of climbing up one day. Fantasised that freedom and worth lay somewhere in that mysterious 'up there' where the lime tree yielded countless fruits for half the neighbourhood.

She sighed, moving the vase of plastic flowers from the table and setting down place-mats to protect the hand-finished wood. Everything changed after Gilbert. All because George didn't know to look ahead. She had not been surprised when Janet took one look at the hurricane devastation and never came back. Their house had been a shell, uninhabitable. The lower slope of the provision ground was washed away and relatives had to come and help build a retaining wall, to stop more of the overhanging slope crashing into the house, as it had done elsewhere on Solon Heights. Of course, they managed to rebuild, but the prosperity never came again. People didn't have money to buy a lot of cosmetics; and George refused to put more effort into farming, seeing that as acceptance of failure. Pearl's dream of climbing to the lime tree at the top of the provision ground moved out of reach, with the make-shift access that had replaced the low slopes.

Needing to lash out, George had taken refuge in blaming Pearl for the helper's desertion. He informed her that it was the way *she* had treated Janet that drove her away. Pearl gave an impatient kiss teeth, pouring the boiled water with such force it splashed back on her hand. She cursed under her breath, feeling even more irritated as she dropped the kettle back on the stove and smeared butter on the stinging spot. 'See how he make me burn meself?' she muttered as she picked the kettle up again and continued pouring more cautiously.

George is just crosses, she decided bitterly, *just see the way he always looking for somebody else to dump every kind a blame on. Look on the way he not going take even one piece a responsibility for the state we in right now. The wonder is he don't come up with some way to blame me for Gilbert too.*

Pearl kissed her teeth again. He was the one who had been too foolish to build a proper retaining wall against landslips and too mean to take out insurance on the house and the land. He was convinced that nothing would ever happen to make paying premiums of two hundred dollars a month worthwhile. Now that it was too late, he sat around complaining about how things always went wrong for him.

If it hadn't been for the money Jean and Jimmy sent . . . Pearl closed her eyes and said a quick blessing to God. They would have lost the house – everything. The Lord knew she shouldn't really complain about Mauvia. If things had got any worse, *she* might be living in a board house and walking clear across town to clean for someone else.

Pearl was convinced it was Jimmy who had saved them, even though Jean's hand wrote the cheques. Not that George would ever accept that. His belief in his sister's generosity was absolute, and his gratitude for each small act of charity only added to Pearl's bitterness. She knew she should be grateful to her sister-in-law, yet somehow she could never get past resentment and the knowledge of the woman's contempt. Jean had taken against her from the minute they met and never made any attempt to hide her dislike, or her feeling that George could have made a better marriage.

Pearl concentrated on the other things she had to do, blotting out the feeling of inadequacy that thoughts of her husband's sister always brought. She had promised to make a pudding for the children, and there was the floor to scrub and the leaves to rake. Jalini's laughter mingling with Aleesa's squeals interrupted her mental list. Pearl's lips tightened on a surge of irritation. 'What going on up there?'

'Aleesa and Jalini misbehaving, Moomie.' Dionne's voice came clear and angry from somewhere at the top of the house.

'Is not true, Moomie.' Jalini's denial was accompanied by smothered laughter.

'Moomie!' Dionne sounded as if she had reached the end of her patience. 'You can talk to Aleesa she just won't hear when a talking and she keep splashing water on the clean floor.'

Aleesa! Always Aleesa! Pearl closed her eyes and counted slowly. She could hear Sylvia's voice, talking to Aleesa, heard the chaos resolve itself; but that only fuelled her annoyance. Her fingers tightened on the spoon in her hand as the ~~other~~ woman's light tread receded on the landing above her, followed by the opening and closing of the spare-room door.

Pearl forced aside the bitter feelings with an effort. It wouldn't do to antagonise Sylvia; not with the arguing with George and the way Jean was behaving.

Pearl nodded as if in agreement with an unspoken thought. Since her sister-in-law came down, the atmosphere in the house had gone from bad to worse. There was something so sharp and on edge about Jean. And why hadn't Jimmy come, really?

Questions buzzed in Pearl's head and she wished she had the courage to voice them, uneasy with the feeling that some unseen drama was playing out around her. Frowning in concentration, her mind sifted through the events of the past few days. Jean was different, quicker to fly into a rage. And she was always talking to herself; having whole conversations that put Pearl in mind of the mad woman who lived in the rotting board house at the junction where the Mountain District Road met the road to Port Antonia.

The noise of children's play increased in volume and Pearl's irritation built up again as she heard Aleesa urging Jalini on.

'Jalini, you don't hear a telling you to get on! . . . You children bathe?'

Smothered giggles were followed by the sound of hurried feet and a slammed door.

Jalini's round face appeared at the top of the landing, a grin lighting up the scrubbed features. 'Moomie, me bathe but Lutie and Dionne don't bathe.'

'A holding the baby, Moomie.' Lutie's voice from the verandah sounded aggrieved. 'You tell me to sit with him till Mauvia come and she don't even come as yet.'

'So why you never put him in the bassinet!' Guilt made her voice sharp. 'Is how long a telling you children you mustn't keep so late for school?'

'He keep wanting to cry when a laying him down, Moomie,' the child was plaintive, 'and Auntie Jean saying we not to let him make noise when she trying to sleep.'

'She say that?'

'Yes, Moomie, she say that we into her nerve all the time and we don't have no home training.'

Who she think she is bout she criticising the children!

45

Pearl's eyes narrowed. 'Lutie put the baby in the bassinet and . . .'

'But he will cry, Moomie.'

'Just do what a tell you!' Her voice rose, irritation spilling over onto the child. 'You children too hard ears, is the self same thing every early morning with the lot of you.' She turned away abruptly, forcing back the words, knowing she was allowing her frustration at her husband and his sister to rain down on her daughter's innocent head.

Jalini shifted restlessly on the landing. 'Moomie, you want that a should come?' she asked in a small voice, the impish smile wiped away by a wary concern.

Pearl wanted to call Jalini and hug her as she used to. But something inside her refused to allow her lips to move, stifled the words of encouragement at birth. Instead she nodded in assent. 'All right Jali, come down and eat some breakfast.'

Jalini's small compact body, clad only in a vest and school pantie, hovered at the top of the stairs. 'Moomie, a can tell Aleesa please to come to the table?'

Pearl nodded absently, spooning porridge into a second plate, her mind already moving to the three days of washing piled up on the floor in her room.

By the time the children were ready and on their way to school it was a quarter to nine. Sylvia and Aleesa had long gone and Pearl felt a bone-deep weariness as she surveyed the debris of the morning. She felt she had been on the go for ever. First Kaona had dragged her out of sleep at four in the morning. Then she had made George's breakfast at five, so he could take the early bus to town for his cosmetics; and straight after that the children had to be woken for devotion. Pearl sat at the dirty table, clearing a space indifferently so she could rest her elbow and support her head. The strain of tiredness weighed heavy on her body and pained her eyes, and she wanted nothing more than to close them and get some rest.

Kaona's cry shattered the silence. Pearl pressed her palms against her ears, trying to block out the sound. But it defeated her, slipping past her hands and drilling deeper and deeper into her brain. Her fingers curled into fists and she felt her control slipping. She wanted to scream and rage, to slap him and shake him and hit him and hit him till he stopped the noise and could never start it again.

The animosity she felt frightened her and she groped desperately for the prayers that were as much a part of her existence as cooking on coal stoves and bleaching clothes under the rays of the hot sun. She was so engrossed in the need for control, Jean was practically standing over her before she realised it.

'What you think you playing at, Pearl?' Jean made no attempt to hide her anger. 'You deaf or something? The baby crying loud enough to wake the dead so go and shut him up.'

Pearl stumbled to her feet, the murderous anger receding, as her spirit shrivelled in the face of the woman's contempt. 'H . . . He did wake you?'

Jean looked at her, incredulous. 'Are you stupid or something?'

She felt hurt and insulted. 'A was only wondering.'

'Well don't! Just go and shut him up. I'm sick to death of you not controlling your kids. If it's not one thing in this godforsaken place is another.'

Pearl was stung by that. 'A don't think you can say that about my children.'

'You don't think period!'

Hearing her sister-in-law's growing rage, Pearl nervously tried to placate: 'Jean, a know you feel a wasn't welcoming enough when you first come.'

'A couldn't care less about your welcome, Pearl.' Jean cut her off. 'As far as I am concerned being here is the

47

worst thing I could think of right now, welcome or not.'

'Jean, a don't think you being fair.'

'Don't tell me what I being or not being!' Jean snapped. 'You think I enjoy coming here? The way this place is so noisy and dirty, is a wonder me and the children don't catch something.'

'Jean, I think you've said enough.' Sylvia's sharp interruption was a welcome one, and the baby's cry was piercing in the momentary silence.

Jean gave Sylvia a narrow-eyed stare. 'This isn't really any of your business, is it, Sylv? And you must admit this place is in a state.'

'Jean, you're Pearl's guest, surely the least you could do is show her some respect.'

'What to her? Come off it, Sylvia. You and I both know this is George's house.'

'I don't know any such thing,' Sylvia snapped, 'and I don't think whatever is between George and Pearl is any of our business.'

Pearl felt her stomach churn as Jean's face contorted and for a moment she thought Jean would hit her. Sylvia stood her ground, facing her cousin down, and finally Jean kissed her teeth and shrugged, 'I know exactly what you up to, Sylvia. Don't think I don't. But a warning you . . .'

She trailed off with another kiss teeth, before turning and stomping off with a final parting shot. 'You better stop interfering in what you don't understand or you could just end up sorrier than you know. *Cho!* You must think Jamaica is England.'

Weary tears formed in Pearl's eyes as she watched Jean mount the stairs. Kaona's crying was more insistent, but *she* was even less able to deal with him now. 'A supposing a have to pick up the baby . . .'

'It's OK, I'll see to Kaona,' Sylvia volunteered. 'I'll

48

just make sure Davian is still sleeping, then I'll pick him up.'

Pearl accepted with gratitude. She avoided looking at the dirty dishes and went out to the verandah, needing to escape the sting of truth in Jean's accusing words.

Chapter 4

Beach days are warm and lazy, Sansee's empty shores inviting, despite the debris of high tide. Sylvia wandered the shoreline with Aleesa and Davian, gathering shells and digging for cockles and sea snails. Other times they scrambled over the rocky headland of Goat Pen.

She loved to watch the way sunlight danced off the clear calm sea, the glare giving a surrealist beauty to the fishing boats bobbing at anchor between the mainland and Carbaritta, known locally as Bird's Nest Island. Sansee was a vivid sunscape painted in golds, blues and greens. A quiet neighbourhood to be at peace in. The water of the Galina River was so low, it warmed to blood heat in the morning sun. Davian fell in love with the sullen river at first sight, despite its murky depths and the unpleasant smell of stagnation where it had dried to sluggish ponds. He jumped in, splashing around every chance he got, and only the built-in floats in his Polyotto costume saved him from drowning. Sylvia warmed to the unexpected sense of adventure behind Davian's shy exterior. He was so much like his dead uncle, she engaged with him despite all her vows of neutrality. The child was everywhere: chasing a family of small black piglets, trying to catch a billy goat's horn. Several times she grabbed his hand on the point of picking up a bee, or laughed at his clumsy attempts to trap one of the slimy-bodied baby toads that were everywhere once night fell. His patience and persistence never failed to amaze her, as did the equanimity with which he took setbacks. He simply smiled when he fell over or missed a lizard's tail, showing a wealth of humour and high spirit behind the absence of words.

In the end Sylvia gave up, allowing herself to be drawn further into his silent world. She searched for shells with him and helped to build sandcastles. And all the time she and Aleesa talked to him. Telling him every single thing they did, or saw or smelt, a constant flow of words cocooning him, and wrapping security around his attempts at sounds.

Some days the beach was so hot it burned their soles but even this failed to douse the children's high spirits. They made a game of it, running from their sheltering place to the cool, wet shore, hopping and skipping through the hot, powdery sand.

Sylvia brought them to the beach every morning now school was out, telling herself it was to give Jean breathing space. It was as good an excuse as any, salving her conscience and satisfying her need to keep them safe, while she waited for Jimmy's response to her last letter.

Thoughts of what she had written brought a sense of guilt. All her training in child protection warred with her loyalty to Jean as her cousin. Sylvia had searched her conscience before deciding she had no choice. Her own departure loomed large, just over two weeks more; and the idea of Aleesa and Davian left exposed between their uncle's hostile marriage and their mother's disintegration was more than she could allow.

In all the years she had known Jean she had never seen her so abusive and out of control; Sylvia was at a loss. She had to admit it now: Jean was showing signs of mental strain. She told herself getting Jimmy here was the right thing to do; it was really his problem –

not hers. But in the meantime she felt the need to shelter Aleesa and Davian, to take them away from that sombre house and keep the laughter and wonder alive for them for as long as she was around.

Sylvia was tired today. Jean had disturbed her rest again, returning home drunk from yet another night on the town. Sylvia had been woken from a deep sleep by a sharp pain, coming awake to find her cousin's elbow digging sharply in her stomach; and the woman cursing and struggling to right herself after overbalancing on the edge of the mattress on the floor.

Sylvia had been forced to undress her, listening with disgust to her raving about being a sinner. She kept a wary eye on the sleeping children, trying to quieten Jean in case they were woken by the noise; and all the time pretending to herself that she couldn't smell the stale odour of a stranger rising from the rumpled clothes she was removing. What those soiled clothes signified didn't bear accepting; and now contempt for Jean warred with an unacknowledged anxiety in case the woman caught anything transmittable . . .

'Will Mum be awake yet, Auntie Sylvia?' Aleesa had discarded her book in favour of doodling abstract patterns in the sand.

Sylvia pinned a bright smile on her face. 'She's probably been awake ages. Do you know what time it is?'

'I hope it's lunchtime, I'm starving.'

She sighed; no point putting off the inevitable. 'Then we'd better wake Davian and get going.'

The smile left Aleesa's face. 'Couldn't we eat in the town, Auntie, at that chicken place?'

She was tempted, she enjoyed going down to the Cool Shade restaurant, liking the bustle and activity in the wood yard that it shared space with. 'What about your mum?'

Aleesa wouldn't meet her eyes. 'We could see her later.'

She squashed the feelings of sympathy with the child's words. 'I think your mum would be disappointed, after all, we were supposed to go to Oche Rios this morning.'

Aleesa's shoulders slumped. 'She never wanted to go really,' she muttered, scratching at the sand with her stick, 'she's only going to come and be grumpy and spoil it for all of us.'

'I'm sure she won't,' Sylvia reassured, wishing she really believed that, 'it's just . . . sometimes your mum gets a bit sad.'

The stick stopped its rapid progress and the little girl looked at her with tear-filled eyes. 'Why don't Mum like us any more, Auntie?'

It was a question the child had asked before and she was still at a loss for a convincing reply. Aleesa was not a child to be fobbed off with shallow answers, Jimmy had seen to that. 'Alli, you know that's not true.'

Aleesa sniffed, and wiped the back of her right hand across her nose, leaving a streak of sand. 'Mum never used to get so cross all of the time and she don't want to hug us any more . . .'

Sylvia chewed uncertainly on her bottom lip. 'Aleesa, are you saying your mum's been unkind? Has she . . . well . . . did she ever hit you children?'

For a moment the child looked trapped, guilty. She dropped her head and avoided Sylvia's eyes, her little shoulders stiff and defensive. 'Let's just the three of us go, *please*, Auntie Sylvia. Mum might still be tired.'

Sylvia felt the questions burning on her tongue. The need to probe deeper into the secrets behind the tense, scared face warred with the desire to gather the child close and heal her pain. So she compromised, giving her a brief warm hug, backing off from a knowledge she suddenly didn't dare to seek.

'I'm sure your mum will be awake by now,' she

reassured gently, 'and I bet she'll be really missing you children.'

Aleesa looked doubtful, but Sylvia didn't give her a chance to object. Bending, she picked Davian up deliberately, automatically soothing his protest.

Aleesa fell into step with her. 'Will Mum really want to see us, Auntie? Will she?'

'Of course.' Sylvia hid her own uncertainty behind a bright, breezy smile, quashing the temptation to use the opening offered by Aleesa's words. Things were bad enough without antagonising her cousin any further. Jean had already accused her of trying to steal away the children's affection and the last thing she needed was another row.

Jean was sprawled on the peeling lounger in the last patch of shade on the small verandah and Sylvia's heart sank when she saw the look on her face. Whoever she had been with last night certainly hadn't sweetened her mood.

'Where have you lot been?' she asked contentiously, eyeing with open hostility the way Davian held on to Sylvia. 'I thought we were supposed to be going to Oche this morning.'

'I wouldn't have thought you'd want to see it again so soon.' The words slipped out before Sylvia realised, a gauntlet between the two of them.

Jean gave her a withering look, turning her attention to her daughter. 'Aleesa, take Davian inside to the toilet, then go over to Miss Lisa and stay with your cousins.'

'But I'm hungry, Mum.'

'Jean, we only came back to ask if you wanted to come down to the Cool Shade restaurant.'

'Please, Mum . . .' Aleesa's voice was querulous. 'We could all go.'

Jean looked guilty, then annoyed. 'Aleesa, not now,'

she muttered impatiently, 'Just do as I tell you and don't bother my soul in this heat.'

The child's eyes filled with angry tears and she glared from Jean to Sylvia. 'I told you we should go without her, Auntie.'

'Aleesa!' Jean's voice held a warning, but the little girl ignored it, too full of disappointment to take heed.

'You never let me and Davian do anything! You're horrible and I wish Daddy was here instead!'

The crack of Jean's open palm against Aleesa's cheek was a shock of sound. The child stumbled back, out of reach, watching her mother fearfully.

'I'm sorry, Mum . . .'

'You didn't have to do that.' Sylvia's arms tightened around Davian's tense body, her own shock registering slowly. 'There wasn't any need to hit her!'

Her cousin's gaze wavered in the face of her outrage, shame and guilt gradually replaced by defiance and challenge. 'I can do what I want with my own children.'

'They're not possessions, you know, Jean, they're as much people as you and I.'

Jean ignored that. 'Aleesa, get going and do what I say.'

The child hesitated, and Sylvia bent to put a reluctant Davian down. 'Go on, Alli, do what your mum say.'

'But I – '

'*Aleesa!*' Jean's eyes narrowed with fury and she made to get off the lounger.

The child looked startled, scared. Grabbing her brother's hand she dragged him away with her.

Sylvia was furious. 'Do you always have to take your temper out on Aleesa?'

Jean hissed air through her teeth. 'What's it to you?'

Sylvia lost her struggle to keep in the angry words. 'The way you carry on it's no wonder the children are afraid of you.'

The tense silence was broken by the clatter of Jean's

feet as she got up abruptly. 'Is that what you trying to do, turn the kids against me?'

Sylvia felt her own anger bubble up. 'I don't need to *do* anything, you're doing a great job of that all by yourself. If this is the way you carry on at home, it's no wonder Jimmy needed a break.' It was a low blow and she regretted the words as soon as they were uttered. 'I'm sorry, I shouldn't have said that.'

'Why not?' Jean looked as if she was about to explode. 'Is what you thinking, isn't it? You did always resent the fact Jimmy like me, didn't you? You think you was the only one should married to a Dyer. A wouldn't surprise if is you make him don't want to marry me.'

She was horrified. 'Jean, you know that's not true!'

Jean gave a humourless laugh. 'You think I born yesterday? You never did think I was as good as you.'

Sylvia was angry with herself for feeling so defensive. 'Oh don't be so stupid. You are the one always putting yourself down . . .'

'Oh yeah?'

'Yes! It's this same insecurity I was talking about when I said you and Jimmy weren't a good idea. Can't you see, Jean,' she spread her hands appealingly, 'so long as you have such a negative self-image, you're going to make life a misery for everyone else.'

Jean sniffed, '*Sure*, is all my fault now, is it? Well, you needn't think you going to get away with that one.'

'What are you talking about now?'

'Don't you come the innocent with me!' Jean's voice was full of scorn. 'I know what you and Jimmy plotting behind my back. But if you think you can undermine me like that you have another think coming.'

For a moment Sylvia thought Jean had somehow found out about her letter and she cast around for something to say. 'Jean, nobody is plotting against you. I admit I am a bit concerned about the way you get at Aleesa, but . . .'

'So what you expect me to do, put up with her rudeness?'

So she didn't know, hadn't guessed. Sylvia breathed in relief, risking another push. If she could only get Jean to loosen up, acknowledge her problem. 'Look, Aleesa isn't really the problem, is she?'

The anger simmering in Jean's eyes boiled over. 'No, *you* are, the way you always trying to make me look bad in front of my own children. You think I don't know what you up to, bout you keeping them out of my way?'

Sylvia shifted uneasily, wishing she had kept her mouth shut. 'Jean, what's got into you now?'

'Don't patronise me. I know what you up to with your sudden *concern for the children*, a mean, when since you turn expert? You and Winston couldn't even bother when you had the chance to have kids, but now I have mine you quick to wanti, wanti.'

Sylvia wasn't going to let Jean rile her. 'Look, I'm not trying to replace you . . .'

'You could a fool me.' The words were provocative, a challenge.

'Of course I'm not.' Sylvia told herself Jean was suffering, that she didn't mean half the things she said, couldn't really help the way she kept lashing out. 'Not that I could anyway. They know who their mother is.'

'No thanks to you, I bet.'

Sylvia shook her head. 'Jean, I'm not going to stay here trading insults with you.'

Jean wasn't accepting that. 'Is Jimmy put you up to it, isn't it?'

Her heart skipped a beat, and she prayed she didn't look as guilty as she was feeling. 'Put me up to what?'

'I know he want my children, but a tell you this for

nothing! Not you or him going to get them. I'll see them dead first.'

The venom rattled her, and she hung on to the reassuring view that her cousin was only speaking in the heat of the moment. 'Look, this isn't getting us anywhere.'

'You damn right is not! Well, I don't need you round my children. We going round to see a friend and you not invited.'

Sylvia watched them go with mixed feelings. She was worried about Aleesa and Davian but right now she needed the space to think. She hadn't managed the confrontation with Jean very well, unable to find distance between herself and the feelings she had for the children. She felt a stab of resentment towards Jimmy. How could he lumber her with this? He of all people knew why she had come to Jamaica, knew what it meant to her. She went for the phone on an impulse, needing to offload some of the negative feelings. It was his mess after all.

She glanced at the clock on the tallboy. What time was it in England now? Seven o'clock, time enough for him to have finished his writing for the day. Sylvia dialled before she had time to change her mind, relieved when the phone was answered on the second ring.

'Jimmy.'

'Yes?'

'It's Sylvia.'

'What's wrong . . . the children?'

She hardened her heart against the worry in his voice, reminding herself that it was his mess. 'Jean's drinking like a fish . . . she's scaring the children. Listen, I know she was berating you continuously when she first got here, but it was when you stopped taking her calls that the drinking got really bad. Couldn't you just speak to her?'

His answer was uncompromising. 'Jean and I went through all there was to say before she left. She know what the situation is.'

'And what about Aleesa and Davian?'

'You mean she's ill-treating them?'

Now she had him on the phone, she wasn't so certain about sharing blame. 'Didn't you get my letter?'

'No, when did you send it?'

Her heart sank. 'Last week . . .'

'Are you telling me she's mistreating the children?'

She didn't have the heart to dump the whole thing on him, trapped as he was by the helplessness of distance. 'She hit Aleesa today and I don't think it's the first time.' She sighed, taking the plunge. 'Jimmy, I don't think she's safe with them. They're with me most of the time, but I'm leaving in just over a week and then what?'

'Sylvia, couldn't you stay on . . . just for a couple of weeks until I can get there?'

This was all she needed. 'I've got a job to get back to, you know . . . look, why don't you talk to George?'

'Are you kidding!' Jimmy sounded frustrated, angry. 'As far as he's concerned, childcare is women's business. Look, I know it's a lot to ask, but you know what it's like getting a flight to Jamaica at this time of year.'

He sounded frantic, and it created new guilt in her – as if the children really were her responsibility. 'Jimmy, you know I can't leave my cases that long.'

He kissed his teeth, annoyed now. 'I thought you was supposed to be in the caring profession. *Jesus, Sylvia man!* You already say Allie and Davian are at risk . . . or don't relatives count when it comes to protecting children?'

The words were like a cage, bringing a sudden anger. They were all so fond of reminding her of her childless state, but it was another story when it suited them.

'You can cut that out for a start, it's not Jean you are talking to now, you know.'

The line hummed in the silence. 'You're right, I'm sorry, that was well out of order. But Sylvie, you are the only person I could really ask.'

'You know I can't . . .'

'Sylv, you can't just up and leave the children, man . . . you know what Winston would say if he was there.'

'Well, he isn't here and you of all people knew how important this trip was. This mess is your fault, you know.'

'I accept that, but your leaving them don't solve anything.'

'You can't offload on me like this, Jimmy, it's not fair. You knew how much Jean was drinking and you must have realised how that affected her mood.'

'I didn't, Sylvia, honest to God . . . Alright, so she never really take much hand in looking after them, but you really think I would leave them with her if I thought she would hurt them?'

Her silence made him swear. 'Christ, Sylv, I can *tell* you about Jean and the kids; she's really good, really loving and patient most of the time.'

She ignored that. 'You mean she doesn't go out all night and stumble in blind drunk?'

His silence gave her the answer even before he did. 'She said she wasn't going to drink any more,' he justi-fied finally.

'*And you believed that?*'

'Sylvia, I'm a writer, for God's sake, not a bloody social worker. When my woman tell me a thing – swear on it – of course a going to believe her.' He sighed. 'What went wrong, Sylvie? One minute things are going really well and the next she's off work so much they asking her to resign.'

'*What!* She's lost her job?' This they hadn't told her. 'You might have let me know about that sooner.'

'How could I when she won't accept it herself? She keeps saying she is on unpaid leave, and insists she going back once Davian start school in September.' He paused and she could almost see him picking the right words. 'Sylvie, a asking . . . no, a begging you, stay a little longer, just for the children. Whatever the right or wrong of this it's not their fault they in this position.'

There was no denying he had a point and she found herself weakening. 'Look, if you can speak to them at work I'll try and get my ticket changed.'

'What shall I tell them?' Jimmy wasn't giving her the chance to change her mind.

'I'll ring British Airways and see if I can get them to give me a later flight date, then I'll get back to you.'

His relief was almost embarrassing. 'Sylvie, you're a lifesaver. I'll make it up to you, just wait and see. I'll be there as soon as I can get a flight, I promise you.'

They said goodbye in the awkward silence that followed.

Chapter 5

Sunlight woke her. Sunlight and the amplified voice of the Sunday preacher exhorting sinners to repent and promising them a warm welcome in Christ.

Jean lay soaking up the morning heat, enjoying the elusive smell of new grass and ripening jackfruit, and drifting with the rousing hymn chorus. As usual, with the sound of the service, her head cleared of critical voices, was filled instead with a kind of peace. The church beckoned, comforted, and for a while she let herself dream of being there, surrounded by all that good will.

Ever since she was a child, younger than Aleesa, she had wanted to go to Sunday church – the forbidden church. And now she found herself wondering if God was giving her a sign at last. Maybe he was saying she needed a church like this, a warmer, less burdensome belief. Sunday church didn't dominate its faithful *too* much. She fancied it easier, a more manageable requirement, that stopped dead at midday and left you free of obligation for another week, apart from optional evening services.

That she could have coped with from the outset. She might never had strayed, never faced the corrupting influence of drink and greed in an atmosphere like that.

Instead of exuberant, undemanding worship, she had suffered the austere fundamentalism of Sabbath keeping, lying to escape public humiliation for her trespasses, until guilt piled up on guilt and lies became a habit.

If only she had known that it had been God's way of speaking to her, of warning her. Jean realised in a rush of optimism that the sign had been there all along. While the Sunday service was being broadcast, she never felt the need to lash out; to hurt the children and keep on hurting them till the pain in her head subsided.

She shook her head, amazed at what she considered her own blindness. Years she had waited and prayed, too honest or too stupid to take the vow of baptism in hope. She had needed the transcendental experience, the knowledge that she had been forgiven for Noel and the destruction she had brought on her father's head.

In the end she had turned her back on the Church, blaming God for setting His face against her. And she had suffered. Alone, cast out from the fellowship of shared belief, she had felt nothing of the balm of God, only his vengeance. New problems surfaced the minute she had learnt to cope with the old . . . double blows, triple blows, driving her to the edge of madness.

The image of the child came back to her, the child bleeding in the shadow of the cross. Jean shivered.

If Jimmy never abandon me I would never be in this state, she thought sadly, *he would never had let me go up Mountain District and suffer through that.*

She rolled on to her side, trying to blot out the images of Jimmy. She could feel depression seeping in again, and feared it would cause the voice of evil to return. Only fear of waking Sylvia and the children, crowded on the mattress below her, prevented her reaching for the bottle in the bag on her side of the bed.

She lay rocking back and forth, arms wrapped tightly around herself in an effort to find some comfort. That was how the child had rocked.

Jean pulled her mind away. She groped for a safer image. But that was another mistake. The new images rolled in, stark and accusing . . . Sansee beach on Friday, where she had sought out Sylvia and the children, under the landmark almond tree.

Something had snapped inside her that day. She had looked at Aleesa's frightened, wary eyes and for a moment saw her daughter merging with that other eight-year-old. It had been scary, terrifying. She had wanted to grab her daughter and run away, keep her pure and safe from the dangers lurking behind the most innocent-looking things. She had been shaking so much it had made her clumsy, and she was too frightened to make sense of Sylvia's concern and the little girl's alarm. Slowly, painfully, she had pulled herself together, forcing the panic down. It left her weak and shaky.

Maybe that was why she had turned to Davian, needing the warm generosity of his silent comfort. But he had backed off, shrinking away, denying her his serenity.

The anger rose sharp and hard, catching her without warning. It pulled her hand back and sent it swinging with a force that knocked the breath from the child.

Davian had screamed and Aleesa had edged away, round-eyed and frightened. Everything seemed to recede . . . the breeze, sounds of the waves, voices over the still air.

Then time started again, loud and roaring. She heard her own ragged breathing, Davian's wails, Aleesa's sobbing; and loudest of all, Sylvia's stunned silence.

The demon voice laughed a bitter sobbing sound, deep and booming in the cavity of her chest.

Sylvia had snatched Davian to her, giving Jean a speaking look. She took Aleesa's hand and led the children away, ignoring Jean's remorseful words and pleas for forgiveness.

Desperation had sent Jean scurrying up to the Sabbath church – the church of her early childhood. The church that had cast a shadow so long, she had fled the country to escape it. She had been out of bed early, full of hope and apprehension. She had been convinced the time was right. Her choices were clear now: living in the greyness of semi-madness, sinking so deep into sin she would be beyond the reach of grace – or repentance and redemption. She had to believe she would find some peace of mind if she prayed hard enough in the cool simplicity of the Mountain District Church; or what else was left for her?

If only she could have found forgiveness, a little compassion. It hadn't been easy, going up to Sabbath church, facing the congregation, facing the past after running so far away from it. And they hadn't given her a chance. She had walked hesitantly through the door and shuffled into the seat next to the side entrance. Slowly, her presence had registered. Hostile stares turned in her direction, scandalised whispers spread through the church and the people close to her shifted away. Unable to bear it, she had rushed from the building.

Pearl's querulous voice rose on the warm air, bringing home the unpleasantness of another day in her brother's house. *No wonder I need to escape*, Jean muttered to herself. *That woman nag so much I hearing her in my dream.*

Jean thought about the bottle again. No. She had finally accepted that one small drink would never be enough. It would take a lot more than that to filter out her sister-in-law's pervasive and unsettling discontent.

The church congregation was singing another hymn. It steadied her, brought back the fantasy of a better place . . . a belief to heal herself with.

She could go – no one could stop her – and Sylvia would be here for the children.

I bet it won't be like yesterday.

Almost without intending to, she was out of bed, reaching mechanically for dress and underwear. It was

65

as if something in that service drew her; calling to the neglected spiritual self somewhere deep inside. Jean paused by the door of the cluttered room, taking a moment to listen to the reassuring sounds. They were singing another hymn now . . . just for her, confirming that to them no sin could be beyond redemption.

Today she didn't linger in the sparse, concrete shower stall. This time she did not need a surreptitious drink. She was buoyant, featherlight, floating on the certainty of that warm welcome. She dressed in double-quick time, keeping a wary eye on the sleeping forms of her cousin and her children.

Pearl was in the kitchen area when Jean came down the stairs. Her face fell into habitual frown lines as she took in the neat floral dress and blue pudding hat. 'Jean, you never did tell me say you was going out this morning.'

Jean shrugged. 'I wasn't aware I was supposed to report my movements to you, Pearl.'

'You know is not what a mean, is just that George looking bout some ackee for your breakfast.'

Jean wasn't going to let her sister-in-law irritate her, not today. 'I will have it when I get back.'

Pearl hovered uncertainly. 'About how long you going be?'

'As long as it take.' The woman was so nosy and intrusive, but Jean wasn't going to let her tempt the anger back, not now with the beneficence of the service ringing in her ears. 'Look, just tell George I'll have a late breakfast.'

Pearl looked as if she wanted to argue, take the conversation further, but Jean didn't wait for more. Every minute she wasted here was a minute lost from the healing words. 'Look, Pearl, I don't have time to talk right now.' She walked to the door, the need to be there in the Sunday church lending speed to her feet, despite the unaccustomed high heels and the uneven ground.

Jean reached the church in time for the main sermon and stood hesitating beside the door, afraid of attracting attention by going in late. Outside the sagging wooden porch, Sunday church didn't seem such a good idea and she wondered whether she shouldn't just hang around a little and then go back.

Then the pastor talked of hating the sin but loving the sinner and she found herself propelled forward, to sit on the back pew, where she was sandwiched between a thin stooped man with a hacking cough and a stout sweating woman. The man leaned across to share his Bible with her as the pastor quoted scripture, and Jean felt the tight bands of tension dissolve from round her chest.

They accepted her, just like that. No shifting of eyes to mark her out, no sudden restless mutter of unease. She relaxed, drinking in the words of consolation in the sermon, buoyed up by the uplifting sounds of prayer and the hymns that followed after. It was as if she had rediscovered belonging; that sense of homecoming that had been so elusive, so lost and swallowed, when her father had abandoned them. It lifted the guilt and failure from her shoulders, leaving her spirit light. At last God had relented, allowed her a belief to heal herself, a guide to lead her safely through the maze of sin.

At the end of the service her neighbours embraced and greeted her in Christ. Jean felt her heart expanding. She stayed where she was, long after the pews had emptied and the beauty of the service was only an echoing memory. She just needed to sit awhile and drink in the peace and the cool serenity.

Why hadn't she come in here before? All those years of mortifying herself, trying to gain acceptance from the pitiless God – the false God of the Saturday church, when all the time, salvation rested just down the hill in the warped wooden structure of the humble Sunday church. She couldn't help regretting all that might have been.

'Everything all right?'

Jean's mood snapped as the elderly pastor sat down beside her. She waited, apprehensive, sure the weighted-down feeling would return, bringing all the destructive poison back.

He held out his hand, breaking the deadlock of silence. 'I am Deacon Davis.'

She adjusted her perception, feeling a release of tension. 'Jean Mackenzie,' she said, accepting the tentative bridge, grateful for this human contact.

The deacon frowned. 'You and Mr Mackenzie up housing scheme related?'

She nodded reluctantly, not wanting to bring her brother into it, needing to keep the world outside, for a little longer.

The deacon smiled, understanding. 'You look like you having troubles.' His voice was gentle, inviting her to share, offering the kindness of a listening ear.

Jean found herself opening up, telling him about Jimmy's desertion and her out-of-control feelings with the children.

'You sure is not just a short time to hisself your husband looking? From what you saying he is a hard-working man.'

'I don't know, Deacon Davis, a just feel he don't want me any more.' She didn't correct the assumption that she and Jimmy were married, ashamed to acknowledge that sin in the face of a man of God.

'A feel you should try and write one letter and tell him bout the way you feeling. If the talking upsetting you it don't make sense for you to keep on doing it. For all that making is a next upset again when he feel say you pressurising him.'

She bowed her head, remembering Davian and feeling a fresh guilt. She wanted to tell him about it, felt the words burning on her tongue . . .

'Something else troubling you?' he asked perceptively.

She couldn't meet his eyes, but the need to unburden herself was overwhelming. This old man, this stranger, she trusted him somehow. 'I hit my little boy, Friday. Knock him down and bruise up the whole of one side of his chest.'

'In punishment?' His expression remained warm, compassionate.

She hesitated, wanting to take the easy way out. Then she remembered the service. The good feelings Saturday worship had never brought. 'No, just because I was angry.'

'What he do to vex you so?'

She wanted to tell him how Davian denied her comfort. How he kept peace bottled away in the face of her turmoil and her need, just like his father always did. Words gathered on her tongue, words to explain the muddled confusion inside her head. An image of Jimmy formed in her mind and she looked at the bright drawing of Jesus on the altar wall. 'Because he is his father's son and I don't know how to reach him.'

'We is all God's children, you know . . . You love your son.'

The 'yes' came without the slightest hesitation. Love was not the issue, had never been. She loved Davian, loved Aleesa and most of all – she loved Jimmy. Jean sighed. 'I would do anything for my children, Pastor, but I just don't know how to reach them. They are always for their father, you see.'

'But if you saying you love them, you is the mother, mother love is a natural thing.'

She couldn't tell this old man what it was like. How could he understand? Him with all his certainty and belief?

69

The old deacon cleared his throat. 'It sounding to me like you needing guidance. Pastor coming down Sunday after next, and a sure he would willing to sit and talk with you.'

Jean frowned and looked into the wrinkled face. 'I'm not a member of your church,' she confessed, remembering, belatedly, how non-members were disregarded in the church of her own childhood.

He shook his head and smiled. 'As a say, we is all God's children, and Jesus was the first to ask that we bring the sinner to him.'

She relaxed, feeling a sense of final acceptance. 'I would like to see your pastor, then, if I may.'

He nodded, looking pleased. 'A will sure and tell Pastor if you want to come.' He hesitated. 'You would like that a pray with you meantime?'

Jean bowed her head in acquiescence, needing that absolution. Focusing on the words of hope she listened as he called to God, begged his blessing for her, asked for a soothing of her troubled mind. Somehow he made her feel better, more positive, closer to the healing she had come here to seek. She said the final Amen with a lighter heart, feeling that the coils of depression had loosened. Now at last she could see a way back to the self she had once been.

When Jean lifted her head it was to a brighter day. The sights and sounds were sharper, clearer than they had ever been. It was as if she had just emerged from a long, long sleep.

'Thank you, Deacon Davis, I feel a lot better now.'

He smiled with pleasure. 'We have service six o'clock tonight, you welcome to join us.'

'I'll think about it.' She was afraid to commit herself. Cautious in case the bad feelings came back.

He didn't push. 'I will pray to the Lord to guide your step and keep you from the devil temptation; and meantime a will talk with Pastor concerning your case.'

70

It was the first time Jean had felt good for longer than she could remember. When she left the church there was a spring in her step, and she found herself returning the hundred and one greetings that were a feature of life in a small place. It was hard to believe that the world was the same depressing place she had woken up in today. The experience of the morning had transformed her so much, she half expected it to have spilt over into the familiar sounds of the housing scheme and the atmosphere of her brother's house.

She shook her head, a little dazed by the evidence of normality. The air was flavoured with the smell of red peas boiling in preparation for the rice which would accompany the traditional Sunday chicken. Children in their best clothes darted in and out of the low concrete houses, chasing each other and getting underfoot. Mr Brown's hens had flown over the fence dividing his garden from George's and were pecking at the dog food drying out in the midday sun, while Miss Lisa's cat stalked a lizard under the pawpaw tree.

Sylvia and the children were on the verandah, playing some sort of word game when Jean finally reached the top of the outside stairs. The sound of their laughter and the children's excitement was punctuated by Pearl's endless litany of complaint. It didn't faze her any more. From where she was standing, newly filled with the spirit of peace, Jean could feel compassion for her sister-in-law, who had to live without grace while trying to pretend she had found favour in the Lord.

'Where have you been?' Sylvia looked puzzled.

Jean grinned, 'Over the Sunday church.'

Her cousin was surprised. 'Wasn't yesterday enough?'

'This was different.' Enthusiasm threatened to bubble over. 'Honest, Sylvie, it was great. I really feel better for going.'

Aleesa looked at her with an uncertain smile, 'Does that mean you won't be angry any more, Mum?'

'Yes, sweetheart.' Generosity welled up, and she reacted to the child without constraint. 'Look, I'm sorry I've been so horrible to you and Davian.'

The child looked grave, unsure. 'Does that mean you won't hurt me and Davian again?'

Jean tensed, feeling remorse flood in, and suppressing the spark of annoyance it brought. *Not now*, she wouldn't let the old bad feelings build inside again. This was the first test of her determination. 'That's right, I won't. Now, how would you like to come to church with me this evening?'

Her youngest niece cut Aleesa's response. 'Auntie, you go into a Sunday church?' Jalini looked scandalised, horrified. 'Moomie say is only Sabbath-keepers can get save.'

Jean shrugged the child's words aside. 'That's not true, Jalini, Sabbath-keeping isn't the only way to worship God.'

'Is true, Auntie?'

Jean nodded, beating a quick retreat. The last thing she wanted was to talk about sabbath-keeping. Yesterday's memory was still raw, still able to leave a bitter aftertaste.

She scooped Davian up, ignoring his wriggling protest. The fear in his eyes pained her new, caring self. She wanted to show him she was her old self, no longer dangerous. His father had trusted her with him and she needed to atone for her failure. So she held him close, trying to tell him without words that she would never need to cause him any more hurt. Finally he became still, passive. Jean missed the feel of his small hands around her neck. The way he used to rest his head on her shoulder and smile reassurance at her.

She pretended she couldn't hear her cousin's footsteps close behind her on the stairs or feel her anxiety. Sylvia would think she really had cracked if she even knew the half of it. She could see her cousin's puzzlement as she turned to face her in the room, sensed her worry, and braced herself for the questions that would follow.

'Jean,' Sylvia closed the door and leaned back against it, 'Davian had a big bruise this morning, so I hope you really mean it about not hitting the children again.'

Jean played for time, fussing over the clothes she was selecting to change into. She pretended she didn't see the way Davian scrambled away from her, going to wrap himself around Sylvia's leg. Not long ago he would have stayed with her in preference to anyone but Jimmy, despite the occasional slap. She tried not to let the hurt of rejection in.

'Jean?' Impatience mingled with the scepticism in Sylvia's voice.

Jean wanted to tell her it had been an accident, that she had not meant to hit him so hard, that Davian was clumsy, had moved, slipped; even that Sylvia had misinterpreted the whole thing. But one look at her cousin's face told her that would be a waste of time. 'I was going through some rough times and I guess I did kind of take it out on the kids.'

Sylvia didn't look convinced. 'How long have you been hitting Davian?'

She felt defensive of a sudden. 'Not long . . . look, I told you it was a bad patch; but it's over now.'

'Does that mean you won't pester Jimmy any more?'

Anger stirred. 'That's none of your business.'

'It is when the children and I have to take the backlash.'

Jean flinched in the face of her cousin's bluntness, irritated by the sense of responsibility it engendered. 'Look, Sylvia, I just told you I was going through a bad patch but it's over now . . . alright?'

'Just tell me honestly, Jean: the problems with Jimmy, are they all to do with your drinking?'

Thrown off balance, she fell back on the old denial.

'I only used to have the odd drink and even that is out now . . . That's what I been trying to tell you . . .'

'Don't give me that.' Sylvia didn't let her finish. 'When are you going to admit you have a drink problem?'

Jean was indignant. 'I don't have a drink problem.'

'Jean, I could hardly miss the amount of times you've been staggering about drunk and if that wasn't enough I found the bottles this morning.'

'What bottles?'

'The ones you stashed away in Davian's suitcase.'

Anger prickled at Jean's scalp. 'You mean you've been searching through my things?'

'No, you forgot to leave out Davian's clothes in your haste to get to church, so I had to get him something to wear.'

Jean took a deep breath, realising how closely Sylvia was watching her. She mustn't let her cousin's disbelief pull her out of control. 'Whatever you might think, I've never had a problem with drink. OK, I admit I have the occasional binge, but that don't add up to alcoholic.'

'So you won't mind that I emptied them down the sink?'

Jean's heart gave a brief skip, but she forced a careless laugh, holding on to the promise she had made herself today. She would be washed in the blood, born anew. 'No . . . I'd probably have done it myself if you hadn't got there first. Sylvia, something great happened today.' The enthusiasm returned, displacing resentment. 'I had the most wonderful experience.'

'What? At church?'

'Yes, I woke up and heard them singing and it was like someone was telling me to come.'

'I thought you said you wouldn't set foot back in a church after the way they cold-shouldered you yesterday.'

She shivered, refusing to tell Sylvia about the *real* trauma of Saturday's visit, refusing even to think of it right now. 'And I did mean it as well, but this is different, these are really nice people, Sylvia, true Christians.'

'And you can tell that after one visit?'

Jean nodded. 'Before that, even, is like I was saying, I was just lying here listening, you know, and it was like something was calling to me . . . I mean, I know it sound silly but I just had to go.'

Sylvia digested that. 'I thought you weren't into religion.'

Jean shrugged. 'I always believed in God, just never found the true way to worship Him.'

The worry was back in Sylvia's eyes. 'You sure it's not just an escape . . . some kind of crutch because you're feeling low?'

It sounded so much like what Jimmy might have said, it made Jean bristle. 'You not in no position to talk, you don't even believe in God.'

'That's true, but Jean, if you do have a drink problem this isn't the way to solve it, you know, hiding in religion is just another form of running away.'

Jean ignored that, turning her back on her cousin's concerns. 'I'm not one of your clients, Sylvia,' she said stiffly, 'I don't have to listen to any of your stupid theories.'

'And what if I'm right . . . tell me that?'

She wasn't going to answer that, not to herself, not to her cousin; wasn't going to get herself into a state where the need for a drink made her ripe for the devil's work. 'Sylvie, just drop it, will you? I'm taking the kids for a walk . . .'

'I'll come with you.'

Jean resented her cousin's suspicious face. 'Do what you like, but I don't want any more of your negativeness.'

Sylvia looked like she wanted to argue. Instead she lifted Davian, shifting her hip to hold his gangling length. 'The kids and I will wait for you outside.'

Chapter 6

Jean had found the Lord! The shock of it reverberated in Pearl's head. The Lord had actually touched *Jean's* heart and given her the call. She could hardly believe such a thing was possible. How could someone like Jean have a sacred experience, an experience that was so powerful it effected an immediate and total transformation? One minute the woman was beating up her children, cursing and swearing on the street and going up the Mountain District church so drunk she could barely walk. Then literally overnight all that stopped, replaced by caring and love for almost everyone.

Pearl found it difficult to accept. It just wasn't fair. *She* had served the Lord for so many years, faithfully and without complaints. It was hard when she was so full of doubts and questions about everything at church. Yet she had overcome every single temptation put in her way, even though her faith was weak. Why couldn't that experience have been hers? She had waited long enough for something to make concrete the beliefs that were more routine than deeply held. God seemed to be touching everyone else, so why not her? Look at George, he was always talking about the vision that led him away from the world to a Christian life. Any opportunity he got, he would describe in detail how he had risen from nothing to gain his Jamaica School Certificate – not that it seemed such a great reward considering the drama he made of it. At least Marcie got a car, a house and a new job and she even managed to marry Pastor and get a *university degree* thrown in.

Pearl sighed. Wishing was futile when it only led to more disappointment and frustration. So she watched Jean instead, secretly hoping to catch her in sin and expose her for the hypocrite she knew she was. But the woman didn't slip once.

Jean had been open and honest about every vice and sin, unlike George who confessed selectively, and kept on in carnal sin with Miss Jourdan over by Southroad. She knew that was where he went on the second Tuesday of every month, when the woman's husband went to Brown's Town market in St Ann. Jean at least gave up her sin, even if she turned the whole thing into sordid theatre.

The drinking had merited the most drama. She must have poured away all the alcohol as soon as she got back from the Pentecostal church that first Sunday. Pearl had watched in surprise as the secret vice of drinking alcohol became a public confession. Jean brought the bottles down two by two, first thing Monday morning, and lined them against the kitchen wall. Pearl had been saddened by the waste as she watched her sister-in-law instruct Mauvia to take them out with the rubbish. Jean might have considered giving the drinks to George; the price foreign spirits were selling in Jamaica he would have made a good profit. As far as Pearl was concerned, it just showed how selfish her sister-in-law was.

Later, Jean buried her head in George's tattered copy of the Schofield Bible, reading passages aloud, and acting for all the world as if she was debating with herself. She had sung hymns as well, raising her voice so high that it woke Kaona, and the children begged to go down to Miss Lisa's house, because they couldn't concentrate to read their books.

The injustice had nagged Pearl all day, till she was

almost at bursting point. Finding the Lord had certainly not mellowed her sister-in-law's attitude towards her, if the provoking way she had been acting was anything to go by. Pearl consoled herself with the knowledge that Jean would have to apologise sooner or later, that continuing with her hostility would only prove her Christianity a sham.

As the woman wandered from verandah to guest room, always with the Bible clutched in her hands, Pearl couldn't help thinking she should have got the holy spirit instead. The way she had suffered George and his sister over all those years . . . she deserved *that* as compensation if nothing else.

On Tuesday evening Jean dressed carefully, singing hymns as she tidied herself in the bathroom. Anticipation caused Pearl's heart to leap, as she wondered if character had finally come to seek the other woman out. But the optimism didn't last. Once her sister-in-law was ready, she heard her trying to persuade Sylvia to come with her to Bible study.

That set the tone for the week which followed. Jean spent almost every day preaching to Mauvia, Sylvia, George and any roadside passer-by foolhardy enough to stop. Then on Friday she gathered all the children, apologising and explaining that she had walked in sin. Pearl felt a sneaking admiration for her sister-in-law as she watched the woman humbling herself. Whatever her faults, Jean had courage. It took a lot of guts to admit to sin in such an open and public way, and to children at that. Pearl wasn't sure she could admit to even a single fault in that way. Just imagine how undermining that would be for discipline. To Pearl's mind it was better that her children saw her without flaw until the inevitable happened and they grew up to find out differently. Still, *she* wasn't one to criticise the foreign ways she didn't understand and she began to relax at the thought that *her* apology had to come too.

Staining the concrete floor with red-oak polish, she fantasised about what she would say to Jean. She would be gracious, of course, forgiving and welcoming. It was the least she could do for a fellow traveller in the Lord. She would tell Jean there were no hard feelings, that she understood the struggle against the call to a Christian life. After all, wasn't it something she endured in all those years with her husband? Look how she herself suffered for her rejection of the Church. It was as if she paid for every individual doubt and question that lay unvoiced in her head. As a child she had never been able to take anything on trust. Had to try things for herself to see if warnings against them were correct. That was why, in the headstrong folly of youth, she had rebelled against the rigid Christian principles Moomie had tried to instil in all of them.

Sounds of footsteps interrupted the memories. She looked up to see Jean coming slowly down the stairs, her whole attention focused on the text of the Good News Bible she was reading. When she reached the bottom Jean looked up as if sensing eyes on her. Pearl smiled encouragingly, expecting some kind word or greeting. She was eager to get her sister-in-law's apology safely under her belt, despite her resolve to be patient. Maybe Jean realised the wrongs were against her and decided to go ahead and talk to her without bothering to wait for George.

Her sister-in-law's eyes narrowed. 'What do you want, Pearl?' The voice was cold, the face shuttered and unwelcoming. 'Is there some in particular reason why you staring at me with that vacant grin?'

The rejection was like a physical blow. 'A was just being friendly . . .' Pearl tailed off, feeling at a loss. She was hurt by the cutting words, but she stayed where she was, bracing herself for the insult.

Jean didn't disappoint her. 'I told you already, Pearl, I neither want or need your friendship. The best thing you could do for both of us is keep out of my way and stop forcing yourself on me.'

That sparkled her temper. 'Me would *never* force myself on nobody, me would a have too much pride for that . . . and sides that a my house this, so if anything . . .'

Jean looked at her sister-in-law, at the dirty kitchen, the flies pooling on the draining dishes. Christian forgiveness was one thing, but Pearl was a joke. She had tricked George into marriage, had never been worthy of him, and her pretence at religion – what a sham. She was wallowing in squalor, rowing with her husband, neglecting her own and other people's children and generally making life unpleasant for everyone. Jean's irritation spilled over.

'Your husband's house, don't you mean? You just tell me what and what is yours, Pearl, so I can avoid using them, OK?'

'Jean, you don't have to be so unreasonable all the time, soh,' Pearl complained, the defiance dying as fast as it had come. 'A don't feel say you have no reason to always treating me so bad. All a trying to do, is make life little easier seeing as how we living together in the one small space.'

'Speak for yourself.' Jean was dismissive. 'There is nothing you can do to make this godforsaken place comfortable. If is not the Johnny punko falling down and getting squashed in the bed, it's the water running out because you can't be bothered to conserve it.'

Pearl felt the injustice deeply. Jean could hardly blame her if the stinky-smelling, hard-bodied worms had a particular weakness for concrete houses. And as to the water, Kaona's nappies had to be washed every day, water shortage or not. 'A really feel say you take set on me for a reason, you know, Jean.'

'You mean you have enough intelligence to work that out?' Scorn was heavy in every word. 'The way you are so thick-skinned, I never would have believed it.'

'*Cho Jean!* You can't come in a my house and abuse my wife so, man!'

For the first time in longer than she could remember, Pearl was relieved to hear George's voice. But relief was followed by a new worry, that he might blame her for having said something to spark off his sister's anger.

'Dear, a was only trying to make Jean feel say she welcome in the house,' she explained nervously, afraid he might turn on her as he had done so often in the past. 'A never did one thing to provoke her.'

George looked suspiciously from one woman to the other. 'Is true, Jean?'

Jean nodded indifferently, giving Pearl a venomous look. Suddenly her face changed, falling into pious lines. 'George, I'm sorry about causing unpleasantness in your house, and while I'm at it I want to apologise for the way I have been behaving.'

If Pearl hadn't seen it for herself she wouldn't have believed it. Jean became a different person in her brother's presence. She could see George's suspicion dissolve. Watched it turn into wary acceptance then total appreciation.

Jean told him about the bottles of spirit she had secreted among Davian's clothes, how she went to the rum shop and cursed like a loose woman and the way she had abused the children. She explained how she had started drinking alcohol and the way it got out of hand.

'Is the weight of your sinning,' George nodded wisely, 'a can see that you was ripe for the harvest of the Lord. All these years a praying for your soul and now the good Lord answer at long last.'

'But I'm not coming to *your* church,' Jean pointed out with a rare touch of humour. 'Going up there only made me want to drink more. It took a visit to a Sunday church to put me on the right road.'

82

'No, man,' George was positive, 'is the softening up that did do it. And anyhows I don't have a problem with Sunday worship. A know plenty in the church feel you can't get saved unless you is a Sabbath-keeper but a think that too narrow. God don't stay so hard, man. He going forgive anybody who sincere and try to walk in His ways. From you seeking fellowship in His name, He will watch over you. A have to admit is not exactly the right way even so.'

'That's exactly how I feel about Saturday worship,' Jean countered on a note of challenge. 'Half the reason I took up the scholarship to England was to get away from Aunt Vi insisting we had to go back to Saturday church once we left the Salvation Army home.'

'A will accept say the church in town did too rough, but you know say is so down there stay.'

Pearl could only stare at this new, understanding George. All she had to do was forget something simple and he was down her throat, accusing her of all kinds of things. Yet here was Jean confessing to carrying the contamination of sin into his house and he forgave without any argument at all.

Jean smiled, 'To tell you the truth, George, it just reached the point where it was Saturday worship, period.'

George was nodding vigorously. 'A did wonder if it was something like that. But while we on the subject of Aunt Vi, she send to tell you say she moving down by Passage Fort come end a week, in case you wanting to pass by when you going town.'

Jean nodded, her mind already moving on. 'It would be nice if you could come to service sometime, you know, George . . . seeing as you Sabbath Baptists don't all believe in being exclusive like the Adventists.'

He made a non-commital response, adding, 'You know, one thing bothering me, what you going do about the situation you in with Jimmy? If you intending to live in the Lord, you going have to give up that sin.'

'The Lord will find a way . . .'

That was as much as Pearl could take. She walked out, leaving the polishing cloths where they were on the floor. On a surge of defiance, she walked down to Miss Lisa's house. Aleesa and Jalini were taunting the woman's young puppies by the front gate. They baited them with pieces of stick while Davian looked on and Dionne, always the mother, tried to stop them. Lutie was under the big almond tree, playing house with Miss Lisa's two children.

Pearl watched the children's antics for a while then hailed Miss Lisa from the gate. She stayed behind after the children started back home with the drinking water, accepting the inevitable tall glass of lemonade.

'Miss Pearl! So what happening make you walking out?' Miss Lisa asked, her round good-natured face falling into unaccustomed frown lines. 'You and Missa George not into a next argument so early on in the day?'

Pearl shook her head, feeling glum. 'Is Jean, you know, Miss Lisa, a trying every try a can and she still disliking me.'

'Maybe you should stop try, try so and just left her gone,' the woman suggested. 'A feel say half the problem with the situation up in that house is the way you letting George sister and him cousin rule you, just through them come from foreign.'

'Sylvia aright,' she contradicted honestly, 'a know she feeling say she better than me, but she have big job, and at least she helping out little with the baby.'

Miss Lisa gathered the sides of her wide skirt and lapped them between her legs, kissing her teeth in irritation. 'Cho, Miss Pearl, man, you too foolish sometime, from the woman make you feel say she better than you, how you can feel say she nice?'

84

Pearl was hurt by the put-down. 'Sylvia never say one rude word to me in the time she there in the house and she is the one always down on Jean to behave and stop disgracing we name down the town.'

The woman frowned. 'You know, if a never know better a would think say Miss Jean under pressure. Is just the other day a see her down the town talking to herself loud, loud, and she just walk past like she never seeing me. Then just through a call out her name, she put down one piece a swearing you see . . .'

'Sorry to cut you, but that not the problem again,' Pearl interrupted. 'Sunday gone she go down the Pentecostal church and from that is pure bad-mouthing a getting up at the house.' She went on to explain how Jean continually denounced her. The way the woman was spreading rumours that she was unchristian.

Miss Lisa listened sympathetically and Pearl felt much better when she finally rose to leave.

The house was silent when she got back and Mauvia told her George had gone up to Mountain District, while Jean and Sylvia had taken all the children down to the beach for a couple of hours. Pearl felt a stab of envy as she stared down at the calm blue waters drowsing under the afternoon sun. She couldn't remember the last time she did something just to please herself.

She straightened from watching Mauvia lighting the coal fire, wiping vainly at the sweat trickling out of her hairline. It would be nice just to wander down to the beach, sit on the warm sand and let the long waves cool her down. She could get herself a soda and some fried fish from the beach shop, and doze under an almond tree when the sun became too hot. Instead she went into the kitchen and started to prepare the evening meal.

They came back from the beach full of high spirits. Pearl felt left out and lonely as the children compared notes on who had been the most daring and how much fun they had. She was glad when the children quietened and trotted off to wash before Sabbath night fell. No doubt things would settle down eventually, once the novelty of Jean's conversion wore off. The problem was managing the consequence in the meantime.

But Pearl's isolation worsened after that first week. Jean became more pious with every passing day, making Pearl feel increasingly more inadequate. These days the woman was a model parent to Davian and Aleesa – too much so, Pearl sometimes thought. It was as if she was driving herself to be the perfect everything. The perfect Christian, mother, auntie . . . everything except sister-in-law. Even Lutie, Dionne and Jali actively sought Jean's help with homework assignments, instead of using it as an excuse to crowd into their narrow bedroom when their aunt was around.

Pearl could not deny the grace her sister-in-law had found and it made her feel even more unwanted. Why was she forced to the periphery until she did anything to avoid being within range of the woman's spiteful tongue? That was how she ended up with the washing, the Wednesday after Jean's confession, leaving Mauvia to the easier job of ironing.

She thought of how Jean sat with the mad woman at Trinityland. The way she went into the heart of the local ghetto, reasoning with the wretched people there. Her sister-in-law seemed to reserve most of her caring for the worst there was, the mentally ill and the destitute, and she was forced to a reluctant admiration. If only Jean would save some of that consideration for her. Lips compressed, Pearl rubbed the blue cake soap against the dirt mark on George's shirt collar with unnecessary force. If anything, where she was concerned, Jean had become ruder and more inconsiderate than before. What had *she* done to Jean to be singled out for tormenting?

She doubled the shirt, wringing out the excess water and spreading it on the zinc sheet to bleach under the rays of the sun, before reaching for Lutie's Sunday dress. The sun had climbed high in the sky and rivulets of sweat ran out of Pearl's hairline, seeping under the collarless neck of her sundress, soaking the fabric and pooling in the creases of her skin. She shouldn't be out here washing in the burning sun. This was Mauvia's job.

If only she hadn't been so defensive on Jean's first day. She could have taken her cue from the woman, returned her politeness with courtesy. Instead she had let her guilty conscience rule her tongue, afraid to explain that George, not she, was responsible for Aleesa's scars. Now, when it was too late, she wished she had told Jean exactly *how* her daughter came to be neglected. Anyway, she couldn't really see what the fuss was about, her children were bitten by mosquitoes all the time. Dionne and Jalini were a case in point. Their feet were full of sores right now, but she wasn't going around quarrelling with people about it.

That thought made her feel better, a little more determined. She couldn't let Jean's disapproval keep pushing her out, forcing her to do Mauvia's work so as to escape the constant flow of condemnation. She could hear Jean talking to Mauvia, filling her head with oppressive ideas about sin and the vengeance of the Lord.

The hissing sound of water running along the pipe distracted her. Pearl froze, listening for a moment to be sure she hadn't misheard. Then everything – Jean, her anger, the injustice of her life – all were forgotten in the urgency of the once-a-week water glut.

Chapter 7

July moved into August, bringing Independence fever to a pitch. Everyone was talking about the big parade in town and the day of events on Sansee beach. Already the dressmakers were sewing furiously, churning out the latest outfits in this year's high-fashion colours as people forgot the misery of poverty and water shortage for a little while. And through it all, the drought sun tightened its grip on the parched and withered country-side. Heat poured mercilessly down on the defenceless land. Jamaica scorching, burning – no phoenix to rise from the ashes with the new dawn.

Sylvia gained a new lease of life, the deep lines of tension and the shadows of misery lifting from her eyes. It was as if she was seeing the world with a new, younger eagerness. Jean tagged along with the children, visiting all the little villages and country towns within two hours' bus ride of Port Juanero. She didn't see any point in it herself, but Sylvia seemed hell-bent on viewing as much of the island as humanly possible in the little time she had left.

Jean consoled herself that she was suffering in Jesus's name as her feet got increasingly sore and her head ached from the fierce heat of the sun. At first she insisted on bringing along the Good News Bible, despite Sylvia's protests, using every minibus ride as an opportunity to bear witness to the glory of God. She was dismayed by the numbers of people willing to make a mockery of her faith; the arguments and quarrels that always broke out when some intolerant soul demanded that she shut up and give them some peace in the heat. Finally she had to admit defeat, singing hymns on the journey and reserving her preaching for a more sympathetic audience.

They spent time in the most extraordinary places. Undaunted by the airless interior of the minibuses, Sylvia squashed up without demur, piling both Aleesa and Davian on her lap whenever Jean complained that she felt faint. Once, she insisted on going with Miss Berta all the way to the market at Linstead. Another time she took two buses to Brown's Town because her mother used to sing a folk song about it.

Sylvia talked to everyone, while Jean stood on the margins, bewildered and excluded. The constant references to the freak weather as God's punishment for the wickedness in the country brought disturbing echoes of childhood superstitions. Granny's stories about Yallah's ponds with their overtones of mystery and vengence. . . Once, a long time ago, two brothers fought, tearing apart their inheritance for individual greed. Each went to court to wrest the land from the other, although twelve hundred acres were more than enough for both. Waking the morning of the judgement to find the great salt ponds – land for nobody. A parallel of the country? Two cousins, fighting . . . trying to settle personal scores. Little knowing or caring when they set the country on the road to ruin . . .

The first week in August was pleasant in spite of that. Jimmy rang to say he had managed to get a ticket for August 19th, three days before Sylvia was due to fly back to England. He spoke to Jean, leaving her buoyed up with optimism, glad to be able to tell him that she was getting on better with Aleesa and Davian. Jean and Sylvia did everything with the children in Independence week – travelled all the way to Kingston so that Aleesa and Davian could see the elaborate floats in the big parade; ate Jerk chicken and ran races on a crowded Sansee beach; even going to the source of the Rio Grande, high in the Portland hills, so they could enjoy the leisurely beauty of a two-and-a-half-hour raft ride.

But for Jean, the best thing remained the fellowship of the church. It kept her feet on the right path, helping her to remain steadfast against the temptation of the bottle. She felt better in herself, about herself. Soon Pastor would be coming, and she would receive his blessing, direct from the Lord.

Her demon voices were just a bad memory, replaced by healing angel ones. These voices brought her to the sea's edge, to the drinking and partying of the ragged people who eked out a living there. Jean was convinced this was a test of her faith, God measuring how well she could resist the temptation to sin.

The tangle of shacks fascinated and repelled her. On the one hand, she hated the endless poverty, the begging mentality and fatalism that were so much a part of the landscape. Yet on the other, she felt the need to seek the poor out and immerse herself in the vibrancy they had. The shanty-dwellers listened to her preaching with amused tolerance. All, that is, except the rastaman.

He fascinated her most. The second time they met, he told Jean his rasta name was Peter, from the tribe of Ash. Privately she thought that was a bit of a cop-out, but her new righteous self forgave him. There was something reassuring about his big capable hands, and the gentleness underlying his 'blood and fire' speeches. He made Jean feel good about herself, listened to her preaching and gave close and serious attention to every-thing she said. Despite the difference in their social status she liked the rastaman. At first she saw friendship with him as a safe, simple game with a sinner. A balm to her battered ego. After all, he knew little beyond his

90

well-thumbed Bible and the visions induced by constantly sucking on his chellum pipe, while she had travelled half the world and acquired an education he could never even imagine. But his open admiration stirred a self-destructive urge in her, a need for more than adoration from afar.

Jean found herself thinking more and more about the dull body beneath the ragged clothes. Peter visited her in feverish dreams and at unguarded moments in the daytime. She could imagine the feel of those hardened fingers against the swell of her breast, a stout leg pressing between her thighs. The dreams gratified her, though afterwards she would be full of guilt and remorse. Ras Peter was good to her, made her feel valued, and the last thing she wanted was to spoil the simple contentment they shared. But however much she admonished herself, she could not shake the growing need. It made her feel soiled and guilty, brought up other images: of childhood rape and of betraying Jimmy with casual drunken sex.

The demon voices she had thought expelled laughed softly and bided their time. Jean immersed herself further into the fellowship of the Sunday church, spending most evenings in worship, prayers and penitence. She reasoned that this was the devil's temptation that Pastor used to warn her to be on guard against. The demon had seen the one small crack and would squeeze through at the least opportunity. Some days she felt as if she was splitting in two: one part of her God-fearing and respectable, the other dark and secretive, feeding on a corruption that ran like a deep vein in her soul. And the struggle between her two selves gradually brought back the need to lash out, until the church and the expectation of Pastor's blessing became all that stood between her and her former chaos.

The praying and soul-searching worked, but not all the time. Far too often she woke up foul-tempered and abusive. Today was one of those days. Jean sat on the verandah to put space between herself and Aleesa's chattering, afraid of the sudden longing for a shot of gin. On the radio, an announcer gave fresh details about corruption in the previous government. She listened, feeling a personal rage out of all proportion to the situation, glad when Sylvia and the children finally appeared. It was a relief to get away from the endless stream of information which underlined the new government's inaction and gave the lie to their claim that they *put people first*.

The walk to Port Juanero was gruelling today. It sapped even Davian's energy, and slowed their progress to a snail's pace. Only Aleesa was her usual cheerful self. Not even the little puffs of hot air, raising dust from the white marl road, bothered her as she skipped ahead to pick ripe soracee berries.

'We're going to Oche Rios today, aren't we, Auntie?' the child asked over and over again, until Jean thought the repetition would drive her crazy.

The heat in the town, much worse than on the hill, finally slowed and quietened Aleesa. Jean pulled the little girl from the side of an open drain, wondering what had become of *her* childhood love for this place. Port Juanero on a airless day only reminded her how her father's gloomy presence squeezed the joy from the most exciting childhood event.

'Daddy, teacher say we going to Castleton for school journey. We going take picnic lunch, and Jeanette saying alligator in Wag Water River and them have one real cannonball tree.'

He sighed, not even raising his head from the paper. At least before Noel died he would have acknowledged her excitement with his attention and a smile.

Jean's mother had haemohrraged to death when Jean was five, after miscarrying her fourth child. Her father had refused to split his children up, rejecting offers of adoption from female relatives, choosing to raise the children himself. He had loved his wife and that had been her last request. Her father's hands, calloused from years of manual labour, had wiped her face when the fever took her. He had bathed her in herb baths and sponged her down with bay rum, made garlic and honey for colds and poured warm coconut oil on her head to ease the ache. He had cooked and cleaned, done everything, while struggling to keep them fed and in school from the five acres of land he had been given by the British government for joining the army in the Second World War – and later, with the six-monthly farmwork programme.

But after Noel died the warmth had gone out of her father, leaving only his sense of duty and the smell of neat white rum. Only now, with hindsight, had she at last begun to understand. Tragedy was the story that had been etched across the deep lines on her father's face.

The images of childhood still had the power to disturb her after all these years. Jean pushed them aside, concentrating on Aleesa's questions about everything she saw.

In the small clearing that went by the grand name of Port Juanero Square, Aleesa stood in the road, gazing with curiosity at the small delapidated monument with the old signs pointing the way to other places.

'Mummy, how far is it to Islington?'

The question shook Jean, bringing disturbing echoes of childhood images. Once, long years ago, she had stood on this very spot, a child like Aleesa, making up stories about all those destinations. Another image intruded: a crying child on a wet March night, standing in the silence while rainwater and blood . . .

She dismissed the thought, annoyed with herself. These roads led nowhere and she had little patience with a child's dream.

'Aleesa, come out of the sunshine, and put your hat back on your head . . . you want to get heatstroke?'

Jean hustled the child to where Davian and Sylvia were waiting in the shade of the ubiquitous Court's furniture store. Aleesa peered into the wide picture window of the store. 'Auntie, why don't we enter that competition and became Court's Millionaires?'

'You have to buy something if you want to enter, Alli.' Sylvia joined in the spirit of the child's fantasy. 'I suppose we could get something small.'

'*Could* we enter the competition, Mum?' Aleesa was in earnest now. 'We could make Uncle George and Auntie Pearl rich and they won't fight anymore.'

The child's thoughtfulness made Jean feel inadequate. What could she tell this little girl, with her simple dream of the world? That the Court's competition fever gripping the country was the stuff of another type of dream? Like quench-aid riddles on the radio, daily, a simple question with no accessible answer, no key to that instant fortune – the local version of American lotteries or the British football pools. Everyone needed the sustenance of dreams, especially those in grinding poverty.

'Mummy, the bus will leave us if we don't hurry.'

Jean frowned, reluctant to face the heat again. 'Aleesa, wouldn't you rather go to the beach?' Her heart sank when she saw the child's mutinous face. 'Look, why don't we go another time?'

'You always say that,' Aleesa muttered. 'Anyway, Auntie Sylvia will take us if you don't want to come.'

The words brought a rush of anger to her head. Jean had to force herself to count to ten, to concentrate on forgiveness as she pressed her nails in her palm to hold back the familiar urge to strike.

'Aleesa, apologise to your mother or you won't be going anywhere.' Sylvia's calm voice steadied her.

'Sorry, Mum,' Aleesa muttered ungraciously, 'but it's not fair . . .'

'I only asked if you wouldn't rather go another time,' Jean interrupted. 'If this thing mean so much to you we might as well get on with it.'

Sylvia gave her a sympathetic look, and Jean ducked her head, the focus of her resentment shifting from child to woman.

'Jean, we *have* been putting off this trip for a while.' Sylvia was watching her closely.

'*Alright!* I said it was OK, didn't I?'

Aleesa refused to be dampened, 'Mum, where *does* all the roads go?'

Jean's eyes drifted back to the old weathered signs.

The road ran in three directions from the square at Port Juanero: to the right it passed Trinityland, gateway to the warm hospitality of Mountain District and the bitter poverty of Jack's River with its frequent murders, and the notoriety of having spawned St Mary's only gunman.

Left, it arrowed straight to Islington. Deep country, where people were clannish and insular. A secretive community. Afraid. Dangerous to strangers. Islington routinely murdered those not its own – an object lesson lost on government planners, to whom country was a place for pleasant drives on Sunday afternoons.

The bridge over the black polluted waters of the Galina River led to the marketplace, and this was where they went now. Here noise, heat and smells mingled in the market-day bustle. This was the main local turning place for the minibuses, the mainstay of Jamaica's ramshackle transportation system. People milled around, clogging the access road and causing traffic to slow to a crawl.

Jean felt even more discouraged when the first bus rattled in. It was old, the white bodywork decorated with blooms of rust that had eaten through in places.

People had been waiting a long time, and there was a frantic rush forward, as the bus reversed and turned.

Sylvia looked doubtful. 'Are you sure about this, Aleesa?'

'Yes, Auntie, quite sure.'

Jean thought longingly of the fallen tree trunk under the protective spread of the old almond tree down at Sansee. 'I doubt we'll get on this one,' she observed, pulling Aleesa back as a desperate-looking man suddenly launched himself through one of the rear windows. He landed in a shower of broken glass, half on the ample lap of an old lady in her Sunday best. A three-way argument broke out. The driver and conductor joining in the spirit of the woman's outrage. The culprit sat impassive, making no attempt to vacate the seat, as others packed tightly around him.

'Mum, is that next bus going to Oche Rios?'

'What bus?'

'The one beside the bridge . . .'

It must have crossed unnoticed, and turned in the square. It was a newer bus, dark-tinted windows promising a more comfortable ride.

Sylvia was already heading for the open door. 'Aleesa, shut up and come on, or we'll never get there today.' The crowd was slow to react, momentarily distracted by the possibility of a fight in the first bus, as the driver and conductor attempted to evict the offending passenger. By the time the rush started they had managed to secure the only comfortable seats, beside the windows at the back. Jean felt a bit better about going now, relaxing enough to allow Davian to climb on her lap as the bus filled up.

The road to Oche Rios had a surfeit of natural beauty. Port Juanero's coastline curved in long, sweeping lines, to the pitted, deep grey of the honeycomb rocks at Galina. Here the sea turned navy blue. Razor-sharp rocks extended far out into deep water while hollows on the shoreline provided natural bathing pools. Aleesa craned her head, bouncing up and down in excitement. She kept pointing out landmarks remembered from other trips, her voice rising with every successful guess. There was the place where unexpected tidal waves smashed sturdy dream houses in their wake. Further on, a ribbon of squatter shacks where a distant cousin lived. Boscobel's pretty white walled villas, Orocabessa's sleepy little market. An old farmer in gumboots, sitting squashed up against Sylvia, leaned forward and grinned at the little girl, asking where she came from. Sylvia engaged him in conversation immediately, pumping him about passing landmarks. The old man was a treasure trove of anecdotes, knowing a story about every little village and hamlet on the way.

Jean felt frustrated and bored. She hated the way others on the bus joined in, vying with each other to own the most outrageous facts. She had never really felt comfortable with the friendly curiosity of country-dwellers, and she was glad when the bus reached Oche Rios. It came to a final rest beside the raised sidewalk near the clocktower, bumping and grinding against the concrete edge as the conductor jumped down and pulled the door wide.

Aleesa scrambled off first, plunging into the tangle of vending shacks and provisions spread across every available sidewalk space. Jean dived after her in irritation, nervous in case she offended someone. She knew how well these people could curse and she had no intention of being on the receiving end.

There was little to do in Oche Rios except wander through the shopping plazas and numerous craft parks. Jean had no appetite for window-shopping. She disliked this town more every time she came to Jamaica and found yet another hotel barring local people from access to prime beach space.

'Right, what shall we do first?' she asked with forced cheerfulness.

'I want to go to the beach, Mum,' Aleesa said immediately.

Jean felt the anger rising again. *So why the hell did you let us come all the way down here?*

The child quailed and Sylvia flashed Jean a warning look. She took a steadying breath, steeling herself as Davian tugged urgently against her restraining hand. 'Look, let's go to Chuckleberry's and have an ice-cream. Then we can see if we can get some stuff at the supermarket.'

'We could go to Dunn's River.' Aleesa recovered some of her daring when the threatened explosion never came.

'That's a good idea,' Sylvia agreed, 'I don't fancy shopping in this heat.'

Jean didn't either, especially with Davian grizzling and unco-operative. Her scalp was prickling and itchy and her body was already dripping sweat under her thin cotton dress. She supposed that was why she gave in so easily, though she still felt conned and aggrieved. Here they were, in the heat and glare of Oche with another uncomfortable bus ride ahead of them, when they could have been comfortably installed at Sansee enjoying a cool breeze off the sea.

Fortunately Dunn's River was only a short ride away, so Jean was in better humour by the time they arrived. Sylvia lingered to examine the carved busts and friezes at the crafts park and insisted on buying them all Jerk chicken to take down to the beach. The park was almost empty, the lull in the tourist trade leaving them with the place almost to themselves. Jean felt more relaxed, able to appreciate Aleesa's ceaseless chatter for a change.

It was nice walking down to the beach along the endless stairs, the shaded, narrow paths pleasant after Oche's hot pavements. The water was cold where the river penetrated, the roar of the falls a constant backdrop. To Jean it seemed to be running faster, the stones feeling more slippery since Gilbert's storm.

The sea was millpond calm. Shallow enough for Davian to walk right out to the point where buoys marked the start of treacherous swift-running currents. Davian delved beneath the shallow water, dredging up little stones and heaping them on his knees, while Aleesa attempted to make castles with the unco-operative sand.

An hour after they arrived a large tourist excursion boat chugged along the reef water, heading for the small jetty at the far end of the short beach.

It fired Aleesa's interest. 'Mum, can we ride on a boat?'

Jean hesitated, remembering the misery of fishing trips in her uncle's boat out at Big Bay. Motion sickness was something she had never really outgrown and she avoided boats at all costs.

'Please, Mum, Davian wants to go.'

He was standing in the water, sand forgotten, his eyes huge and fascinated as he raised his hand. An index finger pointed. 'Boat.'

The two women froze, mirroring each other's shock.

Sylvia was the first to recover. She snatched up Davian, hugging him and laughing. 'Jean, did you hear that! He said "Boat"!'

Davian looked from one to the other, surprised. He smiled uncertainly, not quite knowing what he had done but opening up to the approval.

'Boat,' he repeated, stabbing in the direction of the flimsy craft.

Jean felt a sudden surge of optimism. The sort of transient buoyed-up feeling that comes with the unexpected bonus of a warm sunny day in the middle of a wet and miserable British spring. The let down followed hard on its heel.

One word – so what? One stinking word don't prove a thing.

Davian's little face began to crumple, picking up on her mood. Jean stifled the bitter thoughts, reminding herself of the years of anxiety his silence had generated. The doctors had said that he would talk and Jimmy had believed it . . . But she, she had just seen the child's silence as another punishment for her sins.

'It's a big step, you know.' Sylvia squeezed her arm in reassurance. 'It mean's Davian's going to be alright. It's just a pity Jimmy couldn't have heard it after all his hard work.'

Jimmy, everything with Syvlia is Jimmy! Jean thought sourly. 'Why should he hear it? I've got as much right to experience the kids' growing-up as him . . .'

'I wouldn't for one minute suggest otherwise,' Sylvia offered quietly. 'Jean, nobody ever tried to stop you being a part of the children's lives.'

Jean turned her head, ready tears springing to her eyes as thoughts of Jimmy destroyed the last of her pleasure in Davian's achievement. She watched as Sylvia bent to make a fuss of the child, listened as she pointed out things one after the other, pronouncing the words patiently for him. '*Tree*, Davian, t-r-e-e, and what you're standing on is *sand*, s-a-n-d.' Davian was fascinated. At first he attempted to make the different sounds with varying degrees of success, until the boat attracted him again and he wriggled free of the woman's protective arms.

Aleesa was already running along the sand and Davian chased after her, shouting out his newly acquired word.

'One word don't mean a thing,' Jean muttered under her breath. 'He couldn't even say "tree" properly.'

'Give him a chance,' Sylvia cautioned. 'He's only just starting to feel his way. Remember how quickly Aleesa learned to talk after her first word?'

Jean nodded and tried to smile, but all she could remember of Aleesa at Davian's age was her own anxiety. She didn't dare hope then as she couldn't hope now, in case disappointment resurrected the old rage and brought consequences for her son.

'Jean,' Sylvia was grave, 'if you really believe in this religion of yours, use some of that faith to believe in Davian.'

It was as if her cousin had read her mind, and Jean shifted guiltily under the steady gaze. 'It don't matter *what* I believe,' she muttered, hiding hurt behind defiance, 'they'll never like me as much as Jimmy. I mean, they even like *you* better than me.'

'I doubt that.'

'Of course they do, and you know full well it's true.'

'And that really matters to you, doesn't it?'

She felt annoyed, defensive. 'What do you expect, they're *my* children too, you know. I'm not saying I've always been good to them, but that don't mean I don't care . . . Sylvia,' Jean sighed, rubbing the back of her hand against her brimming eyes. 'I know you and Jimmy don't believe this but I really love those kids.'

'Of course you do!' Sylvia's confirmation came without hesitation. 'Jean, I wasn't for one minute suggesting that you didn't care about them.'

Somehow the assurance made Jean angry. 'Well, you wouldn't, would you, but I know you thinking it most of the time. Well, let me tell you this, if anyone is to blame for the way I can't get close to my kids, it's you and Jimmy . . . the way you keep shutting me out of their lives and turning them against me.'

Sylvia looked worried now. 'Jean, I thought you'd got over all that jealousy thing.'

She shrugged. 'Well, you thought wrong, didn't you? Do you know what it's like? Spending nine years of your life doing for a man, only to be cast aside for someone like you? Do you wonder I resent the children sometimes?'

'That's hardly a healthy attitude. As you say, they're your kids as well.'

'You should tell their father that. I mean, after all I did for him.' The bitterness she had thought resolved, spilled out, and Sylvia listened patiently until it came to an end.

'Jean, what's *really* bothering you?'

Sylvia's quiet question shook her, and she had to swallow hard as disturbing words threatened to spill out. 'I suppose it's the whole thing between Jimmy and me.'

'But none of that is Davian's fault, is it?' Sylvia pointed out with her usual logic. 'That's no reason *not* to believe in him or to help him progress.'

Jean couldn't ignore the reproach. 'You don't understand, Sylvie, it's more than just Jimmy preferring the children, or even . . . well . . . liking your company more than mine.'

'So tell me.'

She smiled, a sad smile, as she fell into step with her cousin, trying to put into words what she was only just beginning to understand a little. She thought about her childish promises in the face of her father's disintegration . . . and that other unspoken thing. *She* was never going to let her children down. Then had come the test . . .

First, there had been Aleesa . . . such a beautiful baby to be so flawed. Jean lived with her guilt and her daughter's pain. Felt it from the very first day when the doctor strapped those tiny little feet and hinted at corrective surgery. After that had come the daily, then tri-weekly, trips on the 109 bus from Brixton for that eight o'clock appointment. Till Jean could not pass St Thomas's hospital at Waterloo in London without feeling anxiety knotting in her stomach.

Standing on the powdery white Dunn's River sand, she felt the eight-year-old anxiety resurrect itself. The guilt that she had not been able to keep up the pace and live with the knowledge of birthing a damaged child. Other women made that daily trek; women whose children had far worse problems than Aleesa's talipes. They spent years walking uncomplainingly along the brick-and-glass corridors of the hospital's Lambeth Wing, into the older, more sombre, closed-in passages of North Wing. Yet she had handed the responsibility over to Jimmy, unable to survive the guilt and despair as weeks slipped into months and the baby's feet did not respond.

She had thought she knew why: God's punishment visited on a helpless child because of her sins. That was why the child had had to endure so much . . . Seven months of trying and trying, physiotherapy that didn't work, the boots that made the baby cry and stole her rest. And that first operation, which left the little legs plastered right up to the hips. Guilt is a self-regenerating state, and Jean could feel it welling up inside. No wonder she had withdrawn, leaving the burden of child-rearing on Jimmy's capable shoulders.

She looked at Sylvia, waiting patiently for her to finish. *What does she know about it anyway?* Sylvia and Winston hadn't even wanted a child, despite all that talk of leaving the best till last. Jean suppressed that thought, feeling mean-spirited and ungracious.

'*Auntie!* Mum!' Aleesa's voice broke through her introspection, relieving her of the need to go on. 'The boatman say he'll take us out for ten dollars, but you have to hurry up and come.'

Embarrassment flooded Jean. She felt the awkward-ness in the silence as it dawned on her how much she had told her cousin. Not since before her father abandoned George and herself in town all those years ago, had she confided so much about her inner feelings.

'Ahm . . . I suppose I'd better go see to the children.'

'Jean, there's nothing wrong with having negative feelings.' Sylvia's voice held sympathy, understanding. 'The problem usually starts when you try to keep them in.'

She smiled uncertainly. 'I suppose so.'

Sylvia touched her arm reassuringly. 'It's not too late to change things, you know. Maybe if you just told Jimmy some of what you're feeling . . .'

If only it was that simple. She thought about the faceless men Jimmy must never know about; the guilty pleasures drinking allowed her to feel. Images of Peter's poorly clothed body rose to taunt her as she silently prayed for forgiveness. How could she tell Jimmy about those things? He had been her first lover, to his knowledge her only one. He was bound to throw her out, laugh at her assertion that those men meant nothing, that until that last stupid binge they always wore a condom.

'Are you thinking about what I said?' Sylvia sounded hopeful.

Jean's smile teetered on the edge of bitterness. She wondered how Sylvia would react if she ever found out about the secrets she carried inside her head.

Her cousin might have read her mind. 'Jean, I know there's more troubling you than you told me about, but it's up to you what to do about it.'

That annoyed her. 'You mean you don't care?'

'No, I mean I can't force *you* to care about your own mental health . . . You have to want to do it all by yourself.'

'Meaning what? You think I'm going mad! Is that it?'

'No, but I think you're under a lot of pressure.'

'You never going to let me forget when I first came down, will you?'

'It's not a matter of that . . .'

'Yes it is. I told you I found the Lord, but no, you can't just accept that. What is it with you anyway? I'm trying to give you the benefit of the doubt but you just want what you want, don't you?'

Sylvia shook her head. 'Jean, don't you think you're being a bit paranoid?'

'Don't you psychoanalyse me, Sylvia, I can be whatever I bloody well like. I'm not one of your clients, you know.'

Sylvia ignored that. 'Jean, I know you care for Aleesa and Davian, however much you also resent them, but unless you do something about all the things eating you up, you're going to lose them, or worse . . . and I don't mean just go to an extra church service either.'

She felt like something was breaking loose inside her head, creaking and straining against a sudden crack in faith, and starting up a low-grade ache. Jean wanted to curse Sylvia, swear at her again before the devil she was sure lurked inside the other woman opened the way for the demon voices to crawl back . . .

'*Auntie! Mum!* You've got to come *now!*' Aleesa's urgent voice restored her equilibrium, made it possible to choke the voices off before they got a foothold. Sylvia waved and smiled, but Jean was still too churned up and impatient for that kind of nicety.

'Hold on a minute, will you?' Jean shouted back, needing to have this whole thing out before it threatened her new peace.

'No, Jean,' Sylvia interrupted, 'if you're really serious about those kids you've got to start putting them first. But you think about what I said, and if you need someone to talk to, I'll be there.'

Jean wanted to tell Sylvia she was the last person she'd turn to, but the woman was already walking off. 'The least you could do is let me have my say,' she yelled in a sudden temper.

Sylvia stopped and turned, but Aleesa cut across what she might have said.

'Come on, slowcoaches!' the child yelled impatiently. 'Hurry up . . . Davian is getting in the boat already.'

'If you're coming, you'd better come now,' Sylvia warned unsmilingly, 'I wouldn't like the children to take it in their heads to go off and leave us.'

Chapter 8

Jean woke late the morning after the Dunn's River trip full of anticipation. She lay still, feeling cocooned and detached as the sounds of morning filtered in. Kaona was fussing next door, while laughter and the noise of children at play mingled with the intermittent barking of the dogs, as they issued warnings to passers-by. She was feeling good in herself today. Last night she had gone to church full of the negative feelings her talk with Sylvia had stirred up, and again it had worked its miracle. She felt washed in the blood, born anew. It had been wonderful, the service. Pastor Simmonds had arrived unexpectedly to lead the congregation and he had preached up a storm in the church. Jean had been caught up in the exuberance, carried along on that tide of righteousness. Before she knew it, she had been on her feet, testifying, witnessing, filled with the spirit. Afterwards Deacon Davis had introduced her to Pastor Simmonds, explaining how much she needed spiritual counselling, and he had agreed to see her this afternoon.

Uneasiness briefly disturbed her serenity as she remembered the involuntary tightening of nerve endings as the pastor's hand had enveloped hers. She asked a silent forgiveness for the unworthy thought. Of course the hand hadn't lingered or suggeste. Pastor Simmonds had an understanding smile and his eyes held a tranquillity that told her he could bring her lasting peace.

No wonder she was so impatient and edgy today. The hours seemed to drag by for ever, the minute-hand of the clock crawled slower and slower as the day wore on. She felt as if she was a child again, waiting for the bittersweet outing to Castleton. She listened to the sounds of the house swirling around her: Mauvia washing tirelessly under the burning rays of the sun; Pearl buffing the concrete floor with red-oak polish and quarrelling with George as he sorted his cosmetics.

Just after lunchtime the roar of the water truck struggling up the heights fractured the silence and broke the monotony of waiting. Jean watched as the neighbourhood came alive, women and children running out with every sort of container, desperate to get enough water to survive to the next trucking. The containers filled every inch of road space, a multi-coloured bloom of desperation in the scorching midday heat.

The water pump coughed to life. Half the precious cargo spilled out through a faulty hose and puddled in the ruts of the pitted road. A fight broke out as several enterprising women attempted to bypass the queue and fill up from the wasting stream, while the less intrepid reviled them for their lack of consideration. The driver tried to mediate, attempting to keep order among the jostling crowd and fill containers at the same time. When the hose ran dry and the pump fell silent for another week, most of the vessels were empty.

The radio announcer spoke the hour and Jean rose from her perch on the verandah, glad to escape the disappointment of the women milling about on the rapidly drying road. Stretching to ease the cramped muscles in her back, she retreated into the privacy of the house.

Pastor Simmonds was waiting for her in the cool empty church. A big, bluff man in his early fifties, his jovial face smiled encouragement as he beckoned for her to join him in the front row next to the altar.

'Perhaps we could begin by saying a prayer together,' he offered.

Jean bowed her head obediently, hands clasped in an attitude of prayer. Pastor Simmonds' hand was gentle on her shoulder as he called God's blessing on her, and begged the Lord to keep her feet on a righteous path. She closed her eyes, drinking in the words of consolation, her Amen heartfelt when he finally came to a halt.

The pastor's hand remained where it was as he forayed into her life. Jean found herself relaxing, opening to him. She told him of her battles with sin, the voice of her conscience that had been nothing but a demonic possession. She talked of her disappointment with Saturday worship and the healing power of the redemption she had found here in his own faith. He listened, grave and still like the white Jesus gazing solemnly down at her from the mortification of the cross.

Maybe that was why she dared to mention Jimmy, to tell the pastor of that sin-shadowed relationship.

The hand on her shoulder tightened fractionally. 'You saying you living in sin with you baby father?'

The weight of her trespass lodged somewhere in her throat. Jean nodded, mortified by guilt. 'But he is the one man I ever live with, Pastor . . .'

'But you was just saying how you fornicating with so much man.' Somehow the voice had lost its note of understanding, had gained an uncomfortable edge instead.

'That was under the influence of drink, Pastor.' She hastened to defend herself, falling into the old pattern of seeking justification as her eyes shifted away from his steady gaze. 'Is like I was telling you: the demon voice was on and on at me and never letting me rest. Until Jimmy, I never once knew a man.'

A shaft of sunlight fell on the image of the white Jesus, tracing a reproach inside her head. Jean pushed desperately at the other memory – the child bleeding in the shadow of the blood-red cross.

'But is plenty man know you now, Miss Jean.' The hand moved along her shoulder with suggestion, hesitated, then shifted further into intimacy when she didn't resist. 'Seem to me what you needing is a laying-on of hands . . . a healing touch. When Deacon Davis saying how you dying to meet me, a could barely believe it.' The voice had altered subtley, the pastor becoming the man. 'A hearing tell about Missa Mackenzie sister from foreign but a never know say you hear bout me.'

The hand had shifted to her neck, along the square line of her sundress, coarse fingers, calloused from years of manual labour, big palm slipping down to cover the weight of her breast. It branded her, shaking loose other images inside her head.

Jean couldn't move, couldn't speak. She was a child again, Pastor's shadow looming over her, as he chastised her for disobeying her father. The hand was hasty and clumsy on her thighs, tangling in the full skirt of her dress. She swallowed hard, once, twice, her heart rate so fast she had to gulp shallow breaths of air, afraid she would pass out.

'You hot for true.' The pastor's voice was rough with anticipation as his hand found the juncture of her thighs and kneeded clumsily. 'But let me close the door in case.'

She barely heard him, barely registered what he was saying. All she knew was that the pain must not happen again. She could not add to the burden of her sins . . .

An eager finger penetrated the barrier, touching accidentally against a nerve that sent a pleasure pain deep inside her belly. The demon voice laughed, an hysterical, sobbing sound, that tore Jean out of her frozen trance.

110

She was on her feet so abruptly that the pastor over-balanced, breaking his hold on her. She had to get away, had to put space between herself and the mad laughter inside her head.

She didn't notice the heat as her feet pounded along the uneven surface of the road. Pain tore through her chest, her breath whistling and gasping, but still she ran. She pushed desperately through the slow-moving crowd, fresh panic welling up as she tore away from the hands reaching instinctively to slow her progress. She was blind to everything – the startled faces, the murmurs of irritation and concern – she just had to get away from the flood of sin and guilt-filled memories streaming into her head. Finally, tiredness and the drag of beach sand against her sandalled feet slowed then stopped her.

Jean dropped to the ground, the roar of the ocean mingling with the noise inside her head. Nothing else penetrated, not the deserted peace of the beach, not the stench from the litter of dead crabs she was sitting on, nor the irritating buzz from the cloud of carrion flies. Her mind was wrapped in the old, once-forgotten memory.

She had just turned eight when it all began, bored and restless in the long school holiday. Her mother had been three-years dead and her father was away on farm work. Jean used to accompany Aunt Vi and Tashi to Port Juanero market on Thursdays. It made her angry that she had to go, while George and Noel were allowed to sit around in idleness or accompany the men tending their father's land in his absence. Maybe that was why she started sneaking away to the library on the green beside the old sea wall. Her father had forbidden it and Aunt Vi distrusted any literature that was not the Bible or scripture-based.

So the library was fascinating for Jean, and the world of books took her far away, beyond the boundaries of

111

her restricted world of Port Juanero Town, Sansee beach and Highgate. She would sneak away the minute her aunt became engrossed in the weekly gossip, slipping into the library, heart pumping as she withdrew her tickets so carefully concealed in her dress pocket. The ritual was always the same: she would head for the Enid Blytons and A. A. Milnes, look hurriedly for titles she had not read, and stand nervous and guilty while the librarian issued the one she chose. Afterwards she would slip out to the sand-bound clumps of grass hidden by the massive spread of the flowering Tunna cactus. Here, high above the crumbling sea wall, where only goats ventured in any numbers, she would sit, feeling a delicious guilt as she immersed herself in adventure. She devoured stories of the Famous Five, lost herself in the enchanted woods, and dreamed that she was living with Pooh Bear and Eeyore in The Hundred Acre Wood.

Jean became expert at judging time from the position of the sun. She would return her book before the library closed and be back at her aunt's market stall in time to watch the last of the packing and get her Bulla cake to eat.

It was when she discovered *The Dream of Sadler's Wells* that the bubble finally burst. She hadn't even noticed Pastor Baker approaching; had been too lost in Rosanna's struggle to be accepted at 'The Wells' to think of a single word of explanation when the book was suddenly wrenched out of her hand and the man stood glowering over her.

'So this is what you up to now you father working away in foreign,' he thundered in his most frightening blood-and-fire voice. 'You is a wicked girl, sneaking round sinning so.'

She could only sit there, shaking, terrified that he would call down God's rage and the Lord would send thunder crashing down from the sky. Pastor Baker was an austere and unsmiling man. Unmarried and solitary, he lived alone at the top of Mountain District, casting critical eyes on the sinning ways of his congregation. The children of the church all feared him, dreading the day they might stand quailing on the receiving end of his disapproval.

'What you doing in Port Juanero?' the Pastor asked when he finally ran out of condemnation.

Jean felt sick with the knowledge of Aunt Vi's disappointment, the weight of knowing it would be stored for punishment when her father returned.

'You don't know to show respect when a talking?'

She swallowed, trying to dislodge the choking thing blocking her voice in her throat. 'A just waiting for Aunt Vi and Tashi to done, down the market, Pastor.'

He looked scandalised. 'You mean to say you auntie allowing you to this ungodly place when Missa Mackenzie forbid it?'

Her voice was small. 'No, Pastor, she never know a was coming.'

The pastor shook his head sadly. 'A should come with you right now and show her your sinfulness.' He paused, watching her fear and apprehension build, before finally offering the compromise. 'However, a thinking you need the guiding hand of a man with your father away so much. A going talk to your auntie about letting Brother Leroy carry you over when he coming up District to see him mother, Sunday.'

He had been as good as his word, and for the first of many Sundays Brother Leroy collected her in his battered old Zephyr and deposited her at the door of the deserted church. She had expected to have to listen to a church service, kneel on the cool hard floor of the meeting room and pray in the forbidden shadow of Jesus and the cross suspended above his head. But Pastor had other ideas.

He told her he had fasted for her, had spoken to the

113

Lord, and that her sins were so great the only remedy would be a laying-on of hands. That time the touching had not made her uneasy, though his insistence that she keep it secret did. Unspoken between them was the knowledge that *he* had kept *her* secret, had prayed and suffered for her in preference to causing her trouble.

It was on the third Sunday that the pattern of his touching changed. The day he silently pressed the shilling into her hand and laid her down on the rough burlap bag he had spread in readiness for her coming. This time no words passed between them. Jean lay staring at the picture of the white Jesus, refusing to accept the reality of those fingers, fumbling in that dirty place between her thighs. Afterwards she didn't meet his eyes, just ran out through the stony yard to the unmade road, clutching her shiny new shilling as she heard the hoarse sound of Brother Leroy's horn.

It went on like that for a month. The touching, the shilling coin and the silent guilt. Then the pastor started telling her things, dirty things, about her sinful ways. How she was leading him to wicked thoughts, forcing him to wrestle with the devil temptation she represented.

It made her feel guilty. The touching made a funny feeling inside her belly now, a squirmy sort of feeling that was shivery and nice sometimes, and sometimes made her want to vomit. Jean was sure it was the evil trying to get out. The mark of Sodom, Pastor told her, was deep inside her stomach.

She grew moody and withdrawn at home, lashing out at her brothers, weeping for no reason. Thoughts of Sundays dominated everything. She felt soiled, weighed down with sin, somehow set apart from other children. Her school work suffered, until her teacher complained about her inattention to Aunt Vi. Worry made her lose her appetite and Granny boiled fever grass and Soracee, sure she was sickening for something.

114

Church became an ordeal. She was sure the white Jesus was reproaching her, condemning her for the evil too deep inside for any of Pastor's endeavours to root it out.

The Sunday before her father came back from farm work, Brother Leroy was late dropping Jean at the church. Pastor was waiting in the doorway of the small meeting-room, anger radiating from every line of the big rigid body. He grabbed her, hauling her into the room and pushing the door shut. Jean was shocked and unprepared when he suddenly slammed her hard against the door. She stared at him, not understanding any of the insults he was hurling at her, and she was shaking and frightened when he finally ordered her to lie down.

This time was different. There was something scary about the way he was looking at her, as if he was thinking real bad thoughts. Her eyes met the blue ones of the white Jesus, met them and refused to acknowledge. The hand between her thighs was hard and forcing. Jean blinked, tears hazing her eyes. Her gaze focused on the cross. She blinked again, frightened to see it tarnishing, turning blood-red under the burden of her sins.

Her body stiffened in terror and rejection, eyes trying to unfocus. She heard the sound of Pastor's trousers' zip and rejected that as well, staring unseeingly ahead, without even the familiar warmth of the shilling coin to keep her company.

It was the weight of his body that shocked her to attention. The crushing heaviness that pushed the breath out of her small chest and made her think her ribs would collapse. He grunted and rolled to one side, fumbling between her legs. Then her hand was being pulled down, forced to touch something clammy and fat, something that wriggled and made her struggle to pull away. Pastor's hand clamped hers to the thing, moved it and squeezed it, while he groaned and

115

squirmed as if he was in a death agony. It was the feeling of something wet and sticky squirting out of the fat sausage thing that made her retch. Pastor was lost in his own distress and Jean used the sudden limpness of his body to wriggle away and run for the door. She felt dirty, as if the white specks on her hand were burning deep into her flesh and staining her for ever.

Her father came that Wednesday and in his benevolent shadow, Jean felt strong enough to refuse to go back for any more guidance. Every day she waited for Pastor to come by and betray the secret that had started the whole thing, but he never did. It made it easier to hold firm against Aunt Vi's coercion and threats, and Pastor's persuasion, which soon gave way to bitter looks.

Every time Pastor caught her alone at all-day church he would threaten God's wrath if she ever told anyone about what happened on the floor of the meeting room. He told her she was sin, that God would punish her for trying to seduce him into the devil's arms. It added to Jean's guilt, reinforcing her belief that she carried the mark of Cain. After all, hadn't the white Jesus, looking down so serenely at the congregation on sabbath day, seen every detail of her leading Pastor into sin? And didn't the holy cross turn blood red in protest at her shamelessness?

The more it troubled her, the more she quarrelled with her brothers, especially with Noel. It was as if something was driving her on, something inside her that sparked off anger at the least excuse. It intensifed her jealousy at her eldest brother's closeness with their father, as she felt more cast out and alone. Sometimes at the height of one of her rages she would wish Noel dead, tell him to die. At that instance she even meant it, though afterwards she would only feel more wicked and beyond redemption.

And then came the day in her ninth year. Right

in the heart of the rainy season, when electric storms unleashed lethal-looking charges into the atmosphere and thunder shook the ground, Granny had gone to town to stay with a sick friend. Aunt Vi and Tashi, taking advantage of Papa's presence, had gone to Constant Spring market in Kingston in the big, brightly coloured country bus, hoping to get better prices than Highgate or Port Juanero could offer.

Confined to the house by the rains, the children had squabbled on and off. Jean resented having to run back and forth from the leaky wooden cooking shed, getting meals ready on her own. Noel and George were both older and they didn't have to help, just because they were boys. The sense of injustice grew and grew until she broke Noel's kite in a fit of malice. He had retaliated immediately, jabbing her in her side and running laughing into the rain when she tried to get him back. That was how he hit on the idea of stealing her mangoes in exchange for his broken kite.

Jean had been indignant, calling down the wrath of God. But she hadn't meant it, hadn't meant for Him to strike her brother dead. She had stayed where she was, on the edge of the verandah, rainwater splashing, unheeding against her thin frock, a high screaming sound going on endlessly inside her head.

She couldn't remember anything after that, just the rain hammering against the new zinc roof. She had felt so cold, shivering and shivering, and waiting for Noel to come in and annoy her because she wasn't feeling good. Time seemed to tilt out of focus, sometimes rushing by, sometimes crawling; while the image of Noel bathed in light, falling silently like a charred stone, replayed over and over inside her head.

She couldn't have said when the women returned. But suddenly the house was oppressively full of people in mourning, people shifting her out of the way, too wrapped in their own grief to comfort her. The charred and twisted thing that had been Noel lay shrouded in its coffin and she fancied everybody knew she had caused his death. She was conscious of the way Aunt Vi and Tashi avoided her eyes, and even Granny wouldn't hug her any more. Now, when her father looked at her, his eyes saw nothing, and she saw the nothingness reflected back at her instead of the regard she had guiltily hoped would transfer to her from Noel.

On the fourth night of mourning she couldn't stand the death talk any more. The guilty secret inside was threatening to burst out of her chest and she felt weepy and upset. It was raining again, the same kind of thunderstorm in which Noel had died. Aunt Vi had her running from house to cooking shed carrying food to the dozens of people gathered to comfort her father. Jean shivered, afraid, muttering prayers for protection as she faced the hostile darkness. Pastor was at the house tonight, glaring at her with the old hostility. Papa sat slumped in the hand-carved settee to one side of the living room, drinking neat white rum and staring at the floor. Tears dripped on the back of his hand, making Jean feel a fresh guilt. The weight of sin settled on her like the heavy cloud weighing down the rainy skies.

She wished Granny hadn't gone over to Miss Vinnie to sleep. But the old lady had been looking so frail and tired, everybody had urged her to rest and save her strength. Jean wished Miss Vinnie would hug her as she had Granny. Would let her curl up beside her great-aunt in the big bed she shared with Missa Brenna when he was home from town.

The false dawn was breaking by the time the hymn-singing and quiet talking died away and people started taking their leave. Pastor was the last to go, making a thing of stretching and talking about the long day he had in front of him, farming and caring for his flock.

Papa had fallen asleep on the settee, and George had long ago sneaked off to bed.

'Jean,' Aunt Vi sat tiredly beside her daughter and her brother on the big settee, 'just take them two plate down the shed then go rest yourself.'

She was glad about that, feeling clumsy and weighed down by her own lack of sleep.

Jean added the plates to the stack in the big zinc tub, upending them in readiness for the washing later on. It was when she was turning to blow out the kerosene lamp that she noticed the man standing in the shadow. Pastor moved, casting a long frightening shadow of his own, and she stared at him in horror.

'You think you going escape the justice of the Lord, ee?' he muttered, moving between her and the door. 'You think making the lightning kill you brother going stop Him righteous punishment? You is a viper from the nest of sin come into the bosom of this good family.' He was coming towards her as he spoke, sounding breathless and upset.

Jean barely noticed, could only stare, mute and guilty, hearing all the unspoken things inside her head coming out of his mouth. She didn't resist when he grabbed her, hardly felt his flesh connect with her unprotected face. This time the coarse fingers brought no shivery feeling, just more of the last time: pain . . . and punishment. She felt his weight, smelt the rum-stained breath. It felt as if he was pressing her to death, and it was a struggle to expand her thin chest enough to take in air. Then all she felt was pain, something hot and burning, something so forceful that it made her think he would rip her in two, tear her apart, leaving all the sin open and exposed. Time and pain ran into each other, on and on and on. She closed her eyes, but couldn't lock out the tranquil blue eyes of the white Jesus presiding over her punishment as he had presided over her sin . . . nor the long thin shadow of the blood-red cross.

The screech of a sea bird jolted her to the reality of

the hot sun beating down on her unprotected head. Jean blinked and shivered, the locked-away memories refusing to go away. Somehow, it had all disappeared after it had happened. She had fallen asleep, there on the concrete floor of the cooking shed, and when she woke it had all gone.

Tashi had found her, seen the blood, the painful way she walked, and hurried to get her mother. Aunt Vi had spoken to her in short embarrassed sentences, telling her she had become a young lady and from now on would bleed every month. She had shown Jean how to tear up old clothes to make comfortable wadding to tie between her legs and catch the blood, admonished her not to let any man touch her, and told her babies could come that way.

Pastor had gone away the following day, one of the deacons taking over until another pastor could be appointed. Jean had bled for days and Aunt Vi insisted she move to Miss Vinnie's house for the rest of the nine nights in case some evil befell her. When her period failed to show the following month, they prayed for her and annointed her with healing oils, but it was five years before she was to bleed again.

Jean shook her head as the sniggering voice returned, trying to deny the vivid memory, but unable to convince herself. She had led the old pastor into sin, just as she was doing with Pastor Simmonds now.

A wail of sadness welled up from deep inside her bowels and she swallowed hard to suppress it. Staggering to her feet, she swayed uncertainly as if she had lost the ability to balance properly. She could not think about those things, not now. Could not accept the guilt of her eight-year-old self. She spun around, once, twice, looking from sea to road, feeling crowded and hemmed in by the same and remembered pain.

She needed a drink. Gin, rum . . . anything! Something to dull the pain and take the sharp edges off the knowledge of the thing her mind was telling her she was. Her eyes lighted on the thatched roof of the Sea Lawn Club, fixed on it. It steadied her, gave her purpose. Almost without her own volition, her feet started to move, one before the other, forward, forward. The noise of the birds, the sharp raw smell of sea water, the trickle of sweat, hot sand burning against her soles as it slipped in through the open sides of her sandals . . . all were forgotten in the anticipation of forgetfulness lying on the other side of the road.

Chapter 9

The ragged woman lived on the main road to Port Juanero, just outside Trinity district in a shack adjacent to fertile cultivated land. No one knew where she came from, or how she got there. Just that one day she appeared with her two dirty straw bags and a pile of old newspapers. The local children saw her as a running joke, her house a magnet for childish cruelties. They threw stones through the clapboard windows, and knocked the weathered wooden walls with sticks, giggling and running off whenever the woman appeared. Sometimes she would chase them brandishing an old rusty cutlass, but most times she would just sit in her sagging doorway and cry.

It made no difference. She was condemned for whatever she did, however sane. If she laughed it was because she was mad; and if she cried . . . they laughed. They would walk past, adults and children alike, joking to one another and poking fun: 'Look how the mad woman a go on, look how she a cry,' as if she had no right to emotions.

Only in the nights did she become an object of desire. A convenience for young male adolescents eager to try out their emerging sexuality and older men who saw her as available and public property. She was tolerated for the most part. A local landmark to be half ashamed of, half amused by; and she had soon been dubbed Miss

Maddy and relegated to something to complain about occasionally or to visit furtively in the night.

George, in a cruel prank of his own, introduced Sylvia and Jean to the ragged woman soon after she first attended the Pentecostal church. Both of them had seen the woman wandering the streets aimlessly, singing and talking to herself, and they did not react as he expected. Instead they sat pointedly outside her house and engaged her in conversation.

Sylvia's heart went out to the woman. To her mind Miss Maddy was more unfortunate than mad. Destitute, she had a degree of mental handicap which made her a natural scapegoat and an object of exploitation. But what concerned Sylvia most was Jean's reaction. Her cousin maintained that the ragged woman's condition was punishment for sins. She joined George in condemning Sylvia's insistence on slipping the woman a little money each time they passed her foraging on the street, accusing her of being patronising and insulting.

Yet Jean often sought out the ragged woman in the early days of her own conversion, going down on some pretext or the other, to sit and engage her in bizarre conversation about the sin of fornication, punishment and repentance. It was as if she was wallowing in some form of mental association; some unhealthy thing that drew her to poverty and despair like a sinister magnet. When tackled, Jean insisted she was doing her Christian duty, though she resisted any attempts by Sylvia and the children to accompany her.

In the end Sylvia had accepted the situation, reasoning that at least her cousin's new peculiarities did not pose a danger to her children. Despite the occasional flash of unprovoked temper, Jean seemed to be pulling herself together well enough . . . until the previous week's trip to Dunn's River. True, she continued talking to herself, but at least it was always some biblical debate.

Sylvia had begun to believe the Church might have

wrought a minor miracle. If it wasn't for the brittle air in Jean's manner, her cousin might almost have been a different person. She had been doing so well with the children, helping to coax more words from Davian and even rising early to explore the local coastline with Aleesa. Sylvia supposed, looking back, it had been just too good to last . . .

At the end of Independence week when tempers were at their worst from the prolonged drought, the council finally took note of local protest and bulldozed Miss Maddy's house. Sylvia had been concerned when she heard, afraid of Jean's reaction. Over the last few days the strangeness in her cousin's behaviour had become more marked. Jean had started drinking again, staying out late and returning in the early morning, stumbling drunk. At the same time her temper was increasingly hair-trigger, raising the spectre of violence to the children once more.

Sylvia suspected it had something to do with the church. Jean had come back from evening service the previous Thursday bubbling over with excitement. The pastor for the area had arrived unexpectedly early and agreed to give her spiritual counselling the very next afternoon. Sylvia had expected her to be more buoyed up after that experience. Instead her cousin staggered in during the early hours of Saturday morning, drunk and abusive.

All Sylvia's attempts to get at what had gone wrong met with cold hostility. Jean's preaching became edged with a bitter kind of irony, punctuated by drinking bouts and stretches of melancholy. She was increasingly obsessed with the idea of punishment for sins and a visit to Miss Maddy was now an essential part of her daily preaching routine.

It was George who broke the news of the bulldozing of Miss Maddy's house to Jean. He seemed oblivious to how wound up and tense she was as he laughed at the memory of how the ragged woman had scrambled around, attempting to save her possessions. Sylvia was disgusted by his attitude, and she braced herself for the explosion she was convinced would follow. Jean surprised her though. She only shrugged and said she had been expecting something like that. Sylvia could not think of a single thing to say as her cousin informed her calmly that the ragged woman had it coming because she failed to heed the warnings of the Lord.

'What eating Jean now?' George asked, his humour fading in the face of stony disapproval.

Sylvia looked at him in surprise. 'Can't you see for yourself, George?'

'I just seeing say she really getting into the fellowship.'

'Is that so,' she gave him a level look, 'and I suppose nothing in her behaviour strikes you as strange?'

'Don't start up, Sylvia, man . . .' This time his laugh lacked conviction. 'The way you look so, anybody would think say Jean a turn maddy stead a walking a Christian way.'

Sylvia just shook her head and walked away, wondering why he so utterly failed to understand.

Miss Maddy just disappeared after the destruction of her house. Sylvia couldn't help wondering about her. She walked over to the broken structure several times, searching through the pitiful ruins in the hopes of finding some clues to the woman's whereabouts. She went as far as asking George if he heard anything; but he like everyone else seemed to have forgotten the woman's existence. Then, one week to the day they destroyed her house, Miss Maddy reappeared. She came in fine style, like a bad omen, on a day Sylvia would be hard pressed to forget. Port Juanero woke that Wednesday morning to find the ragged woman installed in a new location. The house was a mystery. It had sprung up overnight like a fast growing mushroom; a sturdy one-room structure of new wood, that appeared on the commonland between the school and phase one of the housing scheme.

Sylvia had given the beach a miss that morning because of her worries over Jean. Her cousin had announced her intention of going to church the night before, but once again failed to return until the false dawn lightened the moonless darkness. Jean's stumbling progress had woken her and Sylvia found her in the living room, too drunk and disoriented to find the stairs. She had been forced to help Jean up to bed to avoid waking the whole house. Sylvia had wanted to question her, but as usual her cousin passed out almost as soon as her head touched the pillow.

Now Jean was still sleeping off the night's excesses, and Sylvia was too concerned to leave, aware of how unpredictable her cousin could be after a drinking bout.

She was pulling out Aleesa's plaits and half listening to Jalini, Dionne and Lutie bickering about who would get to hold the biggest water bottle, when George appeared at the top of the street steps looking pleased with himself. He was carrying a large sack of oranges and he put it under the shade of a giant croton bush before going to lean against the concrete verandah wall. 'You want some news?'

Sylvia nodded absently, her attention split between Aleesa's hair and Davian's attempt to show her the leaves he was methodically stripping from the mango tree.

Swept away by his own enthusiasm, George was not deterred. 'You know you did asking me bout Maddy last week?'

'You mean the mentally handicapped woman?' Sylvia was attentive now. 'Did you find out where she went?'

'Well, a don't directly know where she did get to first time . . . when the house just pull down . . .' He was playing out the suspense for all it was worth.

Sylvia nodded. 'And?'

George's grin widened. 'Well, she come back, move right out back a the school – new board house and everything . . . you should see the commotion down there.'

Jalini leaned over the low verandah wall. 'You mean the house just come like magic, Daddy?'

He nodded. 'People saying is the man them that use to visit her a night time build it for her.'

Lutie and Dionne crowded Jalini at the verandah rail. 'Miss Maddy living by the schoolyard, Daddy?' Dionne's eyes were wide with fright.

George was immediately stern. 'Yes, and a don't want you children going by her house, lest Mauvia or somebody there with you.'

Three pairs of frightened eyes looked back at him and Aleesa twisted round, curious.

'Miss Maddy going kill we, Daddy?' Lutie wanted to know.

Her father nodded. 'A know the children down soh stoning her house, but you just make sure and don't join in.'

Sylvia felt annoyed. 'I'm sure she can't be that dangerous, George. Surely they would have institutionalised her if she was.'

'From she mad she dangerous,' he disagreed. 'Too much mad people a wander bout the place and not a thing get done . . . she shouldn't allow to live down there, where decent people children going all the time.'

'I not going get drinking water,' Jalini pronounced with finality.

'Me neither,' her more timid sisters were quick to echo.

Pearl appeared at the doorway, her arms dripping soapy water. 'Who not going for drinking water?'

'Moomie, Miss Maddy down the bottom,' Jali offered, 'and she chop one boy already.'

'Stop talk foolishness and go for the water bottle!' Pearl snapped. 'If you left Miss Maddy alone she not going trouble you. She not a danger to nobody.'

George glared at his wife. 'Since when you turn expert on mad people?'

Pearl kissed her teeth. 'Everybody know Miss Maddy not dangerous, George, a wish you wouldn't keep encourage the children to fraid for everything so.'

George squared up to her. 'A telling them not to go down there and a expecting you to make sure them don't disobey me.'

Pearl gave him a bitter look. 'So who going carry up drinking water? George, you know Mauvia staying down by Miss Lisa to wash clothes this morning and not a drop of drinking water leave.'

'So what happen to you make you can't go?'

'You think is simple as that, ee?' Pearl's voice was beginning to rise with temper. 'And who you expecting will watch the baby, you?'

'Pearl, don't start up your foolishness again, is your job to look after Kaona, just like is my job to provision the family. You know your place aready so a don't see why you always a go on bad of a sudden.'

Aleesa shifted restlessly as the volume of the quarrel rose, and Davian pressed closer to Sylvia.

She could feel her own irritation mounting. 'George, I'm sure the children will be all right down there, people with mental illness aren't necessarily dangerous, you know.'

His mouth set in stubborn lines. 'Sylvia man, you don't see you just a encourage Pearl? My children not going near no mad woman.'

Sylvia sighed, refusing to be drawn into the argument. 'What if I walked down for the water with them?'

George looked as if he still wanted to argue, but under Sylvia's level gaze, he backed off.

Pearl gave her a grateful look. 'Sylvia, if you could

a would appreciate that. Miss Maddy not really dangerous, but through she mad and they stirring her up down
there . . .'

'You don't have to explain, Pearl, I could do with
the exercise anyway.'

There was a crowd milling around outside Miss
Maddy's new house when Sylvia and the five children
got down to the flat commonland. She had to pick
Davian up as the noise of the shouting and jostling
made him whimper and cling to her legs. Halfway
through the tangle of people Lutie started to cry and
Dionne refused to go any further.

'Miss Maddy in there, Auntie,' she insisted when
Sylvia tried to coax them on.

'Is fraid they fraid,' Jalini volunteered as she and
Aleesa came back reluctantly when Sylvia called them.
'They always fraid a everything, Auntie.'

'Is not true,' Lutie was stung. 'Is just through Miss
Maddy sitting right in the doorway and she could just
chop somebody the next minute so.'

Sylvia sighed. 'Lutie, how would you feel if you were
that poor lady, with all these people picking on you?'

Lutie looked surprised, and Dionne stopped crying,
but it was Jalini who spoke first, 'I would fight them,
Auntie, a would just knock one a them so and they
woulda never trouble me again.'

'Hush up, Jali,' Lutie said crossly, 'you always talking
bout fighting . . .'

'Yes,' Dionne sniffed, 'and Pastor saying we mustn't
get inna fighting and strife.'

Sylvia stepped in before things got out of hand.
'Maybe the lady is just frightened and if we don't bother
her she won't bother us.'

That seemed to reassure the twins, because they followed when she started walking again, though they
were careful to stay on her right, the side farthest from
Miss Maddy's house.

The ragged woman raised her head as they passed, her eyes seeking a little support. Sylvia looked away, feeling guilty and conspicious. She wished she had the guts to go up to Miss Maddy, stand beside her and ask the crowd to leave. Instead she hurried the children on, ignoring Aleesa's angry outburst that someone should help the lady.

The day was hot and airless, and Sylvia was glad of Miss Lisa's offer of iced lemonade. But her mind remained with the ragged woman and her tormentors on the common. The thought of walking past again made her feel uncomfortable and she had half decided to intervene on the way back, when George drove up.

'Pearl never shoulda agree for you to come,' he explained, ushering the children into the back of the car, 'specially with the times so hot and you not used to it as well.'

Sylvia got into the car, relieved at the reprieve, but she could not suppress the guilty feeling that she had somehow let the needy woman down.

Jean was still asleep when they returned. Sylvia hesitated about waking her then decided against it. Instead she rescued the copy of *Carnival* she had been struggling through the night before and retreated to the relative peace of the verandah. Pearl was engaged in the daily ritual of polishing the floor, singing along to morning worship on the radio. The children had started playing a local version of rounders, confusingly called baseball, and their voices flavoured the warm air with shrill excitement.

Sylvia was in a semi-doze on the fading red lounger when Jean came down, but she snapped awake as her cousin's tension seeped into her consciousness. Sitting up groggily, she mentally searched for something to break the atmosphere that had suddenly formed.

Jean was still in her nightdress, and her narrowed eyes and tight lips promised ill to anyone foolhardy enough to cross her. Pearl came to the door, and retreated prudently after a sour look from her sister-in-law.

Sylvia's nerves tightened and she said the first thing that occurred to her. 'Jean, the ragged woman is back, she's just moved into a new house beside the school.'

'So?'

'Well, I thought you might want to go and see her as you got quite involved with her before they knocked her house down.'

'What you trying to say, Sylvia. That I mad like Maddy?'

'Don't be stupid.' She was horrified by that interpretation. 'I was just trying to . . .'

Jean kissed her teeth, giving Sylvia a bitter look as the words tailed off. Muttering under her breath, she wandered across to the verandah wall, where she leaned against the blue painted stone, observing the children's antics with a jaundiced eye.

As if on cue, Aleesa was run out and refused to leave the game. The argument that followed increased the volume of noise and Davian stared to cry. Sylvia took one look at Jean's face, but her cousin was in the fray before she could make a move.

'*If you lot can't play good together you can stop the game right now!*'

'Auntie, Aleesa get run out and she saying she not going out,' Jalini defended.

'Is true, Auntie,' Lutie supported her sister, 'Aleesa just wanting to bat all the time and if we say no, she take the ball and don't want to give it up.'

Aleesa was indignant. 'That's not true, Mum, I wasn't out.'

'I don't want to hear it, Aleesa!' Jean snapped. 'You give that ball back and come over here right now.'

Aleesa's bottom lip pushed out and she threw the ball on the ground.

Jean was on her in a flash. 'You selfish brat,' she yelled, disregarding her bare feet in her annoyance. 'You think I'm you father or your auntie?'

Sylvia's muscles refused to move as the woman's doubled fist caught the child a staggering blow on the side of the face. She could only stare in shock as Jean's arm came back again, connecting with enough force to knock the dazed Aleesa over.

Lutie, Dionne and Jalini backed away, and Davian's wails reached the edge of screaming. That shifted Sylvia, and she reached Jean as she started hauling Aleesa to her feet, her arm already moving back for a follow-up.

Sylvia caught at the hand in desperation, grabbing her cousin's nightdress in a bunched fist and shaking hard. '*Jean, are you mad or something! Jean . . . let her go! Let her go right now!*'

At the shock of the unexpected assault, Jean let go of Aleesa and Sylvia stepped between them, shaking with reaction. Somehow she managed to keep her voice steady, taking command. 'Children, go inside . . . you too, Aleesa, take your brother and go with your cousins.'

Jean glared at Sylvia. '*Aleesa, you dare!* You better stay right where you are until *I* say otherwise.'

The child scrambled to her feet, stood trembling and uncertain as her eyes moved fearfully from one adult to the other.

'Go on, Aleesa,' Sylvia coaxed, reaching out to give the little girl a gentle push, 'go and look after your brother for me.'

'But Mum said . . .'

'It'll be OK, I'll have a talk to your mum.'

Jean turned on Sylvia then. 'You think I'm mad like Maddy, so you can come with your psychology and have me eating out of your hand?'

'I don't think you're mad Jean, but I think you need help.'

'*Help from you?*' The words were a provocation.

Sylvia didn't rise to the bait. 'I don't care who you get it from, but you can't go on like this.'

'Says who?' Jean's voice rose in angry challenge. 'You better take your nose out of my business if you know what's good for you, Sylvia, or . . .'

'Or what? I'm not a little eight-year-old you can bully, you know.'

'What I do to my children is my affair.' Jean took refuge in bluster. 'If I want to take them out of here today not you or anybody else could stop me.'

Sylvia struggled to keep her voice from rising to match the other woman's growing anger. 'I couldn't let you do that, Jean, and you know why as well as I. Look at you, coming in at all hours and drinking God knows how much. The children aren't your property and if you still think you can do what you like to them, you're not a fit mother to have them.'

'Who you talking to like that?' The belligerence increased, curling Jean's hands into fists, and she took a threatening step forward.

Sylvia tensed but stood her ground. 'Jean, I have no intention of getting into a fist fight at my age.'

'You mean you too fraid to back up all your fancy threats?'

She wasn't rising to that. 'Let me just say this so we both know where we stand: lay one more finger on either of those children and I'll see you're prosecuted the minute you step foot back in England.'

'*You can't help it, can you!*' Jean's anger threatened to spill over. 'You just can't keep your faas social-working nose out of my business.'

'Think what you like, Jean, but Aleesa and Davian are my cousins and I'm not going to have them mistreated because you haven't got the guts to face up to your own inadequacies.'

For a moment they squared up to each other, two antagonists with hostilities finally raw and open. Then Jean's face contorted. 'You going to regret this, Sylvia, just you wait. No one – not you, not Jimmy – going to walk over me ever again . . . and don't think I going to forget this.'

Sylvia watched her storm back into the house, feeling hopeless and deflated. How could things have deteriorated so fast? It was as if Jean had regressed overnight. If anything she was worse than before. She had never been so out of control, so much on the edge of violence. It made Sylvia doubt her own judgement, wonder at her ability to sense impending crises. To think she had even been toying with the idea of changing her ticket again . . . going back to England without waiting for Jimmy to arrive. She already felt guilty about neglecting her own clients and the hundred and one problems waiting at work.

She chewed on her bottom lip. What to do now?

She thought of ringing Jimmy, then dismissed that out of hand. The way the house was constructed Jean would be able to hear every word; anyway, what could Jimmy do from England? She would only cause him unnecessary worry and run the risk of further antagonising her cousin at the same time.

She felt isolated, alone. If only Winston was here. He had always been the person she talked through her ideas with. Self-pitying tears threatened and she steeled herself against them.

'Sylvia, is everything all right?' Pearl hovered at the doorway of the house, keeping a cautious eye on the stairs. 'Is just that, a couldn't help but overhear you and Jean arguing.'

Sylvia forced a reassuring smile. 'Yes, everything is fine.'

Pearl hesitated, twisting the tea towel nervously in her hand. 'A hope you don't mind, but a let the children take Aleesa and Davian down by Miss Lisa.'

Sylvia felt a surge of gratitude. 'Thanks Pearl . . . was Aleesa alright?'

'One side of her face bruise up bad and she have a cut lip, but a put some ice on it and give her one kisko to stop the swelling.' Pearl came further out, looking worried. 'Something wrong with Jean?'

It was difficult to know how to answer diplomatically and Sylvia opted for partial truth. 'Jean hasn't been herself for a while and she sometimes gets a bit annoyed with the children.'

Pearl didn't look convinced. 'She seeming to get vex for the least little thing . . . is something to do with Jimmy noh?'

'Miss Sylvia, is you that?' Miss Berta's voice was a welcome interruption and Sylvia turned, grateful for the relief.

'Hello, Miss Berta, how are things?'

'A can't complain, Miss Sylvia, but how you managing with this drought heat?'

'Well, Miss Berta, I keep telling myself it's better than a wet English summer.'

Miss Berta mopped her brow with a fluffy pink flannel, pulled her hat off her head and fanned it from side to side. 'A just see the children down by Miss Lisa. Is what happen to Aleesa, she get inna fight?'

Sylvia was hunting around for an appropriate response when Pearl stepped in. Moving to the verandah edge she gave the trader a polite smile. 'Hello, Miss Berta, how is business?'

'Hello, Miss Mackenzie,' Miss Berta's smiled cooled a little. 'Things not as bad as they could be, mam.'

'And the children?'

'They doing OK, Bernice get some day's work and

she look like getting a position with a lady down in St Catherine.'

Pearl nodded. 'A glad to hear that . . . tell them howdy for me, will you?'

'Yes, Miss Mackenzie.' Miss Berta moved on with a wave and Pearl turned back to Sylvia. 'A hope you don't mind but is best they don't know the fullness of what happening with Jean.' She looked significantly towards the common, where the crowd around the ragged woman's house had started to disperse.

'Thank you,' Sylvia looked at the other woman with new respect. The way Pearl had handled Miss Berta was a study in manipulation, and yet she wasn't even aware of it. 'I didn't have a clue what to say to her.'

Pearl looked pleased and embarrassed by the implied compliment. 'Is nothing when a think how you put up with us . . . Sylvia, a just wanting you to know say a grateful.' She scurried away before Sylvia could respond, retreating back to the safety of her kitchen as Jean reappeared.

The cousins eyed each other warily, their earlier animosity alive between them. Jean had put on the shorts and cotton blouse from the previous day, and Sylvia realised that she hadn't even bothered to wash herself. It increased her irritation as she wondered if Jean was trying to provoke her.

'Are you feeling better?' she asked, keeping her voice calm.

Jean kissed her teeth. 'Who said there was anything wrong with me?'

Sylvia pushed her rising anger down. 'I'd rather believe you didn't deliberately set out to hurt Aleesa.'

'I only gave her a couple of slaps. Christ, Sylvia, anyone would think that I beat her up or something.'

She couldn't let that pass. 'That's exactly what you *did* do, Jean, the whole of one side of Aleesa's face is bruised.'

'She must have hit herself when she fell.'

'No, Jean, you did it with your fist. You have to accept that, because the next time you could really damage that child.'

Jean burst into tears. It was as if something broke inside her, releasing a stream of misery. Sylvia wished she could feel sympathy, a little kindness even. But images of the woman's fist connecting with Aleesa's defenceless head kept intruding.

So she just sat there, watching her cry, feeling more and more resentful of the whole situation. Why did *she* have to end up in the middle of this mess? That wasn't what she came here for. All she had wanted was a chance to say a private goodbye to Winston and their joint past. But even that peace had become over-shadowed by everyone else's personal tragedies.

Ironic really. On the surface, Jean and Pearl had everything she didn't. Between them they had six children, and settled relationships. Yet the bitterness in their lives was something she and Winston never knew.

Sylvia wondered if it was because he died before things turned sour. Dismissed that. They had fourteen good years before he died. Years in which they learnt how to communicate, talking out disagreements rather than allowing them to become festering holes in the fabric of their marriage. That thought only served to increase her irritation with the sobbing woman beside her.

Jean sniffed, catching Sylvia's attention. 'You don't care, do you? You couldn't give a damn about me . . . you're just like Jimmy.'

Sylvia looked at her in resignation. 'Jean, I just don't know what to say to you any more. If you want to talk of course I'll listen, but right now I have to admit I'm not feeling very sympathetic.'

'So you don't want to know what happened last night?'

'I didn't say that.'

'Well, I'll tell you anyway.' Her mood had become ugly again. 'I went to bed with a man.'

Sylvia held up her hand. 'This is none of my business.'

Jean continued as if she hadn't spoken. 'And it's not the first time either. You know the day Aleesa was coming here? I didn't bring her to the airport because I was with someone else . . . all night!'

Sylvia was appalled, but she listened as Jean poured out the story of her drinking blackouts. When her cousin finished speaking she could only spread her hands and ask why.

Jean looked miserable again. 'Sylv, I really tried, you know. I really thought the Church was the answer, but you was right in the end. They just as bad as the rest of them. Just because you make one mistake when you little, every man think you is easy meat.'

Sylvia was totally at a loss. 'But what happened last night, Jean? I thought you were really getting on well at church. I mean, you *did* go to church, didn't you?'

Jean kissed her teeth. 'I don't want to talk about it. Them people was just one big waste of time . . . and Pastor Simmonds the worse.'

'Oh, stop feeling so sorry for yourself!' Sylvia's temper snapped. 'Why can't you think about someone else for a change? I'm sick to death of hearing all the things other people have done to you. Supposing you just stop for one minute, Jean, and consider what *you've* been doing to Jimmy, and your children . . . and to me.'

'*You!*'

'Yes, me.' Jean's surprise fanned the flames. 'It might not have occurred to you, but I had my own reasons for coming to Jamaica, and nursing you wasn't one of them.'

'Well, I'm sorry you feel like that,' Jean responded

with wounded dignity. It made Sylvia feel a fresh guilt and she backed down.

'Look, I'm sorry, I shouldn't have gone on like that.'

'*Sorry?* You think I want your pity?' Jean yelled. 'You take my man and you take my children . . . you always have everything you want and then you tell me "sorry" and want me to *talk* to you.' She got up and headed for the roadside stairs, only pausing to give her cousin a last bitter look. 'I don't need you to listen to me, Sylvia Dyer, I can find plenty people out there who will. I can find man like you could never even dream. You think is just now they wanting me?' she hissed through her teeth. 'Cho, you could never understand with your wither-up self and your sour face.'

She stopped abruptly, turning to plunge down the steep roadstairs. Sylvia could only sit and stare, feeling utterly stunned.

Chapter 10

Jean was lying naked in a strange bed, wedged between a rough wooden wall and a man's body. The smell of tainted air and garbage mingled with the rawness of fish and seaweed. It overwhelmed her, making her gag until her brain adjusted to it. There was a stickiness between her thighs. That and the scent of stale sex told her what her mind could not recall.

She felt no alarm, no shame; only resignation. She had even gone beyond the panic of wondering if the sex had been protected. She no longer really cared about the risks. Her mind was emptied of any sense of responsibility. What did it matter anyway? If she was pregnant it couldn't be any worse than before. She already knew about being an unmarried mother living without the security of a wedding ring. If she caught something she might die, but right now she couldn't see much in life to hang on for.

She smiled vacantly, *Who say I isn't the one passing out disease?* she wondered, choking down a sudden urge to giggle. *With the sin I weighted down in and the amount of time I been in this self-same position, I can't expect to stay lucky . . . specially the way bad luck following me all my days*. It was as if everything was conspiring to send her down, keep her down, and somehow it just didn't matter any more.

The man's back was turned towards her. It was sun-baked and dry-skinned taking on a greyish cast in the shadowed room. Jean's gaze took in the rough, scaly-looking elbow, before lingering on the rusty-red appearance of the locks that made him seem somehow familiar. It didn't make her curious to find out for sure. None of it did. All she wanted was to stay here, where nothing and no one could reach her.

She hoped he wouldn't wake up. That she did not have to put up with his sexual attention now her mind was clear. Yet she just continued lying there, making no move to leave the bed and put some distance between them.

The man shifted, mumbled and turned over in his sleep. Jean tensed as a counterpoint to the vibration in the bed, pressing back hard against the uneven texture of the wall to avoid contact with him. She stared at his bearded face incuriously, not even surprised to see that it was the rastaman from the squatted land. What was his name again? *Peter* . . . Yes, that was what he called himself: *Peter from the Tribe of Ash*. He was a con artist, she remembered that as well. She knew enough real rastas to recognise a hustler when she saw one. But he at least accepted her for what she was, even admired her for what he thought she had achieved. She felt a brief pleasure at her feat of recall, but even that petered out, taking her back to the flat featureless state she had been in before.

It occurred to her that she must be in the rastaman's dilapidated wooden house. Several clues fell into place and that pleased her briefly too. No wonder she had thought the sea sounded close enough for her to stretch out her hand and bury it in the wet sand of the shoreline. While she drifted in and out of sleep, that had been a comforting thought. Like being cocooned and nurtured safe from the pain of real life.

One foot was becoming numb from lying too long at an awkward angle. Jean shifted experimentally, waiting to feel the usual queasiness. When it didn't come *that* puzzled her as well. Hadn't she been drinking? Surely she must have been to end up here. The prickling sensation in her foot left it feeling weak. She rubbed at it to get the blood circulating, idly trying to remember the events that brought her here. She let her mind drift backwards, grappling for a focus of recall.

Yesterday – what had happened then? She had woken up feeling sick and depressed with the mess her life was in. Hearing the children's laughter had been like a goad, a mocking counterpoint to her depression; tantalising her with a joy she could no longer share. She had only gone downstairs to ask them to keep the noise down, nothing more. Her brows wrinkled as she remembered Aleesa's defiance and what she saw as her cousin's inter-ference.

It's all well and good Sylvia talking about girlchildren having freedom. She not even a mother, and she sure as anything not going have to take the shame when Aleesa turn rude and slack. Is bad enough the way Jimmy spoiling them children, but with Sylvia and George around I can't do a thing with them, not one single thing. She sighed, her mood tilting further into depression. *Why can't Sylvia see I was being firm for Aleesa own good? Attempting to save that wilful child from the thousand and one sins of pride? The good Lord knows I could write a book about sin,* she decided sadly, *I feel so loaded down with them myself, is like a festering corpse on my back sometimes.*

A strange, desperate sort of laugh bubbled up inside her. Jean gulped it down and wrapped her arms around her stomach. She rocked back and forth in an attempt to keep the sound at bay, then froze on a sudden thought. Supposing something had broken loose, some elemental malfunction somewhere in her belly? She was afraid in case that strange laughter boiled over. What if it kept running on and running on till it emptied her altogether of the possibility of humour?

Jean shivered despite the heat. She fancied that all

her emotions were in flimsy containers waiting for an accident. She could just imagine the little goodness and all that badness spilling over and getting all mixed up. It caused a sudden surge of panic. Supposing the good drained away, leaving her with all that sin exposed?

The thought made her shift uneasily, the movement setting up a vibration in the sagging bed that woke the man. He blinked, once, twice, focusing on her with bloodshot eyes. A smile split his face, showing significant gaps between his teeth.

'Good day, Miss Jean . . . A did tink you would gone by this.'

Jean didn't bother to smile back, afraid to waste emotions she was sure had started leaking away.

He lay where he was for a long time, just looking, admiration and pleasure in his eyes. Jean stared back, feeling nothing. She wasn't even dismayed that he was awake, with every intention of continuing where he'd left off the night before.

One of the man's hands came out to rest on her stomach. It was a big hand, long-fingered and bony, the nails discoloured by nicotine and dirt. Jean lay still, neither accepting nor rejecting. It made him press on, fingers tugging gently at the sparse hairs that grew between her navel and her pubic line.

Jean stared at some point far beyond him, feeling a sense of futility. The gesture reminded her so much of Jimmy it brought a sting of tears to her eyes. She quashed those feelings down at birth, angry all of a sudden. Why should Jimmy matter anyway? He didn't want her now he was *somebody*, he'd made that clear enough.

This man . . . *Peter*, he liked her. His every look and gesture told her just how lucky he considered himself to have merited her attention. Yes, Peter wanted her and as far as she was concerned, he could never in a

143

hundred years reach the point where *she* wasn't good enough for him.

That was enough to relax her tensing muscles and she didn't resist when he raised himself on one arm and urged her to lie on her back. But Jimmy still managed to cheat her. He kept intruding in her mind – his loving, the conversations that accompanied it – till she couldn't kid herself that this man could be a substitute.

Peter was a gentle kind of person even so, his hand moving over the skin of her belly with a strange, patient insistence. It felt comforting, soothing to her battered spirit and she opened her legs willingly to accommodate him when he finally rolled on top of her. With her eyes closed tight, she could pretend Jimmy was the one that held her, that it was his beard tickling her neck, his mouth closing warm and wet on first one breast and then the other.

The fantasy was arousing. Jean wrapped her legs tightly around the scrawny waist pulling him deeper inside her. Her hips rocked with the urgency in him, while the fantasy image drew a groan of satisfaction from deep inside her.

Afterwards he returned to stroking her belly, a self-satisfied smile in his voice, 'You like me, ee? A did know it from the first, you know.'

Jean kept her eyes closed, feeling the let down heavily. The smells of poverty were suddenly oppressive, and she had to breathe deeply to still the panicky feeling of entrapment. She could feel him moving about, guessed that he was getting dressed, but felt no desire to go searching for her own clothes.

The bed depressed as he came to sit beside her. There was the scratching and spurting sounds of a match being lit and she smelt the aroma of ganja as a spliff was thrust into her hand. She opened her eyes then, looking at the fat cigarette doubtfully. She had never messed around with drugs, but Peter was watching her expectantly.

Jean looked at the spliff again. It didn't smell too bad, a bit herbal really. She put it to her lips on a sudden decision, inhaling deeply. The smoke irritated her throat, making her cough. Peter slapped her on the back and produced a carton of juice from somewhere. Eyes watering, Jean eyed the spliff doubtfully. She'd never smoked anything before in her life.

'Try again noh,' Peter's voice egged her on, 'the thing is not to draw on it too sudden.'

She put it to her mouth again, gingerly. This time she managed not to cough. After that it was not too hard to hold in the strange blue smoke. The mellow feelings were surprisingly relaxing. Her insides didn't seem so fragile any more. Jean felt good, Peter looked good. She smiled, thinking he was really quite handsome underneath it all.

He told her about his frustration with his life. She sympathised, feeling the echoes in her own. He had wanted to go to America, but his sister over there didn't want to know and his one aunt in England had never answered his letters. He knew he could make good money from selling ganja up in foreign. But down here it was a hand-to-mouth business because the local market wasn't saying anything.

By the time she had gone through a third of her spliff she was feeling relaxed and clear-headed. She couldn't imagine how she could ever have been against this thing; ever believed what she now considered foolish talk about psychosis. Her brain seemed to have sharpened, all the thousand and one problems fading to insignificant specks.

She found herself telling Peter about Davian and Aleesa; how her son could barely say two words at the age of three, Aleesa's arrogance and the way Sylvia thwarted every attempt she made to bring them up in the disciplined ways of old Jamaica.

He listened patiently, full of sympathy and understanding. Why had she failed to realise just how bright he was, what a fine mind lay beneath that rough exterior? She listened, rapt, as he encouraged her with a mixture of scripture and his own view, finishing with the profound observation that all her sufferings would make her stronger.

'In the end is for you to follow what inside your heart,' he suggested when she asked what she should do.

'But I told you,' she explained again, 'Sylvia is just the one to get me arrested. You don't know how much power people like her have up in England. She can just come one day and take the children and next thing you have to go up to the law court and they put you in prison for child abuse . . . just through you want to grow them right.'

'She caan do that, man!' Peter shook his head. 'You is the youth dem mother before Jah, nobody can change that, cause he sees it all and he knows it all.'

'You don't know her; she and Jimmy is together in this thing. She was married to his brother and from Winston dead Sylvia is all over Jimmy and the children, with me shut right out,' she explained earnestly. 'He write this book, see, and then he didn't want me any more.'

'What, you mean he did want the book stead a you?' He laughed uproariously at his own joke.

Jean shook her head, admiring his wit but unable to share the joke as memory dampened her drug-induced contentment. 'No, he want the children, but he can't have them all to himself with me there, you see. So he and Sylvia start to spread all these stories about me not being right in the head – like Miss Maddy, you know – and they going to arrest me in England.'

'So why you have to go back a England? From you have US visa, you can go anywhere you want.'

She hadn't thought of that and she looked at him with new respect. 'I could, couldn't I? I mean, Aleesa and Davian are my kids . . . she's the one who didn't want any because she was too busy building a career.'

'Who?'

'Sylvia – my cousin, remember? She want to steal my children.'

He rambled off again, giving her a different set of advice, but Jean was no longer listening. All her resentment against Sylvia rose up larger than before. She fancied that her cousin always disliked her, that she and Jimmy had deliberately set out to turn the children against her. The voices sniggered in her head, calling her an idiot. They pointed out that she had done nothing thousands wouldn't . . . had punished the children out of love and the need to save them from the devil's temptation and the deep pain of unshriven sin. Jean nodded frantically, wanting to acknowledge every word. She agreed with it, all of it. Thinking about it now, she felt she had done nothing but the best for the children out of the purest of motives.

Her mind was jangling with sounds, the anger growing inside her, threatening to explode her chest. Jean sucked desperately on the spliff, needing to get the mellow feeling back.

The knock on the door interrupted her self-pitying recollections and brought the clamouring voices to an abrupt halt. Jean frowned as a woman in a faded floral sundress poked her head around the door, wondering if Sylvia had sent *this one* to spy as well. In her mind, her cousin was growing into something big and evil with tentacles spreading as far as she could hope to reach on a small island like Jamaica.

'Ras Peter,' the woman said apologetically, her uncertain manner unknowingly calming the naked woman on the bed, 'somebody out here say she wanting to see the lady.'

Jean just had time to pull the worn sheet over her exposed body before the door opened wide and Sylvia walked in. Her cousin stopped abruptly as she took in the occupants of the room, her eyes disbelieving and angry as they settled on the spliff in Jean's hand.

Jean squashed the tendrils of shame before they could take root, revelling in a sudden vicious satisfaction instead. '*Sylvia*, come in,' she said mockingly, relieved when the noises peopling her head did not return; she needed total control for this. 'What you saying, cousin?'

Sylvia's lips curled in distaste, her eyes taking in the soiled clothes on the floor and the tumbled bed, before coming to rest on Ras Peter. 'I would like to speak to my cousin in private if you don't mind,' she told him pointedly.

He drew deeply on his spliff, eyes narrowing as he met the woman's challenging and contemptuous gaze. 'So you is the cousin trying to tief way Miss Jean children. Nobody don't tell you is unnatural to remove a youth from him mother? You think you can set your face against Jah and win?'

Sylvia's face shuttered over. 'I don't know who you are, Mr . . . ?'

'Just call me Ras Peter. You know you trouble, Miss Sylvia, you living too much of your life with the wicked. Now, why you don't leave Miss Jean and her children alone, mam? Is not right to interfere between a one and her youth them.'

Sylvia looked at him impassively, waiting for the speech to end. 'I didn't come here to trade words with you, Mr Peter, so if you could just step outside for a few minutes . . .'

Ras Peter didn't take the hint. 'You know is unnatural for a queen not to have a youth unless Jah wither her womb in punishment; that is what bring forth jealousy and envy. You should find a king and breed you own youth, steada trying to take what belong to Miss Jean here. You is a presentable woman, plenty king would consider you . . . even if you tainted with the wicked.'

Jean smiled with malicious pleasure at Sylvia's obvious annoyance. She drew deeply on her spliff, holding the smoke for a long minute before blowing it deliberately in her cousin's direction.

Sylvia looked even more grim. She marched further into the room staring at Jean with a mixture of contempt and scorn. 'I don't know what you're playing at now, and I don't care. But if you have to screw around, can't you find somewhere that isn't right under your brother's nose?'

That caught Jean on the raw, brought the dormant guilt feelings tumbling in. Her bitterness towards her cousin increased as all the old grievances were prodded to the fore. 'Why shouldn't I do what I want? I'm not George's keeper, Sylvia, I don't tell either you or him how to live your lives so just keep your nose out of mine, right?'

Sylvia glanced at Ras Peter in frustration. 'Look, Jean, we need to talk about the children . . . privately.'

Jean stared at her, weighing up the words. Inside she knew she was afraid of being alone with Sylvia, afraid that the unvoiced condemnation would spill over into words the minute there was no one else present.

'Jean,' Sylvia persisted, 'I think you do still care about Aleesa and Davian despite the way you've been carrying on recently. So I'm asking you to talk to me . . . *please!* Give me ten minutes for their sake.'

Trust Sylvia to push the knife in, Jean thought bitterly. She gave a nervous laugh. 'Surely I can sleep out one night without you coming to search for me like a lost soul?'

'One night?' Sylvia looked puzzled. 'Jean, what are you talking about? You've not been back to George's in three days.'

For a moment her mind couldn't grasp what Sylvia was saying . . . all those nosy people gossiping inside her head and not one mentioned *that*. 'What you talking about now, Sylvia?' she demanded, half deciding it was a bluff.

'*You*, Jean . . . disappearing for three days without a single word to anyone. You, leaving your children and just going off to find some low-life sex.'

Ras Peter made a sound of annoyance, but both women ignored him. Jean was having enough difficulty of her own, grappling with the shock of what Sylvia had said. 'This is some kind of a joke . . . right?'

Sylvia shook her head. 'Do I *look* like I'm laughing? Jean, none of us knew where you were until Pearl caught sight of you last night. Can you imagine how worried everybody was?'

She felt a stab of fear; panic started to rise and she stared at Sylvia with real dislike. 'You're lying, aren't you . . . You're just trying to get back at me because I have kids and you don't.'

'Jean, you know fully well I wouldn't do that . . . If you have any sense left in that blocked-up head of yours you'd realise that everybody was worried about you.'

'What, even the children?' Jean taunted.

'Yes, even the children.'

Fear made her lash out. 'Sure! I bet you for one was glad to see the back of me, I bet you couldn't wait to get on the phone and tell Jimmy all about it.'

'Jean, I'm not prepared to discuss this with an audience.' Sylvia's mouth set in stubborn lines.

Jean knew her cousin wasn't bluffing. When Sylvia got that look there was no shifting her position. 'Ras Peter, you could give us some time?'

He shrugged again, taking another puff of his spliff. 'Sure thing, Miss Jean, if is how you want it.'

She nodded, her whole attention fixed on Sylvia now, fear fighting the anaesthetising effect of the ganja weed.

There was no denying that the woman was in deadly earnest; Jean knew her cousin well enough to realise she wouldn't make up something like that.

Three days! How could she have three whole days missing from her life? What on earth had she been up to?

Sylvia walked across the uneven floor to perch awkwardly on the edge of the bed, 'Jean, I want you and the children to come back to England with me. I phoned British Airways and they can get us all on a flight on Tuesday.'

That frightened her, resurrecting the suspicion that her cousin meant to have her arrested. 'You're kidding, aren't you?'

'I'm serious,' Sylvia persisted, 'I just feel you'd be better off in England at this point in time.'

I bet, she thought sourly, but she was careful to keep it to herself. 'Why?' she asked aloud instead.

'Jean, look at you!' Sylvia's annoyance began to show. 'Jamaica was supposed to be straightening you out, but if anything you're worse than when you came.'

'What do *you* know?'

'I know that you're not always in control of your actions . . . Just look at yourself, lying naked in some strange man's bed . . . puffing away at a spliff as if it was second nature, and you can't pretend you haven't been hearing voices.'

Jean chose to ignore the last part. 'Why don't you say what you mean, Sylvia? It's not so much that he's a stranger, is it? More that he's poor and a rastaman to boot.'

'I meant just what I said,' Sylvia responded briskly. 'But if you must know, this place stinks . . . and don't tell me that have something to do with poverty. There is no excuse for filth.'

'You're such a snob, aren't you? There's nothing wrong with a bit of honest dirt.'

151

'Well, I can't stop you wallowing in it,' Sylvia said brutally, 'but I don't intend to stand by and watch the children suffer because you're too selfish to give a damn.'

Anger was white hot in Jean's chest. How dare this woman come here and start laying down rules about *her* children? 'This isn't England where you can just come and take away people's children for any and every little thing, you know,' she almost shouted, 'so don't come it with me. And if you said all you came to say you can leave right now!'

Sylvia gave a strained smile, putting a break on the escalating conflict. 'Look, getting into a slanging match isn't helping the situation any, is it? Why don't we start again and try discussing this reasonably.'

'You trying to say I not reasonable?'

'Not at all,' Sylvia placated, 'I'm just saying trading insults won't help anything.'

'Why you so interested in the children welfare anyway? You been like this since the day I step foot in this Jamaica, even before I get a chance to say dog. Jimmy been talking to you, haven't he?'

Her cousin seemed to weigh her words carefully. 'Well, since he couldn't get down himself, Jimmy did ask me to keep an eye.'

'*Spy on me, you mean?*' She could hear the panic colouring her voice. 'That's it, isn't it, he ask you to get him some evidence, didn't he? How long have the two of you been plotting together eh?'

'No, Jean! That is not it. Nobody is spying on you; and you know as well as I that Jimmy isn't like that.'

Jean felt fresh bitterness. She should have guessed he was behind it. They were in it together, just as she thought. Jimmy and Sylvia were trying to steal her children by proving she was an unfit mother.

'You never did like me, did you, Sylvia, ever since I had children and you didn't? You is the one been plotting against me all along. You is a hypocrite, you know that? Smiling up to my face with your "family is family" nonsense. I bet you couldn't wait to tell Jimmy all the gory details.'

Sylvia got up abruptly. 'I can see there's no point talking to you in this mood.'

'What's the matter, Sylvia . . . can't you take the heat?' Jean taunted as her cousin made for the door.

Sylvia stopped, turning back to face the bed. 'I don't intend to play infantile games with you, Jean. I can see you're not yourself. So when you dry out a bit and decide to start taking your responsibilities seriously, I suggest you find your way back to the house and give some serious thought to seeking professional help.'

Jean wasn't going to let that pass. 'And why should I need help?'

Her cousin sighed. 'You lose three days of your life and you can ask me that?'

'What you trying to say, that I getting mad, that I can't even remember what I was doing from one day to the next? Well I have news for you, I stayed away deliberately. You can look at me anyway you like. You think I'm going to let you and Jimmy tell *me* what to do?'

'Well, Jean, if that's the way you feel, there isn't much left to be said, is there?'

Jean watched the other woman go, feeling a poisonous triumph. Then depression rose like a wave to swamp her. Three days. What had happened to all that time? She wondered if her cousin had been telling the truth? Could she really trust any of them up there? After all, Sylvia spent years pretending to have her interests at heart; and all the time she was there plotting to steal her children. They were all the same, smiling to her face and looking to destroy her the minute her back was turned. Well, she was wise to their game now. None of them could fool her again.

Ras Peter came back through the door. 'Things aright?'

Jean nodded automatically, still caught up in the worry of those lost days. 'Peter, how long have I been here?'

He looked at her, surprised, 'Just since yesterday, What happen, you forget aready?'

'No, of course not; is just something Sylvia said.'

'Oh, you mean when she talking about you staying out a the house three days. A wouldn't wrong you if is so them treat you up soh.'

'But don't you see, I couldn't have been gone for three days. I had a bit of a row with Sylvia, that's why I came down here.' She didn't tell him about not knowing the details of how she got from the Sea Lawn tavern – the last place she had any recollection of – to his house.

Peter nodded in sympathy. 'You did look well rough when you come by yesterday.' He grinned, looking at her naked shoulders appreciatively, 'But you looking aright now.'

She smiled back automatically, not really listening. She should have guessed Sylvia was lying. How could anybody lose three days? Hours yes, but *days*! Relief mingled with a growing fear of her cousin. To think how she had trusted Sylvia, even though she didn't like her. Jean shook her head; when would she learn you couldn't trust anyone? Every last one of them let you down, went out of their way to try and hurt you.

Look at Jimmy, the way he caused her to get sick; and Sylvia with her lies. It had been the same with Noel, the way he went and got himself killed just so the blame would fall on her. It wasn't as if he hadn't known lightning would strike you dead if you stood under a green tree in a thunderstorm. *He was the one did make Pastor put the pain in me belly so the sins couldn't escape again.*

154

She gulped back a sudden need to cry, pulling on the stub of the spliff one last time. *Papa was just as bad*, she thought sadly, *he never love me one bit. Look at the way he just dump me and George in that terrible charity home, just cart us up to town and dump us . . . none of them did care what Pastor did.*

Jean sniffed, the self-pitying thoughts refusing to be stemmed. *Aunt Vi couldn't even have the conscience to take us when Papa dump us . . . just through Tashi go America and she thought she was above us.* Jean shook her head again, hopelessness eating away inside. *If you can't trust your own father, who you going to trust?*

Ras Peter walked over to pat her clumsily on one shoulder. 'You mustn't make your cousin upset you, man, you don't see is what she wanting?'

'She want to steal my children away,' she confided in him, taking the new spliff he offered. 'She always wanted them and now she going to try and take them.'

He raised his head and contemplated the glowing tip of his own spliff, watching the spiralling blue smoke that writhed around his head and hung on the air. 'You know what you going have to do? You have to decide one time about the youth them and just do it.'

Jean sucked on the end of the spliff, allowing the smoke to escape through her nose. 'I wish it was as easy as that,' she told him glumly. 'You have to understand Sylvia, you know. She came to tell me she want to take the children back to England . . . and you know she had the nerve to expect me to come back with her too.'

'You make her walk all over you too long,' Ras Peter observed. 'What you have to do is show all a them you don't need to listen to what they saying. If you man don't want you back you could even stay on down here in Jamaica.'

That idea excited her until the practicalities intruded. 'But what would I do? My work is up in England.'

'So what? You have education and you talk nice . . .

155

a fine lady like you would soon get a next work down here.'

Something was nagging at the back of her mind, but immediate worries were too pressing for her to explore in that direction. 'You think a could really do that?'

He nodded. 'Yes man! A don't think – a know so . . . you don't have no one back over in England now your cousin turn on you.'

'But where would I live? I couldn't stay up at George's, and accommodation is expensive.'

'You coulda even stay with me.'

She looked doubtfully around the mean-looking room, and he laughed, 'Not here. A have a place down in town that me mother dead and left me. It don't amount to much at present, just a old nog-house. But a aim to fix up and build a good house one day.'

She liked ambition in a man; wasn't that one of the things that had made her fall for Jimmy? But still the doubts persisted. What if she couldn't settle here? The island irritated her so much already, it was bound to be ten times worse if she was to stay on permanently.

'What happen if me and you fall out?' she wondered aloud.

He shook his head in instant denial. 'That not going happen, man . . . and from you have US visa a could even introduce you to some ways and means to make a money.'

She was faintly annoyed by his persistence. 'I want to see how things go when I see Sylvia again . . . and anyway I can't just up and move to Jamaica.'

'You think on it then,' Ras Peter's voice cooled a little, 'but if you go a prison inna England, might as cheap you stay a Jamdung and you with US visa and all . . . plenty a ways to make a money in that.'

Jean pinched off the end of the spliff as she had seen him do and deliberately uncoiled from the bed. Ras

156

Peter might be good for her ego, but she had no intention of throwing herself away by moving in with him.

Chapter 11

Sylvia retreated from the tangle of baked mud paths and board houses as fast as her feet could move in the heat. She could see groups of children pointing, heard their derisive shouts of 'English' and 'foreign lady!' Several women, washing clothes around a standpipe, paused in their work, attracted by the noise. They whispered and shook their heads, eyes brimming with laughter Sylvia decided was at her expense. With her fingers digging into her palms, she had to make a deliberate effort to keep walking as if she didn't care.

What she really wanted to do was march right back into the mean-looking shack and drag her cousin out. *How could Jean! How could she!* The thought went round and round inside her head. *How could she make a fool of me like this?*

That brought a fresh wave of anger, put another spurt of energy into her feet. Instinct told her she needed to put some breathing space between herself and Jean, to organise and come to terms with this new reality.

Pangs of guilt gradually replaced anger as the distance between herself and the squatted land grew. *I shouldn't have just left like that*, Sylvia thought with remorse, her feet slowing as the heat began to take its toll. *I shouldn't have let her throw me like that. What on earth do I tell Jimmy now?*

The recollection of her brother-in-law's trust brought a sense of failure. He had asked her to keep an eye on

Jean, had even mentioned his suspicion that his lover was getting ill. *I had to know better, didn't I?* Sylvia shook her head. *What's the point in having all that training if I couldn't see this coming?* The thought was key to the Pandora's Box of her memory. Now she was focused on it, all the warning signs came tumbling out.

She felt guilty all over again, remembering her original concerns about Jean's mental state. Why hadn't she acted on her suspicion that her cousin's religious conversion was no more than a cry for help? Jean had recognised her own decline, had made one last deliberate attempt to stop it. While *she* had been so glad to be relieved of responsibility she hadn't questioned too hard.

It made her uneasy to think of Jean clutching vainly to a futile hope while she remained wrapped in the solution to her own old grief. An image of the mean one-roomed shack rose to mock her, burning itself inside her head. The shock of seeing Jean – naked, dirty and uncaring – twisted her stomach into knots and made her feel sick and disappointed. Seeing that stark and sordid evidence, she could no longer avoid acknowledging just how far gone her cousin was. 'How long has she been sleeping around?' Sylvia wondered aloud, concentrating on the obvious when the sense of failure threatened to weigh her down.

She frowned, remembering Jean's mention of an incident in London; the strong smell of stale sex the woman always brought back along with the alcohol and vomit in the early hours of morning. She could no longer deny the evidence, had to accept promiscuity as another part of the problem.

Sylvia's heart sank as thoughts tumbled over each other. *What if Jimmy finds out about this? How could Jean sink so low? When did it start? Why? If I hadn't seen it with my own eyes . . .*

She shook her head again, reliving the shame of

159

seeing her own cousin – fastidious Jean with her repressed sexuality and her modesty – perched naked on that soiled bed; the oversized spliff clenched between her teeth like some obscene gesture. It was like a bad joke . . . except Sylvia never felt *less* like laughing. Instead she focused on the dilemma it presented her.

Jean needed Jimmy's support, now more than ever. But could she in all conscience keep her cousin's casual drunken sexual encounters from him? Despite his liberal attitudes, she couldn't imagine her brother-in-law putting up with such rampant infidelity, whatever the excuse.

What to do? Supposing she kept her mouth shut and Jean got an infection and passed it on to Jimmy? Sylvia wavered from one position to another, with no clear right and wrong in sight. The morning sun burned like a brand against her exposed neck and arms, and caused a band of pain to tighten her scalp and send shooting pains behind her eyes.

Trudging miserably beside scum-ringed pools of stagnant water she skirted small piles of assorted rubbish before crossing the Islington Road. As usual there was a group of men congregating on the low wall dividing the road from one of the few intact drainage channels she had seen in Port Juanero. They were horsing around, exchanging trivial bets and making lewd comments at passing women. Today their cries of 'nice English lady' failed to cause the usual irritation. Sylvia's mind was too firmly caught up in Jean's situation. *Why didn't I notice?* she asked herself again as she started the steep climb towards the Heights. *Surely I could have done something before things got so bad?*

Her cousin had the manic, intense look of someone on the edge of disintegration; erratic swings of moods that suggested a fragile grip on reality and self. Sylvia felt suddenly overwhelmed and desperate. Jean needed help badly, help she very much doubted would be forth-coming in this country.

Struggling up the badly rutted road of the housing scheme, Sylvia tried not to dwell on the universally negative reaction to people considered mentally ill that she had found in Jamaica. She suppressed the image of Miss Maddy weeping and cowering outside her wooden house, focusing instead on the discomfort she was feeling in the hot airless day. Her throat was dry and aching and she wished she had bought a box of iced milk from the board shop at the bottom of the hill road.

Shading her eyes, Sylvia paused in the welcoming shadows of a flame tree as she contemplated the long walk still ahead. She had to work something out . . . some way of getting Jean back to England before she deteriorated any further. The decision made her feel better. It eased the ache in her throat and the burning along her nose lining and behind her eyes. It was a false euphoria and she knew it. But that didn't stop her feet moving easier through the clinging heat when she restarted her walk.

George was loading boxes of cosmetics into his car boot when she finally reached the house. 'A was just going come look for you,' he said anxiously.

Sylvia smiled apologetically. 'The heat is so bad today it was all I could do to get here at all.'

George made a sympathetic sound in his throat. 'A should a think bout that, next time call me, you hear, and I will carry you where you want to go.' He straightened. 'What about Jean, you never get to see her?'

'Well, yes . . . sort of, but I didn't make a very good job of it, I'm afraid. Look, George, would you come down with me later and try talking to her? At least you don't irritate her as much as I seem to do at the moment.'

'*Me!*' He was incensed. 'I don't have *one* thing to say to her.' He kissed his teeth, grabbing another box from the pile on the grass verge with an abruptness that underlined his impatience. 'Imagine how she shame me, man.'

Sylvia stared at the rigid lines of his back in dismay. She hadn't realised until now how much she had been counting on George's understanding and support. 'George, getting mad at Jean isn't the answer. You have to understand that she isn't responsible for her actions right now.'

'Don't tell me that, Sylvia. You see Jean,' he gave another kiss teeth, 'she just get everything into her lap so. She go live in foreign and even get education. Take me now: I never get a thing, not one solitary thing a don't break my back to earn.'

Sylvia was appalled. 'George, that's all well and good, but Jean is suffering. You have to understand that if you want to help her.'

'If anybody needing help is me. You think it easy with the four children? And Pearl, she, she just on my back from morning till night about one thing or another. Nothing no wrong with Jean, Sylvia man. She just worthless and good for nothing from time.'

His bitterness took her by surprise and she could only stare at him as her mind tried to grapple with this new setback. 'George, I understand that things haven't been easy for you, but to put it bluntly, I think Jean is having a nervous breakdown.'

'You think is she one? Is just this last school term I get elected to the school board and she did have to come here and do this. You know what that look like?' He took a calming breath as anger increased the volume of his words. 'Last evening a was down by the market, and Dorrie telling everybody say Jean living down near seaside and fornicating with some tiefing rastaman.'

'Look, I understand that.'

'No, Sylvia man, you don't understand, cause ten days' time you a go back a England. And is just so Jean going ups and go when she finish shame me. But I don't have nowhere to ups and go, so is me one going leave to face down her slackness. Down Port Juanero not like town, you know. Them kind a things matter here, man.'

It wasn't that she didn't sympathise with him, but somehow she had to make him see things from his sister's point of view. 'George, I *do* see your point but . . .'

'No "but" no inna it.' His face set in stubborn lines. 'All I know is Jean always doing something to mash things up for me. First time, she get a good man like Jimmy but can't even get him to married her and now she fornicating with some dirty, tiefing rastaman right where everybody can see it. If you ever know how much people come up to me and talk about it – when Dorrie tell me where she was, a shame, a shame, you see.'

Sylvia realised that nothing would be gained by continuing with the discussion. They were going round in circles, which only served to feed George's resentment. 'Let's leave it for now and talk later,' she suggested, 'the sun is giving me a headache and I really have to find some shade.'

'Now or later not going to make a difference,' George warned, slamming the car boot with ominous finality. 'Jean is my sister so a not saying she not welcome in my house, but if she wanting to live in sin she going just have to go do it somewhere else.'

She watched him drive away in a cloud of dust, then climbed wearily up the street stairs. One of the dogs came from her sleeping place underneath a croton bush, yawned and stretched before slinking off again.

Pearl and Mauvia were hanging the washing at the back of the yard, shaking out creases from the bed sheets before pegging them on the high line. Sylvia was glad they were too busy to notice her; Pearl had been

163

very supportive over Jean's disappearance but right now she didn't have space for any anxiety outside her own.

She slipped into the house, thankful that the children were nowhere in sight. She needed a breathing space, time to marshal her thoughts and come up with some new plan of action.

Aleesa would want to know where Jean was; despite her fear, the child had a highly developed sense of responsibility towards her mother. She blamed herself for Jean's disappearance, linking it in her mind with her refusal to relinquish the ball during that ill-fated game. Aleesa had been so relieved when Jean was located, convinced that somehow her mother would return and everything would be alright again. Sylvia sighed, crossing the living room with heavy steps. She was not looking forward to coping with *that* disappointment.

The spare room was cool and inviting, smelling strongly of red-oak polish and beeswax. The bed had been spread with fresh sheets, the mirrors cleaned and the dressing table tidied and brought to a high shine. Sylvia suddenly realised how tired she was. She had slept badly over the past few days, worry and guilt keeping her awake till the early hours of morning. The pain in her head had worsened and she lay down, intending to rest her eyes for half an hour.

Chapter 12

Voices woke her. Shrill voices, flavoured with anxiety, intruding on disturbing images of Winston's coffin disappearing down that deep, dark hole with a naked laughing Jean balanced precariously on top as she puffed defiantly at the fat spliff in her hand. Sylvia blinked awake, the noise of the coffin knocking against the pulley struts resolving into a softly insistent rapping on the door. A faint hint of ganja remained in the air, and she wondered if her brain had imprinted it there.

'Who is it?' she called out as the knocking became more frantic.

There was a whisper of children's voices. 'Auntie Sylvia,' Lutie's voice came timidly through the door, 'Moomie say you must please to come.'

'What's wrong, Lutie?'

It was Jalini who answered, sounding scared but making an effort to disguise it. 'Auntie Jean come and she bring a rastaman from down Sansee and Moomie saying she turning like Miss Maddy. Auntie, you can come quick?'

A whispered conference followed the sound of adult footsteps, then Pearl's voice: 'Sylvia, a can come a minute?'

'Yes, come in.'

Pearl entered looking nervous, leaving Lutie and Jalini hovering outside the door, 'Oh, a sorry, a didn't realise you was sleeping.'

'That's fine . . . what's the matter?'

'Jean downstairs with the rastaman from down Sansee and she acting strange. A couldn't help but over-hear what you was saying to George bout the way she getting mad and a was wondering . . .'

Sylvie sat up, swinging her legs to the floor. 'Jean isn't mad, Pearl, you needn't worry about that, but she isn't well either.'

Pearl didn't look convinced. 'Is just that she acting strange, and with the children and the baby . . . and through she did hit Aleesa and her face still bruise up . . . well, a was wondering if you would talk with her.'

'Give me five minutes and I'll come down.'

'You couldn't just come a minute now?

Sylvia's headache was worse than before she went to sleep. She couldn't think of anything she wanted less than another confrontation with Jean and her new man. But the fear in Pearl's eyes and the memory of the fading bruises on Aleesa's face were enough to send her feet searching for her sandals.

They were sprawled out across the living area, Jean with her shoes on the polished coffee table. She wore the same clothes she had walked out in three days before, but now they were soiled beyond redemption. Ras Peter reclined in George's favourite seat, puffing contentedly on a spliff. His eyes roamed with careful interest, resting assessingly on everything of value.

Mauvia, Aleesa, Davian and Dionne were huddled by the kitchen table while Pearl, Lutie and Jalini stayed on the landing. Sylvia felt a surge of anger as she met the mockery in Jean's eyes. Her cousin was doing this on purpose, deliberately bringing the rasta to frighten Pearl and the children, and to goad her.

'Jean, what are you doing here?' Sylvia asked cautiously, reminding herself that the woman probably couldn't help her behaviour.

166

Her cousin smiled and sat up. 'Hello, Sylvia, I've had a think and I've decided to come for that little chat after all.'

'What! Here?' Sylvia looked around doubtfully, catching the atmosphere of fear in the house. She was torn between her need to reach Jean and her awareness of the fear the woman's presence brought. 'Look, why don't we walk down to the beach or something?'

Pearl came to stand at the bottom of the stairs, emboldened by Sylvia's presence. 'Jean, a could ask your friend please to take what he smoking outside the house.'

Jean looked at her insolently. 'Why should he? This is my brother's house, and Ras Peter is my guest.'

Pearl stood her ground. 'This is a Christian house first off, so if he wanting to stay he going have to put out what he smoking.'

Jean smiled unpleasantly. 'Why don't you go and take a running jump or something, Pearl.'

Sylvia was annoyed. 'Jean, there's no need for that. This is Pearl's home after all . . . and as for you, Mr Peter, I thought you rastas had more respect for other people's viewpoint than that.'

The man gave her a speculative look before shrugging and gazing off into space. He took the spliff out of his mouth with slow deliberation and snuffed out the end.

That was when George came in, the look on his face telling Sylvia that the neighbours had already alerted him to his unconventional visitors.

'What going on in here?' he asked belligerently, eyeing the spliff in Ras Peter's hand with outrage. 'What you doing in me house . . . a don't want no ganja-smoking rasta in my house.'

'He's my friend, George.' There was a quiet challenge in Jean's voice.

George dismissed that. 'How you can so shameless a

bring him inna the house in front a your own children? How you think this going look on Jimmy?'

'I couldn't care less,' Jean muttered, though she looked less certain now. 'Jimmy don't own me, George, none of you do.'

Pearl looked out from Sylvia's protective shadow. 'Jean, you can't come in here and talk to George like that, man.'

Jean turned slowly, giving her a malevolent look. 'But wait! You still here, why don't you go and kill yourself or something.'

'Jean . . .' Pearl tried again.

'Drop dead, Pearl.'

'There's no need for that,' Sylvia said, but Pearl was already walking back up the stairs, ushering Lutie and Jalini in front of her. 'You children go on outside and stay up back of the yard,' she told the others. 'Go with them, Mauvia.'

'What happen, Pearl? You fraid I'm going to contaminate them?' Jean mocked her retreating back.

Sylvia moved further into the room. 'Jean, why don't we try sitting down and talking like reasonable people?'

'Reasonable people now, is it?' Jean's laugh had a high-pitched quality, an hysterical edge. 'Did dear *cousin* Sylvia tell you she think I'm going mad, George?'

Her brother refused to be deflected. 'I don't want your manfriend in this house, Jean, and if you don't ask him to leave right now a going call Missa Mandrake to arrest him.'

'*Arrest me!* Arrest me for what?' Ras Peter was alarmed. 'You see me here peaceable as anything – what a do to you people . . . tell me that, ee? What a doing to you make you want to call policeman fe go lock me up and shoot me?'

George snorted. 'You don't hear say ganja illegal in Jamaica? This is a Christian house and you just walk in with your heathenness and pollute the place with that dirty drug.'

Ras Peter was on his feet. 'A never come here for no trouble . . . a did just walk out with Miss Jean to be company. But a will bid you good day and be walking on now.'

Sylvia breathed a sigh of relief. Maybe they could get somewhere now Jean no longer had someone to impress.

It was short-lived: Jean got to her feet too. 'If my friend not welcome in your house I can't be welcome too, truth George.'

George scratched his head and sat down on one of the dining chairs. 'Jean, a don't know why you always having to bring trouble so. A mean, you get everything. It did always you with Papa from start to finish and still you don't satisfied.'

'That's what you always saying, George.' Jean gave him a sour look though she did allow Ras Peter to leave alone. 'But if you did work harder at school and spend less time chasing women you would have something to show for it now.'

'That not true and you know it. Papa did always rate you more than me, from even before Noel dead. Look how he make sure you would aright . . . and from you get the scholarship is like a could never good enough for you again.'

'So *you* have a grudge against me too, George? You and every other body – but if you ever know . . .' She shook her head and gave a short bitter laugh. 'Cho, I don't even know why I staying here talking. You couldn't wait to jump in Jimmy's plot, could you?'

George looked puzzled, 'A don't directly know what you talking bout, but if is so you behaving to Jimmy is no wonder he don't want to married you.'

Jean kissed her teeth. 'That's his loss. You think I care what he do now? But if you think I will stand by and let you lot rob my children from under my nose you making a sad mistake.'

Sylvia stepped in quickly, seizing on that. 'Jean, I think we should talk about the children . . .'

'I already know your views, thank you very much.'

Sylvia could see the rejection forming clearly in Jean's eyes, and she used the first thing that came into her head. 'Look, I really don't want to have to tell Jimmy what's going on over here, but if that's what it will take to make you see sense I will.'

She knew she had said the wrong thing the minute the words were out. Jean's face had an unforgiving bitter look to it. 'What you expect me to do now, Sylvia? Shiver in my shoes? I don't care about Jimmy, I don't care about any of you. You think a don't know why you want me to go back to England so bad?'

'Jean, be reasonable . . .'

'*Reasonable!*' Her cousin rounded on her with open aggression, her voice rising to the edge of a scream. '*Stupid, you mean!* Look at you – you so shrivel up you can't even find a man to breed children with . . . that's why you so set to steal my two. You think I don't see the disgusting way you eyeing Jimmy these last two years? Is him you think will give my children over to you eh? Is him you want to warm up you bed now Winston escape?'

Sylvia closed her eyes and counted slowly. She had to stay calm. Her anger would only make the situation worse. 'Nobody is trying to steal your children.'

'So, is only Aleesa you want. I should a guess. Davian not good enough true he isn't talking.'

The conversation was disintegrating as it had done in the morning at the wooden shack. Somehow most of Jean's antagonism centred squarely on her cousin. Sylvia cast about for a way to save the situation and came up blank, while Jean ranted on, documenting a catalogue of grievances, real and imagined.

170

'I don't even know why I talking to you,' Jean finished finally. 'I come here to see my brother, not some cousin two times removed.'

George cleared his throat. 'A don't really know what eating you, Jean, but a can't see what difference you expecting talking to me going make. You know how a feel bout your sinning ways already, and don't think a going accept the fornicating right where the whole world can see to point finger.'

'I come here to talk bout the children, George, but if you don't want to, I will just take them and leave right now.'

He looked sceptical. 'The way you always a dump them on Sylvia a surprise you even come at all. A don't know what wrong with you, Jean. Deacon Davis was just saying how good you coming on and next thing Pastor Simmonds talking how you just reject him blessing in preference for the sins of the flesh.'

Jean looked chastised. 'Is the whispering, man, they start point at me and talk about sin just like up the mountain.' She rubbed her belly, staring earnestly at her brother. 'The sin did in there from long, long time – honest to God, George. I did pray, but is like nobody was there to answer.'

George was unsympathetic. 'Cho, Jean, Pastor Simmonds bend over backward to draw you in him fold. Look how he try counsel you on the wages of sin when he find out say you living with man and don't married.'

'Is not like that, George,' Jean pleaded, 'I never mean to raise temptation to his eyes. I never had one single thought of sinning with him. But is the first sin you see, he start to touch me and it just come back.'

'What you talking now?' George cut her off impatiently. 'Pastor Simmonds is a man with not one single blemish to him name, whatever bad-minded people saying, so a hope you not intending to bear false witness.'

171

'But I wouldn't do that, George.' Desperation crept into her voice. 'Is the same thing was happening as before.'

'A don't know what you talking bout and a don't want to.' George was increasingly impatient. 'Everybody trying to help you and is like you just can't hear.' He shook his head in disgust. 'Is the devil alright, him claiming you for himself right from the start.'

She gave him a cunning look. 'Is Sylvia, you know, George! Is she do it.' Jean pointed accusingly at her cousin. 'Is like from Winston dead she start on me. You wonder a did need the little drink? She and Jimmy, man, you never see anything like them – the way them was at Winston till him turn fool and get in car crash . . . Is that kill him, you know?'

Anger caught Sylvia off-guard, mingling with a resurgence of guilt. *How dare Jean pick on Winston's memory – mix him up in her sordid breakdown?* She had to get out of there, needed some release for her own bitterness.

'Yes, go on, get out,' Jean crowed triumphantly as Sylvia turned and walked away. She laughed, the sound jarringly off-key and out of control. 'Run away, you selfish old cow, run and see if truth can't follow you. Think you can grab Jimmy in place a Winston and I going keep quiet?' The laughter pealed out, following Sylvia through the door with a final taunt. 'If you can't take heat you shouldn't light fire.'

Pearl was hovering on the street side of the verandah when she emerged. 'Sylvia, you alright?' she asked in concern, '*Wait!* But you trembling . . . Is anything a could do?'

Sylvia looked down at her hands, surprised to see that they *were* shaking. 'I'm fine.'

Pearl chewed on her bottom lip. 'A sorry a never stay in there. You think she will alright?'

What was the point in pretending? 'I don't know,

Pearl, I just don't know . . .' she tailed off as a rush of tears filled her eyes and threatened to colour her voice.

Pearl caught hold of her hand, squeezed reassuringly. 'Is not your fault, Sylvia, these things happen for a reason and nothing you could really do would prevent it, from is the Lord's will.'

Sylvia smiled at the other woman gratefully, comforted despite her own lack of belief. 'I think I'm going to just take a walk. Do you mind keeping an eye on Aleesa and Davian?'

'You know a don't mind,' Pearl was eager to be of service. 'Possible if is never for the help you always giving me with Kaona since you come, a could be the one like Jean now . . . a did feel so bad since he born.'

Sylvia shook her head. 'I doubt that, and things are a bit better now, aren't they?'

Pearl shrugged. 'To tell the truth, a still don't feel good for him, but it don't dig into me head so much when he crying, and the play you show me to play with him start make him smile a little too . . .' She broke off, embarrassed. 'Oh, but a shouldn't so selfish and into talking about my small worries when you having so much crosses on your head.'

Sylvia didn't deny that. 'I'll just tell Aleesa I'm going, in case she gets anxious when she realises I'm not here,' she said instead, summoning up a reassuring expression as she left the verandah.

Aleesa was terrified when she heard Sylvia was going to leave her behind. 'Auntie, can me and Davian come with you?'

'No, Alli, you have to stay here.'

'But what if Mum hit me again? Auntie, please don't let me stay.'

Sylvia was tempted, but she knew taking the children would only antagonise Jean more. Squatting down, she tried to explain to Aleesa, 'Look, your mum isn't very well right now, so sometimes little things make her cross and you coming with me might just do that.'

'But she will hurt me, Auntie . . .' Tears shimmered in Aleesa's eyes.

'Of course she won't, and you have Mauvia, Auntie Pearl and Uncle George to look after you.'

The little girl was crying in earnest now. 'I don't want to stay here, Auntie Pearl don't like me and Mummy is going to beat me up.'

'Aleesa, that's not fair to Auntie Pearl.'

'You said she didn't like me, I heard you telling Uncle.' Aleesa was defiant through her tears.

Sylvia looked her in the eye. 'I was wrong to say that and I'm sorry, but Auntie Pearl has been really nice to you, hasn't she?' The little girl nodded reluctantly and Sylvia pressed the advantage. 'You stay here and be good for Auntie Pearl and I'll let you talk to Daddy on the phone when I get back.'

That mollified Aleesa and she even waved obediently when Sylvia finally reached road level.

On the road, she considered walking to the top of the hill, remembering its deserted peace. She liked to sit on the cliff edge, shaded by a guava tree, and watch the birds wheeling and swooping in the sky above Carbaritta Island, or stare at the white flecks of broken waves against the blue-green band of the reef water. It was easy to lose track of time up there, to see only the beauty of the surrounding land and forget underlying problems. So she turned downhill instead, rejecting the coolness and the peace in favour of the scorched and arid lowlands.

She only went as far as the sea road and back, the airless, ovenlike quality of the heat driving her to shelter under the same royal ponciana as the morning. Once her anger and pain subsided, Sylvia's thoughts returned to Jean and her own sense of failure. *Why didn't I realise just how much pressure coming to Jamaica without Jimmy would give Jean?* she asked herself again, finding no more answer now than she had all day. She felt a brief resentment towards Jimmy. He had known the state Jean was in, knew the way people in Port Juanero would react to the woman's behaviour. *Why on earth did he send her down here in that condition?*

Sylvia shifted uncomfortably, remembering her brother-in-law's frantic attempts to get her to see Jean's problems and her own scepticism in the face of his concern. She had only been able to see the issue in terms of Jean's constant attention-seeking.

She chewed on her bottom lip. *I knew she took it badly when Jimmy refused to get married, but I didn't realise how she felt about her awkwardness with the children, though even that is not enough to account for her illness. It has to be something else, probably something that happened before . . .*

It all made perfect sense to her, but she was no nearer knowing what to do. Sylvia thought of ringing Jimmy, rejected that out of hand and couldn't think of a single thing instead. She rubbed a finger along the bridge of her nose, feeling isolated and hopeless.

The sound of stone knocking stone alerted her to someone approaching. Sylvia turned to see Miss Berta labouring up the steep incline towards her.

'Miss Sylvia, you walking out,' the woman observed, coming to a breathless stop and offloading a variety of bags and packages around her ample form. 'That alright for you young people but the times too hot for my old bones.'

Sylvia nodded. 'They were saying on the radio that it's the hottest it's been for twenty years.'

Miss Berta wiped her neck under the wide, open collar of her sleeveless floral dress with the ever-present flannel. 'You can say that again. So where you walking to? Is Miss Jean you visiting?'

Sylvia ignored the avid interest. 'Actually I was just on my way back up the hill.'

175

'Wait little then and a will walk part way with you if you carry three a them scandal bag.'

Sylvia agreed reluctantly. She had problems enough hauling herself around in the heat, much less to carry the bulging carrier bags nicknamed 'scandal' because they were thin enough to show their entire content.

'So how Miss Jean doing?' Miss Berta asked, mopping at her face with her flannel. 'Is true she turn maddy?'

Sylvia was taken aback. 'Where did you hear *that*, Miss Berta?'

'Port Juanero is one small place, man; and Miss Jean going in rum shop and tavern a drink everything in sight. Is same way the father did go, you know.'

Sylvia sighed. 'Miss Berta, is there *anything* you don't know?'

The woman laughed, then sobered. 'A did know Miss Jean and Missa George father long time before him take to the white rum . . . that is a family with troubles, man. Them luck stay like some bad-minded smaddy obeah them.'

Sylvia hesitated. Jean had always resisted talking about what became of her father and now she wondered if she could find some clue to her cousin's present state somewhere in that information.

The professional in her surfaced. 'Miss Berta,' she said carefully, 'Jean isn't very well right now.'

'Just like the father,' Miss Berta agreed, as Sylvia hoped she would. 'Is same so he did stay. Grab the bag them noh, Miss Sylvia, a have to reach over by Richmond come evening.'

Sylvia picked up the bags obediently, falling into step with the big woman. 'What do you mean when you said Jean is like her father?'

Miss Berta nodded as if agreeing with something. 'That family well bad lucky, man. The madda dead left Old Missa Mackenzie with the three children them, but

176

he did love the big one, Noel, so till he foolish . . . and when him dead in the lightning strike, Old Missa Mackenzie just start on the white rum.'

'You mean he became an alcoholic?'

'A wouldn't know bout that, Miss Sylvia, but him turn drunkard. Then one day him just take the children go a town and leave them in one children home down there . . . and next we hear is Bellevue them send him go take out most a him brain. Is funny . . .' She paused to adjust the weight of her various parcels. 'A did always think is Missa George it woulda happen to, what with Miss Jean going foreign and getting through with the education and the big job, and him so wild as well. But then he did get save and go in the church and even go back a night school and pass JSC.'

The trader tailed off as they reached the chain-link fence surrounding her property. 'Bernice, come take some a this load, and tell Marta to pour some lemonade, Miss Sylvia visiting.'

Miss Berta's oldest daughter came out, smiling shyly at Sylvia. Her hair was covered by a shower cap to keep her wet-look hairstyle moist. 'Hello, Miss Sylvia,' she said, relieving her of the scandal bags, 'A did see you down the beach with Aleesa and Davian yesterday but you never see me.'

Sylvia smiled in acknowledgement, following Miss Berta on to the cool verandah and reaching gratefully for the long glass of iced lemonade the younger child brought.

'It drink aright?' Miss Berta asked, easing herself in the slatted canvas chair beside Sylvia.

'Yes, it's nice.'

'A did get the lime them from Missa George lime tree.' She drank deeply, waving the children away. 'Now, Miss Sylvia, what you wanting to know about Miss Jean family?'

The woman's store of knowledge didn't disappoint

her. Miss Berta had lived close to the Mackenzies in Cromwell land, had known the family all her life. By the time Sylvia left, she thought she understood some of the tragedies that had helped to shape her cousin's present mental state.

Chapter 13

The smell of seasoned chicken frying and red peas boiling in a thousand kitchens was magnified by the hot afternoon air. Sylvia's stomach heaved, a nagging sense of uneasiness causing her to increase her speed as much as the heat would allow. Sweat sprang up at her hairline, ran in converging rivulets across the contours of her face and oozed from her pores till her clothes cling hot and clammy to her skin.

She knew something was wrong long before she got to the house. Sensed it even as the faint crying of a child reached her. At first she thought it was Aleesa and the rapid tattoo of her heartbeat slowed a little. Then she realised it was more than one, heard the note of panic and alarm that often coloured Lutie and Dionne's speech. Finally she was close enough to recognise Jalini's voice raised in complaint and misery. That sent a surge of adrenalin pumping through her body on a new wave of anxiety. Sylvia felt faint as excess oxygen restricted her breathing.

Calm down, she told herself, recognising the signs of hyperventilation and forcing herself to take slow, even breaths. She stopped in the road below George's house, reluctant to start the long climb. The queasiness of impending crisis lodged somewhere inside her stomach. It spread so fast that for a moment she thought she would be physically sick. She tried to rationalise away

179

her fears. *Surely nothing could have happened? George would still be there if it had and there was no sign of his car.*

The dogs, both present for a change, ran halfway down the ungraded front yard then up again, their restlessness giving the lie to her attempts at self-delusion. Sylvia wondered why the children were crowded at the road end of the verandah. She wanted to shout at them, tell them not to lean at such a danger-ous angle. Expectation outlined Aleesa sandwiched between the tall gangling twins. No, not Aleesa, Jalini. Sylvia counted again, more slowly this time, refusing to accept her young cousin's absence.

Had Jean upset Aleesa? A hundred and one other possibilities flashed through her mind. Perhaps the child had been hurt in some way. In her mind she saw Jean's fist connecting with the small face, raising to follow through with another blow . . . *Could that be why George wasn't here? Maybe Alli was hurt – really hurt!*

Her feet were moving now, shifting rapidly up the uneven stairs. The closer she got, the more alarmed she was. The three children looked so cowed, so frightened.

Lutie spotted her first, crying even harder when Sylvia forced a smile in her direction. 'Auntie!' She squeezed past her silent twin, leaning down so far that Sylvia's heart skipped a beat, 'Auntie Jean gone, and Moomie try and stop her.'

'Yes, Auntie,' Jalini sniffed, 'and Aleesa never did want to go through Auntie Jean give Davian a big clap for crying, but she just clap her too and say she had was to come.'

What were they talking about? Sylvia's mind couldn't take it in for a moment. Aleesa was here . . . she had to be. Maybe she and Davian were upstairs waiting . . .

'Auntie, they gone long time,' Jalini inserted, 'and we waiting and we waiting, and Moomie send Lutie down the road and you don't come.'

Fresh wails of distress from the twins accompanied a

sense of guilt Sylvia couldn't cope with. It threatened to overwhelm and paralyse her. She retreated inside herself and focused on the children instead.

'Don't lean over so far, Lutie, you too, Jalini, or you might lose your balance and fall on the concrete.'

Lutie's head disappeared and Sylvia heard her calling out to Pearl. That galvanised her, got her up to the house in double-quick time despite the sweat stinging her eyes and the heat-burnt thirst in her throat.

As she climbed breathlessly on to the verandah, Pearl came out of the house, a fussing Kaona in her arms. 'You children go down by Miss Lisa and ask her please to give you dinner.'

'Moomie, a want to stay,' Jalini disagreed immediately. 'Me and Aleesa did turn good, good friend and is me Auntie Jean clap through me tell her say she must leave me cousin alone.'

Pearl's kiss teeth was a sign of impatience, betraying her own anxiety. '*Jali, do as a say and don't trouble me head this day, hear!*'

'Yes, Moomie.' Jalini was subdued.

'Moomie, what if Miss Lisa gone out?' Lutie was practical as ever. 'We should come back straight way?'

'A just this minute ring her and she expecting you. And please to tell your father to carry you back up, when he come to collect him cosmetic money from her.'

'Yes, Moomie,' the three children chorused.

Sylvia watched them running down the road for a long minute. She couldn't accept, couldn't take in what the children had been telling her. Jean hurting Davian, hurting Aleesa, taking them away, exposing them to heaven knows what – and this after *she* promised the little girl she would be safe.

Lutie, Dionne and Jalini finally disappeared around the bend in the road, taking away her excuse for putting off the inevitable. Sylvia turned reluctantly to face Pearl, still needing to deny the stark truth of yet another failure. 'Have Aleesa and Davian gone with George?'

'Sylvia . . .' Pearl sounded hesitant, guilty and sympathetic at the same time, 'Jean take Davian and Aleesa with her when she leave.'

She had heard it from the children, of course, but that didn't stop the news, relayed with such finality, impacting in her stomach. She sat down hard on the lounger, needing the support. 'You mean you let her take them out somewhere?'

Pearl shook her head. 'She not just walking out for a little while, Sylvia, she pack one suitcase and take them.'

That information had her on her feet and running for the guest room. It wasn't that she didn't believe Pearl, just that she needed the activity, the faint hope, to stop despair closing completely over her. The sight that confronted her brought Sylvia to a dead stop.

The room was a complete mess, all her belongings deliberately thrown about and damaged. Her clothes had been pulled off the hangers in the wardrobe and trampled underfoot, while the drawers had been taken out and left in a tangled heap. Loose face powder and lipstick were ground into everything, and her handbag lay upended on the pile, the purse gaping and empty close by.

She felt stunned, unable to come to grips with this vicious act of petty spite. What terrible thing did her cousin's disturbed mind fancy she had done to deserve this?

There was a rustling sound underneath her feet. Sylvia looked down, feeling as if a giant hand was squeezing her heart when she saw what she was standing on. She bent to pick up the ripped pieces of the photograph and stared disbelievingly at Winston's face. It was the final indignity. Sylvia walked slowly across to the bed and dropped down on the only available empty space.

Jean had done this to her. Had systematically gone through her things, robbed her, then deliberately ripped her last memory of Winston in half. It numbed her, momentarily robbing her of the ability to rationalise . . . even to think.

'Sylvia, a sorry about this.' Pearl came gingerly through the door, her own shock vibrating in her voice, 'A never expecting she would do this. A just never think to look.'

Sylvia stared dazedly at her, surprised to see how wavering and misted she seemed. Something wet dropped on her cheek and ran down to the corner of her mouth. She looked up in surprise, almost expecting to see rain pouring out of the cloudless sky. What did her mother used to say about the sun and the rain again? *The devil and him wife a fight.*

'A should a come and make sure she never do this,' Pearl said apologetically, trying ineffectually to sort out some of the soiled and jumbled items of clothing. She gave up after a while, letting the garments slide back down into the tangle.

For a moment she just stood where she was, looking impotent. Then she seemed to come to a decision. Picking her way gingerly through the debris of her sister-in-law's visit, she cleared a space and sat beside the other woman. 'A know is not a excuse but the children did fraid for Jean, and then George just up and leave, through he did have him cosmetic rounds.' She trailed off as she caught sight of Sylvia's face, putting an awkward arm around her shoulders. 'Sylvia, don't upset yourself. If a did know . . .'

'It's not your fault,' Sylvia reassured automatically, 'it's mine. I should have taken Aleesa and Davian with me.'

She was disconcerted to hear the sound of tears in

her voice, and she touched the fall of water again. Imagine crying now! Just when she had finally reached the point where she could start to celebrate Winston's life. How could she sit here crying over a torn photograph? It wasn't even as if she didn't have a lot more back in England.

Pearl cleared her throat. 'A did try to get Missa Mandrake to come over when Jean was taking the children but he did out on police business, but a leave message with him helper for him to pass by soon as he reach back.'

Sylvia wiped her eyes with the back of her hand, focusing on Pearl with an effort. 'Where is Kaona?' she asked, noticing the child's absence for the first time.

'Mauvia sitting with him.'

It occurred to her to ask what Mauvia was doing there on a Sunday, but the need to do something about the children made the moment pass. 'Pearl, if you don't mind, I think I will go down to that rastaman's house and see if the children are there.'

Pearl got to her feet, 'A did pass by already.'

'*You?*' The last thing Sylvia would have expected was for Pearl to go to the squatted land. Her cousin's wife always seemed so conscious of what little status and position she had, clinging to it with the desperation of a woman who had little else to her credit.

'A was worrying about Davian and Aleesa,' Pearl said defensively, 'and through you leave them with me a can't help but feel responsible for what happen.'

The need to reassure Pearl briefly overcame Sylvia's own misery. 'Look, don't feel that way. If Jean was determined to take them there wasn't a lot you or anyone else could do.'

'They not down there,' Pearl blurted out. 'A did ask one and two people and they say the rastaman gone with Jean and they never come back with the children.'

She felt like every turn she made was a dead end, but

she still needed the optimism of doing something. 'I think I'll go and check anyway. You never know, maybe they went somewhere else first.'

Pearl agreed reluctantly. 'Alright, but you can't walk back down all that way, in the hot sun, specially as you upset and you don't used to it. A will get Miss Brown son to carry you – him run one taxi car.'

It turned out to be a wasted journey. As Pearl said, the children weren't there and Ras Peter's mean-looking house had an air of desertion. Sylvia searched out the woman she had spoken to in the morning, asking her if she knew where they went.

The woman proved to be as friendly as before but had nothing helpful to tell her. 'One next woman come look for them already,' she said sympathetically. 'A know Ras Peter mother leave him house when she dead.'

'*Where?*'

'A don't directly know that, mam, him just say is in town, over by Sandy Gully way. A feeling say them gone there, through the lady don't like the living down here.'

Sylvia tried to press her, but although she seemed to genuinely want to help, she could offer no further clues.

On the way back up the hill they passed Dorrie, Miss Berta's friend who traded outside the school in term time. She called out and waved, stopping them. 'Miss Sylvia,' she puffed when she caught up with the car, 'a was just coming to find you. A see Miss Jean and that good-for-nothing Ras Peter.'

Sylvia sat up straight. 'Did they have the children with them?'

'Yes, man, them carry Aleesa and the baby. Them did just getting on the bus to Highgate and Miss Jean give Aleesa one bitch lick on her face, a did sorry for her.'

Sylvia felt a resurgence of hope, though her anxiety

for the children's safety increased. 'What time was that, Dorrie?'

'Long time now, is just through Miss Lisa saying how she just take the children and Miss Mackenzie never find them, that a was coming to see you.'

'Thanks, Dorrie. Is there another bus to Highgate tonight?'

'A think the last one gone early through is Sunday . . . but a couldn't swear say they going in Highgate.'

'But you said . . .'

'A know, Miss Sylvia . . . is just that is town bus them take, the one that go Highgate and Richmond, then back round the Junction to town.'

Sylvia thanked Dorrie, feeling less overwhelmed. At least now she had somewhere to start looking.

'A can't take you to Highgate tonight, mam.' The taxi driver might have read her mind. 'A have to carry a man go airport and a don't eat dinner as yet.'

'Look, you heard what Dorrie said.'

'A sorry, mam, but is one hour a have and Highgate couldn't do in the time.'

It didn't matter what she said to convince him, he refused to budge. As far as he was concerned he already had a fare and there was no other taxi available that night. In the end she had to let it rest.

Pearl was cooking dinner when Sylvia got back and there was a stout man in police uniform sitting in one of the carved easy chairs and drinking lemonade. The man got up as soon as she walked in and Pearl introduced him as Mr Mandrake. Sylvia shook his proffered hand, sitting on the heavy settee as he resumed his seat.

The policeman took out a small spiral notebook and flicked it open, pen at the ready. 'Miss Mackenzie say Ras Peter take you small cousin them,' he said by way of opening. 'You have any idea why?'

Sylvia hesitated. 'Well, actually their mother took them and went off with Mr Peter.'

Mr Mandrake frowned, closing the notebook. He finished his glass of lemonade before getting to his feet. 'You know, that put a different complexion on this thing.'

Pearl put down the large metal spoon she had been using to stir the pot and came across. 'Missa Mandrake, if you could just stay and listen to what Miss Sylvia saying a would grateful.'

The man still looked doubtful, but at least he sat down again. 'Alright, but we don't really have authority to interfere between a mother and her children them.'

Sylvia told him something about Jean's condition and her erratic moods. She explained her fears for the children's safety, and her qualifications to judge the risk.

Mr Mandrake sat impassively through it all, giving her the impression he was barely listening. He didn't even show a flicker of interest when she talked about the way Jean had abused Aleesa and brutalised her small son.

When she finally stopped speaking he shook his head discouragingly. 'Seem to me like your best thing is to get the father down from England, then we could be talking.'

'But you don't seem to understand,' Sylvia pressed on, surprised by the casual dismissal, 'we're talking about child protection here, the children could be at risk.'

He wasn't in the least impressed. 'A can't see the problem, Miss Sylvia. The mother decide she don't want to stay here so she take the children, nothing wrong with that.'

'And what happens when she hurts one of the children, kills one even?'

'A don't know what you trying to say,' his back was well and truly up now, 'but that sort a thing is a crime in Jamaica same as in any other place. If one a the children dead, the person responsible would go to trial for it and might even hang. Same so it did happen when that man over Greenhouse District chop him wife and kill one a the children, him hang for that, no true, Miss Mackenzie?'

Pearl's assent did nothing to allay Sylvia's fear for the children's safety. What was the point of punitive action after one or the other of them was harmed? She didn't want someone to hang for the children's possible death. She just wanted them back so she could deliver them, unharmed, to their father.

'Missa Mandrake,' Pearl pleaded, 'you sure you can't do nothing for us on this thing?'

'Sure a sure, Miss Pearl. You think is the first somebody from foreign complain about man and woman taking they own children to a next place? They don't understand say things different in Jamaica. Over here we don't just jump down people throat the minute they don't raise children how we like.' He laughed, shaking his head at the thought. 'If a so we woulda inna plenty argument all the time.'

'So you are not prepared to help me find them?' Sylvia asked evenly, assuming professional briskness to hide her anger and disappointment.

'A never said that.' The man gave her an assessing look. 'If you could excuse us, Miss Mackenzie, a would like to talk to Miss Sylvia in private a minute.'

'You could use the verandah. Mauvia gone up and the children staying down Miss Lisa house so you shouldn't get disturb.'

Sylvia was on the offensive as soon as the heavy door closed them out on the verandah. 'You've already said you were not prepared to help, so what's the point of this, Mr Mandrake?'

'If you wait and listen, Miss Sylvia, you will find out what a offering.'

'But you already said there was nothing anybody could do.'

Mr Mandrake got straight to the point. 'If we could come to an arrangement a would more than willing to help you get back the children. A have some contacts, you see.'

Sylvia eyed him with suspicion. 'What kind of arrangement?'

'A was thinking maybe a thousand dollars. Is not for me of course.'

'Of course,' Sylvia echoed sceptically, 'I suppose helping me will cause expense.'

'That right. You see, a couldn't really do it in police time, and depending on where they staying a might have to get a next man to help. Everything cost money you know.'

'So if I said yes, when would you start looking?'

'A would need the money up front,' he warned, 'for if a going look for the children, a going need something to pay out with, when a trying to get information.'

'I don't have a thousand dollars on me.'

He wasn't to be deterred. 'Well, what you have?'

'Very little, just a few dollars and some cents.'

'What about foreign money?'

She had no intention of telling him about Jean stealing money from her purse. 'I have enough money for a taxi when I get back to London and that's it.'

'But you have traveller cheque though.'

She nodded warily. Fortunately her cousin had made no attempt to take either her traveller's cheques or her foreign currency.

'That alright then.' Mr Mandrake became expansive. 'The bank opening tomorrow so you can go down and get it change first thing. If you come down by the station and ask for me, them man them will tell you were I is . . . though most time a just sitting outside.'

'Have you any preference as to how I should get the money?' she asked sarcastically.

'Well, I would prefer US dollar but otherwise just how it come.' He grinned at his own humour, walking back to the door. 'Miss Mackenzie, a going over now . . . when Missa Mackenzie come, tell him later, you hear?'

Pearl came to the door. 'All right, Missa Mandrake, tell Miss Mandrake a say hello.'

He paused at the verandah edge. 'Till tomorrow, then, Miss Sylvia.'

She watched him go with a new sense of outrage, not wanting to believe what had just happened. Aleesa and Davian were out there in danger somewhere in this place, and all the man could think of was making some easy money.

'He can help you find the children?' Pearl asked hopefully,

Sylvia gave her a bitter smile. 'If I pay him a thousand dollars in advance he'll see what he can do.'

'*So much?*' Pearl was affronted. 'But you must can get it for cheaper.'

Sylvia looked at her incredulously. 'He tried to get me to bribe him, Pearl.'

'But the money he asking too much, man. A will go and see him tomorrow when Mauvia come. He only asking that kinda money just through you coming from foreign and he think you rich.'

It was hard to credit what she was hearing. Pearl was talking about the policeman's dishonesty as if it was an everyday occurrence. 'Pearl, two children are in danger and that policeman will only help for a bribe, what kind of thing is that?'

Her disapproval penetrated finally and Pearl seemed embarrassed. 'You have to understand, Sylvia, Missa

190

Mandrake is not a bad man. Is just so life is over here. People expecting to make a money whichever way they can find. Is through the police pay so bad and everything so expensive. The only thing is how much he asking. It way far too much.'

Sylvia shook her head slowly. 'I can't pay a bribe, Pearl. I'd rather look for the children myself than get involved with dishonesty.'

Pearl nodded. 'A don't wrong you; possible Missa Mandrake only going to have a little time . . . and come to that a sure George would glad for the chance to help you.'

George echoed that sentiment when he brought his own children back an hour later. He sent them to their mother, and stopped to talk to Sylvia on the verandah.

'Sylvia, a hear what happen,' he said as soon as the children went through the door. 'A frighten when Miss Lisa tell me, you see. Just make me know anything you feel a can do . . . anything, man.'

'Well, Dorrie said she saw them on the Highgate bus, and I was wondering if you could give me a lift over there tomorrow?'

'You talk to Missa Mandrake?'

Sylvia nodded, her expression ironic. 'He will help me if I am prepared to pay him a thousand dollars.'

'So much? No, man, him can't do that. Tell you what. A will talk to him tomorrow first thing. Him have to be reasonable, man. Just through you come from foreign don't mean he should ask a money so big, that not fair at all.'

'George, I'm not going to pay a bribe.' Sylvia repeated what she had said to Pearl. 'I think it's dishonest and I don't intend to encourage it.'

George looked at her patronisingly. 'Is the only way people survive in this hard time, Sylvia. Missa Mandrake can't hardly live on what they paying him.'

'I don't care, George. Aren't you the one who's

always complaining about how corrupt the Jamaican government is? How officials take bribes and the ruling party only give jobs and money to their supporters?'

'That true . . . but is a different thing. You have to see say man like Missa Mandrake is small fish, him have to feed him family one way or another.'

'He's corrupt, George, and if I start paying him then I am approving of his corruption. You have to make up your mind: either it's right for the government to only give the country's resources to their supporters, or it's wrong for Mr Mandrake to take a bribe.'

'So how come is now you start see it as wrong doing?' George sounded sulky. 'You don't see is how everything go in Jamaica. If you want a water, you pay a man a little something over by water commission . . .'

Sylvia refused to be placated. 'George, that's terrible. If that's how you've been getting water it's not right.'

He hissed through his teeth. 'Cho, Sylvia man, *right* is what you can pay for in this Jamaica. Look how much tiefing a go on in government and all them place. You think any a we did see dust from all that Gilbert foreign aid? If is war you waan make a them you should go see, stead a bothering bout small man like me an Missa Mandrake who haffe hustle little to keep on.'

That made her uneasy; she had seen enough, read too much, heard too much about the endemic corruption among the rich in Jamaica not to admit he had a point. 'But following a bad example doesn't make you any less bad, does it, George?'

'Have it your own way,' George shrugged, clearly surprised by her vehemence, 'but you going find it hard to do one single thing down here if you don't prepare to do as do is.'

'Are you saying you don't intend to help, George?'

'*Me?* No, sah, from I in the Lord I not into that kinda asking for bribe thing Missa Mandrake and the other

192

sinner them using. Just say the word, man . . . anytime. If is Highgate you waan reach we will leave first thing and we will look as long as it take. What Jimmy saying about this whole thing anyhow?'

Sylvia had hoped no one would ask that. She had been putting off ringing Jimmy since coming back and finding the children gone. 'It's too late in England to be ringing now,' she excused herself, 'so I thought I would stay up and ring him later.'

'What you think he will say?' George persisted. 'Any chance he could reach down sooner? For through he is the children father, police would bound to help get them back if he directly ask.'

Pearl came to stand in the doorway. 'George, you can come? A putting your dinner on the table.'

George went obediently and Sylvia breathed in relief. She sat where she was, thinking about the children. Jimmy had trusted her to look after them, just as he had trusted her judgement with Jean. Recently she didn't seem to be able to make a single right assessment.

She thought about Aleesa's pleading, the desperation in the child's eyes. Why in heaven's name hadn't she listened? If only she hadn't been so caught up in her own selfish need. If she had only come back sooner, not met Miss Berta on the road. She closed her eyes, unable to resist the transient comfort of pretending she had taken them along and they were both upstairs now getting into mischief with their cousins.

'Sylvia, you would like that a dish up some dinner for you?'

She shook her head, feeling a fresh prick of tears. 'No, I don't really feel hungry.'

Pearl came to sit beside her on the weathered wooden bench that ran along one side of the verandah. 'Is so a feeling as well . . . a keep thinking a shoulda stop Jean taking the children. A shoulda stand up to her and they would be here safe right this minute.'

'Don't blame yourself, Pearl, they weren't your responsibility.'

The woman shook her head. 'Is my care you did leave them in.' She hesitated. 'Sylvia, a know it never always looking like a take to Aleesa, but a really like her, you know. Is just that a did sometime feel a jealousy through she more forward than Lutie and Jali at school.'

'It's all right, Pearl.' Their roles were reversed now, Sylvia in the more familiar one of comforter. 'I know you didn't harbour any malice against Aleesa.'

'Is since the baby you see,' Pearl persisted, 'sometime a did only feel to sleep and cry and not a thing else. A don't know why, Kaona was the easiest of all a them to born and he never give me even one bit a trouble in the whole pregnancy. If it wasn't for you helping, you see . . .'

Sylvia patted her hand reassuringly. 'It was probably just a touch of postnatal depression,' she responded automatically. 'It happens to a lot of women after a baby.'

'But a never feel this way when a did have the other three. To tell the truth, a don't directly know if a ever going feel the same for him as for the other children.'

'It happens like that sometimes.' She silently willed the other woman not to start reciting the history of her pregnancy.

Pearl must have read something of her feelings in her face. 'A sorry about going on like that, a know how having Aleesa and Davian missing must paining you.'

'That's all right.'

They lapsed into an uneasy silence, then Pearl cleared her throat. 'Sylvia, a was thinking, you know my brother Lawrence is a councillor for the district – why a don't ask that he help you?'

'What could he do?'

'Well, the MP for down here is a minister of government and Lawrence is like him right-hand man. Him do all sort a things for him, and when things like Christmas work come out, is Lawrence say who and who to get it.'

'Pearl, I don't quite see . . .'

'He could help, a sure he could.' Now the idea was out, Pearl was eager to sell it to Sylvia. 'Lawrence is a important man down here, you ask George.'

Sylvia smiled, touched despite herself. 'Thanks for the offer, Pearl, but I can't see how a local politician can help me find Aleesa and Davian. For a start, it's hardly going to help his personal standing one way or another, is it?'

'Lawrence would want to help, man.' Pearl was adamant. 'You know how he like Aleesa and he was even saying he wanting her to come and stay by him house when my three go up there a morning time.'

She could feel herself wavering, clutching at a straw of hope. Suppose Lawrence really had useful contacts, surely it wouldn't hurt to hope? 'I don't know, Pearl, could he get the police to help?'

'Lawrence can do that and more.' Pearl couldn't hide her pride. 'Down here everybody rate him and none of them going want to get in wrong with him.'

George came back to the verandah, belching appreciatively. 'Who you talking, Pearl?'

'A was just telling Sylvia how Lawrence could maybe help get Davian and Aleesa back for her.'

He nodded, picking out the food lodged in his teeth. 'That true but he up in town with the minister right now.'

'He coming back mid-week though.'

Would she be searching for the children for that long? Surely not. 'Well, if we haven't found them by then, I'll ask him when he comes down,' Sylvia conceded.

'We will find them, man.' George stretched out on

the lounger and closed his eyes. 'When you go in, just close the light noh.'

Sylvia felt a stab of irritation. Anyone would think he didn't care what happened to the children; despite his exaggerated words of concern he was going on exactly as normal. She stifled the thought. George was taking her to Highgate, giving up his selling-time to go with her. That certainly wasn't the action of someone who didn't care.

Chapter 14

After the endless weeks of waiting, the drought showed
signs of a crack that night. It started with a rising wind
which blew in off the sea down at Sansee. Zinc roofing
sheets on George's concrete water tank flapped madly,
causing a racket that triggered off a frenetic spate of
barking among the dogs. Lightning followed swiftly,
periodic jagged flares accompanied by the deep reson-
ance of thunder, rending the thick darkness of the
country night.

Then the rain came. Sheeting down with a roar to
rival thunder, it poured out of the sky. Hour after hour
it fell. Sylvia moved restlessly in her nightmare as the
heavy, moisture-ladened rustling of banana fronds and
mango trees penetrated the dream.

By the time the false dawn painted the first grey
fingers in the sky, the rain had relented and the wind
begun to die down. Water ran off the sloping concrete
roof, along the stairs and down to the road below.
Rivulets slid off asphalt and white marl, disappearing
into the greedy earth, the land thirsting still.

Morning came early to the uplands. A flurry of
breathless movements, as night creatures handed over
yard and bush, roadside and gully, to the frenetic
activity of the dawn wakers. Cock-crow was muted
today, smothered by damp vegetation. One by one
dogs, roaming in packs through the dark hours, slunk

home to take up duty positions before their unsuspecting households awoke.

Sylvia woke, Kaona's whimpering bringing her from sleep to full alertness without transition. It left her feeling unrefreshed, her head heavy and woolly from too little rest. She lay still, listening for Jean's soft snore and the children's snuffling sounds. There was only silence. She opened her eyes, flooded by memory. The children were gone, taken, heavens alone knew where, by their increasingly unstable mother. Reluctantly, she turned her mind to the day before.

Pearl had persuaded the twins to help restore the guest room while Sylvia was searching for Jean and the children at Ras Peter's house. They had returned the drawers to the dressing table, and cleaned off the lipstick marks, sorted out the few untouched clothes and sent the rest with a passing motorist to a woman who took in washing up in Mountain District. Pearl had even tried to stick the torn photograph of Winston together again, putting it in a makeshift frame.

Sylvia had been touched when she returned to find the room tidy. She hadn't expected that kind of sensitivity from her cousin's wife. It warmed her towards the other woman and steadied the panic inside her a little. Pearl had surprised her in the last few days, showing a strength and tenacity Sylvia had never suspected lay behind her timid outer shell.

She had been a silent support after Jean's disappearance, and she had been full of practical advice the evening before. It was Pearl who had dredged up the names of several minibus operators servicing the Highgate-Kingston route. She had rung them one after the other, often making several phone calls to get the right person. Somehow Pearl managed to persuade all the bus operators to be on the lookout for Jean and the children. It made Sylvia feel better, as if something was happening, even though she couldn't be out there physically searching for herself.

Her sense of defeat returned now, as her mind focused on the new day. Sylvia had not felt this overwhelmed since Winston died. She deliberately thought of the mundane steps she needed to take, in an effort to stay in control.

She had to phone Jimmy for a start. She had not been up to it last night, too emotional herself to be able to take his inevitable anger. Now, she mentally squared up to the task. She peered at the luminous hands of the travel clock, wondering what time it was in England. She did a quick calculation . . . ten o'clock. She had to get a move on. Jimmy wouldn't thank her for disrupting his concentration.

Yesterday's feelings of failure returned with a vengeance. Sylvia squashed them and walked purposefully for the door. She couldn't afford self-pity, not now; and Jimmy had a right to be angry that she had failed to keep his children safe.

The line was busy when she finally connected with London, and she was tempted to put off her unpleasant duty a little longer. She steeled herself, dialling again with unsteady fingers. Jimmy was the children's father, their chief carer. He had every right to know what had happened to them.

She got through on the third attempt, her stomach starting to flutter with the first ring. Jimmy picked the phone up almost instantly, his voice disembodied by the distance.

Sylvia wiped a suddenly clammy palm against her cotton trousers, feeling as if her voice would strangle in her throat. 'Jimmy, it's me . . . Sylvia.'

'Sylvia, what's wrong?' He was immediately alarmed. 'Why you phoning at this time . . . has something happen to the children?'

She swallowed hard. 'Jean hasn't been too well . . .' She was playing for time and they both knew it.

'Sylvia, what is going on down there and don't tell me you got up five o'clock in the morning just to let me know that Jean isn't well. It's the children, isn't it?'

No point prevaricating any longer. 'Jean took them yesterday.'

'Where to?'

Puzzlement joined the rising alarm in his voice and Sylvia felt her guilt increase. 'I don't know exactly, but we do know where she was heading.'

She could imagine the stunned look on his face in the silence that followed. 'Sylvia, you saying Jean walk out with my children and is *now* you decide to tell me?' He asked the question slowly, as if he thought he had somehow misheard.

She felt terrible. 'Jimmy, I was trying to see if I could get them back.'

'You make them sound like a misplaced handbag . . .' Another brief silence followed. 'I can't believe it's my children we're talking about here . . . that you let Jean walk off with them just like that.'

'You think I am feeling any better about it? I keep telling myself I shouldn't have gone off and left them, that if I hadn't spent so much time at Miss Berta's it might not have happened. But dwelling on might-have-beens doesn't help the situation any, Jimmy. I should know that, I've been through the whole range of them.'

There was a tense pause as he let that sink in and his voice was calmer when he spoke again. 'Was she alone or with someone else?'

The question threw her, coming sooner than she expected. Sylvia took a deep breath. 'Actually she was with a man called Ras Peter.'

'Not old brother Peter from the shanty by the sea-shore?' Jimmy's voice was heavy with disbelief.

'Well, he's about middle-age and he has shoulder-length locks . . .'

'And a lot of broken and missing teeth?'

'Yes, that sounds like him.'

He hissed air through his teeth and she could almost see his disgust. 'Well, I don't care what Jean do with herself – not any more – but I want my children away from that man. I'm coming as soon as I can get on a plane and I don't care how long I have to wait around for a stand-by ticket to do it.'

'Jimmy, you must understand that Jean isn't well.' She controlled her own anger at the memory of the damage she had suffered at her cousin's hand; she had to keep Jean's illness firmly in mind and try to make him see. 'A lot of what she is doing is the result of that illness.'

'That's a bit of a change for you, isn't it?' he asked bitterly. 'Wasn't it you who was so convinced she was only seeking attention?'

She was glad he couldn't see the guilt she was feeling. 'I'm sorry about that – I should have listened to you . . .'

'No!' he cut in sharply. 'I'm the one should have listened. I'm tired of making excuses for her, Sylv, tired of hanging on waiting for her to turn back into the woman I used to know.'

'Jean needs you,' she said instead, hoping the words sounded more convincing than they felt.

'Well, I'm beginning to realise I don't need all this hassle,' he countered. 'The truth is, Jean is irresponsible and I blame myself for not seeing it before.' He sighed, the sound loud enough to travel across the distance. 'Sylv, just get Alli and Davian back for me, will you?'

It was on the tip of her tongue to remind him that most of this mess was his fault. That if he hadn't sent Jean alone with the children none of it would have happened. But she contented herself with the foremost concern. 'The trouble is, with Jean being the children's mother, it's going to be difficult to get any kind of help from the authorities unless you as their father are here.'

'Well, I going to try my hardest . . . but Sylvia, I'm begging you to try and find them. If anything happen to the kids I don't know what I'll do.'

Her heart went out to him. Jimmy had taken care of Aleesa and Davian almost from the day they were born. She had seen how he made time for them and the way he structured his life around them. That was why she still found it so hard to understand how he could let them come to Jamaica under Jean's uncertain care.

The house was coming awake when she finally hung up. George appeared at the top of the stairs, buttoning his shirt before disappearing again. Pearl brought the baby down and shouted for Dionne to come and take him. 'Sit out on the verandah so he will get some fresh air,' she told the child before busying herself with the breakfast.

The children were subdued, sitting down with more than usual docility for the morning devotions. Afterwards they went about their chores, their voices barely above a whisper.

Sylvia sat on the side of the verandah overlooking the road, needing to escape the misery. She watched Mauvia toiling up the hill, walking from side to side to ease the steep climb, and wished fleetingly that her life could be as uncomplicated.

'Mawning, Miss Sylvia,' the helper greeted, fielding the dogs as she came up the stairs. 'Miss Jean and the children back yet?'

Sylvia shook her head. 'Good morning, Mauvia, how are you?'

'Managing, you know, mam.' She spotted Dionne about to take the baby in. 'Dionne, wait little bit, let me wash me hand.'

She went across to the outside pipe, coming back

with her hands dripping wet. 'You did hear the thunder last night, Miss Sylvia? A hoping Miss Jean and the children never catch up in it . . . Come, give me the baby, Dionne, and go bathe. Pastor coming to carry you up Mountain District today.'

Sylvia watched them go, before turning her attention back to the road. A stream of early workers were making their way down the road, moving aside for the vehicles driven at breakneck speed. A minibus went by, honking on its horn, the driver shouting out a cheery 'good morning' to those he recognised and stopping to take on a passenger wherever he was flagged down.

Dionne came out half an hour later accompanied by Lutie and Jalini. The three of them were dressed in their Sabbath best, an assortment of bags stuffed with clothes and books between them.

Jalini came to sit beside Sylvia. 'Auntie, if Aleesa and Davian come back you will send come tell me?'

Sylvia looked down at her in surprise. 'Of course I will.'

'You think they going alright, Auntie?' the child asked in a whisper, as if afraid to voice concern aloud. 'A did hear the big, big thunder in the night and a know say Davian don't like it.'

'Don't worry, Jali, I'm sure they'll be fine.'

The little girl stayed close by her, reassured. Sylvia wished *her* fears could be as easily allayed. The build-up of tension inside left her feeling wound up. Her whole impetus was to be out there searching, making some effort to bring the children back. The forced inactivity of waiting was creating annoyance in her and she was glad when George finally appeared.

He came to an abrupt stop at the door, looking at her in surprise when she rose, eager to be gone. 'You never need to ready so soon, you know. A just going to carry the children up the mountain and then a will carry you over Highgate.'

Sylvia frowned. 'I thought your pastor was coming to take them.'

'That was the decision first time, but Pastor did need to get a early start for town, so a tell him say he needn't worry himself.'

She couldn't believe what she was hearing. 'When did all this happen, George?'

'We agree on it Sabbath gone.'

'So why didn't you tell me about it last night when you promised to take me to Highgate first thing this morning?'

'Cho, Sylvia man, don't fret yourself. A tell you a going to take you and a mean it.'

She sighed, shaking her head. 'George, it's eight o'clock, I can just as easily take a bus. There seem to be a lot of them this time of morning.'

'No, Sylvia, a can't make you do that, man. Look noh, a will carry the children up right now. Fifteen minutes is all it going to take, fifteen minutes – you watch and see.'

She watched him go, the children trooping obediently behind him, hauling their bags and packages. Sylvia was in two minds, but in the end she decided to stay. George knew St Mary as she could never hope to and he seemed to have contacts everywhere. To be truthful she had no idea where to start looking, and the thought of searching on her own brought the familiar sense of inadequacy.

By ten o'clock she realised he wasn't coming back in a hurry. Sylvia paced up and down, checking the clock on the tallboy every few minutes. Her head was filled with the terrifying dangers that could be happening to the children while she hung around waiting for George. It made her irritated and on edge. The image of Jean sitting on that soiled rumpled bed came back to haunt her. It stiffened her resolve, refusing to allow her to contemplate the possibility of not finding Aleesa and Davian safe.

Pearl looked up from polishing the floor on one of Sylvia's endless trips to check the time. 'George don't reach back yet?'

She shook her head, trying to smile despite her irritation. 'I think I'd better take the bus. At this rate I'll miss any chance I have of finding Jean and the children . . .'

'*Miss Mackenzie? Miss Sylvia?*' Miss Berta's voice hailed from the roadside. 'Anybody up there?'

Sylvia trailed reluctantly behind Pearl, hoping the trader didn't want to talk to her. She just didn't feel up to exchanging banter with Miss Berta, however helpful the woman had been the day before. Time was already pressing and she wanted to be on her way.

'Somebody can hold the puppy let a reach up?' Miss Berta asked, hovering anxiously at the bottom of the stairs.

Sylvia moved to block the dog's attempt to make a run for the woman, fully intending to tell Miss Berta she was on her way out, once she was safely at the house.

'A could get you a glass of lemonade, Miss Berta?' Pearl offered as the woman puffed on to the verandah.

Miss Berta nodded. 'As a matter of fact is Miss Sylvia a come to see. A did mean was to come last night but it did late when them boy them did carry me over from Highgate.'

Sylvia's ears pricked up, any thoughts of making a quick exit forgotten. She could tell by the look in Miss Berta's eyes that she had important news. 'You know where Jean and the children are?' she asked hopefully.

'Yes, man,' Miss Berta grinned triumphantly. 'Miss Mackenzie make a call to Blue boy and ask him to look out for Jean and the children and so he just question one and two a the man them that do the evening run to town. A see him on the road up Highgate last night and him send to say Miss Jean them go town in Missa Samuel bus. And him say Missa Samuel say him see them get on a Papine bus when them reach Plaza.'

'Thanks ever so much, Miss Berta.' Sylvia could have hugged the beaming woman.

'Don't mention it, but if is Papine you goin search, you best to try down place like Kintyre and August Town, where Ras Peter have relative . . . though them place *rough*, you know, Miss Sylvia.'

'That's OK,' Sylvia reassured her. 'If there is any likelihood of them being in those places, that's where I have to look.'

George came just as Miss Berta was ready to leave. He was full of apologies and excuses. 'A did want was to get away, but you know how it is. You can't just ignore people when them hail you . . . If you ready now, a just need a fresh, then a want a quick five minute to call down Trickster garage on the way.'

Sylvia was too buoyed up with new hope to be angry with him any more. 'Do you think we could go to Kingston instead?' she suggested eagerly. 'Miss Berta said Jean and the children went there in a Mr Samuel's bus and . . .'

'Kingston!' George looked at her as if he thought she was mad. 'A can't do that today, Sylvia man . . . is new month and a can't miss a collection day at the minute. If it was next week now, that would be a different story.'

'George, carry her no, man!' Pearl was indignant. 'Last night you promise you would take her anywhere, and sakes a you she still here when she could just as cheap take the bus.'

'Pearl, none a this concern you. Jean and her children is my family so a would appreciate you not interfering.'

'Is so? Then how come you not up and searching for them? Miss Berta say Jean them gone to some bad area in town and you can't see fit to miss one collection day.'

'Pearl, why you not minding your business left me and my family out a it!'

Sylvia saw red. 'Look, I'm fed up with the two of you arguing all the time. George, Pearl *is* right. You did promise to take me to Highgate first thing this morning, and I would have much rather you be honest from the start and say you couldn't do it, than have me waiting around in expectation.'

'But you don't see, is for a reason.' He was not prepared to accept that he was at fault. 'Probably the Lord guiding my step, cause, see here now, if we did go a Highgate we wouldn't get to see Miss Berta and find out say is town Jean them gone.'

Pearl kissed her teeth. 'George, you too quick to form fool with the Lord name. Any one a them man them who always hang round by the bus stop would tell you which part them go.'

George gave her a bad look. 'So how come you know so much bout man out a street?'

'Is common knowledge, George, and you know it, too . . . a feel the least you can do is to carry Sylvia go a town.'

Sylvia couldn't cope with this any longer. 'Pearl, if George don't want to drive me into town that's fine, I haven't got any problems with taking the bus.'

'No man, Sylvia, don't say that,' George was offended. 'A will drive you to town the minute the busy time over.'

'No George, I can't afford to waste any more time. I will get the bus.'

'But you never going to manage to get back down from you leaving so late,' George pointed out.

'That's all right, I can stay in a hotel overnight.'

Pearl looked at her with concern. 'Don't hotel price nearly expensive like motor car?'

'It will only be for one night, Pearl.'

'You needn't do that,' the woman said firmly. 'A have a sister living down by Cassava Piece and a next one up Mannings Hill, a will give you their address in case.'

Sylvia looked at her for a long time and Pearl almost willed her to accept the offer. She felt so guilty about this mess. She should have stood up to Jean, done anything to stop her walking away like that. It shamed her that until Sylvia pointed out the obvious she hadn't even thought about the possibility that Davian and Aleesa could be in danger.

'Please, Sylvia, a would feel a whole lot better if you would go and stay round by one a me sister them.'

Sylvia frowned then nodded. 'Alright, I'll do that if I can't get back. If you'd let me have the address I'll be on my way. Oh, and by the way,' she added, as Pearl scribbled the addresses on the back of an envelope, 'could you possibly tell Mr Mandrake I won't be need-ing his help after all?'

George was not to be outdone. 'Don't bother with that, Sylvia man. Just wait on. If you determined to go a town a will drop you down the bus stop after a have a fresh, and we can pass by the police station and talk to Missa Mandrake one time.'

Sylvia made no comment, but as soon as she heard the shower running, she grabbed her bag and said goodbye.

Pearl hugged her impulsively. 'A will sure and tell Missa Mandrake for you.'

As she watched Sylvia go, Pearl wished with all her heart she had the courage to go with her, but she had Kaona, and there was George's dinner . . .

She gave a last wave, turning on a sigh. Who did she think she was fooling? She was frightened of West Kingston, pure and simple. It was alright for Sylvia, she was used to dealing with rough people in her work.

Also the other woman talked so pretty, everybody would know straight off that she was a lady from foreign.

That did little to appease Pearl's guilt. Whichever way she looked at it, Sylvia had left the children with her and she had let her down. All day the feeling nagged her, following her down to Miss Lisa for drinking water and keeping her company over the dinner preparation. By ten o'clock she was sure Sylvia would not be back. Pearl phoned her sisters in town but neither of them had seen her. She wished there was something she could do. She felt trapped and impotent, alone with Kaona in the house.

It was nearly midnight when Sylvia finally got back. She looked defeated and exhausted, and Pearl contented herself with fussing around, getting her something to eat and drink. She decided not to ask anything until the morning, the other woman's depression giving her some inkling of how badly the search was going.

Sylvia was gone when Pearl woke up the next day, leaving a note to say she had arranged to take an early bus. She found it just as footsteps heralded George's return. Pearl's anger died at birth when she saw who was with him.

'Morning Miss Mackenzie.'

'Lawrence! But wait, when you reach back from town?'

He grinned. 'Last night, man . . . you mean Miss Sylvia don't tell you we was on the same bus?'

'She did really tired . . . but how you know a was wanting to talk to you?'

'A never know, a just come to borrow a phone call.' His narrow face was suddenly wary. 'Pearl, you know a can't abuse my position as district councillor so if you asking a favour it better be one a can deal with.'

'You know a would never do that,' Pearl said

reproachfully. 'A just wondering if you could help Sylvia with looking for Miss Jean.'

He nodded thoughtfully. 'Yes, them man down Port Juanero tell me she get mad and run a town with the children . . . that a real pity.'

'But you will help her?' Pearl asked eagerly.

'Can't do that. If she did in St Mary now it would be a next thing . . . but town,' Lawrence pursed his lips and shook his head, 'a can't do a single thing.'

'But you must know people down there? What about the government people in town – they might able to help noh?'

George made a sound of irritation. 'Pearl, you don't understand he can't help.'

She looked at him in annoyance. 'Is not you a was talking to, George.'

'But what George saying true.' Lawrence exchanged an amused look with his brother-in-law, tucking his shirt further down into the narrow waist of his trousers. 'You can't just up and ask a favour just through a woman decide to move her children from country to town. Now if Mr Dyer was here, that would be a different story.'

Pearl felt let down. 'Lawrence, you sure you couldn't help? Jimmy might not reach till next week and Sylvia sure the children in danger.'

'Don't worry about Miss Sylvia,' he admonished, 'she will have everything under control. You have to understand, woman from foreign different from woman down in Jamaica, Pearl. Now a have a urgent phone call to make so you have to excuse me.'

She watched him dial the number, wishing she had the courage to tell him how angry and disappointed she was feeling. But years of conditioning held her back. Why did she always have to be afraid of saying what she was thinking, of doing anything that might draw unwelcome attention to herself? Cursing her timidity,

Pearl busied herself with tidying the kitchen and preparing Kaona's second feed. If only she had the courage to face Lawrence down, pressure him to help Sylvia. But he would only accuse her of being unnatural and anti-woman.

She wished she could be more like Sylvia. Sylvia was so direct, and she didn't care what men thought of her attitudes and opinions. But Pearl was so *anxious*, all the time. The knowledge of it nagged at her all day, feeding her disaffection. She had spent most of her growing years afraid of one thing or another, she thought. Her mind drifted through some of the million and one things to be afraid of . . . because she was a girl.

First it had been the thunder-storms so frequent in the mountains. She could remember huddling in bed, pressed up against Marcie and Angie during bad night storms. But rainy mornings were the worst. She would lie shivering in bed, dreading Moomie's impatient summons to devotion on the shadowed verandah. After that her younger sister got sick, and she had been afraid then too, frightened that the thing eating the substance from Angie might creep into her one day; frightened that God might punish her for being glad when death finally took Angie away from pain.

Pearl shifted restlessly. Why did she have to be the way she was? She tried prayers but found no comfort there tonight. Sylvia was out there somewhere, searching for the children, while she cowered in the security of this house. She wanted to help, wanted to so bad. She wished she could think of something concrete, some way to help Sylvia now Lawrence had refused her.

She fell asleep no nearer to any practical ideas of support. It was a restless, unrefreshing sleep, punctuated by strange dreams, though for once Kaona's whimpering comforted rather than annoyed. Morning brought no answers either, just a depressing sense that this was yet another day, like all the days before.

Sylvia was back early that afternoon. She climbed on to the verandah looking hot and exhausted and Pearl was quick to offer the only comfort she knew. 'Sylvia, a could get you something to drink?'

Sylvia closed her eyes and sighed. 'A cup of tea would be nice but could I have a shower first?'

Pearl watched her climb the stairs, wishing she had something more to offer. She busied herself with boiling water and raiding a teabag from George's precious box of Red Label, before buttering some water crackers to go with it.

Sylvia looked a lot better when she came down and she drank the tea gratefully. 'Thanks, I needed this.'

'H . . . how you get on?' Pearl asked hesitantly.

Sylvia shrugged, her face looking drawn and defeated. 'Not very well; nobody in Kingston seems to know Ras Peter. One man sent me down to Helshire and a policeman at Crossroad offered to arrest him for a price.'

'A sorry,' Pearl couldn't meet the woman's eyes. 'A wish there was a way a could help.'

Sylvia put her cup down. 'Actually, I was thinking about that on the way back down here. You see, the problem is that I sound too English. I think maybe somebody who sounded Jamaican would probably have better luck.'

'Who, me?' Pearl was amazed. 'But a don't think so you know, Sylvia, a can't talk good like you and a don't brave like you. A don't know if a wouldn't fraid to go in West Kingston.'

'It's not too bad in the daytime,' Sylvia refuted, 'the people seem quite nice on the whole.'

'But is bad area down there,' Pearl couldn't help pointing out, 'plenty killings always going on . . . You know when George go there in May he did see two young boy, little bigger than the twins, a wheel one dead man in a store trolley.'

Sylvia didn't seem particularly impressed. 'That was unfortunate, but it doesn't mean the whole place or all the people in it are necessarily violent, does it?'

Pearl conceded that, but she was still not convinced. She wished she had Sylvia's ability to take things in her stride.

An image of the provision ground rose in her head. The lower slopes on which she used to stand before Gilbert put paid to that. The idea came slowly, forming a daring picture in her mind. It was exciting, frightening and she felt a brief exhilaration. Pearl wondered if she dared carry it out. For years she had been trapped by her inability to attempt new things, do anything with an element of risk. Now she felt a longing to break out and take a chance at something.

'Sylvia, you really think a could do some good?'

'Don't worry about it, Pearl,' Sylvia sighed, 'I didn't mean to pressure you.'

'Is not that a don't want to help,' Pearl insisted, coming to a decision. 'As a matter of fact, a was thinking if a can get Mauvia to stay late down, and you can maybe pay her something for the extra, a could come with you tomorrow.'

The relief on Sylvia's face heartened Pearl. She wasn't convinced that somebody like her would have any chance of succeeding where someone with Sylvia's education failed, but she couldn't spend all her life refusing to try. Pearl looked out at the hill land, just visible through the partially open kitchen door. There was something she had to do first, something that couldn't wait, not if tomorrow was going to make a difference to her life.

Chapter 15

Beyond the washing lines, the back of the yard rose sharply in a steeply eroded landscape. It stood as a monument to bad planning. A legacy of carelessness dating from the time when the large estate was subdivided for the housing scheme. And now the land towered above the two stage structures, threatening and dwarfing.

Far above was the high provision ground where George now cultivated fruits and ground provisions for the table since Gilbert washed away the lower, more fertile slope. It was a part of her home, yet for all Pearl knew of what lay up there, it might as well have been another country. As far as she was concerned the provision ground was just another battlefield in the ruins of her marriage. Just one more place for George to assert superiority and heap humiliation on her.

George considered that he worked his fingers to the bone so his children would never be in want. He was always boasting to his neighbours about the high yields of his pineapple suckers and the size of his yam and eddoes; yet the only time he willingly brought her any of that bountiful harvest was in expectations of night favours or because he had guests to impress. Most times when she needed something from the land it was another story. George would complain about the way she was always harassing him and march off in annoyance. She long ago lost count of the times she had to swallow her pride and beg, or get Mauvia to go up and dig provisions for her. It underlined her sense of uselessness, the feeling that she was trapped between that towering landscape and the hostile world outside.

Pearl stood in the shadow of the rising land, peering up with bitterness. She could have put up with his malice if it wasn't for the limes. They represented all her repressed anger and frustration of the last twelve years. Limes were a staple and the thing George claimed he hated picking most . . . even though he had no difficulty providing half the women in the neighbourhood with them.

It had become a daily ritual. Pearl would ask and he would refuse. He saw no reason for a daily excursion, yet would not increase the amount he picked with each reluctant capitulation. Pearl had tried everything, begging, bribing, even threatening to not make the lemonade he insisted on having every day. Everything except her secret fantasy of getting there herself. *If a could get there for myself . . . maybe a wouldn't need him for a next thing again.*

Access to the provision ground was by way of a tortuous climb. It meant scaling the half-finished construction of the breeze-block retaining-wall, then shinning up an almost vertical hill. This was what had barred Pearl all those years, even before Gilbert washed away the lower reaches: the insurmountable obstacle of that vertical climb.

Now she stared doubtfully at the two tree trunks embedded almost perpendicularly into the rising land. This was the test she had set herself, the fantasy of independence she had nurtured for ten years. To be able to climb this slope and get her own limes instead of waiting on George's pleasure.

Pearl's smile was bleak. *To think that is all a hoping this past years. Just to climb up top a one little hill.* She shook her head, retreating back to the house. *Mayhaps if a could reach up by the lime tree and do a good service to Sylvia tomorrow, then a could even do a next thing again and a next one after that.* The possibility excited her, even though she had no clear idea of what those other *things* might be.

Although she found it difficult to restrain herself, Pearl waited until Mauvia was safely inside with the ironing and tiredness drove Sylvia to take a nap, before making her attempt to scale the hill. This way it was her private battle, a challenge to herself – for herself.

Scrambling on to the low wall, she gritted her teeth and set her left foot in the hollow between the two dead trunks. It wasn't too bad at first, wood insects and the weather having eroded natural handholds in the splintered parts of the bark. But that soon gave way to smooth surfaces which had Pearl clinging with desperation at the thought of the ground below.

The climb seemed endless now, full of obstacles and dangers. Doubts crowded in even as her hands searched for purchase on slippery wood and crumbling soil. Tragic outcomes dominated her thoughts: if she fell, smashed her head against the rough concrete of the house wall, who would look after the children then? She and George used to talk about what would happen to the children if one of them died, but she no longer had faith in his promises of putting their needs before his own.

The slope seemed to rise for ever, promising little possibility of a quick end now the climb had begun. Pearl forced her mind from its morbid track, angered by her lack of courage. She had to do this, had to prove that she could stand up by herself. She would be thirty-four years old in October; if she didn't attempt this hill now, was she ever going to try?

Just above her head, a guava tree clung with tenacity to the steeply rising land, within touching distance of a dwarf coconut palm. She reached for it, then slipped, sending a shower of earth and stones rattling against the wall below. Her face slammed against the crumbling hillside, pain and shock nearly loosening her grip and sending her crashing into the concrete house. For a timeless moment she hung suspended by one arm, the fingers of her free hand clawing desperately for purchase on the lower stem.

The pain from a cut lip barely registered, though a graze on the side of her face stung where sweat trickled into it as she managed to get a secure grip on the guava bush. Closing her eyes in fright she pressed her body flat against the powdery earth, as if that would somehow prevent a fall. Her body shivered with reaction, her heart racing so fast she had to gulp for air. Pearl stayed motionless for a few minutes, waiting for the pounding in her ears to stop and the fear pains in her chest to ease.

She wondered if she should go back. Maybe George was right and this climb was not suitable for a woman. Her left foot actually started feeling downwards again before she even realised it. She pulled the foot back, telling herself she could manage. After all, Mauvia managed this climb whenever she felt inclined, and Jean had shinned up on any number of occasions, picking jellynuts for herself and the children. Thoughts of her sister-in-law brought back images of the woman dragging her reluctant son along, a terrified Aleesa walking shakily beside them. It stiffened Pearl's spine, strengthening her resolve. She edged upwards a little, using the sturdy branches of the guava to pull herself to the point where her feet found a small ledge to rest against. Sweat poured down her face, mingling with the dirt and making her eyes smart. She didn't dare look down, sure she'd lose her balance and go crashing back.

The side of her mouth was throbbing now, the pain bringing tears to her eyes. She had to force her body to keep moving, inch by painful inch, past the first dwarf palm, to a second, much older specimen. This palm made a sturdy handhold, the land behind it flattening out a little. Pearl gradually pulled herself around the root, lying prone, kneeling, till finally she could stand up straight.

She leaned against the bole of the palm, trembling with relief. 'A do it! A reach here," she told herself over and over again, 'a never fall down.' She surveyed the ground ahead, noticing how much less steep the incline was up here.

Her finger traced the scratch on her cheek and gingerly outlined the split side of her lip. *It worth it*, she decided, bracing herself and straightening from her leaning position, *the worse over and done with now so a must can make the rest of the climb.*

The feeling of triumph she experienced made up for every fearful moment on the side of that hill. She hardly noticed the grazes on her hand, or the wide streaks of dirt that soiled the front of her dress. The going was easier now, even though she stumbled on the freshly tilled earth and tripped over the root of a fallen ackee tree. Pearl plodded on, stopping periodically to wipe the sweat from her eyes with the skirt of her dress. At last she reached the top of the incline, finding herself on a slope gentle enough to walk upright. She stood and stared in amazement.

Ten years she had lived in this place and she wasn't familiar with what lay just behind her house. She shook her head, realising for the first time just how trapped her daily life had been. Her eyes took in the young naseberry plants sharing space with bananas, plantains, pineapple suckers and two hurricane-damaged ackee trees. It was strange not to have known how fat and prolific the ribbon canes really were or even that there were two star-apple trees and not just the one she used to glimpse from the lower slope. Up here was another world, leafy and cool, a place to linger and be at peace . . . no wonder George wanted to keep it all to himself.

Pearl had to remind herself she still had a way to go, tempted just to sit on the loamy ground and take in the tranquil beauty. She forced herself to go on. To finish the climb and get the limes for the lemonade she had promised herself she would drink, in celebration of her safe return.

The lime tree stood higher up the hill, half in shade, at the point where three properties met. It was surrounded by half-hearted cultivations of okra and cherry tomatoes. Wild vines twisted round its thicker branches and cow itch grew in a tangle at its base. The lime tree was the great survivor of both flood and drought. Three years ago lightning had split its smooth grey trunk, leaving a scorched black line. Yet it grew on, sending out new strong limbs from either side. It bore prolifically all year round, not needing a dormant period like the other fruit-bearing plants. Pearl stared at the tree in fascination, feeling an overwhelming sense of achievement. It was heavy with fruits in various stages of maturity, while a carpet of over-ripe limes lay browning under the sheltering spread of low branches sweeping along the ground. She breathed in deeply, enjoying the scent from the sun-warmed blossoms and large green limes.

Her eyes followed the twisted line of new growth as it silhouetted against the pale blue sky. Then she looked down, far down to where the new zincs on the house top were just visible. She wanted to dance around, sing, shout. To do something crazy with that bubbling sense of freedom. Instead she climbed gingerly on to a low branch and started to gather limes.

Night was falling by the time she finally came down from the hill and Pearl felt as defiant as a child after an illicit day out. She didn't feel guilty about abandoning

Kaona, knowing Sylvia and Mauvia would care for him between them. Just this once she had done something for herself alone, and she felt exhilarated by the experience.

Sylvia was playing with Kaona on the verandah and Pearl stiffened, expecting censure or at the least disapproval. Instead the woman looked surprised, then smiled. 'Pearl, where did *you* spring from? I didn't realise you were still here.' She gave a double take, registering the cuts and bruises and the swollen lip. 'Good grief, what happened to you?'

Pearl's grin was lopsided but she didn't care. 'A just went up back to get some lime.' She cradled the plastic bag of limes possessively, feeling as if her chest would burst with happiness. 'A went up back to get some lime,' she repeated, enjoying the sound of her triumph.

Sylvia was puzzled. 'Did you fall or something? Is that why you were so long?'

Pearl needed to share the sense of achievement welling up inside. 'Is the first a ever go up there. You know up there so pretty a did just want to stay little.' She perched on the edge of the bench. 'All the time a was needing any provision or vegetable kind a did have was to ask George. Is like a couldn't do a single thing for myself.'

'So that's why you felt you had to go up there,' Sylvia acknowledged quietly.

Pearl shook her head. 'Not directly, but from the first it did something a fraid for through a don't too like the height and woman not really encourage to climb or do them kind a thing.'

'You really lead a restricted life, don't you?' Sympathy mingled with surprise in Sylvia's voice. 'I can't imagine how women over here put up with it.'

'Is not ever woman in the same boat?' Pearl dismissed, not wanting to be distracted from the triumph. 'From the first a come to this house a did have ambition to climb up the back, but a never could find the courage, not even when the low slope did still out there. Is like something that did bar me from trying a next thing.'

Sylvia seemed impressed. 'Climbing that hill was a real achievement, Pearl. I doubt very much I could have done it.'

Pearl felt a glow of pleasure. 'What directly make me do it was true you was wanting me to come town with you tomorrow.'

'I don't get you.'

'You see, is through a did wonder if a really could of some use, from a never do much else but breed and raise children aside from the little part-time job over in Highgate before Kaona come.'

Sylvia nodded, understanding dawning. 'And now you feel you can do other things as well. You don't have to explain to me, Pearl.' She leaned across and squeezed the woman's arm. 'I'm glad you managed it.'

The euphoria lasted until Pearl went through the door and caught sight of George. He was at the kitchen end of the living area sorting out cosmetics and he looked up from the box he was rearranging as she walked across the room.

Impatience crept into his expression when he spotted her. 'Pearl, where you get to, man? Mauvia saying she never know where you was and Sylvia did have was to bathe and change the baby.'

Pearl's own irritation rose, overshadowing her sense of achievement. 'George, a asking you please to sort your cosmetics on the verandah.'

'This is my house, Pearl, and a can sort it out where-soever I want. And a don't get answer to my question yet – how you can just up and leave the baby so?'

It was as if the house was closing in on her again. Climbing the hill had wrought no miracle and George's implied criticisms still made her feel the same inadequacies as before. Pearl fought against the defensive anger. 'A was up the back getting some lime for your lemonade.' She went over to the plastic container they used to store the limes, emptying out her bag before facing him once again. 'You always saying how you too busy to pick lime so a decide to save you a trip.'

That annoyed him more. 'What you trying to do, Pearl? Why you want people to think a can't provision my own family?' He looked at her closely now, noticing her cuts and bruises for the first time. 'You see you face!' George's voice rose in alarm.

Pearl's voice softened and she mellowed a little at what she saw as his concern for her welfare. 'A knock it against the hillside.'

George's eyes narrowed impatiently. 'Pearl, what you trying on now? You go knock your self round, up a hillside and next thing a going hear say is beat a beating you and forcing you to climb steep, steep hill. Cho, Pearl man, why you always a do this?'

She shrugged, trying to pretend his attitude didn't hurt. 'George, a only go up back and get some lime. Mauvia go up there all the time, and a don't recall you quarrelling when Jean did go up for jelly coconut.'

'That different and you know it.'

'Different, how, George?' Pearl planted her hands on her hips. 'You think say something the matter with me make a can't do a single thing for myself?'

'You shouldn't have to. In a marriage man have him job and woman have hers,' he insisted stubbornly. 'A mean look at you, Pearl . . . your clothes them dirty so till and the whole a your face cut up. What you think people going say?'

His reaction disappointed her, pushing her back into the old pattern of lashing out. 'A don't care what you or any other bad-minded somebody say, a going up to bathe then a going make lemonade with the lime a pick from the tree.'

'And when you intending to cook?'

222

'Some food leave from yesterday, a could warm it up for you.'

He gave her a cutting look. 'You know a don't like to eat day-old food . . . you saying to me you couldn't cook through you go up back for two lime?'

'Is the first a going up there,' she offered by way of explanation. Her face was suddenly feeling very tender, and the whole of her body came alive with pain.

George was not impressed. 'And what about tomorrow, ee? How long it going take to look vegetable kind if lime take up the whole afternoon?'

'A glad you mention tomorrow.' Pearl's shoulders straightened and she savoured the revelation, feeling advantage slipping back to her. 'For a going to town with Sylvia. But you needn't worry, Mauvia will cook you a meal for she going work late down, and Miss Claudia say she will come in the night and sleep over if we too late coming back.'

He looked at her as if she had suddenly become a stranger. 'You can't do that, Pearl man, you know a don't like Mauvia cooking.'

That was a joke. Pearl thought of the many times she had cooked dinner and it just sat on the stove or in the fridge and spoiled. Then there was the snide remarks some of the women in Mountain District made about her cooking. Remarks that could only have originated with him. Recollection brought a sudden humour at his expense instead of the usual bitterness. 'George, if any thing you can eat up Mountain District or get something down Cool Shade.'

'You really serious about this thing?' George was incredulous.

'A don't see the problem. Is plenty time you eat up the Mountain and don't say one word to me till long after the food done cook.'

'You know full well that not what we talking bout.' He shook his head, still unable to accept these sudden

223

acts of defiance. 'I don't know how you can just ups and go a town without one word?'

'George, I don't know where you get to from one day to the next and a don't complain,' Pearl pointed out reasonably, 'but that is not what a talking. A going town to help look for Davian and Aleesa, true a worrying like Sylvia and a want to help get them back.'

He bristled at the implied criticism. 'You think is you one worrying? If anything a worrying more, but you know that a can't just leave the collecting go a town, somebody must leave to earn the money you love spend so much.'

Pearl wasn't having that. 'Sylvia paying for this trip, true she asking me to help her look for the children.'

'Sylvia ask *you* to help search for the children?' George didn't even try to hide his surprise. 'But you know you not really able, Pearl.'

His certainty made her resolve waver, and she wondered briefly if he might be right. After all, apart from working in a board shop, she had done nothing but bear children and raise them, in the seventeen years she had been out of school.

Then she remembered the lime tree. Felt the sweat and pain of her exertion and the taste of that triumph. 'Sylvia feel a can of some help, George, and that good enough for me. Now if you will excuse me, a going bathe and change.'

He was gone when she came back down and Pearl was relieved she had got off so lightly. She got some ice from the fridge and made a pack, holding it against her cut lip while she heated up some of yesterday's stew for Sylvia and herself.

Pearl waited until the other woman changed Kaona and settled him for the night, before serving the food. Once they were seated at the kitchen table, she restrained herself long enough to mutter a swift blessing before digging her fork into the steaming plate of stew,

224

peas and rice. She enjoyed every last mouthful, hungrier than she had been in a long time. Today she had reached a milestone in her life and it felt good. It made everything else seem so much better, so much more possible.

For the first time in many years she went to bed looking forward to the new day. The activity and the achievement improved her rest, keeping her sleep pleasant and dreamless right through until morning.

Pearl was up an hour before dawn, Kaona's feed ready and waiting by the time he stirred awake. The baby's early morning cries didn't seem to irritate her any more and she was amazed at the difference it made to him. He laughed and blew bubbles at her, splashing about contentedly in his small bath. His happiness was easy to respond to and she was almost sorry to take him out of the water and even found herself trying to make a clumsy game out of dressing him.

The only person that seemed to have the power to annoy Pearl, whatever the circumstances, was George. He had come in late again last night, but this time the gesture was lost on her. She had been deeply asleep and had been surprised to find him beside her in the morning. Now she hoped he wouldn't wake until they were gone, afraid he would simply start up yesterday's argument all over again.

When she heard him moving about in the bathroom her heart sank, but he surprised her. Instead of complaining and arguing, he simply made himself some tea, then insisted on taking them to the bus stop once Mauvia arrived.

The minibus was half empty and they were able to pick and choose their seats. It felt strange not to have to battle for entrance, or struggle through a tangle of bodies to find a space to wedge into. Pearl enjoyed the novelty of having a whole seat to herself, enjoyed the privacy of being able to speak to Sylvia without providing entertainment for a dozen other ears.

The sun was still low in the sky when they reached Halfway Tree in Kingston. Pearl loved the freshness in the air at this time of day, the sense of space and leisure that she knew would disappear once the heat came on and the fumes from rush-hour traffic mingled with the city waste. She would have liked to linger, to peer into the inviting windows of the boutiques in the miles of inter-connected plazas, but her companion was impatient to be on her way. Sylvia told Pearl she had met a man who might know where Jean and the children were and she didn't want to run the risk of getting to Kintyre late, only to find him out.

They had no problem getting a bus; it was as if half the city transportation plied the university route. Pearl felt the old anxieties resurface when they alighted at the Papine stop. It was busy here, the air alive with the colourful persuasion of traders vying with each other to attract the few customers available so early in the day. Others milled around, waiting to board the buses that would carry them to the downtown market, or on into St Thomas.

Sylvia made straight for the steeply plunging Kintyre road the minute she left the bus. Pearl followed reluctantly, feeling an instant dislike for the area. Right now she wished she was anywhere else, certain that at any minute she could find herself in the middle of a shoot-out or a knife fight. What had seemed like a good idea in George's provision ground yesterday, seemed foolhardy now. She thought longingly of the peace of Port Juanero, where any small incident was a long-term talking point.

At the bottom of the incline the road snaked around a wide shallow gully, dried out now from the lack of rain. The bed was treacherous and uneven, large rocks brought downstream by earlier floods marooned with smaller river stones. Pearl hated the smell and sounds of this place. It reminded her of her own childhood in the sagging nog-house her grandfather had built, and brought to her mind the media images of poverty and local violence.

Sylvia must have noticed her tension. 'Are you alright, Pearl?'

Pearl nodded uncertainly. 'Is just that a don't come down this way before.'

'You don't need to worry,' Sylvia reassured her. 'The people down here seem friendly enough, and if it makes you feel any better I haven't seen any sign of violence.'

Pearl was uneasy: Sylvia didn't understand how rough some of these areas could be. She knew, she had seen for herself when she had been pregnant and staying with Marcie over in Cassava Piece. And as if that wasn't enough, the *Gleaner* was always brimming with stories about places like this. Gory tales of gratuitous violence and murders that had become so everyday they were more like a listing than hard news. She didn't need Mauvia's stories, gleaned from a cousin in town, to tell her how dangerous this area was.

'I doubt anything could happen in broad daylight.' Sylvia gave Pearl an understanding smile as she started at the sudden barking of a dog. 'Apparently this area only becomes unsafe in the nights.'

That was cold comfort, but Pearl clung to it in the absence of anything else.

The man Sylvia had met lived on the far side of the gully and it took them a good fifteen minutes to walk around. Pearl answered cheery morning greetings with wary suspicion, twisting her head to watch each person, making sure they didn't double back as the villains always did in the American movies she was so fond of. By the time they had located the sturdy wooden house she was a mass of nerves.

The man they had come to see was old and slow. He needed the aid of a walking stick as he hobbled to the verandah rail to verify who they were. His eyes were

227

bright and intelligent though and they rested on Sylvia with recognition. 'You is the foreign lady come here the other day.'

Sylvia nodded. 'You said you were going to try and find out something for me,' she prompted.

'Truth,' he nodded, 'come up and rest yourself. A see you bring your friend with you this time.'

'I hope you don't mind,' Sylvia responded.

'That alright. You want to know if anybody see a rastaman and a lady with two England children?' He shuffled back to the still-moving rocking chair once they were comfortably seated.

'Have you found out anything?' Sylvia asked eagerly.

The man ignored her haste. 'A did live in England first time, in Brixton, you know it?'

Sylvia nodded impatiently. 'I used to live close by.'

'A suppose it change a lot since my day. A did in the war you know.'

'I was wondering if you found out anything.'

He gave her an assessing look. 'What you want to find them for. You say the children did with the mother.'

'I think they might be in some danger.'

He scratched his balding head and pursed his lips. 'A don't know about that, you know. People round here don't like nobody faasing in them business.'

Pearl listened for a while, watching as the man became more and more unsympathetic. She was surprised at Sylvia's lack of perception. At the rate she was going, the woman would only succeed in upsetting the old man and raising his suspicion to the point where he would refuse to help.

She cleared her throat. 'Excuse a little, I am the children auntie and is they father wanting to find them.'

The man looked at her in surprise. 'You is from down here?' It was more statement than question, but she took it as the latter.

228

'As a matter of fact a coming from St Mary.'

His eyes lit up. 'You don't say, is there a born, you know. You know a place name Rock River?'

'Yes a know it good, a have a school friend who did come from down there.' Pearl said a silent thanks to the Lord. 'But a born and grow up Mountain District . . . close by Port Juanero.'

'Yes a know Port Juanero well . . . a use to work down the hotel near Little Bay. What it call again . . . Casa Juanero.'

Pearl exchanged information with him for a while, allowing him to tell her several anecdotes from his young life in St Mary. Afterwards she obligingly swapped family information with him so he could satisfy himself that they were not related, before finally bringing the conversation back to the point of their visit.

'Miss Sylvia was saying you did sight the two children.'

The man wasn't so easily drawn. 'You say the father wanting them . . . but if is the mother have them I don't see why he hunting them.'

'Truth,' Pearl agreed, hoping her candidness would disarm him, 'and in the normal course of things a would agree with you, but the mother not too right in the head and that worrying everybody.'

'So is not quarrel the two of them quarrel make she run way with a new boyfriend?'

'No sir, nothing like that,' she assured him. 'The children father love him baby mother and give her all she wanting, but is like a madness take her and she start do a whole heap of strange things.'

'A can understand that,' he was all sympathy again. 'That rastaman . . . him say him name Peter from the Tribe of Ash, him mother leave him a house just down the long road you passed back so. You can't miss the house for it have a big rock right out front of it.'

229

Sylvia would have got up then, but Pearl stopped her. 'You know when they likely to be in?'

He scratched his head again. 'The lady who living in the next house say they come by, but they leave back again. She think they gone to a place over in Spanish Town – a get her to write down the address.' He rummaged in his pockets, finally coming up with a neatly folded piece of paper from a child's exercise book. 'Read this out and a will tell you if is the one.'

Pearl took the paper eagerly, relieved when the man confirmed it was right. She got to her feet. 'A can't thank you enough for this.'

'No need man,' he grinned. 'St Mary people have to stick together – and anyway if the mother not too right and the father want the children is so it should go.'

Once they left the old man's house, Sylvia turned to Pearl. 'I just don't know how to thank you for this, Pearl.'

'A never did do much,' she denied automatically. 'Is just that you have to careful how you talk to people lest they think you is police or something so.'

Sylvia looked at her in surprise. 'Pearl, I spent hours talking to people over the last two days without getting anywhere. I even went round to the woman he was mentioning, and she swore she didn't know who I was talking about . . . don't you see – it's your accent.'

She was relieved that Sylvia was pleased rather than jealous. 'Well, a suppose it help a little in place like this, where man good to rob you as talk to you.'

'Don't sell yourself short,' Sylvia insisted gently, 'you have a real talent for getting people to trust you.'

The implications of the words sank in slowly and they were almost at the top of the steep road leading to Papine before it hit her. *She* had got that address. She, Pearl Mackenzie, who George considered good for nothing outside the house, had done what Sylvia with all her education couldn't do.

She anticipated the rest of the day would be like that. Had fantasies of finding the children and taking them back to Port Juanero. But the reality proved surprisingly barren. The old man in Kintyre was their only success that day – if she didn't count the sighting by two schoolboys out to get money for tastee patties.

When they got back to Papine, the buses were beginning to fill up with workers on their way to the city. Fumes belched from faulty exhausts and were trapped by the rising heat, and horns blew constantly. It took a long time to get on a bus for Spanish Town and that broke down just before it reached Halfway Tree. By the time they finally arrived at the old town square, most of Pearl's optimism had trickled away.

When they finally located the house, a half-dressed, surly-looking man opened the door in response to their knock. He stood discouragingly in the doorway, eyeing them with suspicion and hostility. Pearl saw the flicker of recognition in his eyes as Sylvia thrust the picture at him, but she was relieved when he grunted a negative response and slammed the door in their faces. She could sense the woman's anger and to placate her suggested they show the photographs and ask around in the market and the town square.

Sylvia was mollified but Pearl started to have second thoughts when the long fruitless hours of their quest only strengthened her companion's determination. She found wandering around the market a disheartening experience. Several people claimed to recognise the children, but none could remember where they had been.

By three o'clock Pearl had had enough. Her feet ached from the unaccustomed exertion and the glare of the sun caused bands of pain to tighten across her unprotected head. 'A think we should finish for the day lest we can't get a bus out of town,' she suggested

231

finally. 'If we come early tomorrow we could mayhaps try Kintyre again.'

Sylvia nodded reluctantly, visibly trying to put a brave face on things and control her desperation. Pearl suspected it was only the woman's own exhaustion that led her to capitulate, but she herself was too tired to feel even a twinge of guilt.

Chapter 16

Fly noises were everywhere, increasing and decreasing in volume like the sound of sea on sand. The insects became bolder as she made no move to disturb them. One perched on her nose, stopping to clean its mandibles before walking around to poke about at the entrance to a nostril. Jean moved her head in a half-hearted attempt to dislodge it. Somehow she just couldn't sum up the energy to raise a hand and brush the irritating presence aside as it foraged deeper into the opening.

The voices in her head were getting louder, arguing with each other in an attempt to get her attention. She tried to focus on the good ones, to listen to Granny and Aunt Vi and filter out the wicked things the others were trying to tempt her with. But the good voices were getting weaker, draining away.

How did I get here? The question popped into her head, shifting her attention and quietening the clamour a little. She couldn't remember one single thing about life outside that ragged door, couldn't even recall what she was before. All she knew was she had to stay alert, had to keep herself safe until help came. Jean concentrated hard, trying to remember why she needed help, but her mind just kept wandering from subject to subject, thwarting any effort to focus on one thing.

Her eyes swept indifferently across the opposite side of the mean little room, not registering much. She

233

knew the contents as if she had been there all her life. On the facing wall was a soiled pallet bed whose mattress had seen better days. Over by the door was a chipped and worn enamel chamber-pot, while a kerosene lamp hung from a crooked rusty nail in the doorway, squeaking and scraping with every stray gust of wind.

Something was watching her. The knowledge jolted through her system. It freed her head to turn about, her hands to flail at the flies that seemed to mass like so many lost souls, right on top of her. *Something was there alright*, lurking just outside her line of sight. She knew it with a certainty that chilled her, and made her eyes dart frantically from side to side, bringing old fears and superstitions crowding in. *They had found her again!* Searched through the whole of Jamaica until they could pinpoint her location and continue her torment.

The thought made her break out in a cold sweat. One slip, that was all it would take, one moment of inattention and she would be lost for ever. Somehow she had to get out of here, run away to a new safety somewhere – except she couldn't summon up the energy to move. Maybe if she remembered how she had got here, she might find her way out again. She racked her brain, groping along the hazy lines of memory.

She had been with the rastaman . . . at his house. Yes that was it! They had been smoking ganja and he had told her all manner of wisdom. Deep lines furrowed her brow as she tried to make the connection between the man and herself.

An image formed in her mind. Leathery palms encased in bittersweet chocolate. Long fingers cool against her hot flesh. Images of Jimmy smiling encouragement, smiling arousal . . . fulfilment. Jimmy dark and beautiful, skin on her skin, flesh inside her flesh.

Jean frowned, feeling a brief regret as the beauty of

the image dissolved, leaving another one in its place. That rastaman – what had been his name again? *P-e-t-e, Peter . . . Peter from the Tribe of Ash*. Yes that was it, Peter Ashman. She felt relieved at that feat of recall. Pleased when it proved to be the dam behind which other memories lurked.

They was all against me, she decided, *right from the start they were against me. Even that hypocrite Deacon Davis, skinning his teeth in a plastic smile and all that time a whisper, whisper about me every little chance. All of them so backstabbing, just waiting to put the dagger in.*

The old desire to laugh nearly caught her out. Jean gulped and swallowed, afraid of the violence of the emotion dammed up behind the need. She felt a rush of bitterness as the wild laughter fought to get out through her tightly sealed lips. It was *their* fault, all of them. If she listened hard right now, she bet she could hear that two-face deacon clear down Port Juanero town, su-suing about her, telling people how she and Jimmy was living in sin and about the way she try tempt Pastor.

To think he let that bad-minded woman call my name right in front of the whole church. She shook her head violently, then held it still as the laughter threatened to rip loose. The voices inside her head laughed instead, a wild clamorous noise that had her pressing both sides of her skull and rocking back and forth to bear the pain. *To think, eh.* She sighed as the laughter subsided, her mind focusing a little better. *If Miss Berta did tell me what they was planning, I would never just walk in there without a suspicion. And all the time that Deacon Davis plotting my downfall with Pastor Simmonds just through they know a was struggling with the sin.*

A tear meandered down her cheek. *They all wanting Jimmy to leave me; but they making a sad mistake if they think they going rob my flesh and blood from right under my nose.* She shook her head again, more cautiously this time as she brooded on the perceived injustice. *All that time I was there trusting in the deacon and he was broadcasting my business. No wonder ungodly woman like Miss Berta could repeat the self-same thing to me out a street. They were all in it together. All of them – Jimmy, Pearl, Sylvia and the rest.* That was what made her head hurt most. Them and the things surrounding her and wailing out because she was too smart to let them snatch her soul. She cried out her own defiance as the voices inside her head rose to a crescendo. Shaking her fist at those unspeakable things she was sure had crept a little nearer.

She could hear a good voice now, cutting through the clamour and malice to restore some order to the confusion in her head. Jean nodded as if she had been asked a question, relieved to find the empty memory spaces filling up in her mind. They thought she wouldn't remember, but she had fooled them again.

Despite all the bad things they were whispering about Ras Peter she already knew the truth. He was the only one who ever did a single thing to help her. Ras Peter really rated her. He looked up to her foreign ways and the education all the others hated her for. Look at the way he brought her here to hide after he helped her escape from Port Juanero with Áleesa and Davian . . .

The children! What happen to me children?

Jean's eyes swivelled round, making a wide sweep of the shadowed room, taking in the wooden shutters, tightly closed against the light digging in through the glassless hole that passed for a window. A stray sun-beam caught her glance, distracting her for a moment. She followed it with her eyes, sure she could see a whole ballet of little people dancing on the floor. Her mind emptied of panic, of fears about misplaced children and fanciful evils. The whole of her attention refocused on this new absorption.

The sunlight shifted finally and the dance evaporated

in front of her eyes. Jean frowned, at a loss again. *Now what was it I was supposed to be doing?*

A whimpering sound from the opposite wall caught her attention and brought back the previous quest. She looked across, her scalp tightening when she saw them. They sat huddled together on the narrow bed, looking for all the world like Aleesa and Davian, but she knew better. They couldn't fool her. The stab of inadequacy she felt was her very own warning system. If they had been her children she would feel love, out-and-out love and a desire to protect them. But those – *things* – sitting motionless on the far edge of the bed repelled her so strongly, she recognised them for what they were. They had replaced her children and drained Jimmy's love for her, like the demon vampire things they were.

Her eyes narrowed as she tried to work out the mechanics of the switch. Sylvia must have come in the night and stolen her real children again, just after she found them as well. *Yes, it had to be Sylvia*, she decided. It was just the sort of vindictive thing that woman would do, take her lovely children and leave those demon things instead. *She was jealous from the day Jimmy first interested in me*, Jean reasoned. *She was never satisfied with Winston one, she did always want to have his brother as well.*

That thought made her head hurt all over again, and she prayed Ras Peter would hurry up and come back. She had to be patient; he had helped her before.

She felt a sudden urge to giggle and she had to swallow it down, realising how much laughter still bubbled away inside. Laughter was not a thing in endless supply and she couldn't let it all escape in one go, in case she deflated and shrank like the empty skin of a balloon. Better to concentrate on how to get the children back. Ras Peter would help. When he returned he would give her something to strengthen her insides so she wouldn't be so brittle any more; something to smoke that would make her strong enough to drive the demon things away for ever.

The boy thing . . . so much like her beautiful Davian to look at, started to cry and she felt the sound deep inside her brain, boring in and in, tempting her. Jean squeezed her palms against her ears, fighting the need to react. She wanted to cross the room, put her fingers around that small throat and squeeze and squeeze until sound no longer came out of it. The desire was so great, resistance caused a sheen of sweat to break out across her forehead and prickle along her scalp. Her back bowed with the effort of staying where she was. Jean gritted her teeth, determined. They would really love for her to go over to where they were. It would suit them just fine if she lost control, smashed them to pieces and tumbled into the eternal fires of hell.

She was sure they knew about the evil things lurking just outside her line of vision, waiting for just one more sin, to drag her down with them for ever. Probably they were all in league together: Sylvia, those two and the ones who drilled into her brain, making wicked suggestions to her and refusing to allow her peace so long as she resisted.

She tried to pray but the words slipped out in a jumble and then she forgot why she was doing it anyway. She abandoned the effort as she shifted on a suddenly cramped leg. Something rustled beneath her and she looked down, almost expecting to see the serpent crawling towards her on the floor. Instead she found a bag of holey bullas, next to an open bottle of 7-Up. It made her feel hungry all of a sudden, and she grabbed the bag, pulling out one of the small ring cakes with impatient fingers. She remembered that Ras Peter had left the food behind, as she chewed urgently and it increased her warm feelings for him.

A movement from the bed caught her eyes, whispered conversation halting her as she reached for a second bulla. She looked up with a snarl of warning. Snatching up the bag and the half-full bottle of flat, warm 7-Up, she cradled them protectively against her chest. *Let them come, let them just try and take my things.* She glared at them, challenging and expectant. If they came now she could pound them, grind them into dust and pulp and there wasn't a single thing the lurking demons could do. Whatever she did would be self-protection and no one could blame her for that.

They were on their feet now, and she watched with silent hostility as they edged cautiously along the wall, before backing over to the far corner. The girl helped the little boy with his trousers' zip, and held the chipped white enamel chamber-pot while he discharged a stream of urine.

Disgust rose like bile inside Jean, mingling with a new alarm. She fancied the stream of urine was going on and on, spewing out of that tiny organ like a river of doom. She could see it clearly through suddenly transparent enamel, reaching halfway, three-quarters then brimming up and flowing over the edge of the chamber-pot. It came across the floor as a trickle at first, snaking towards her in a sizzling, corrosive stream. She could hear them laughing, both of them. The sound penetrated deep inside her head and lodged with the voices already there. Jean scrambled backwards, the bottle falling with a loud thud against the sagging wooden floorboards. She felt the stream of liquid reach her, splash her. Felt it burning and burning, till it was a massive effort to stop the screams welling up from those dark and dangerous recesses of her stomach. *She was going to burn alive!*

The thought panicked her, but she dared not move too quickly. Dared not run in case disaster happened to what she fancied was the fragile state of the emotions contained in the cavity of her chest. *Why don't Ras Peter hurry up and come back? What had she ever done to deserve this?*

Images of Noel superimposed themselves on Davian's features. Noel under the mango tree, one minute stretching up, the next minute all covered in the bright, bright light. She could see it like an instant replay, smell the charred and burning flesh, her father's terrible grief, the unspoken accusation in Aunt Vi's eyes . . . The child bleeding on the muddy floor of the cook house in the painful, searing shadow of the blood-stained cross. It added fuel to her fear. *She had to get out of here!* Find the way out before she burned and shrivelled like Noel. He was there now, standing like some charred evil, come back to haunt her. She watched as a hand raised, pointing charcoal fingers at her in bitter accusation while the voice in the ruined, exposed throat wailed out and goaded her with taunts.

Jean scratched frantically against the wooden wall, gouging and digging at it. Splinters flaked and pierced the tender skin under her torn, ragged nails, causing the blood to well up, bright scarlet oozing past the crusted dirt.

The pain steadied her, pushed the nightmare images away for a moment. She stared at the deep crimson of the welling spots of blood, watched them spread, merge, turn into a trickle and ooze faster and faster, staining the side of the fingers, soaking into her palm. Blood on her hands . . . Noel's blood, her father's blood . . . pain inside, stretching, splitting, tearing her belly apart.

A peal of laughter bubbled in her stomach, fighting to escape. She had to stop it in case it opened the floodgate to damnation. Whatever else happened, she had to avoid *that* catastrophe at all cost. That was what they were watching and waiting for. Once all the good had finished trickling out of her and everything positive had evaporated they would make their move. She could imagine them burrowing down inside her, distorting her soul for ever. It made her scratch at the wall again, scratch and pound until her fingers were raw and her arms were heavy and numb.

The howls came from deep inside her. One followed by another and another coming out of the murky well of sins that just seemed to be growing all by itself. She crouched against the wall, shuffling away from the pool of burning liquid, a cornered animal in her confusion. Noel seemed to be growing bigger and bigger, towering above her. Jean shrank away, pressing her back hard against the wall. She fancied if she used enough force she could merge with the wood, be surrounded and protected by it. She tried to watch the whole of the room at once. Eyes, fear-filled and rimmed with tiredness, darted incessantly, hardly daring to blink in case the demon people used that instant to make their move and corrode the pitifully small amount of good remaining to her.

It was as if her vision had fractured, and everything came through in fragments. Jean stared at the flies circling above her head. She traced the lines of decay from the hole in the wall where the age knot had fallen out, to the ribbon pattern of termite infestation near the shuttered window. But all the time she kept a cautious eye on the demon things standing between her and the door.

Her eyelids grew heavy, her head sliding against the wall as the room blurred. The things around her stirred and whispered, the sound jerking her back to alertness with a warning snarl. They thought they were so clever trying to make her sleep but she wasn't having that. She shifted purposefully, easing her bottom into a more comfortable position. If only she could remember what she was doing here. It had been some kind of sin, had to be. This was the torment the old pastor used to mutter about as his fumbling fingers pinched and hurt . . .

It was so hot in here, so full of bad odours. The blue- and greenbottle flies kept up a crazy buzzing chorus right in her ears, an accompaniment to the two demons wailing so loudly on the other side. Every so often the taller demon thing would move closer, try to talk to her, tempt her to go out the door. But she was cleverer than they thought. She would never escape if she went that way. They wanted to lead her further down the byway to hell.

If only she dared close her eyes, just for a few minutes, if she had enough faith to go to sleep and trust God to keep her safe. That seemed funny somehow, and she giggled, gulping the noise back down when it threatened to spill over into a dangerous belly laugh. God had abandoned her for sinning with the old pastor. He blamed her for Noel and her father just like the rest of them did. That had always been the trouble with the Lord: He was just too short-tempered, quick to threaten her and throw her out of the fold. Jimmy was a bit like that, him and Sylvia both. Unaccountably that thought made her want to giggle too, and she had to swallow hard, tears of merriment brimming in her eyes. Imagine the whole of them so down on her like that!

Suddenly it didn't seem worthwhile fighting any more. The need to sleep came like waves, rolling heav- ily into her. It made her feel sluggish and light-headed at the same time, though her mind continued skipping round from thought to thought. She let her head slide down until she was lying prone, all the time keeping the two things in sight. If only someone would tell her what to do.

Her eyes were beginning to feel weighted, resisting all her attempts to keep them open and alert. She could hear the things whispering and shuffling around on the floor, but somehow she couldn't move, couldn't get the command to sit up past the cotton-wool feeling in her brain. The effort was too much, far too painful to sustain. *What did it matter, anyway, if they gobbled her whole or filled her with evil?* She was nearly that already. That thought released her from the need to stay awake and she relaxed her mind and let the sleep take her.

Chapter 17

Sounds of voices woke her, the babble of children and adults all talking together. Jean lay where she was, too many half-formed images chasing each other inside her head to think of anything at first. But then thoughts started to coalesce, sounds solidified to make sense. She recognised Sylvia's restrained annoyance, Pearl's high anxious voice with the converted whine of childhood, Aleesa, sounding so full of fear, Davian's tearful, formless chatter . . .

Jean shifted cautiously, worried that the half-remembered sense of fragmentation would return. Her head remained clear and she breathed a silent prayer. She stayed where she was, not daring to move in case it triggered off the altered images and brought the bad voices back.

'Jean, are you alright?' Sylvia's face swam into view, tense and concerned. 'Jean, can you hear me? Can you sit up?'

She sat up slowly, her eyes instinctively narrowing against the harsh, afternoon light streaming through the open door. Everything about her felt shaky, even her voice when she finally settled on something to say. 'Sylvia, what are you doing here?'

'I've been looking for you and the children for days.' Anger crept into Sylvia's voice, clipping the edges of the words. 'What do you *think* I'm doing here? I've come to get the children, of course.'

That galvanised her, bringing her up straight. The still-damp skirt clung to her legs, a welcome coolness in the heat. One of her legs felt sore and cramped, and she bent to rub the knee before shifting her weight on to it. The movement brought Pearl into her line of sight – Pearl, slipping off with her children like the thief Jean had always suspected lurked under that pious exterior. She made a lunge towards the woman, but Sylvia was there between them, blocking her way and refusing to move. Pearl had been keeping a wary eye on her sister-in-law, and she cried out in alarm when she saw the threatening movement.

'Take the children out, Pearl!' Sylvia ordered when the woman froze. 'Go on, take them down to the bus stop like I told you.'

Pearl still hesitated. 'But what about . . . ?'

'Just do it!'

Jean watched, helpless and frustrated, as the woman disappeared through the door. She wanted to rush at Sylvia, to knock her out of the way, but something in her cousin's expression scared her. Instead, she backed away, trying to find some way around Sylvia. The voices inside her warned against touching Sylvia, jeered and taunted her with what would happen if she did. Moving restlessly from side to side, she tried to think of ways of getting past. Somehow she had to extend herself to the point where she could stretch and stretch till she could grab at Pearl's retreating back.

In the end she gave up, retreating to the wall and pressing her back hard against it as she tried to control a sudden need to cry. 'You can't do this, Sylvia – just come like that and steal my kids.'

'Jean, no one is trying to steal your children.'

She could hear the effort Sylvia was making to control her impatience and it saddened her. Sylvia spent half her life trying not to lose her temper, projecting that *reasonable* social-work image. The thought warmed her to her cousin, wiping away her suspicion.

Poor old Sylv, the wonder is how all that splendid control don't mad her. That struck Jean as funny, and she giggled. Chewing on a torn fingernail, she gave her cousin a sly look, a broad smile replacing laughter. 'Look, Sylvia, I wasn't too good recently, but Ras Peter took the sickness out and a feel a lot better now.'

Sylvia didn't return her smile. 'Jean, mosquitoes have made a meal of the children and Aleesa said you haven't given them anything to eat for two days.'

She scratched her head vaguely, trying to remember. 'You mustn't believe everything Aleesa say, Sylv,' she offered finally, 'you know how much lies children that age tell. I'm always feeding them, you know. I think they have worms, either that or a demon the way they eat so much.'

Sylvia took a deep breath, then wrinkled her nose. 'I'm sure you tried your best,' she offered finally, 'but I suspect you haven't been feeling too well yourself?'

Jean nodded, warming to her cousin even more. Sylvia wasn't so bad really. Imagine noticing how bad she was feeling. 'I think it must be something a eat, probably that Jack fish Jimmy buy, and ever since then a haven't been myself, you know. I must have swallowed some down the wrong way.'

The thought of the fish stranded somewhere in her stomach released another giggle. But Sylvia only nodded. 'Well, something is going wrong and only a doctor can help you.'

That made perfect sense to her. 'When you say Jimmy coming down?'

Sylvia frowned. 'Tomorrow afternoon, he had to get a flight through Miami as all the direct flights were booked up.'

That animated Jean, filled her with a sense of energy. 'So what time is the flight? I need to know . . . there's so much preparation, the ironing, packing the children for the move down to Trelawney,' she ran her hand through her matted hair, 'and a must wash and style my hair and we don't want to be late meeting him, do we?'

'I don't think it's a good idea for you to go to the airport, Jean.' Sylvia picked through her words as if they were a minefield. 'You haven't been too well . . . and anyway you'll see him when he get to Port Juanero in the evening.'

Jean felt the anticipation drain away. Couldn't Sylvia see that was just what they wanted? 'I can't come back down to Port Juanero, Sylv, so many of the people down there envy me it's hard to find somebody not plotting against me.' She grabbed the other woman's arm, leaving flakes of dirt and blood. 'You don't see is what Pearl want?'

Sylvia's attention shifted to Jean's torn and battered fingers, losing the thread of the conversation in a new concern. 'What happened to your fingers?'

A gleam of malice lit Jean's eyes and she suddenly looked very sly. 'Is Pearl, you know . . . just because she was jealous of me, she come early on and just mash them up like this.'

Sylvia hesitated, sighed. 'Jean, you can't stay here. Look, your Aunt Vi came with us and she is waiting outside, would you stay at her house instead?'

She cocked her head to the side, thinking about that. 'Aunt Vi used to live with us, you know,' she offered conversationally. 'She used to always favour Noel over George and me. Just like Papa.'

'Jean!' Sylvia was getting impatient again. 'Do you want me to call her? She's living at her daughter's house as Tashi is still in America. It's out on Red Hills Road and she wants you to come and stay with her for a while.'

That was strange. Jean's brow wrinkled in a frown.

'But she wouldn't take us in, you know. She said from our father put us in the Salvation Army home, it was for him to come back and get us. She blame me for Noel like all of them.'

'She doesn't blame you for anything, Jean. Look, why don't you talk to her, ask her yourself?'

Did she dare, after all the years she had avoided Aunt Vi, afraid of the accusation she was sure the woman carried in her eyes? But Sylvia was right, she couldn't stay here waiting for Ras Peter. He was probably in league with all those people who were out to get her. Why else would he just abandon her in this dump with a bag of stale, holey bullas and a bottle of 7-Up?

'Well, shall I get your aunt or not?' Sylvia's impatience was back with a vengeance. 'I can't just leave her standing out there while you make up your mind.'

'Alright, she can come in.' She said it before she could change her mind, prompted as much by Sylvia's displeasure as by any wish to see the woman. 'A might as well stay with her as anywhere else.'

Sylvia was out the door in a flash, returning a few minutes later with the old woman. Jean stared, curious despite herself. Aunt Vi was greyer, a little more stooped and slower than the last time Jean had seen her. That and the age warts blooming with profusion on her chin and above her eyes were the only things that were different. Essentially she remained the same. The eyes were sharp and direct with the underlying warmth that always made her brisk manner bearable and the face was as round and welcoming as it always had been.

Jean studied the old woman closely, looking for the slightest flicker, the slightest gesture which would hint at blame. All she found was welcome and a compassion that folded her against the ample chest. Somehow they were out of the closed-up and oppressive atmosphere of the small one-roomed house, out into the late sunlight and the old remembered smells of baked earth and boiling peas.

She was content to go along, Aunt Vi's concern wrapping like a balm around her troubled mind. If she closed her eyes she could block out the ugliness around; the whispers about some unfortunate mad woman, and the furtive giggles that followed them through the dilapidated street. Aunt Vi was promising to pray for her, to take her to the balm yard, all sorts of things that went way over her head. All she needed was the thought that someone cared. Someone who had known Noel didn't blame her for his death.

Jean had no clear impression of how they got to Aunt Vi's comfortable old house. But suddenly the sun which had started to pound inside her head was replaced by the shadowed cool of stone walls and the smell of lime and oranges, so much a part of the memory she carried of her auntie's presence. The old woman stood her under the shower and bathed her as if she was still a child.

Later Aunt Vi slipped one of Tashi's nightdresses over Jean's head and trickled warm coconut oil across her scalp, before massaging the ache away. And all the time she hummed church hymns, old remembered songs coming out on a slightly off-key note, punctuated by admonitions to God to heal and bring peace to a troubled soul.

If only Sylvia would go away, Jean thought wistfully. She could pretend her father was out in the bush with Noel, George was fetching drinking water and Tashi was grating coconut under the ancient almond tree. If she closed her eyes she could see Granny waving that big old hat of hers to try and stir a little breeze. This could be her second chance. Time to do things right, not lead Pastor into temptation, goad Noel under the mango tree or call God's attention by talking death.

But Sylvia was still there when she opened her eyes

and the noises filtering into the house were the bustle and snapping impatience of town life, not the lazy relaxed pace of the St Mary countryside. Soon even Aunt Vi's hands stopped their healing touch, the old lady sitting up and stretching her back to ease its ache.

'A going boil some fish tea give you,' she announced finally, 'it will help build back your strength; and a can see Miss Sylvia here wanting to have a private word with you.'

Jean watched Aunt Vi leave, feeling lonely and abandoned again. She ignored the light touch of Sylvia's fingers on her arm, refusing to turn round when her cousin sighed.

'Jean, what do you want me to tell Jimmy?'

Anger sparked inside her. 'What you mean tell him? After all he done to me I barely even want to talk to him much less.'

'That's hardly constructive.' Sylvia sat on the side of the bed. 'Earlier on you were all set to meet him at the airport.'

'That was before.'

'Before what?'

Jean gave Sylvia a sly look. 'You think you can find out that easy? Don't think I don't know what going on with you and Jimmy. Is you put the people them in my head, isn't it, Sylvia?'

'Oh stop being such an idiot! No one put anything in your head, and there's nothing going on between Jimmy and me.'

Jean laughed, she couldn't stop herself. It just bubbled up and overflowed before she could do a thing about it. She gulped it back before it finished altogether. 'Who you think you fooling, Sylvia? From Winston dead you looking to take Jimmy away from me.'

Sylvia shook her head and stood up. 'I can't see any point even trying to talk to you just now.'

She hardly heard that, her mind already moving on. 'When Jimmy coming to see me again?'

Sylvia took a deep breath. She looked at Jean, her wild expression, her bruised fingernails. When Jimmy had sent Jean to Jamaica she might have been drinking and degraded, but he was really going to be shocked by this. It certainly wasn't going to help Jean if he reacted with disgust.

'I don't think it's a good idea for Jimmy to come just now,' she said quietly. 'He'll have had a nightmarish journey, the children will give him a lot to cope with. I think we should sort you out a bit before you see him.'

'You not going to tell him where to find me!' Jean accused indignantly.

'Don't be stupid.' Sylvia avoided her eyes. 'I suspect Jimmy will be anxious to see you as soon as you're well enough.'

Jean knew her cousin was lying, knew it as sure as she knew she could never go back to Port Juanero. Sylvia wanted Jimmy for herself. *Why hadn't she seen that before*! It had been there all along. All the time she was waiting for some glamorous stranger to snatch him away from her and the threat was her own cousin. She wanted to argue, be angry, say something; instead, a stray smile popped out before she could prevent it.

'Jean,' Sylvia said with new purpose, 'I'm not going to let you keep putting Jimmy through the wringer. If you want to see him you're going to have to come down to Port Juanero yourself, because I'm certainly not going to encourage him to keep running around after you.'

'But Sylvia, I don't feel good,' she retreated into regression, 'you self-same one saying how bad I looking.'

Sylvia's stony expression didn't change. 'What you need is a doctor, not Jimmy. I'm trying to arrange for you to see somebody on Friday, and if you're really serious about Jimmy you'll make the effort to come.'

Jean felt cowed, deflated by what she fancied was new evidence of her cousin's lack of care for her. She curled into a defeated ball, closing her eyes to lock out Sylvia and her treachery, not even bothering to resist when the voices crept back inside her skull one by one.

Chapter 18

Had she made the right choices? That thought dogged Sylvia like a silent companion. It followed her back to Port Juanero on the overcrowded minibus, and stayed with her as she tended to Aleesa and Davian. Worry picked and frayed at her temper. It caused her to snap at George for making light of Aleesa and Davian's ordeal, and to shut his children out when they tried to tell her about their stay at Miss Lisa's house.

Sylvia wished she could talk over the decisions she was making. Explore all the issues and reassure herself she was acting with the best of all intentions. The questions buzzed away inside her brain. Was she doing the right thing for the right reasons? Was it really ethical to make decisions about Jean for Jimmy, even if it was in the children's best interest? The pressure made her head ache and resentment creep in. This was supposed to be her holiday of a lifetime, a time to store new memories to supersede the old, not grapple with the daily questions of her working life.

Port Juanero was a small community steeped in old habits of mutual support, where every family crisis became a matter of public concern. Everyone knew of Aleesa and Davian's disappearance and news of their return brought a stream of well-wishers crowding into George's small house, bringing an air of celebration. Even Mr Mandrake dropped by with his roly-poly wife to shake Sylvia's hand, congratulate her and bring cheese trixes for the children to show there were no hard feelings.

Sylvia sat on the verandah with Pearl, Miss Lisa and the two traders, wishing she could share her worries with them. The women's generosity had surprised her. Miss Lisa had taken Pearl's children with matter-of-fact efficiency when Mauvia reported in sick, and they would never have found Aunt Vi's address without Miss Berta and Dorrie's help. The women refused Sylvia's clumsy offer of money to compensate them for their time. Brushing aside her thanks, Miss Berta only said that women had to stick together, while Dorrie had a few choice adjectives for George's lack of involvement and support.

She knew they understood the responsibility she felt for keeping Jimmy's children safe, but she could not talk to them about Jean's life. It wasn't that she thought they would betray her confidence. She knew them better than that now. Miss Berta only gossiped about superficial things, bits of information that were common knowledge. Other things she kept within herself, holding them secret like so many precious articles of faith.

The complexity of her moral dilemma was a different issue though. Sylvia stared reflectively at the garish orange fruits of the soracee vine, rioting along the wire mesh fence. *They wouldn't understand*, she thought regretfully, not even attempting to test that theory, *they just don't have the educational background or the knowledge to grasp that kind of moral question*.

To her mind, however admirable and selfless Pearl and the other women's actions were, they had been motivated by gut instinct rather than a rational view of moral responsibility. She thought wistfully of good friends and work colleagues in England. People who shared her views and her concerns. If only she had one of them with her now, someone who wouldn't pile the endless burden of his own preoccupations on her shoulders.

Sylvia withdrew inside herself, suspicious and overwhelmed by the amount of help on offer. She had only non-commital responses for all of them, vague statements that Jean was visiting in town in answer to questions about George's sister's mental state.

The moon was high by the time the stream of visitors trickled off and the crowd of well-wishers finally started to drift away. Lisa stayed behind to help Pearl with the clearing up and Sylvia retreated to the spare room. She sat on the side of the bed, watching the sleeping children in the moonlight filtering through the open shutters, troubled by the decisions she was imposing on their mother.

She saw her whole working life as devoted to safeguarding choices for her clients, allowing them the freedom to make their own mistakes, when it would lead to growth and not destruction. Now here she was, moving Jimmy's life around like so many chequers on a board. It didn't matter how many times she told herself her plans were for the best. The question *Best for whom?* refused to go away. It kept her awake long into the night when only the stray bark of a dog and Davian's heavy breathing punctuated the silence, till she abandoned her attempts at rationalisation. *I'll just have to do what I think best and live with the consequences*, she decided.

Sylvia held the children close, savouring their warmth and the small sounds they made in their sleep. She hadn't realised just how empty her arms were, how much she ached inside for a child of her own – a daughter like Aleesa, even a son like Davian, with his impish smile and the shades of Winston in his eyes.

The false dawn found her out of bed, too restless to continue struggling with her insomnia. Sylvia walked down to the shore, enjoying the dewy freshness of the morning and the peace of her own company. The tide was going out, the beach stretching damp and unmarked in either direction. She perched on a log embedded in the wet sand, listening to the rhythm of the sea and watching as the first orange rays of sunlight spilt over the rim of Cabaritta Island to bathe the fishing boats in a perfect, painter's light.

In the optimistic brightness of the new day, she was able to convince herself of what the sleepless night failed to do. That leaving Jean with Aunt Vi *was* in everyone's best interest. The old lady seemed to have a calming effect on her niece and Jean desperately needed her unconditional acceptance.

Anyway it was only for another day. Just until she could take her cousin to see the psychiatrist she had found listed in the phone directory and get some medication to stabilise her. Jean could then fly back to England with her when Jimmy arrived. Sylvia was sure they could find a flight with two seats free, people were always extending their stay on the island. Jimmy wouldn't have to know. In fact it was much better if he didn't in case guilt and obligations prompted him to intervene and spoil everything. Better for him to see Jean *after* she received the care she needed and had moved past her present destructive spiral.

The early morning commuters were on their way to work when she finally got back to the house. Most of them called out a greeting or stopped to ask how the children were. It made her feel good, gave her the illusion of belonging to the community.

The euphoria lasted until she heard the first strong thud of stone against wood. Sylvia hesitated in the act of mounting the road stairs. She turned, looking automatically towards the commonland behind the primary school. Three teenage boys were stoning Miss Maddy's house with real intention. Sylvia could almost visualise the expression of hostility and spite on their faces. That was how the people in Kingston had looked at Jean. As if she was contagious and they were in danger of catching a fatal disease. Sylvia was shaken by the realisation of how deep and lethal the vein of terror ran in Jamaicans when it came to mental illness. The quality of violence was too much at odds with her image of a gentler, more accepting way of life than the one she knew in England. God alone knew why, but somehow she thought attitudes of intolerance in the Caribbean had passed away with the colonial reality of her parent's generation.

Miss Maddy's voice rose on a wail of fear, and that reminded her of the wounded sounds Jean had made. No doubt if she went down there, she would see the city people's hate and fear mirrored in those young boys' eyes. She was angered by their ignorance, wished there was some way to force them to realise the suffering they were causing. Everybody, even the most educated and knowledgeable in Jamaica, seemed to poke fun at the mentally ill. It was like a massive moral cancer seeping into the social fabric and eating away at its humanity from the inside out.

Sylvia hadn't intended to interfere but somehow her feet carried her down the hill. Down past the crowded goat tract, the small patch of commercial calaloo nurtured by rejected American pesticide, the grave of the last owner of the Solon Plantation, to the place where Miss Maddy's house stood, looking incongruously prosperous against its grey and sagging neighbours. In her anger she barely noticed the rising heat or the way the bumpy surface of the badly rutted road dug through the soft canvas of her sandals.

The three boys grinned and selected new stones when they saw her. Close up they were older than she had thought, on the adult side of teenage. She ignored their tacit attempt to draw her into their ranks, marching forward to stand in front of Miss Maddy's house.

'Stop it right now, do you hear me! Why don't you go and find something constructive to do instead of stoning a poor defenceless woman?'

The boys looked at her in astonishment. 'Is Maddy living in there, mam,' the shortest one, with a young paunch and patches of dry skin, volunteered finally. 'She don't care whatsoever we do.'

Sylvia folded her arms and glared at them. 'Have you ever asked her?'

The young spokesman exchanged puzzled glances with his companions and scratched his head. 'But she mad, mam, she can't feel no way.'

She was disgusted by the casual dismissal, yesterday's anger spilling over to engulf them. The boys listened in amazement as Sylvia lectured them, dropping their stones and edging away when she threatened to have them arrested if they continued their harassment. She watched with contempt as they beat a hasty retreat. What else could she expect from a gang of louts who got their kicks from picking on a helpless woman?

Sylvia felt good because she had not ignored the woman's terror. This time she had come down to the commonland and stood up for what she believed in.

She smiled faintly. *At least I managed to do something for Miss Maddy, even if I didn't manage to stop them taunting Jean yesterday.*

She squared her shoulders under the influence of achievement, half expecting the ragged woman to come flying out, full of praise and gratitude. When nothing happened, Sylvia knocked tentatively on the thick wooden door, puzzled by the lack of response. 'Miss Maddy, they've gone now, you can come out if you want to.'

Still nothing. She tried again, rapping knuckles sharply against the sturdy frame. This time the door opened a crack, just enough for an eye to peer suspiciously at her.

'It's OK now,' Sylvia repeated kindly, sure the woman was too terrified to open the door fully. 'They've gone and after what I said, I doubt they'll be bothering you again.'

The woman opened the door, her face angry and spiteful. Clearing her throat she spat a stream of saliva directly at Sylvia. It just missed contact, and she followed up with a string of invective that left her self-appointed rescuer disturbed and shaken.

'Look, I was only trying to help you,' Sylvia said indignantly as the tirade died down a little. 'The least you could do is show a little gratitude.'

The woman kissed her teeth. 'Who ask you?'

Sylvia couldn't believe her ears. 'I didn't have to come down here, you know. I could have left those boys to smash up your house . . . Is that what you wanted?'

'Me never ask you fe no help,' the woman insisted, 'them never troubling me.'

Sylvia looked at the ragged woman in disgust. She wanted to grab her and shake her, force her to stop bowing under the endless indignities. All her pent-up anger against Jean threatened to spill over and she had to take a deep breath in an attempt to push it back. 'It seems to me that you are getting a considerable amount of trouble from the majority of people around here,' she managed finally.

The woman looked at her uncomprehendingly for a moment. 'A never get none a that,' she said a little more belligerently. 'The gentleman them who come look for me gi me money and whole heapa nice, nice something, and them even buy Junction chicken and ice-cream cake give me.'

'That is not the point.'

Miss Maddy blinked. 'A don't know what point you talking, mam, but my gentleman them good to me, them come make house fe me when bulldozer mash

259

down the next one over by Trinity district and them talk sweet to me come night time, so why you did drive them way?'

'But you can't let them use you like this.' Sylvia's revulsion was instinctive. 'They have no right to take advantage of you like that.'

The woman kissed her teeth again. 'What you know bout anything? Who ask you fe come faas in a my business make my gentleman them run gone?'

'Miss Maddy, you must try to understand . . .'

'Me no want understand a thing! Me never ask you fe no help, me no want no foreign lady help. You no hear say me is mad woman? Why you no left me gone?'

The door slammed on that last tirade and Sylvia was left staring at the solid wood, feeling awkward and embarrassed. She could hear smothered childish giggles behind her and it added fuel to her annoyance. *Ungrateful woman!* she thought sourly, turning and marching away. *She don't even have enough sense to know when somebody is trying to help her.*

The sun was higher in the sky and it was hot work toiling back up the hill now she no longer had righteous indignation to sustain her. Sylvia felt aggrieved. She had gone all the way down to the common and the woman didn't even have the sense to be grateful. *Some of these women are their own worst enemies.*

Jalina waved at her when she was halfway up the hill, skipping down to meet her at the bottom of the house. 'Auntie, Aleesa and Davian still sleeping,' the child said anxiously, 'and Moomie saying not to wake them till you come . . . a could wake them up now, Auntie?'

Sylvia felt hot and irritated. 'No, Jalini, they need to sleep.'

The child fell into step as Sylvia started climbing the stairs. 'Auntie, is true Auntie Jean get mad like Miss Maddy and try to chop Moomie?'

Sylvia looked down at the child in shock. 'Jalini,

where did you get such a foolish story? Of course your auntie didn't try to hurt your mother. She's not well, that's all.'

Jalini looked sheepish. 'A did just wondering, Auntie.' They had reached the verandah and she chased one of the dogs who was trying to follow them into the shade.

Lutie was sitting with Kaona, bouncing him on her skinny knees and pulling faces to make him laugh. 'Is mad Auntie Jean mad, Auntie Sylvia?' she asked curiously.

Dionne appeared in the doorway. 'Auntie Jean going come back and kill we when we sleeping, don't?' she asked worriedly, her eyes brimming with ready tears.

'Of course not.' Sylvia had to struggle to control her irritation. 'Your Aunt is not well and she is staying in Kingston until she gets better.'

But it took a lot of effort to reassure the children and by the time Sylvia finished, her mood had worsened. Annoyance made her cut off Pearl's attempt at conversation with a curt 'good morning' and George fared no better. He ignored her bad mood in his eagerness to discuss the idea of throwing a welcoming party for Jimmy and she told him bluntly to get off her back.

George was not to be deterred, persisting until Sylvia stopped impatiently beside the stairs and listened.

'For God's sake, George!' she snapped when his intention sank in. 'Can't you show a little sensitivity? Jean is sick and you're here talking about throwing a party for Jimmy.'

'Sylvia, is what you want from me, man? Is not my fault Jean always causing trouble.'

'She's ill, George, not causing trouble. The least you could do is show a little compassion.'

'Compassion, my back foot! A not arguing with you, Sylvia, through a know things little different in England, but Jean causing all manner of tribulation from she go get herself mad.'

'That's hardly fair.'

He ignored that. 'Everybody wanting to see Jimmy. It mean plenty to people that he get through so good.'

Sylvia swallowed her own response, knowing that her bad temper was partly a result of the frustration and anger that Jean and the ragged woman had caused her. 'You do what you like, George. I have to go and see to the children.'

They were awake, hands linked. Aleesa sat protectively on the side of the bed, while Davian lay wide-eyed beside her. Sylvia felt the pain of their suffering as if it was her own. They were silent and withdrawn, and she had to force herself to allow them space. This was when she really felt her lack of experience with children, wished she and Winston hadn't found so many reasons for postponing parenthood. She washed Davian while Aleesa took a shower, then sat with them as they ate porridge and brown bread.

The house was solemn and tense around them, despite the normality of Pearl at the kitchen sink and her children baiting the dogs from the verandah. Sylvia felt the need to escape the oppressive atmosphere.

'How about us spending the morning on the beach?' she suggested.

Aleesa was immediately animated. 'Can the cousins come?'

Pearl's children appeared as if by magic, crowding into the doorway. Jalini pushed her way forward. 'Auntie Sylvia, we can come beach with you?'

Sylvia wanted to refuse, irritated by the clamour. She was tired of always doing for someone else or their children. Since coming to Jamaica she had scarcely had a moment to herself and she was fed up with that, too.

'I don't know about that,' she muttered, 'I'm not sure I'm up to putting up with all of you today.'

Pearl turned from the sink, her eyes unconsciously mirroring her children's appeal.

'Sylvia, if you could take them a would grateful. Mauvia not coming down today and a having to go to Oche.'

Sylvia felt a sense of obligation to Pearl and that made her even more irritable. 'I can't take the baby, Pearl,' she warned.

'That aright,' the woman wore an air of suppressed excitement, 'Miss Lisa taking him for the morning, a having to pass by and leave him on the way. Is just the big one them you see. She can't take them this morning for she having to . . .'

'Alright, I'll take them,' she interrupted Pearl's rambling explanation, 'just don't expect to make a habit of it, that's all.'

'Sylvia, a wouldn't ask if a could find a next way,' Pearl said quietly.

That shamed Sylvia. 'I'm sorry, Pearl, I didn't mean to imply you were dumping them on me. Alright, you lot, go on up and get your swimming costumes.'

Pearl waited until the children were at the top of the stairs before coming across to the table. 'A going to look a job down by the new Palm Springs hotel. They looking people to do maiding and the pay not too bad.'

Sylvia was impressed. 'You mean George don't mind?'

'Well a don't directly tell him as yet. A was thinking if a was to get it the money would be a help.' She hesitated. 'You think a doing the right thing?'

How could she tell the other woman that? She had never been in the position of negotiating a relationship with a man of George's inadequacies, so she compromised. 'I think . . . if it's what you want and you think it's for the best, you should go for it.'

Pearl smiled, relieved. 'You think a could get a chance and get through?'

She could see the uncertainty clearly now. The lack of self-assurance that years of being pushed to the margins had bred. 'Pearl, you have as good a chance as anyone else.'

'But a don't really work since a get the part-time job before a did pregnant with the twins. The two hour down by Miss Chung after Jali start school never really count . . .'

'Work is work,' Sylvia interrupted, 'and believe me, Pearl, running a house and raising four children *is* pretty hard work. If you think about all the planning you have to do, the cleaning and the buying in . . . you probably have enough experience to do the manager's job.'

Pearl laughed, some of the tension leaving her face. 'A too dark for that job. Probably the tourist will think the hotel don't run good if they see a black manager and instead they will leave go to a next one with a clear-skin manager.'

'Do you really believe that?' Sylvia was diverted, shocked by the acceptance implicit in the casual words. She had heard many variations on this very same theme, *but for Pearl to think it normal enough to joke about it!* This was what Jean had been trying to tell her about colour gradation racism. It was so endemic it had become normal and unchallengeable.

'Everybody know is only clear-skin people get good position in this country. Probably if a even have a education a couldn't get good job like them through a so black.' Pearl was serious now. 'You know how Marcie dark?' She waited for affirmation. 'Well, is same reason she saying, why she don't get the manager job. Them call in one clear-skin lady and give her even although she don't have so much exam as Marcia and she not working as long . . . and is Marcia having to do the work still, through the lady can't directly manage from it so hard for her.'

The story was so familiar it appalled her. 'So why doesn't someone do something about it?'

'Nothing can do,' Pearl shrugged, resigned, 'is just so Jamaica stay. Even Lawrence saying how new government just as bad as the old one in them ways. Is from is only pure clear-skin and white people a run things you see. Every one a them from government right over, down on the black-skin people. Marcie say is through them fraid to lose the life they living if black man ever get what due to him.'

Sylvia was uncomfortable and angry. Today everything seemed to irritate her, make her feel a personal sense of affront. She supposed it was the strain she was under, the sense of her own vulnerability in the face of her cousin's disintegration. She was glad when the children's return put paid to the conversation and the feelings of impotence it generated within her. Turning, she took the bag Aleesa thrust into her hand, checking automatically to make sure they had everything they needed.

'I got your bathing suit and your swim hat,' the little girl said importantly, 'and I didn't forget the cream and the sting relief, and Davian and me found our pocket money from before last week so we took it to get the cousins something from the shop.'

Sylvia smiled, softening in the face of the child's customary generosity. The bad feelings generated by the conversation were lost in the scramble for departure and she suddenly found herself looking forward to the outing after the hassle and tension of the past week. Pearl gave her the spare keys in case they returned before she did, and packed mangoes and cheese trix for snacks in a silent expression of gratitude.

Chapter 19

Solon Heights was alive with noise when Sylvia and the children returned in the late afternoon. Petrol fumes hung heavy in the air and the drowsy peace of the hill had been replaced by a bustling excitement and a cacophony of sounds from cars crawling upwards in nose-to-tail formation. Engines revved to keep from cutting out on the steep gradient, and horns set up a discordant symphony as drivers jostled for position on wider stretches.

The further up the hill they went, the more congested the road became as vehicles stopped to allow smartly dressed pedestrians a right of way. Verges were choked and crowded with cars of all varieties: ageing Cortinas and Chevrolets, dilapidated Datsuns and Toyotas, parked end to end, many with their bumpers touching. As they came up to the flame tree by the agricultural station, more cars trundled past, excited occupants disgorging eagerly and hurrying across the road with only a cursory greeting.

The human stream converged on George's house and Sylvia guessed from the sounds of revelry that Jimmy had arrived. His presence had obviously triggered off the party her cousin had been threatening to organise and her nerves tightened as the culprit's voice came pompous and self-important across the thick air.

'They going up the house, Auntie,' Jalini volunteered unnecessarily, grabbing Aleesa's hand and pulling her forward. 'Come, Aleesa, make we go see, Daddy keeping dance.'

'Don't run off, you two.' Sylvia managed to pull them to the side of the road as yet another car trundled past. 'You can't go on the verandah anyway until you wash the sand off your feet.'

Davian chose that moment to break free of Sylvia's loose clasp and dart in front of a nearly stationary car. Lutie, Aleesa and Jalini gave chase, yelling and screaming for him to stop. They fell into step when he started labouring up the road stairs, vying with each other to help him over the high riser that marked the halfway point.

Dionne slipped a shy hand in Sylvia's. 'Is true Daddy keeping dance, Auntie?'

Sylvia shook her head absently, still debating on whether to make the effort to catch up with the other children. 'Your Uncle Jimmy must have arrived from England and he's having a small gathering to celebrate.'

The child's face lit up, but she hesitated on the verge of chasing after the others, looking uncertainly at the woman. 'A must walk and not run, don't, Auntie?'

Sylvia hid a smile. Of all George's children, Dionne was the most timid. The one with the most of Pearl in her. Quick to cry, the little girl agonised about every small action in case it was the wrong one. Sylvia always had the feeling Dionne wanted to blend into the background so she need never be singled out for either decision or criticism.

'Go and catch up with the others,' she said finally, 'but be careful on the stairs.'

She watched Dionne weave through the crowd of well-wishers making their way to the house. Sylvia was reluctant to be a part of what she saw as a tasteless exercise. It was inconsiderate of George to plunge Jimmy straight into this after the journey he must have had; as if having to fly standby, burdened with worries

267

about Jean and the children wasn't sufficient stress. She paused by the verandah long enough to say a brief hello, before ducking round the side of the house to wash sand and sea salt from the children's skin under the outside pipe. Afterwards she left them to climb the verandah stairs, going in through the kitchen door herself, in preference.

Pearl looked up from making a fresh batch of lemonade, excitement animating her features when she saw who it was. 'A get through with the job, Sylvia,' she whispered gleefully, looking around nervously as if she expected to be overheard. 'A starting a week from Monday. The man say he think a going to get on good with the work.'

'That's great,' Sylvia was pleased for her. 'But how did George take it?'

Pearl looked sheepish. 'A don't directly tell him as yet.'

Sylvia was sympathetic, sensing all the other unspoken things. 'A week doesn't give you much time, does it?'

'Is hard to find a right time,' Pearl agreed, 'specially now, with Jimmy reaching and everybody wanting to see him.'

'He isn't staying here, is he?'

'No, he letting the children sleep over and he staying down by the San Juanero hotel, true he only really come down from England to carry them back. But you don't know how George stay when Jimmy in Jamaica, he going to round there every spare minute, till late down in the night.'

'So what do you intend to do?'

'A going to take the job. If the time not right to tell him, a just going have to work in secret and tell him when a can . . . but we needing the money and a needing the work.'

The baby's crying punctuated that statement and

Sylvia nodded, understanding. 'You must do what you think is best. Don't worry about Kaona, I'll see to him.'

Pearl smiled with gratitude. 'He don't long feed so he probably wanting to bring up wind.'

Resettling the baby, Sylvia marvelled at the difference in Pearl's relationship with him. Kaona's crying no longer brought trapped desperation to his mother's eyes, and he smiled a welcome for her every time she came into his line of sight.

Sylvia retreated to the spare room in preference to joining the general celebration. She had had enough of back-slapping congratulations the day before, and it struck her as macabre that people could make merry, knowing about the tragedy that had overtaken Jean.

Busying herself with sorting through what was left of the children's clothes, she wondered how Aunt Vi was coping with Jean. She had tried ringing early in the morning, but the line was constantly engaged. Her fingers closed jerkily on one of her cousin's elegant floral print dresses as she remembered the wreck this room had been. She had to ring Aunt Vi later, when the crowd dispersed, give her some guidance on dealing with Jean's illness and remind her about the morning appointment with the psychiatrist.

The noise downstairs quietened at last, tailing off with a final shouted exchange between George and Lawrence, followed a few minutes later by a car engine roaring into life. Sylvia breathed a sigh of relief, getting off the bed and heading for the door. The packing was long finished and she was becoming bored with her own company.

Jimmy was sitting on the verandah lounger, Davian on his lap and Aleesa cuddled up close to him, while George perched on the low wall. Sylvia went to sit on the green canvas chair, ignoring the censure in her cousin's gaze. 'Is everyone gone?' she asked innocently.

Jimmy smiled, but George didn't share the humour.

269

'Sylvia, you do me bad, man,' he complained. 'Everybody was asking after you. Even Lawrence saying how you just cut all a we today.'

'George, I told you what I thought of this party idea.'

'But from it happening nothing say you couldn't just come for a five minute.'

'George, I'm sure those people came to see Jimmy, not me.'

'Well, you could at least come talk little. That way they couldn't leave here thinking you scorning them.'

She shrugged. 'Most of them saw me yesterday – anyway, I wouldn't have thought you'd feel much like celebrating,' she added quietly, pressing home her earlier point. 'Jean is your sister, you know, George.'

'You think you have to tell me that!' He got down from his perch on the wall, hissing through his teeth, 'From the day Jean born is just pure grief she a bring . . . A don't even want to think bout the thing them she do me, clear from when we did young.' He turned to Jimmy, his annoyance with Sylvia swallowed by his larger grievance against his sister. 'Look no, a will catch you later, a have to go up so to check one and two people and a want to reach before night catch. Sylvie, you coming for the ride?'

'I don't think so.' Her abruptness narrowed his eyes and she forced herself to continue on a calmer note. 'I want to try and get an early start to Kingston tomorrow so I need an early night.'

'A never planning on staying long,' George wasn't taking the hint, 'and as a matter of fact one a the reason a passing by is to try and look some jelly for all of you.'

'I'll come, Uncle George,' Aleesa volunteered, 'me and Davian can help you carry the jelly coconuts.'

'Me coming too,' Jalini announced immediately.

'Daddy,' Lutie looked disgruntled, 'if Jalini coming, me and Dionne going have to come, don't?'

George made an impatient sound. 'All a oonu stop the nonsense. Lutie go with Dionne and Jalini, go help your mother tidy up.'

Jalini looked like she wanted to argue, but Pearl called them at that moment, and she trailed reluctantly behind the other two.

Aleesa didn't give in that easily. 'But Davian and me can still come, can't we, Uncle George?'

George looked trapped. 'No, man,' Sylvia could hear the strain in his voice as he attempted to remain pleasant, ' a couldn't carry you today not unless your auntie coming.'

'No, George, I have to talk to Jimmy and I'm not sure if I'll see him before I leave as I intend to be on the first plane out I can find seats on.'

'Well, why we don't all go?' George tried again. 'Jimmy, that rental car you have down the road would reach faster than my runaround.'

Jimmy shook his head. 'I want the children to have an early night tonight, and to be honest with you, man, a could do with one myself. A had to wait around for nearly nine hours for a seat on a plane out of Miami and then the first rental I got broke down, which was another long wait. So right now I'm really feeling wiped out.'

Despite the explanations George still tried to get them to change their minds until Sylvia suggested he took Pearl and his own children. That sent him scurrying off and she smiled grimly, wondering if he would ever learn.

'Aleesa, take your brother upstairs and have a wash,' Jimmy said, lowering Davian from his knee as soon as George had gone.

Jalini appeared instantly. 'A could help Aleesa bathe Davian, Uncle Jimmy? A can do it good, good now, you know. A even help Moomie bathe Kaona Sabbath morning.'

Jimmy acquiesced and the children went off, leaving a shared silence on the darkening verandah.

'George and Pearl still not getting on so good?' Jimmy asked finally – more, Sylvia suspected, for something to fill the silence than out of any real interest at that moment.

She shook her head. 'But Pearl is beginning to stand up to him a lot more. She was really good when the children went missing, you know . . .' She tailed off, aware that she was skirting too close to the subject that lay unspoken between them.

'Where's Jean, Sylvia?' Jimmy changed the subject abruptly, tapping into her guilt.

She hesitated, debating how to put what she had to say. 'She's being cared for in Kingston.'

'Cared for – why? I mean, I thought as the children were back she had started behaving . . . and with the party and everything – George didn't say anything about her still being ill.'

He seemed to have aged a lifetime since she saw him at the beginning of the summer, lines of worry scouring deeper grooves in his forehead and around the sides of his mouth. Sylvia's heart went out to him, her resentment against Jean hardening her resolve. 'Jimmy, I told you on the phone that she was mentally ill.'

'Yes, I wanted to ask you about that. Are you saying she was having a breakdown when she came over?'

She was glad to see how well he was taking it now, half expecting stony rejection of her cousin after his outburst on the phone, but a part of her felt a twinge of envy that Jean could have a man like this and not appreciate him. 'I'm not a psychiatrist, Jimmy, so I couldn't say exactly what is wrong with her, but I'd hazard a guess that it was a bit more serious than that.'

He digested that, then nodded. 'So when can I see her?'

Sylvia had to brace herself to tell the lie, praying it

wouldn't come tumbling down around her head. 'Right now she doesn't want to see you.'

'Does she know I'm here?' He sounded hurt, suspicious.

'Yes,' she was on firmer ground now. 'I told her you were coming today, but she blames you for her illness. It's just the way some psychoses work.'

'I thought you said you didn't know what was wrong with her?'

'I don't, but I do recognise some symptoms and they seem to be consistent with what I know of psychoses.' She could hear defensiveness creeping into her voice. 'To tell you the truth I don't think it will do a lot of good dwelling on exactly what Jean's illness is. It's better to work out the best ways in which you can help her now, rather than waste time trying to find somewhere to throw the blame.'

He scratched his head and sighed, just as Aleesa called out to him from the bathroom: 'Daddy, will you come upstairs and dry Davian, he keeps wriggling and won't let us do it.'

Jimmy gave her an apologetic smile, getting up tiredly. 'Look, I can't take this on just now. Why don't you walk out with me later on, when the children are sleeping and we can discuss the best course of action.'

Sylvia agreed willingly, glad of the reprieve. She needed time to sort out the renewed uncertainty in her mind. She had thought all her decisions were made. But in the light of Jimmy's pain and his obvious concern for Jean, she found herself agonising all over again. Did she really have the right to keep Jean's whereabouts from him? Shouldn't he make the decision on how involved he wanted to be for himself?

It was late by the time the children were asleep and Sylvia didn't feel much like going for a walk. Her sleepless nights were catching up on her, so when Jimmy suggested they had a drink in his hotel she was quick to agree. The last thing she wanted was to walk out in this dark night, considering the amount of crabs and other scuttling things that could be lurking underfoot.

They sat on the balcony of his room, Jimmy insisting on knowing everything that had happened. Sylvia explained something about Jean's erratic behaviour and her uncertain temper.

'What I can't understand,' he burst out, 'is how she deteriorated so quickly.'

'Jimmy, you parented the children from the day they were born until now, then suddenly you dumped them on Jean and expected her to cope just like that.'

'She was always good with them.'

'In small doses, yes; but just imagine how frightening it must have been to suddenly have sole responsibility for their care and welfare, especially when she was under so much pressure already.'

'So it's my fault for asking her to be a proper mother to them, is it? And what about your responsibility? You were supposed to be keeping an eye on things.'

That brought her own resentments to the surface. 'Jimmy, getting into an argument isn't going to help anyone. I'm not saying you didn't suffer, but I spent three days looking for Aleesa and Davian in a country I don't know the first thing about, where everybody in a uniform or a suit seems to be on the lookout for a bribe. So don't come throwing out accusations at me about . . .'

'I'm sorry,' he put a placating hand over hers, 'I shouldn't have said that. The truth is, I've been really scared for the kids. And then not being able to get here as well . . . I should have seen it coming, shouldn't I?'

What did he expect her to say? Of course he should have seen it coming, but telling him that now would only add to the weight of his guilt and lead them off at another tangent. 'As you said, it all happened very quickly. One minute she was in with the Pentecostal people and the next she was totally gone.'

He wasn't really listening to her now. He just sat there, staring over the balcony at the moon-silvered leaves of the poui tree as if it was some private landscape of his own. He seemed bewildered, as if he couldn't understand what he had done to deserve this pain. Sylvia's heart went out to him, her own irritation forgotten in the face of his misery.

She took his hand in hers. 'Jimmy, it really was nobody's fault, Jean's problems went back too far for that. Even the drinking was almost inevitable, given what happened to her father.'

Sylvia told him what she had learnt from conversations with Miss Berta and Aunti Vi. How Jean had blamed herself for her brother's death. The way that tragedy drove her father to the bottle and left Jean and George stranded in a children's home . . .

'I suppose she sees something of her father in you,' she finished uncomfortably. 'Certainly she was always comparing the two of you and how inadequate you made her feel . . .'

Sylvia tailed off, realising his attention was still focused elsewhere. 'Look, it's getting late and you're tired, so I think I should go.'

Jimmy stirred. Pulling his hand away from her, he rubbed it against his face as if he was coming out of a long sleep. 'I always knew there was something, you know. I even tried to tackle her about it once or twice.'

'Maybe she didn't want you to think badly of her.'

'I can't accept that,' he shook his head in denial. 'She knew she could always count on me. We were good together nine years, Sylv, we were a team, man.'

'No, you weren't,' she contradicted. 'I bet you didn't even know how much Jean wanted to get married.'

'*Married!* How come she didn't tell me if it meant that much to her?'

'Because you told her from the start that you didn't have time for that kind of foolishness . . . remember?'

He looked shocked. 'Jean knew I was committed to the relationship. If she said she wanted marriage I wouldn't have made any objections.'

She sighed. 'I just wished you'd told her that. I have to say I was against the relationship from the start – most everyone was. As far as we were concerned Jean needed marriage and you were dead set against it.'

He snorted. 'That's really rich. Jean is the one who wasn't committed to the relationship. You know how many times she came home smelling of other men?' He shook his head. 'The worst of it was the way she didn't even attempt to hide her slackness. I'd wake up in the morning to find that she hadn't even bothered to take off her stale clothes.'

'You knew!'

'Of course I knew. What do you take me for, Sylv? My lover crawls into bed in the early hours with another man's semen on her and I couldn't tell?'

'I thought . . . well, I didn't realise it was that bad.'

He dropped his head in his hands. 'Things were bad a long time.' There was no disguising the bitterness now. 'You know, one night she came in reeking of sex and booze and wanted to carry on where the other man left off.'

She sucked in her breath in horror as he continued. 'I could have killed her, Sylv. I wanted to just take a pillow and smother the drunken grin on her face for what she was putting me and the kids through.'

'Why didn't you leave her?' The question slipped out before she could stop it.

He shook his head. 'I guess because I didn't want to be another statistic – another black man abandoning his woman and children. And to be truthful I wasn't sure I'd get custody of the children, as we're not married.'

'That wouldn't have been a problem. You should

have said something to me, you know . . . told me how bad things were.'

His smile had an edge. 'I tried, remember? You said I was over-reacting, and that was one of your kindest comments. Sylv, this might sound strange, but I do care for Jean. I care for her a lot despite everything, but judging by the way she's been treating me, this thing is just a one-way street.'

'Can't you see she was acting that way because she wasn't well?' It sounded lame, but she had to say something in Jean's defence. 'When people get a mental illness they tend to behave out of character.'

Jimmy wasn't impressed. 'More like character coming to look for her, if you ask me. George told me she ran off to sleep with old Ras Peter before she came and took the children.'

She remained silent, unable to think of a single new thing to say in her cousin's defence. She hadn't realised how long or how frequently Jean had been having casual sex. 'Look, there's no point getting into another set of recriminations. What happened, happened and there's nothing anybody can do to change that.'

He accepted that. 'So where do we go from here? To be honest with you, Sylv, I don't know how much more I can take from Jean. My inclination is to just take the children and go, and I worry about what all this is doing to Davian and Aleesa.'

'Jean is staying with her Aunt Vi at the moment.'

'Aunt Vi? Are you sure? Jean has never spoken to her in all the years we've been together.'

Sylvia nodded. 'Well, the old lady seems to have a calming effect on her, and with Jean refusing to come back here it was the best I could do till something could be worked out.'

'I suppose I should come and see her.'

'No point in that right now.' The uncertainty in his voice strengthened her determination. 'I'm taking her to see a psychiatrist tomorrow and I doubt your being there will aid anything.' She pretended not to notice the relief on his face, continuing neutrally, 'With any luck, they might be able to give us something to stabilise her condition, at least sufficiently for her to come back to England.' She stretched, trying to relieve the pain in her lower back. 'Now I really have to go, I've got an early start in the morning.'

He stood up with her, following her into the room. 'What about you, Sylvia? How are things with you?'

The unexpected question brought a rush of tears and she blinked them back in surprise. 'Not too bad, I suppose.'

He put out a detaining hand. 'I know how much this trip meant to you and I suppose we did dump everything on you. But . . . well, did things work out as you wanted?'

The tears were hot in her eyes, stinging the hidden corners and producing a flow. It made her angry all of a sudden. '*Work out for me!* How could *anything* work out for me when I was running around sorting out everybody else's problems?' She bit her lip hard, trying to stop the shakiness from getting into her voice. 'Let's just say I've had better holidays, OK?'

'Sylvia, I'm sorry.' He sounded so regretful, it caused another welling up of tears. Sylvia resisted the urge to wipe her nose, bowing her head in dismay.

Jimmy didn't say another word, just took her in to his arms and held her, giving her comfort and allowing her the privacy of his silence.

Once she started, the tears just kept coming: for the children's pain, for Jean and the inevitability of her disintegration, for the destruction of her Utopian vision of Jamaica . . . Jimmy's arms were like a cocoon to rest in, someone to hold her and allow *her* pain some space. He eased her down on the settee, stayed close beside her and just rocked her. Finally the flow of tears slowed, ebbing away and leaving her wrung out and ashamed. Sylvia wanted to move away from him, put back the polite mask of distance and pretend it had never happened, but his arms were warm and she suddenly realised how little human comfort she had received since Winston had died.

Jimmy rested his chin on the top of her head. 'Do you want to talk about it?'

She was tempted, so she retreated further, remembering belatedly who he was. 'Sorry about that,' she said awkwardly, wiping her eyes and blowing her nose with the tissues he provided. 'Can't imagine what came over me.'

'Sylvia, you can't be strong all the time,' Jimmy said quietly, 'none of us can. I realise how hard Winston's death hit you and I know you've never had the space to grieve properly and really come to terms with it. After all, that's why you came down here in the first place.'

That made her want to cry all over again and she took a deep breath to stave the feeling off. 'Winston has been dead for two years, Jimmy.'

'And you were there for everyone when it happened. You know, it's become such a habit to dump on you, no one ever take the time to wonder who is there for you. I'm right, aren't I?'

That caught her attention, calling to the lonely empty space Winston's death had left inside her, the void still present despite her new acceptance of his passing. It made her want to reach out to Jimmy, hold on to him, be a part of him in a way that shamed her.

'I have to go, it's really late and I need to get some sleep.'

Jimmy got up with her. 'Why not stay here?'

She hesitated, thinking of the empty hours until morning.

'Sylvia, you're not in much of a state to put up with Kaona's crying and George and Pearl bickering.'

'And *you're* in no fit state to put up with my self-indulgence,' she countered in half-apology.

He shook his head. 'Sylvia, you've done so much for me . . . for all of us, I'd like to feel I can do some small thing for you. Stay and talk to me; the spare bed is comfortable and I can arrange a wake-up call in the morning so you don't oversleep.'

She wavered, and he held out his hand. She thought about the silent years behind her, the long lonely years in front. She had expected Jamaica to help her come to terms with her loss but it hadn't proved to be that simple. Taking a purposeful step forwards, she placed her hand in his outstretched palm, allowing his warm fingers to close on her decision.

Chapter 20

Early morning in town is the best time of day. The sun, spilling over the rim of the encircling mountains, pierces the dull dawn sky and animates the cityscape. It triggers birdsong and brushes tropical colours into concrete grey. The smell of damp earth leaches into the air. Rich and loamy, it mingles with the fresh clean scents that drift down from adjacent hills.

Jean sat on the side of the bed in her borrowed clothes, as full of apprehension as a young woman waiting for her first lover. In her mind that was what she was, miraculously transformed to the days of innocence when thoughts of Jimmy were a breathless flutter in her stomach and a bubbling uncontainable joy. He was coming for her today, coming to get her and make everything all right.

She hugged the memory close. *To think he come all the way from England just to get me back . . . he's such a romantic.* It made her feel like giggling and dancing and skipping all at once. How he must love her to be doing all this for her, to be leaving the writing that meant so much to him because he knew she was in danger. A brief frown wrinkled her brow. Maybe it was wrong of her to force him to choose between her and the book; but she'd make it up to him. She'd be everything he ever needed, all he could ever want.

The indignant braying of a passing donkey distracted her, draining the images of Jimmy and romance from her head as if they had never been. Now her whole attention focused on the noises of a city coming awake.

The merging textures of sounds fascinated her: the deep defiant roar of provision trucks, and long-haul commercial soft-drinks carriers, so different from the sleek, low, throbbing hum of the oil and fuel tankers. She could distinguish Japanese-made town buses from the clumsy, growling old country ones, with their heavy burst of foghorn sound as they laboured round each bend in the twisting road and moved towards downtown. Cars chugged, purred and wheezed. Bicycles squeaked and jangled.

The sounds of pedestrians merged with the traffic; the time they passed by marking their place in the social hierarchy – the precise level of respect their position would command. At the early end of morning came the market traders and farming peasants, following on the heels of the higglers, overloading decaying, gaudily painted country buses with their bigger market loads. Then came the manual workers and those on their way to the slave-labour conditions of the free-trade zone. And after that the dainty-stepping, high-heeled shop and office workers, still too marginal to own the ultimate status symbol of some kind of working car. Finally, the schoolchildren, laughing and giggling. And interspersing it all, the occasional clip-clop of the old-time donkey dray-carts and the plaintive calls of the paper and kiscopop vendors.

She remembered the sounds from somewhere far back. She had been town-bound, brought all the way from St Mary with a reluctant George and dumped some place on the margins of the city. She tried to pick out and explore that memory, but it proved elusive and slipped away. So she focused on the comforting smell of boiling chocolate-tea and nutmeg. Aunt Vi always started her day this way: chocolate tea, seasoned with salt and nutmeg, sweetened with condensed milk, accompanying ackee – when it was in season – with yesterday's boiled dumpling and thick wedges of hardough bread, dripping butter, to mop up the excess.

Jimmy coming to get me this morning! She remembered as if for the first time but without the previous euphoria. *He going come with Sylvia and carry me go a doctor so they can give me one medicine for me head pain. Then he going hold me like him used to and kiss me and listen make me tell him all the things them that gone wrong since the evil take set on me. And after that he going tell me never mind and promise him not going send me away again.* She hugged herself in an excess of joy. *Yes man, Jimmy going make everything come right and he never, ever going left me again.*

She smiled in fresh anticipation. She was so lucky to have Jimmy. He was the kind of man you only found once in a lifetime and when they got married he would be hers for ever. She hugged herself again, giggling like a child. They would have two children – no more than that, but not yet. Not until she had had him to herself for at least a year . . . maybe two.

A stray thought nudged at her and she frowned. *Supposing he didn't come? Supposing he left her hanging on and hanging on till she grew old and dusty and shrivelled away inside?* That depressed her, and a fresh bout of giggling shook her as her attention shifted to the rhythms of the house.

Aunt Vi's familiar patterns brought more echoes of past memories. Vague pictures of sitting on the old stone verandah, bickering with Tashi and George. The sound of ceramic and cutlery clinked together and the religious hymns on the morning radio service mingled with the noise of hoe on stone as her father and Noel gathered provisions for the harvest table.

This time Noel and her father didn't bring a flood of guilt and Jean grinned with relief. Her aunt had prayed for her the day before, going down on her knees and begging the Lord, until she was filled with the Holy

Spirit and could drive the demons out. It had given the good voices that Jean fancied shared space in her head, a chance to show what they could do. They had tried to help her by keeping her spirits up. Telling her funny stories that made her roar with laughter while they mended and resealed the nice feelings left in her stomach. But now the bad ones had started creeping back. She had heard them crawling around the room all night. They spent hours looking for a way back in, before giving up and oozing out through the concrete, and she had actually believed she had finally defeated the evil in herself. But the minute it started to get light they came oozing right back, popping up just out of sight as soon as they thought she wasn't alert.

It made her want to scream out for Aunt Vi, but she was afraid to do that too. Suppose they trapped her auntie instead, drilled into *her* head and put the pain there? No wonder Granny kept whispering about how selfish she was and urging her to pray.

'Jean, a laying the table just now . . .' Aunt Vi's strong voice was reassuring.

She was glad to escape the menace of the room, practically scurrying out and slamming the door to keep them trapped inside. It was a relief to know that God was in too many places in the body of the house for them to follow. Jean made sure she sat right under the picture of the Last Supper, feeling relief at the thought that a black Jesus was watching over her.

Aunt Vi brought the breakfast on a battered tray, putting a heaped plate on the place-mat in front of her and a mug of aromatic chocolate beside it. 'Make haste and eat,' she urged, sitting on the other side of the table. 'You cousin coming to carry you go a doctor this morning and a promise her a going have you ready nine o'clock sharp.'

Jean picked up the fork, but before she could put it

in the food, the ackee came alive right in front of her eyes, heaving and crawling and laughing at her.

She dropped the fork, scrambling to her feet. 'I can't eat that.'

Aunt Vi looked at her in surprise. 'Jean, what happen to you now? You know how much you always liking ackee and boil dumpling.'

'But look at the plate, Aunt Vi – you can't see them?'

The old woman pulled the plate towards her, staring at it intently. 'Where? What you talking?'

Jean pressed her back hard against the wall, right under the Jesus picture. '*The ackee! Look at the ackee!*'

The woman looked from the plate to Jean in concern. 'Nothing wrong with the food, child. A tell you what, you set yourself down and a will dish you out some fresh.'

Aunt Vi was humouring her. Jean could hear it in the woman's voice and see it in the sympathetic glance. 'I tell you something is making it move,' she insisted stubbornly, but the old woman only nodded and smiled before taking the plate back to the kitchen.

Jean stayed where she was, feeling defenceless and alone. *A could never have imagine they could get round so well. Not even cooking seem to can get rid of them.* She looked at the picture above her head, eyes widening with horror as it changed right there in front of her eyes, the colour peeling away shade by shade.

Jean closed her eyes, shaking her head violently. It had to stop, the Jesus had to stay the same. If it changed . . . if it became the white one Aunt Vi would see her shame exposed, would see her naked and bleeding in the shadow of that blood-red cross.

She took a deep, shaky breath. 'Get thee behind me, Satan!' she muttered over and over again, relieved to see the picture of Jesus reverting to its original colour when she dared another glance. Feeling a little braver, she gave the tranquil face a longer look, allowing the bitterness to seep inside her. 'Not even you strong enough to cast the demon out,' she muttered in annoyance, 'not you, not anyone strong enough.'

It worried her that Aunt Vi was so sceptical. *How I can feel safe when not a one of them believe me?* she wondered unhappily. *The very people who should must can protect me and not a one of them can do more than call me madwoman, like they can't see is sane a sane.*

The old woman came back with her plate, urging her to return to the table, 'Come sit, man, and a will bless the table a next time, before you eat.'

Mollified, Jean went forward reluctantly, sliding cautiously back into her seat. She kept her eyes opened a crack as her aunt went into a marathon prayer, afraid to close them completely in case this new plate hid other nameless dangers.

Jean was relieved when the food on her plate didn't start the same mad dance, but she nearly choked when she saw that Aunt Vi's food was heaving in its place. She curled her fingers into fists not daring to say a word in case it added fuel to her aunt's suspicion that she was going mad. Why didn't the old lady notice? Why did she sit there eating the revolting mass as if she couldn't see it seething and wriggling on her fork? Jean reached for the enamel mug with a shaky hand, eyeing it suspiciously, maybe the things had drowned in the thick chocolate tea and lay buried under the sediment at the bottom. That turned her stomach, making her push the drink aside.

Aunt Vi stopped eating, watching her in puzzlement. 'Why you not eating now? You don't like ackee again?'

Jean shook her head, unable to find her voice. She wanted to snatch her aunt's plate, squeeze out the things already in her throat, stop the contamination reaching inside the old woman. She fancied she could see clear through to the other side of Aunt Vi's head, see the things wriggling at the back of her mouth, the top of her throat, getting ready to start eating into her head. This couldn't happen to her auntie, she couldn't let it. She edged her chair sidewards, inch by inch, never taking her eyes off the wriggling things. They were poised to strike now, lapping up pearls of blood oozing round their pincer-like grip. She had to be slow and cautious, a sudden movement was all it would take to send that first evil arrowing to the centre of the old woman's brain. Jean's hands opened, moved forward, her fingers extended, flexed . . .

'Miss Vi, you dey dey?' A woman's voice, sharp with enquiry, came from the vicinity of the front door. 'You can hurry with the things them, mam?'

The sound startled Jean, jolting reality back into focus. She picked up her fork and reached for the mug of chocolate, wondering if she really could eat such a large helping of ackee.

'Excuse a minute,' her aunt said, unaware of the drama playing itself out next to her. 'That lady coming for the washing Tashi friend leave and a having to make sure she taking everything.'

Sylvia arrived just as the washerwoman was leaving and she stood aside politely as the woman balanced the bundle of dirty clothes on her back. Falling into step with Aunt Vi, she came to an abrupt halt at the door of the main room when she noticed her cousin pushing the food around the plate with her fork.

'Jean, aren't you ready?' Impatience crept into her voice.

Jean looked past her, feeling fluttery and excited. Any minute now and he would come through the door, smiling and winking at her.

'Jean, we have to go, the appointment is at half nine and it's nearly five past now.'

Why wasn't he coming in? She pushed away her plate and wandered to the door; maybe he was waiting behind it to shout 'Boo' and give her a fright.

'Jean, what's wrong with you?' Sylvia grabbed hold of her arm, halting her progress.

Jean blinked. 'Where's Jimmy meeting us?'

Her cousin didn't quite meet her eyes. 'He can't come, Jean, he has to stay with the children.'

'What children?' She didn't believe that for one minute. Jimmy didn't have any outside children. 'You mean you stop him from coming. You was always trying to steal him away, wasn't you, Sylvia? Just through you kill off the man you did have.'

Aunt Vi came bustling over. 'Hush up you mouth, Jean, and stop bad-mouthing your cousin so. You just rinse off your face and make Miss Sylvia take you go a doctor.'

She subsided, feeling even more resentful. Sylvia was just like George and Noel, always getting her in to trouble with Aunt Vi and Papa. Still, she would go with her for now, but once the doctor gave her the medicine to stop her head pains, she was off. No way was she staying around and putting up with this.

Jimmy would find her somehow, she could depend on that. He was always there for her, every time she needed him. No doubt he was sorry about the way he just sent her off to Jamaica by herself. That was why he flew all the way from England to get her, because he could never forgive himself for allowing the demon things to bore up her head and make her ill.

The doctor's surgery was a short busride and a fifteen-minute walk from Red Hills Road, tucked away in the marginal streets bordering the Constant Spring golf course. Jean stuck close to Sylvia, afraid, cowed by the hostile stares and loud whispers she fancied her presence sparked off. The bad feelings hit her the minute she entered the crowded bus, making her shake and tremble as she swayed with the other two women who were jammed with Sylvia and herself on a seat constructed for two.

By the time they reached the surgery Jean was holding herself tightly in control. She felt as if her head was expanding from the throbbing inside, threatening to burst her skull like an over-ripe breadfruit.

The doctor was American-trained with a calm matter-of-fact approach. Jean was suspicious of him at first, especially when he insisted on seeing her on her own. She perched on the edge of a hard wooden chair beside the door, in case he turned out to be one of *them* and this was just another demon trap to drag her down.

Except he wasn't like that. He didn't think she was mad, like some of those rude people calling her mad woman and jostling and pushing her every time she dared to venture out alone. Or even Aunt Vi, humouring her because *she* was too ignorant to see what was right under her nose. He understood about the voices and the temptation to sin. She could feel his sympathy, his caring, and they soothed her.

If he wasn't so clear-skinned, this man could almost pass for Jimmy. It didn't matter that he was a bit older and a bit fatter round the middle, it was the sensitivity that counted. She wondered if he was married. Jimmy wouldn't marry her, didn't think she was good enough for him now his book was published and he'd become *somebody*.

'Do you think Jimmy let you down?' the doctor asked, when she told him about it.

'Is not his fault,' Jean was quick to defend, 'it's the sin, you see. The one that happen since before Noel.'

He tried to get her to talk about that, but she couldn't tell him. She could never tell anyone how much blood was on her hands. Jean spread them out, looking at them, sure she could see the redness welling up under the skin to leave a condemning stain on her palms. She pushed them behind her quickly, afraid the doctor would notice and condemn her too. Maybe that was what had happened with Jimmy. He must have seen it when she wasn't too careful, must have guessed the guilty things she had thought hidden too far inside her for anyone to dig out.

The doctor started talking again and she tried to focus. But somehow the words came out distorted, his mouth moving out of time and sequence with the sounds. She could only stare at him, unable to believe anyone could talk so fast; it was like a record playing at the wrong speed, the voice so high and squeaky it made her snigger.

Not that he seemed to notice, just continued talking as if everything was just fine. When he finished, he motioned her to the door and she got reluctantly to her feet, looking at him without comprehension. Wasn't he going to give her something to take the pain away? A medicine that would expel the things drilling inside her head and make her whole again? She opened her mouth to enquire, then changed her mind. No point asking when nothing he answered would make sense.

Sylvia rose when they came out, and the doctor said something to her.

She nodded and frowned. 'Jean, do you mind waiting her while I have a word with Dr Graham?' she asked.

Jean nodded in relief. She had half expected Sylvia to sound the same as the doctor, expected that all the world would sound like that, leaving her excluded and isolated.

'I shan't be long,' Sylvia assured her, 'just stay here and don't wander off.'

Jean had intended to do just that, wait there until Sylvia came to take her back to Aunt Vi. But they left the door open and she couldn't help hearing what they were saying. Jean couldn't believe it. They were going to send her to madhouse. Sylvia was sitting there, cool as you please, talking about an institution.

Jean tried to hear what the man was saying, but the words remained a fast, bewildering jumble. Not that it mattered. Her cousin was the betrayer, the Judas; the doctor was just another pawn like Jimmy and Winston.

'So she think I belong in Bellevue, ee?' Jean muttered. 'Well, she in for a shock when she come out a that room, for I not going hang round and wait for them to cart me off.' She grinned as she visualised Sylvia's surprise, then just as suddenly burst into tears. 'A not so mad a don't know what they doing,' she sniffed. 'Everybody know how Bellevue stay, the way them lock up decent people till them dead and how them even take way your brain and beat you with cat-o-nine from morning till night.'

It was no wonder Sylvia hadn't brought Jimmy to town with her. No way would he let them even think of that. The tears ebbed away and she frowned, no longer even sure of that. Supposing it was his idea? He was the one always writing stories, supposing he had dreamt up this one to lock her away so he was free to be with Sylvia? Maybe they were all in it together – the whole wide world against her.

She got up stealthily, looking at the wary receptionist sitting behind her desk and the two old women on opposite sides of the room. Sylvia was probably paying them to watch her. No doubt they would pounce on her the minute she tried to escape. She racked her brain, trying to find a way out. Somehow she had to come up with a cunning plan, something so simple they wouldn't see through it.

Jean straightened her shoulders and cleared her throat. 'I'm just going to the toilet,' she announced to the room at large, 'a want to wee wee, you see.'

She stretched with a nonchalance she was far from feeling. Her heart beat fast as she started moving across the room, terrified they would see through her ruse. She walked boldly to the door, relieved when the three women remained seated. She was sure they would soon realise she wasn't coming back, but by the time they gave chase, she would be far far away.

As soon as she got out the street door, Jean began to run. She didn't care where she went, only that she put distance between herself and this new threat. She ran and ran, losing one of Tashi's borrowed shoes along the way, and kicking off the other when the uneven gait slowed her down. *Sylvia never going find me now.* The thought made her laugh wildly, full of her own cunning and her daring.

By the time she slowed to a walk she was completely disoriented. She didn't care; she had long ago lost the thread of where she was trying to reach and her throat was burning with the more immediate need for a thirst-quenching drink.

She spotted a jelly-coconut vendor and headed over to him. 'Give me a jelly . . . not too soft,' she ordered.

The man eyed her suspiciously, looking from her well-groomed hair to the sweat stains on the borrowed dress and the dusty, shoeless feet. 'What happen to your shoes, mam?'

'Them fall off, now give me the coconut noh – you can't see that I thirsty?' Her voice automatically mimicked his language.

He complied with the authority in her tone, though he kept an eagle eye on her as she drank it. The water soothed her throat and filled her belly. Jean dug eagerly into the creamy white jelly when he split it open for her, wiping her mouth with the back of her hand when both halves were completely clean.

'That's four dollars,' the man said, taking the husks from her.

Jean kissed her teeth. 'Four dollars for what?'

The man's eyes narrowed. 'Cho, mam, no gi me no trouble, you hear, you eat off me jelly so you going have to pay for it.'

Who was he trying to fool? 'So when since you can

make jelly coconut? If I want jelly all I have to do is climb coconut tree, you know, so a not paying no four dollar for something you pick up off a roadside.'

The fury in his face warned her of his intention, and she was halfway down the road, roaring with laughter before he could attempt to catch her. *That man must really think I born yesterday*, Jean thought sourly. *Imagine trying to tell me say him coulda make coconut.* She gave another kiss teeth, slowing as she came to Mary Brown's corner.

Which way now? She could go back to Aunt Vi, but Sylvia might be there and these days she no longer knew who she could trust. Jean wandered about aimlessly for a while, not quite sure what she wanted to do. If only she knew where Jimmy was.

She didn't for one minute believe Sylvia's lies about him having outside children. Jimmy would never do that. They had decided to wait until after the wedding before even thinking of children and he had assured her he hadn't fathered any on another woman. What she had to do now was find some way to see him. They were trying to keep them apart, she could see that now. But once she found him and he knew what they were up to, everything would be fine.

Somehow her feet took her back to the district where Ras Peter had left her, the place where Sylvia had found her. Jean wandered the streets, stepping indifferently into bad-smelling drains and keeping up a monologue to herself.

Occasionally a car swerved to miss her, as she walked in and out of the road, oblivious to danger. Jean stopped where she was, shaking her fist and trading insults as the shaken driver vented his anger on her head, before reversing and manoeuvring around her.

Towards mid-afternoon she began to feel hungry and she foraged around, picking up discarded snack bags and shaking the crumbs into her palm. She went systematically along the roads, up one side and down the other, till she came across a half-eaten common mango near a chainlink fence. Jean gnawed hungrily at it, standing in the middle of the sidewalk to better appreciate the taste.

She was sitting on the high pavement picking the mango fibres from between her teeth and sucking the last sweetness off her fingers when she saw the rastaman walking past on the opposite side of the street. Jean recognised him immediately, feeling a sudden rush of joy.

Fancy that, eh! He had told her he would come back and she hadn't believed him. Imagine, she was sitting here thinking of ways to find him and he was right there across the street. She scrambled to her feet, running out into the traffic and just missing an oncoming car. Jean ignored the driver's bad-tempered cursing, her eyes fixed on the striding figure of the rastaman.

'Jimmy! It's Jean . . . Jimmy, wait up noh!'

The rastaman continued walking, oblivious. Jean frowned, increasing her speed as he turned the corner. If she lost him and he found out she hadn't trusted him to come back, that would be the end of any chance she had to keep him. 'Jimmy!' she shouted as he came in sight again, then she remembered, something else . . .

This whole rasta thing was a disguise. Jean felt mortified; fancy forgetting that. What was the rasta name he was using? She racked her brain, slowing a little as a stitch started in her side. *Peter!* That was it, Ras Peter from the tribe of Ash.

'Ras Peter!' she tried again, the stitch forgotten in the renewal of excitement.

He slowed a little, looking around uncertainly before speeding up again.

'Ras Peter, it's me!' Jean yelled, elbowing through a slow-walking family group as she started to gain on him. 'A right behind you.'

This time he stopped and turned around, a frown furrowing his brow as his eyes moved uncertainly from side to side before coming to rest on her running figure.

She waved gaily. 'Good thing a saw you,' she panted to a stop, 'otherwise you would reach back at the place and found me gone.'

The rastaman looked at her in stunned surprise, edging away as she moved forward again. 'Go way from me, Maddy!' he shouted angrily, pushing her with rough panic when she tried to get hold of him. 'Move yourself before a burst your head.'

Jean looked at him in bewilderment. 'Jimmy, it's Jean, not Miss Maddy.' Why was he doing this? What had Sylvia done to make him think she was anything like that ragged, mad woman down Port Juanero town? She looked at him appealingly, willing him to understand. 'I'm sorry a forgot your pseudoname but you have to understand how much pressure I been under. It's Sylvia, she's the one . . . You never going guess what she try to do to me this morning.'

He just kept backing away. 'You don't hear, a say go way!'

She tried to grasp his arm but he jerked it out of reach, pushing through the crowd that had gathered from nowhere and walking off at a near run. Jean made to follow but someone tripped her and a hard kick landed in her side. She stumbled, grabbing hold of a woman's dress to stop herself from falling. The woman screamed and a foot crashed against her shoulder, loosening her hold. She was on all fours now, crawling, dragging herself forwards in time with the screams of terror ripping from her throat.

The blows rained down like so many stings but suddenly she was free of them. Jean was just in time to see the rastaman turn the next corner, and she ran after him, needing to catch him and explain.

Somehow they were making a big mistake, confusing

her with that mad and stupid woman. She was different, she had lived in foreign for years and had education and everything. They should be looking up to her, not laughing and jeering at her.

She managed to keep him in sight at first, dodging around pedestrians and darting across busy roads. He twisted and turned, going into areas that had vague familiarity and others with a brooding menace alien to her.

Desperation kept her going. If she didn't catch him and he left her stranded in this hell-place, she would never regain herself, never find her way back home again . . .

In the end her legs failed her, slowing her down as he increased the distance between them and got further and further away. Finally they wouldn't go another step and she just sat down where she was, feeling defeated and abandoned.

The howls welled up inside and escaped without her noticing, coming faster and louder as she sat crouched against a yard fence on the baked mud path.

'What happen, Maddy? Something do you?' Her heart leapt at the thought that he had returned, but it wasn't him.

This man was stout with short, uncombed hair and a beardless face. Jean watched him cautiously, wondering if *they* had sent him to finish her off. But he smiled pleasantly enough, despite the gleam of malice in his eyes. 'What you want?' she asked suspiciously, adding in a wheedling voice, 'I looking for Ras Peter but I lost him. You know him?'

The man nodded, looking as if he was trying not to laugh at a private joke, 'A know just where you wanting to go, just follow my lead and a will look after you.'

She stayed where she was, watching his retreating back with dull eyes.

The man stopped when he realised she hadn't moved. 'You coming or not?'

She moved forward reluctantly, not really wanting to go, but unable to think of one good reason why she shouldn't. 'You know where Ras Peter will be staying?' she pressed him as she followed his lead along the warren of mud paths.

'A tell you already, mad lady, a know everything.'

She hesitated as they came to an abandoned and deserted patch of scrubland, hanging back as he stepped over some thorn bushes to the sandy ground beyond. The man hissed impatiently through his teeth and muttered under his breath. Jean shrank in on herself, expecting a blow, but all he did was pull out a half-bottle of rum and offer it to her.

She took it with a wary hand, gulping greedily. It seemed like such a long time since she had had a strong drink and suddenly she realised how much she needed one. She drank again, deep and long this time. 'This taste nice but my usual drink is gin and vodka.'

He looked sceptical. 'And a suppose you living in a big house?'

'I live in foreign if you must know,' she corrected with dignity. 'England, to be exact, and a did go to university and have education.'

The man laughed and shook his head. 'But oonu mad people can tell some story ee.'

She put the bottle to her mouth taking another gulp. 'I not mad, you know. Is Sylvia do this to me – she make people think I mad so she could tief Jimmy away.'

'Say what you want, lady, but just come,' he was irritated now, 'a couldn't care less if you was queen a England so long as a get some sugar.'

She followed obediently, cradling the bottle close when he tried to retrieve it. He shrugged, grabbing her arm and pulling her down to the uneven ground behind a clump of dusty-looking bushes.

She lay incuriously as he fumbled under her skirt and pulled her panty down, watching passively when he unzipped his flies. She felt his hands clutching at her, hard intrusive fingers poking and jabbing in her body with painful brutality. The image of the cross flickered a moment, wavered and dissolved.

It barely registered on her conscious mind. Nothing did any more. Soon he would be finished and she could sit up, drink her rum and wait for him to take her back to where she knew Jimmy was waiting to take her home.

Chapter 21

The small roofed area on the viewing gallery of Norman Manley Airport was full to overflowing with passengers and their relatives in multi-coloured disarray. Ample-breasted women wearing their best outfits sat enthroned in regal splendour, stirring the air with elaborate straw fans. Younger female relatives bustled around serving pre-packed lunches and herding straying children back into the shade while the men engaged in passionate discussions about politics, religion and the state of play in a current cricket match. There was no breeze and the fumes of aviation fuel mingled with atmospheric pollution in a thick, unpleasant stew. The tourists, dripping with sweat and silenced by discomfort, perched awkwardly at the margins, on the line of shade where the heat penetrated as fiercely as full sunlight.

Sylvia felt alien to both groups. She stood with Jimmy in the direct sunlight of the viewing platform, trying not to feel embarrassed by the uninhibited display of Jamaican life she had thought so wonderful only a week ago. The sun was a burn on her exposed arms – 102° the weatherman had said. Dry heat, hot enough to create mirages and put distance into nearby conversations. She ignored the scalp-tightening discomfort as the sun penetrated the protective straw hat, wanting to remember only the boldness of its presence in case she never returned. Her attention drifted aimlessly, focusing at last on the activity below.

The last few passengers of a small Cubana jet were disappearing out of sight, as a Boeing 737 started loading passengers. Sylvia watched the stream of people walking across the tarmac, speeding along as if they were afraid the big Air Canada jet would close its door and leave without them. Her gaze shifted as an Air Jamaica flight dropped out of the bleached blue sky to land elegantly on the long runway. The roar of the engine was drowned by the air-splitting noise of a Liat propeller plane kicking into life. She found the spectacle fascinating, a dream of childhood come to life. Watching the big jets take off and land brought a sense of poignancy: echoes of standing in the viewing gallery at Heathrow, holding tightly to her father's hand and waving at the BOAC plane taking her mother to this far, far place. Jamaica had been faded sepia prints, picture postcards from Jimmy and Aleesa, posters on the curved walls of London Underground and books purchased or borrowed from the local lending library.

There was little traffic this afternoon, and soon the last of the passengers had disembarked from the Air Jamaica flight, and the Air Canada and Liat planes had disappeared over different horizons. Sylvia shifted her attention back to the viewing gallery, conscious that she had checked in her luggage early so she could spend a little time with Jimmy and the children.

Davian was chasing Aleesa, who had joined a strange tag-like game with a group of other children at the far end of the exposed gallery. Both the children had recovered well, shrugging off the bad experience with nothing but the odd nightmare to resurrect what had happened in Kingston. She wished she could say the same for herself.

Ever since Aunt Vi had phoned to ask about Jean, the doubts and questions had come to nag at her again.

300

Sylvia could still hear the distress in the old woman's voice. She had returned from the peace and silence of the hilltop to be greeted by Pearl's anxiety.

'Sylvia, George auntie from town phoning the whole afternoon long, she wanting you to call her back soon as you reach.'

Sylvia's fingers had been shaking as she dialled the number Pearl gave her.

Aunt Vi answered immediately, 'Miss Sylvia, is you that?'

'Yes, Miss Mackenzie.'

'And Jean dey with you in Port Juanero?'

The guilt Sylvia had rationalised away that morning came rushing back. 'No, I left her in town.'

'But she don't come back as yet, you know, Miss Sylvia. A fretting about her all the day. Is just so her father did stay when he getting sick. You could tell me where she is?'

'I don't know. She ran out and left me when I was speaking to the doctor.'

'A suppose you never find her again true you not use to in town.' The old woman's voice held understanding.

Sylvia kept silent, shamed. How could she tell the old lady that she hadn't even looked? Suddenly her actions didn't seem so reasonable.

'Anyway,' Aunt Vi persisted, 'a was wondering if she mention anywhere she might go to.'

'No, not that I can remember.'

'Don't fret yourself, then.' Aunt Vi was apologetic which only made her feel worse, 'a going get them boy to go look down at the board house where she was staying first time.'

Sylvia made a non-commital response, putting the phone down with relief when the old woman finally rang off.

Now the guilt pressed in on her. Maybe she should

301

have made some attempt to search for her cousin. Jean could hardly be blamed for her actions. Trouble was, she had been too angry when she had come out of the surgery to find the woman gone. *What else could I do?* she asked herself again. *I just can't keep taking responsibility for her.* Anger and resentment resurfaced, mingling with the guilt. *Why should I have to feel I'm the one who failed her?* Jean had been dumping on her from the moment they had met. Sylvia sighed, *I did the best I could in the circumstances, and I'm just going to have to keep telling myself that. Feeling guilty isn't going to help the situation.*

Despite her mother's dementia, she had never really faced mental illness this close to home. Her mother's illness she could rationalise: she was old, it was hereditary. But never, despite the textbook knowledge and all her years of mental-health work, had she considered that anyone in her family could become like Jean. Maybe that was why she kept thinking Jean would snap out of it. That her cousin would not melt back into the warren of West Kingston in preference to the comforts of her aunt's house. Not that it would have mattered too much if she had known, she acknowledged silently; Jean had just pushed her that one step too far.

Sylvia felt echoes of the fury that had gripped her when she realised her cousin had just walked away after all the effort everyone had put in to finding her. It didn't matter how much she told herself Jean was sick. Anger, and the pent-up hostility from years of being understanding, burned inside and she cursed Jean all the way to New Kingston.

Sylvia shifted against the chest-high barrier that ringed the viewing gallery, wondering why she felt so little remorse. Her hand strayed to the outside pocket of her shoulder bag where the torn pieces of Winston's photograph lay. Pain tightened the corners of her mouth, bitterness welling up at the memory of Jean's desecration.

'How long before you have to go through?' Jimmy's question diluted the uncomfortable feeling.

Aleesa's voice rose bossily above the other children's and Davian had wandered across to the rail, chattering inconsequentially to himself. Sylvia checked her watch, part of her marvelling at the amount of words the child had learnt since that first optimistic outburst on Dunn's River's sands.

'Another ten minutes or so.' She gave him a reflective look. 'Jimmy, what will you do – about Jean?'

'Nothing personally. Try to get people to keep an eye out for her, I suppose.'

That surprised her. 'But . . .'

'Sylvia, I've thought about this for a long time now, and, bad as this sounds, I just feel – well . . .' He scratched his head as he always did when he was ill at ease. 'Jean made her bed and she's going to have to lie in it. Anyway, we've had this out before. I told you to stop worrying about her and get on with your life. If she chose to run off like that there isn't much you or anyone else could do.'

Sylvia braced herself, needing to come clean. 'I might as well tell you, I didn't really look for her. I was so annoyed that I went to the airline office to change my ticket, then got the bus back to Port Juanero.'

'I don't wrong you.'

'You really mean that? I thought you'd be mad as anything.'

He shrugged. 'Why should I be?'

'Aren't you concerned about her?'

'Of course I'm concerned, but what do you want me to do? I've spent years bailing your cousin out.'

'Will you still try to find her?'

'Sure, but I doubt I'll manage it. Sylvia, Kingston is

303

full of mad people . . . few more days and I doubt anybody would even recognise Jean.'

Sylvia conceded that. Jean had been filthy when she was found after only a few days, despite receiving help from Ras Peter. She doubted anyone would be willing to lend her cousin a hand, now she was so obviously disturbed.

'What if you don't find her, will you stay on?'

'No chance.' He was firm on that. 'Sylvia, nobody over here going to take the disappearance of a mad person – even a foreign one – seriously.' Jimmy unconsciously echoed her own thoughts. 'So I've not exactly had much luck getting official help.'

She nodded, remembering the expectation of bribes when the children had gone missing, the indifference when Miss Maddy disappeared. 'But what about you?'

'I don't know, Sylv, I just don't know. Sometimes, when I think of what she did to Alli and Davian I'm not sure I ever want to see Jean again.'

She resisted an urge to wrap her arms tightly around him and offer the same comfort he had given her the night he arrived; instead she slid her hand in his and squeezed reassuringly. 'You have to do what feels right to you, Jimmy. You can't forever be thinking about how things look from the outside, when you're the one suffering on the inside.'

Jimmy smiled sadly. 'Thanks for that. You see I've been thinking . . . about Jean, me, the kids – the future I suppose – and the truth is, however much I'd be prepared to help if she's found, I'm just not sure I could carry on as before.'

She digested that, adjusting her perception when she heard the bitterness in his voice. 'I still don't understand why you put up with the situation as long as you did.'

He thought on that for a while. 'Who knows? I suppose I still have a lot of feelings for her and then, as I said the other day, the children were a complication.'

He smiled bitterly. 'I kept telling myself that other black men were too quick to walk out on their responsibilities and I wasn't going to be like them.'

He had said that before and she'd let it pass, but this time she met his eyes squarely, letting him see the admiration she felt for him. 'Jimmy, you're the one that's always taken on responsibility for the children. Nobody could *ever* say anything to fault the way you've cared for them.'

'Truth, but she might still have got them, mightn't she? If we had a split up, I mean.'

'Not necessarily. After all, they are registered in your name and you've always been their chief carer . . .'

'Well, anyway,' he cut in, 'I felt it was important for the children to have two parents . . . not that Jean has been much of one recently, but I thought if she came to Jamaica, cared for them a while, she might learn to appreciate them again and we might have salvaged some of the good things we had.'

'And you don't think you still can?'

His denial was emphatic. 'I put up with a lot from Jean, loved her through all those difficult months when she was drinking so heavily, but I don't think I could ever forgive her for what she did to the children. Whatever grudge she was holding against me she should never have taken it out on them.'

She wanted to probe further, help him to deal with the pain, but he suddenly shook his head and straightened. 'Look, can we talk about something else?' He paused, looking at her closely. 'How about the way *you* are feeling now you're on the way back to England – do you still think you didn't get anything out of this trip? Last Thursday I had the distinct feeling you thought it was one big waste of time.'

Sylvia frowned, thinking about that. 'No, it wasn't that. Jamaica has been great – in a way.' She gave a strained laugh. 'I suspect I was probably expecting too much.'

'But surely you got *some* of the things you came for?'

That was true. Being here had given her some insight into what had made Winston the person he had been, helped her come to terms with the memory of his death and appreciate what they had had together. It had also brought her a different closeness to Jimmy . . . though that was something still to be resolved within herself.

'To tell you the truth,' she confessed, 'after seeing you and Jean, and Pearl and George, I really value what Winston and I had. I hadn't realised just how many good times there were until now.'

He didn't take offence. 'You two always had something special.'

Sylvia wished she could offer Jimmy similar consoling words. 'What happened to Jean was inevitable,' she repeated. 'In fact, it probably would have come sooner if she hadn't found somebody like you.'

Aleesa marched over, tired of the running game. 'Auntie, when is your plane coming?'

'It's there already, sweetheart, look.' She pointed to the big wide-bodied jet with the sober British Airways colours. 'I'm just waiting till nearer the time for them to start boarding before I go.'

'We're coming home on Wednesday, aren't we, Daddy?' the child offered.

Jimmy nodded. 'But it probably won't be in the same plane.'

Aleesa wrinkled her nose. 'I'm glad we're going home. Jamaica is a nice place to visit, that's all . . .' She looked wistful. 'I just wish Mum would come back and be like her real self again.'

It was the first time she had mentioned her mother and both Sylvia and Jimmy reached out together. Sylvia stepped back, embarrassed, but Jimmy smiled understandingly as he gathered his daughter to him.

'Sometimes things happen that none of us can help,' he told the child gravely. 'I guess your mum is under too much pressure to come to us right now.'

'Will she ever come back? If she did I would love her just the same, Daddy, honest I would. Davian and me forgive her already.'

He stared sadly across the airfield and Sylvia wondered if he was thinking of the end of *his* ability to forgive, but all he said was, 'We'll just have to wait and see what happens, Alli.'

The little girl nodded, mollified for the moment. 'I hope she don't live in Jamaica for ever, though. I don't like it for living in.'

Sylvia put a hand on Jimmy's arm as Aleesa wandered off. 'Are you OK?'

'I'll have to talk to Alli about Jean sometime, though I haven't the faintest idea what to tell her.' He straightened, changing the subject abruptly. 'She's got a point, you know.'

'What about?'

'This place,' he responded, gesturing around. 'When I was growing up I didn't even notice how racist and corrupt over here was, or perhaps that was because it wasn't so bad – the corruption, I mean. But now . . .'

'Jamaica has a lot of good points.'

'Oh, I know that. At least, the average working-class person still have a lot of kindness.'

Sylvia nodded in agreement. 'I've never really felt so accepted anywhere else. I mean, look at the way everybody helped when the children were missing, and then the party they threw last night.' She still felt emotional about that. They had come round to see her, people she had done no more than pass the time of day with. All of them had brought something to eat or drink, a memento and a blessing. They made a party from scratch, right there in George's small living space.

It made her feel they valued her, had taken her in and opened their hearts to her.

A paper-vendor came by selling the *Sunday Gleaner*, his cry breaking the thread of her thoughts. Sylvia bought a copy to read on the plane.

'At least you gave them something back.'

'What?'

'The women . . .'

'What women?'

'Pearl, Miss Berta, Dorrie – the ones you pulled together. Don't you see the way they're getting on now, instead of isolating themselves in their own separate part of the poverty hierarchy?'

Sylvia didn't quite follow his meaning. She hadn't helped anybody . . . well, maybe Pearl a little. She had seen her cousin's wife move from the rut she was in, start to gain in confidence and reach out for her own needs. Mind you, Pearl had been the one to make the decisions for herself, showing a rare bravery Sylvia admired.

She smiled, remembering the last argument George had had with Pearl. It was on Friday night and George had jumped in feet first as usual when he overheard Sylvia telling Pearl that she had managed to get her ticket changed to this flight.

'So soon?' he had launched into her. 'So how come you on so much haste to leave of a sudden?'

'George, I told you I was going to get my ticket changed.'

'But you never say it going to so soon, a was hoping you would come up so Sabbath coming – everybody wanting to see you up the church and is like you malicing them from you come.'

Sylvia didn't intend to get into this argument again. 'George, I'm not interested. They know where I am if they want to see me so badly.'

'But is Sunday you leaving,' he countered, 'and with

tomorrow being Sabbath nobody really have time to organise a thing with the day coming up so soon.'

'George, left Sylvia no, man,' Pearl had joined the fray. 'She having to reach back for her job, and anyways if she not wanting to go church you shouldn't try force it on her.'

He looked at his wife, 'Why you starting up again now, Pearl? A talking to you? Why you don't keep out a what don't concern you?'

'Everything in this house is my concern. I live here and Sylvia is a guest here, so she concern me too.'

George gave her a sour look. 'Hush up your mouth, sun must a turn you fool.'

Sylvia seated herself at the kitchen table in resignation, recognising the futility of trying to interfere. But to her surprise Pearl put a stop to it, not spiralling off into bad-tempered abuse as she usually did.

'A not arguing with you day and night so, any more, George,' she said abruptly. 'It affecting the children and it not serving any purpose.'

George looked astonished. 'What you saying?'

Pearl kissed her teeth. 'If you don't know, a sorry for you. A telling you this straight, George, a not sitting down on my backside so, make you walk all over me again. A living in this house and a doing my share, so if anything going on, is my business same as yours.'

'When since?'

She gave him a level look. 'Since a could fetch lime and ground provision for myself from up back, and since a go a town when you did too fraid to look for your own sister.' She paused nodding her head before delivering the final blow. 'And since a starting work Monday week.'

'*What!* You telling me you get *job* and don't even say dog bout it?'

'A telling you bout it now, George.' Pearl gave another kiss teeth, dropping the knife and the yam she was peeling. 'Cho, a not going stay here and take no more insult. You children, put on your shoes and come.'

George could only stare in shock. 'Pearl, man, you don't know is Sabbath evening?'

'A know it, George, but when since you ever observe it? A going down by Miss Lisa, and any reckoning to make, God will call me to account himself. He don't need you to do it for him.'

Leaning back against the guard rail, Sylvia smiled, amused by the memory as she told Jimmy about Pearl's stand and George's meekness the following morning.

'It's high time she stood up to him,' Jimmy agreed. 'Men over here have the exact same attitudes as their fathers and their fathers before them.' He shrugged. 'Just goes to show that nothing will change in Jamaica, unless the women cause it.'

Sylvia nodded, checking her watch again. 'I'd better go, I promised a woman at work I'd get her some perfume in Duty Free.'

She hugged all of them one after the other, Aleesa, Davian and Jimmy, feeling a sudden rush of emotion at the thought of leaving the island. 'Don't bother to come down with me,' she said, when Jimmy grabbed Davian's hand, 'I think I might do something stupid, like cry.'

Jimmy smiled in sympathy but it was Aleesa who broke the mood. 'If we stay here will you wave to us?' she asked cheerfully.

Sylvia nodded. 'And I'll see you when you get back to England.'

Boarding for BA Flight 264 was announced as soon as she got through to Duty Free, leaving very little time to browse. Sylvia followed the other passengers through the massing soldiers in the airport building, standing patiently in line for yet another American-ordered search.

310

The plane was airborne and levelling out when she finally opened the bulky Sunday paper. She was flicking through, idly wishing she had brought a magazine, when an article caught her eyes. It was about a woman found dead on some scrubland in a part of Sandy Gully she recognised from her frantic search of the city. It jolted her, bringing home the danger that had been too abstract to appreciate, despite George's dire warnings and Pearl's obvious fear. She folded the paper, reading on with the curiosity of someone who had been there.

Something snagged inside her, squeezing her heart as she read the description of the unknown woman. Her eyes moved over the words so fast they blurred together and only certain phrases lodged inside her brain. The green dress, that strange haircut. *Could it be?*

The hum of the jet engines was suddenly very loud in her ears as she stared at the printed words. Sylvia's stomach churned, her fingers shaking as she tried to read the article again. She could feel her heart racing as she searched for the final clue. It wasn't there – no striking foreign shoes – *the woman was barefoot, without identification. Police believed she was probably an itinerant from somewhere in the country . . .*

Sylvia folded the paper with unsteady hands, swallowing hard to relieve a sudden pain in her throat. *It couldn't be! It just couldn't be!*

Should she ring Jimmy when she got back? Get him to find out definitely? She squashed that idea at birth; if it wasn't Jean – and she could not allow herself to believe it could be – then she would be worrying him for no good reason but to appease her own guilt.

'Are you all right, miss?' the kindly middle-aged man beside her asked in concern, his voice taking on a faraway sound through the drone of the aircraft.

'Yes . . . fine. I thought I saw something in the paper about somebody I knew, but the description didn't match.'

He smiled, turning his attention to the flight attendants coming along with the drinks trolley. 'That is the trouble with the *Gleaner*, you can't believe a word you read in it.'

She focused on that, using it to help calm herself down.

'Something to drink, miss?'

Sylvia looked up at the smiling attendant. 'Perrier if you have it.'

She took the glass, taking a deep draught to lubricate her throat. She couldn't believe it was Jean – didn't dare to . . . or how would she ever live with herself?

The plane came down in the Bahamas for a brief stopover and she watched the landing activity as her neighbour gathered up his belongings to disembark. He hesitated, clearing his throat to get her attention. Sylvia turned to find him looking longingly at the paper in her hand. 'You still have use for that?' he asked hopefully.

She looked down at the paper for a long, long time . . . wondering. Then she held it out to him, coming to a decision. 'You have it,' she offered. 'There is nothing in it to concern me.'